Samantha Young is a *New York Times*, *USA Today* and *Wall Street Journal* bestselling author from Stirlingshire, Scotland. She's been nominated for the Goodreads Choice Award for Best Author and Best Romance for her international bestselling novel *On Dublin Street*.

Visit Samantha Young online:

www.authorsamanthayoung.com
www.twitter.com/SYoungSFAuthor

By Samantha Young:

On Dublin Street
Down London Road
Before Jamaica Lane
Fall from India Place
Echoes of Scotland Street

Hero

Castle Hill (ebook novella)

Hero

SAMANTHA YOUNG

piatkus

PIATKUS

First published in the US in 2015 by New American Library,
a division of Penguin Group (USA) LLC
First published in Great Britain in 2015 by Piatkus

A CIP catalogue record for this book
is available from the British Library.

ISBN 978-0-349-40878-1

Printed and bound by CPI Group (UK) Ltd, Croydon CR0 4YY

Piatkus
An imprint of
Little, Brown Book Group
100 Victoria Embankment
London EC4Y 0DY

An Hachette UK Company
www.hachette.co.uk

www.piatkus.co.uk

Heroism feels but never reasons, and therefore is always right.

—Ralph Waldo Emerson

Hero

CHAPTER 1

Boston, Massachusetts

This wasn't happening.

This couldn't be happening.

I curled my hands into fists to stop them from shaking as I made my way through the hallway into the open-plan living area of the penthouse apartment. It had high cathedral ceilings and a wall of windows that led out onto a huge balcony. The water from the harbor glistened under the sun. It was a beautiful building with a gorgeous backdrop and I could not appreciate any of it because I was too focused on finding *him* there.

My heart stopped at the sight of him standing outside on the balcony.

Caine Carraway.

"Alexa!"

My head snapped around from Caine's direction to the kitchen area where my boss, Benito, was surrounded by two laptops and various other equipment for the photo shoot. This was supposed to be the moment I smiled in greeting and told him to direct me where he needed me.

Instead I looked back at Caine.

The orange juice I had drunk that morning sloshed around unpleasantly in my stomach.

"Alexa!"

Benito was suddenly in front of me, frowning and glaring at me.

"Hi," I said, my voice flat. "Where do you want me?"

Benito cocked his head to the side, looking up at me in a way that was almost comical. I was tall at five nine. He was only five six. But what he lacked in height he more than made up for in personality. "Please"—he gave me a long-suffering sigh—"tell me I've got my normal Alexa back. I cannot cope with the Mother's Day–disaster Alexa. Today I'm shooting Caine Carraway for *Mogul* magazine's Top Self-Made Men Under Forty. Caine is to grace the cover." He shot a look over his shoulder at said cover model. "An obvious choice." He raised an eyebrow at me. "Today's an important shoot. In case you don't know, Caine Carraway is one of Boston's most eligible bachelors. He's the CEO of Carraway—"

"Financial Holdings," I said softly. "I know."

"Good. You'll also know he's horrifically wealthy and incredibly influential. He's also a very busy man and a hard man to please, so I have to get this shoot done right and done quickly."

My attention drifted over Benito's head to the man who had successfully started a private bank immediately after graduating from college. From there he eventually expanded his company, building a diversified business portfolio involving everything from corporate banking to home mortgages, insurance companies, investment trusts, securities trading, asset management, and so forth. Now Caine himself was CEO of a major holdings company that was home to a board of directors of influential and wealthy businesspeople.

According to reports, Caine had managed all this through ruthless determination, eagle-eyed attention to his organization, and power-hungry ambition.

At the moment Caine was busy talking on his phone to someone as Marie, a beauty assistant, smoothed the lines of his tailored suit. The designer navy suit fit his body to perfection. Caine was tall, at least two, if not three, inches over six feet, broad-shouldered, and visibly fit. He had a strong profile, with sharp cheekbones and an aquiline nose, and the hair he was now impatiently batting Marie's hand away from was thick and as dark as my own. Although it was pinched tight right now, I knew from photographs that he had a sensual, brooding mouth.

Definitely cover model material.

And definitely not a man you crossed.

I swallowed past the lump that had formed in my throat.

How ironic that he should be standing there, right in front of me, after all the ugliness my mother's recent and sudden death had brought to the fore . . . and he was a part of that ugliness.

Six years I'd worked as a personal assistant for Benito— one of the city's most successful and temperamental photographers. Of course, Benito was never melodramatic around clients, just his employees. Yet since I'd worked with him for a long time, I should have felt secure after all these years. I didn't.

Strictly speaking, I *used* to feel like I had job security.

But losing my mother three months ago had caused my family issues to rear their ugly heads, and unveiled some harsh truths I often wished I didn't know. I went on with work, putting on a brave face. However, it's not possible to be that strong when you lose a parent, and unfortunately I'd had a bit of an emotional breakdown during a photo shoot for a major women's magazine. It was a shoot for Mother's Day.

Benito had tried to be understanding, but I could tell he was pissed. Instead of firing me, though, he told me to take a much-needed vacation.

Thus a few weeks later, here I was with a mighty fine tan courtesy of the Hawaiian sun, and upon my arrival this morning I'd had no clue what this photo shoot was about or for whom.

I'd received a clipped e-mail from Benito when I'd returned from my trip with the address for the photo shoot but no other information. I was his PA and I had no clue what his latest job entailed—that didn't sound good to me.

So I was tan, yes, but I still hadn't really sorted my head out about my mom, and was now seriously worried that the job I'd been busting my ass over for the last six years was seconds away from being flushed down a very expensive penthouse toilet. Today had to go well for me.

My anxiety had increased tenfold when I strode out of the elevator and caught sight of the people buzzing around the hallway and in the open double doors of the apartment. There were way more people at the shoot than usual, suggesting we were shooting someone particularly important. I was panicked, then, when our intern, Sofie, relayed to me that the person we were shooting was none other than Caine Carraway.

My whole body had jerked in reaction to the name and I'd started to tremble.

I hadn't stopped trembling since.

Caine suddenly looked sharply at me as if he'd felt my gaze on him. We stared at each other, me struggling to hold on to my emotions, while he finally let go of my eyes so his could travel over my body.

Benito believed that dressing casually around celebrities

impressed upon them that he and his people were not intimidated because we were on the celebrity's level talentwise. He believed that attitude made his clients respect him more. I thought that was superficial bullshit, but it meant I got to wear whatever I liked, so I didn't air that opinion. On shoots I often opted for whatever was most comfortable. Today that was shorts and a T-shirt.

The way Caine Carraway was looking at me right now . . . I might as well have been naked.

Goose bumps prickled along my arms and a shiver ran down my back.

"Alexa," Benito snapped.

"Sorry," I apologized, attempting not to think about Caine's heated gaze or the burning ache that was forming in my chest.

My boss shook his head impatiently. "It's fine, it's fine. Just . . . here, take the BlackBerry back." He slapped the device in my hand. I'd given it over to him before I left for vacation so he could give it to the temp. Benito's world was in that BlackBerry. It had all his business contacts, e-mails, his work calendar . . . everything on it. I saw the e-mail icon already had fifteen unread e-mails this morning. "Get the crew organized first before you get to work. We're shooting on the balcony with the harbor as a backdrop. Then inside in the sitting area. It's a little darker there, so set it up."

From there I went into autopilot. I knew my job inside and out, and that was the only reason I managed to do anything competently, because my head was not on the work. It was on the man I could barely look at as I directed one of our guys to set up Benito's camera and laptop out on the balcony and got the lighting crew to set up in the sitting room for later.

Caine Carraway.

I knew more about him than I should because for the last few months if I heard his name or saw it in print I paid attention. Call it morbid curiosity.

Orphaned at thirteen and put into the system, Caine beat the odds and went on to graduate from high school as valedictorian and continued his education at Wharton Business School on a full ride. He'd barely graduated from college when he started up the bank that would lead to Carraway Financial Holdings. By the time he was twenty-nine he was one of the most successful businessmen in Boston. Now at thirty-three he was feared and respected by his peers, welcomed into the fold of Boston's high society, and one of the city's most eligible bachelors. Although he was immensely private, the society pages took snapshots of him whenever they could, mostly at glamorous events. He was seen with beautiful women all the time, but the same one was rarely pictured with him after a few months.

All of that said *alone*, *lonely*, and, *closed off* to me.

That ache in my chest intensified.

"Alexa, come meet Mr. Carraway."

I felt my breathing increase exponentially and turned from Scott, our lighting technician, to find Benito standing beside Caine.

Trying to control my emotions, I walked slowly over to them both, my cheeks burning under the heat of Caine's black gaze. On closer inspection, I could see his eyes were actually a deep, dark brown. His face was a perfectly blank mask, but his eyes were more expressive.

I shivered again as they raked over me.

"Mr. Carraway, this is my PA, Alexa—"

"Nice to meet you." I cut off my boss before he could say my last name. "If you need anything, give me a shout." And before either Benito or Caine could respond, I quickly darted back across the room.

Scott was staring over my shoulder, and when his eyes returned to me they informed me that Benito was not pleased by my behavior. "What's with you?" Scott said.

I shrugged at my colleague, not sure how to explain why I was acting like a teenager. It would be a long explanation. Too long. Too personal. Because what was with me was that only three short months ago I had discovered my father was to blame for destroying Caine's childhood.

Now he was right there in front of me.

At Benito's snap of my name, I spun around to find him scowling at me and gesturing me out onto the balcony. The shoot was starting.

Standing behind Benito, looking at the photos on the laptop, and glancing up from those to the real man in front of me, I was able to safely study Caine. Not at any point did he smile. He stared broodingly into the camera and Benito didn't dare to ask him to change his countenance. He directed him to turn his head and body this way and that, but that was as courageous as Benito got with the guy.

"He's got that brooding thing down pat," Sofie murmured in my ear as she handed me coffee. "If I wasn't happily engaged I'd try to put a smile on his handsome face. You're single. You should so go there. I definitely think you could put a smile on his face."

I covered a reactive blanch with a smirk. "I think it would take a gymnast and her twin sister to do that, babe."

We looked at each other, laughter we couldn't quite hold down bubbling up between us. It was a relief to laugh under such intense circumstances.

Unfortunately our laughter drew Caine's attention. We

knew this because everything went quiet and we turned to find him staring curiously at me while Benito . . . Well, he appeared to be trying to fry both Sofie's ass and mine with the heat of his glower.

Sofie skittered off.

"Let's take a break." Benito sighed and approached the laptop. "You've been acting strange all morning," he said under his breath. "Am I missing something?"

"No." I stared at him, trying not to give away the truth. "Coffee?"

He nodded, no longer angry, just slightly disappointed. Which was worse.

I wisely hurried back into the apartment and headed to the bathroom. I thought a splash of cold water on my face might do me good. My hands shook as I cupped my palms under the tap water. "Shit," I whispered.

I was a mess.

Again.

Enough was enough. My job wouldn't survive another public outburst. Sure, it was a crappy situation, but I needed to pull myself together and act like a professional. Resolved to do so, I strode out of the bathroom with my shoulders thrown back and almost walked into a coffee cup.

The coffee cup was clasped in a large hand that belonged to Caine.

Staring up at him, I was struck mute. Mostly because my pulse was racing so hard it was difficult to concentrate on anything else, let alone words.

Caine raised an eyebrow and pushed the coffee toward me.

I took it, completely unable to keep the bafflement off my face.

"A peace offering," he said, and I shivered again at the

sound of his deep, cultured voice. "It would seem I scare you for some absurd reason."

Our eyes locked, and my pulse was racing for an entirely different reason now.

"What *are* they saying about me these days?"

For a moment I forgot everything but what it was like to be lost in his beautiful eyes. "Lots," I answered softly. "They are saying lots of things about you these days."

He grinned, proving me wrong—he did *not* need a gymnast and her twin to put a smile on his face. "Well, you have me at a disadvantage. You know me, but I don't know you." He took a step forward and I suddenly felt overwhelmingly, deliciously surrounded by him.

Oh God, oh God, oh God. "There's not much to tell."

Caine dipped his head, his dark eyes liquid with a heat I felt between my legs. "Somehow I doubt that." His eyes flickered to my lips before returning to mine. "I want to know more, Alexa."

"Um . . ." The old cliché "Be careful what you wish for" suddenly floated across my mind.

He seemed to mistake the fact that I was a flustered panicked mess for deliberately being enigmatic, because he warned, "I'm not finishing this shoot until you tell me something about yourself. Time is money." He smirked. "Gotta keep the boss happy."

Was he referring to himself or Benito?

I stared at him, feeling my palms turn clammy as my heart rate increased, speeding up by the mounting seconds of silence stretching between us. And that was when it happened. Overwhelmed and thrown by his sudden appearance in my life after only having just discovered he was the little boy who played victim to my father's villain, I went into meltdown. "I know you," I blurted out. "No, I mean . . ." I stepped forward, edging us farther down the hall where we had more privacy. The coffee cup trembled in my hands. "My name is Alexa *Holland*."

Shock moved through him.

To witness it was awful. His whole body jerked like I'd hit him, and the powerful businessman visibly paled before me.

I forged on. "My father is Alistair Holland. I know he had an affair with your mom and I know how it ended. I'm so—"

Caine's hand cut through the air between us in a gesture to silence me. Fury had replaced the shock. His nostrils flared with it. "I'd stop if I were you." His words were guttural with menace.

I couldn't.

"I just found out. I had no idea until a few months ago that it was you. I don't even—"

"I said stop." He stepped forward, forcing me back against the wall. "I don't want to hear it."

"Please, listen—"

"Are you fucking kidding me?" He slammed a hand against the wall above my head and I saw past the cultured, ruthless gentleman everyone else saw to a man who was far less polished and way more dangerous than anyone truly realized. "Your father seduced my mother and after introducing her to drugs, left her to OD in a hotel room because trying to save her meant watching his precious inheritance go up in flames." His face was so close to mine now I felt the warm puff of his breath on my lips. "He destroyed my family. I want *nothing* from him or you. I certainly don't want to breathe the same air as either one of you."

He abruptly pushed away from the wall and marched out of the hallway.

Most women would probably be in tears after a verbal assault like that. Not me. Growing up, I'd watched my mother succumb to tears in every spat she ever had, and I'd hated that. When she was angry she cried, when all she really wanted to do was be angry.

So I never cried when I was angry.

And I was pissed at my estranged father for putting me in a position where I'd be painted with the same disgusting brush as him.

Caine's last words penetrated through my thoughts.

"Oh, shit." I rushed out of the hallway.

Caine was speaking to Benito in the kitchen.

My stomach flipped as Benito flinched at whatever Caine said. He looked over at me, bewildered, before turning to respond to the other man.

Caine glowered and whipped around, searching the room for someone. His eyes locked on a young man dressed in a stylish suit. "Ethan, I want a different photographer." His voice carried across the room so everyone heard and caused them to halt in what they were doing. "Or I don't do the cover."

Ethan nodded militantly. "I'm on it, sir."

I was horrified; my eyes flew to Benito, whose mouth had dropped open in equal horror. Caine didn't stick around long enough to witness that, though. He was already striding toward me, and as he passed me to head for the exit, he didn't even look at me.

I felt sick.

Benito's tone was quiet, surprisingly calm. His words were not. "What the fuck did you do?"

My friend Rachel moved the restless child in her arms from one side of her lap to the other. "It's been five hours. Calm down. Your boss will call you to clear this whole misunderstanding up."

I eyed her daughter, Maisy, with growing concern. "Should Maisy's face be that purple?"

Rachel frowned at the subject change and looked at her daughter. "Maisy, stop holding your breath."

Maisy stared up at her stubbornly.

"Uh . . . she's still holding her breath." Why Rachel was not as worried by this as I was, I did not know.

Rachel made a face. "You won't get a toy if you keep holding your breath."

Maisy let out a comically long exhale and then grinned at me.

"She's the devil," I murmured softly, eyeing her warily.

"Tell me about it." Rachel shrugged. "Apparently I pulled the old holding–my-breath-to-get-what-I-want trick when I was her age."

I glanced down at my half-eaten lunch. "We can leave and go for a walk through the gardens if she's getting restless."

"We're not finished calming you down." Rachel waved at a passing waiter. "Two more diet sodas and an orange juice, please."

I didn't argue. Out of all of my friends, Rachel was the most persistent and overbearing. That was probably why she was the only one of them I still saw on a regular basis.

There had been four of us, close friends, in college: me, Rachel, Viv, and Maggie. Out of the four of us, I was the only one not married, and I was childless. Between them they had four kids. I'd lost contact with Viv and Maggie over the years, and now I only saw Rachel every few weeks. I'd been so busy with work and socializing with colleagues that I'd never bothered to make new friendships outside of the old or outside of my career.

If that horrible gut feeling I had turned out to be true, if

Benito fired me, I was looking at a very grim future of no money, no pretty apartment, and no social life.

"Maybe you should make mine a vodka," I grumbled.

Rachel heaved a sigh. "Benito is not going to fire you. Not after all your hard work. Right, baby?" She bounced her daughter on her knee.

Maisy giggled at me and shook her head, her dark curls flying into her mother's face.

"Great, even the three-year-old knows I'm fucked."

Rachel grimaced. "You can't say *fucked* in front of a kid, Lex." Our drinks arrived and she pushed mine toward me. "Now calm your shit so we can talk about me for a while."

I smiled a real smile for the first time in a week. "Only if you tell me one more time I'm not going to get fired."

"Lex, you're not going to get fired."

"Alexa, you're fired!"

My stomach dropped at the irate beginning to the voice mail message Benito had left me.

"I don't know what the fuck happened this morning, but you are done. And not just with me. Oh no! Do you know what you cost me today? You pissed Caine Carraway off so badly I lost *Mogul* and two other magazines from the same media company! My reputation is on the line here. After everything I've worked for! Well . . ." His voice lowered, which was even scarier than the shouting. "Consider yourself fucked, because I'm going to make sure you never work in this industry again."

I pinched the bridge of my nose and sucked in a shuddering, teary breath.

This was bad.

This was so, so bad.

CHAPTER 2

I stared stubbornly at my phone as I sipped a huge glass of red wine. "No."

My grandfather sighed loudly, causing the speakerphone to crackle. "For once put your pride aside and let me help you. Or do you want to move out of that apartment you love so much?"

No, I did not. I'd worked my butt off to be able to afford to rent a place like my one-bedroom condo in Back Bay. It was beautiful with its high ceilings and tall windows that looked down onto the treelined street. I loved the location. I was a twenty-minute walk from my favorite part of the city—the Public Garden, Newbury Street, Charles Street . . . Location was everything, but the fact that my apartment was cute and homey was icing on a very nice cake. It was the kind of place I'd always wanted, and I had hoped that someday I'd have saved enough for a deposit to buy the apartment or one in the same neighborhood.

Material goods didn't mean a damn thing. I knew that.

But I just really needed my pretty apartment right now. It was a comfort thing.

Did I need it enough to sell my principles?

Unfortunately no.

"I'm not taking your money, Grandpa." I knew it wasn't Edward Holland's fault, but the diamond fortune he'd inherited from his family and gone on to expand with wise investments that diversified his business portfolio was the very thing that had polluted my father. I didn't want anywhere near something so toxic.

"Then I'll have a word with Benito."

I thought about the fact that my grandfather had kept his relationship with me secret from the rest of his family. No one outside the family knew that Alexa Holland was *a* Holland—my dad had managed to keep the indiscretion with my mother that led to my birth from his family, excluding his father—and Grandpa certainly hadn't confessed to them that he'd reached out to me when I was twenty-one and all alone in Boston.

I understood that it would have caused drama and irritation for him to reveal the truth, but I couldn't say it didn't hurt. Sometimes it felt like he was ashamed of me. Like it or not, though, he was all I had now and I loved him.

I bit down my resentment. "You can't," I said. "Benito has a big mouth. He'll tell everyone who I am."

"So, what, then? You find another job . . . Doing what?"

Any other job would come with a major pay cut. As an executive PA to a successful photographer, I made a nice income. More than twice that of standard PA positions. I sipped at my wine, looking around at all my pretty things in my pretty home.

"I didn't even get to apologize," I muttered.

"What?"

"I didn't even get to apologize," I repeated. "He blew up in my face and then ruined my life." I groaned. "Don't even say it. I recognize the irony in that. My family ruined his . . . tit for tat."

Grandpa cleared his throat. "*You* didn't ruin his life. But you did take him off guard."

Guilt suffused me. "True."

"And I already told you my attempts in the past have failed. It isn't our place to apologize."

"I know that." I did know that. I wasn't disappointed, because I couldn't apologize for my father's sins. I was disappointed because in that moment, when Caine realized who I was, I saw a pain in his eyes that was so familiar to me. Seeing the pain that was clearly still raw for him, I felt a sudden, overwhelming sense of kinship with him. We were both part of a tragic legacy. I'd never been able to talk about it with anyone because of the secrecy of it all. For years I'd been left to bear the burden of the truth all by myself. Then three months ago my mom died and all the ugly shit came crawling to the surface, and during a tirade on the phone to my grandpa he'd finally let slip the name of the child who had been wronged.

Caine Carraway. The only other person besides my parents and grandfather who knew the truth. The only other person who could possibly understand.

I couldn't explain the connection I felt to him. I just knew that it was possible I was the only person who could understand his pain, and . . . I found I wanted to be there for him somehow. It didn't make sense. I barely knew him. I knew that. But I couldn't help feeling it all the same.

It was gut-wrenching then to have him look at me like I was part of the problem. Like . . . I was to blame. I hated the idea that he could think that of me, and I didn't want that to be the last time we ever spoke. I didn't want to be part of a bad memory. "I should go over there and apologize for ambushing him. While I'm there I could ask him to fix this. One call to Benito and he can make this go away."

"Alexa, I don't think that's wise."

Maybe not. But I was desperate for my job back and to change Caine's opinion of me. "Ever since Mom . . . I just . . . I need him to hear me out, and I see no harm in asking him to call Benito while I'm there."

"That sounds an awful lot like what you need and not what he needs."

I shoved that truth aside and rationalized, "Have you met Caine Carraway? I don't think that man knows what he needs."

The receptionist was staring at me as if I was ridiculous.

"You want to see Mr. *Carraway* of *Carraway* Financial Holdings without an appointment?"

I knew it wouldn't be easy to walk into the huge rose-granite-walled building on International Place and expect to be escorted directly to Caine's office. Still, the receptionist was treating it as if I were asking to see the president. "Yes." I curbed my natural instinct to return her question with sarcasm. She didn't look like she'd respond well to that.

She sighed. "One moment, please."

I glanced over at the security guard who was manning the metal detectors situated before the elevators. Carraway Financial Holdings shared the building with another company, which meant there were security cameras everywhere. No matter what I tried to pull here, I was going to get caught. It was all just a matter of timing. I was okay with getting caught . . . as long it was *after* I got in to see Caine.

I sidled away from the reception desk while the pinchy-mouthed receptionist lady frowned at her nails. While her focus was elsewhere I smoothed on a fake look of nonchalance and began to walk toward the detectors.

"ID." The security guard held out a hand to stop me from going any farther.

I stared up into his bearded face and noted the alertness in his eyes. Damn my luck. I couldn't get a clichéd, unobservant security guy?

I smiled innocently. "The lady at reception told me they've run out of visitor ID passes. She told me to go on up."

He narrowed his eyes in suspicion.

I gestured to her. "Ask her."

He huffed and looked over at reception. I realized right away he was going to yell the question at her so he didn't have to move from his post.

It was my only opportunity.

I skittered past him and rushed through the detectors and heard him shout just as I was hurrying into the elevator that would take me to Caine's floor. The doors shut as the security guard's foot came into view.

"You've lost it," I murmured to myself as the elevator climbed. "You've actually finally lost it. You should have taken the therapy when it was offered."

I heard a snort from my right. I was sharing the elevator with a guy who grinned at me as if I was hilarious. "It doesn't work for some people," he said.

I was confused. "What?"

"Therapy," he explained. "Works for some, not for others."

I took in his sharp suit and expensive watch. He was good-looking with perfect light brown hair and vibrant blue eyes, and I could tell with just one look that along with the designer

suit he wore designer confidence. He was also vaguely familiar. "Did it work for you?"

He shrugged, his grin wicked. "My therapist worked for
me."

I laughed. "Well, at least you got something out of it."

His smile widened and he nodded at the elevator buttons.
"Carraway Financial Holdings?"

I nodded and my stomach flipped nervously at the thought
of seeing him again. "I need to speak to the CEO."

"Caine?" The guy's eyebrows rose before his gaze roamed
over me. "Should I tackle you and let security have you?"

"Mr. Carraway would probably prefer that, but he *needs* to
let me have my say."

"Uh . . . who are you?"

I shot him a wary look. "Um . . . *who* are you?"

"A friend. I'm supposed to have lunch with him."

The elevator doors pinged open. "When I have it I'll give
you my firstborn if you let me cut into the first five minutes of
that."

He stepped out and I followed him. His gaze was apprais-
ing.

I waited, my eyes darting nervously to the receptionist,
who looked awfully concerned by my sudden appearance.

"I'll tell you what." Elevator Guy drew my attention back
to him, amusement lacing his words. "The detectors didn't go
off, and it's clear you're not carrying a weapon." He gestured
to my tailored shorts and tank top. "So I'm going to take you
in to see Caine. But"—he cut me off before I could give him
my relieved thanks—"I get to accompany you. I'm curious to
hear how Caine knows someone like you." He put his hand
lightly on my lower back and started guiding me toward
reception.

I wrinkled my nose, not sure if I'd just been insulted or complimented. "Someone like me?"

"Mr. Lexington." The receptionist shot up from his chair, his voice high with panic. "I believe that woman just dodged security."

"It's fine, Dean." The guy, who I now recognized from the society pages as Henry Lexington, the son of Randall Lexington, one of Caine's business partners, waved away the receptionist's concerns. "Let Caine know we're on our way."

Bemused, I let Lexington lead me down a corridor of offices. Near the end of the hallway, the space opened out and a glass desk as stylish as the reception desk we'd previously passed was positioned aside two large double doors. A brass plaque on the door declared that the room beyond belonged to Caine Carraway, CEO.

There were no windows into the office on this side, affording Caine complete privacy.

The young man I'd seen at the photo shoot stood up from behind the glass desk as we approached. His eyes darted to me and then widened with recognition. "Uh, Mr. Lexington—"

"I'm expected." Lexington threw him a debonair smile that definitely worked for him and reached for the door.

"But—"

The PA was cut off as Lexington led me inside Caine's huge office. While there were no windows behind us, there was a wall of them opposite us and along the right side of the office. Light streamed into the modern but sparsely decorated space.

I barely took anything in, however, because my gaze zeroed in on Caine.

He looked equal parts enraged and baffled by my presence as he shot to his feet from behind a huge antique desk.

There was another dip in my belly, this one a little lower than the last. Although I'd already witnessed it, the power of his presence continued to surprise me.

"Henry, what the fuck?"

Lexington's eyebrows rose considerably at Caine's reaction to my appearance. He looked down at me and smirked. "Seriously, who are you?"

"Get out."

Both our heads whipped back in Caine's direction.

Of course he was talking to me.

"No." I took a step toward him despite the menace emanating from him. "We need to talk." The muscle in his jaw flexed at my refusal to be cowed.

Inwardly I was pretty cowed, but he didn't need to know that.

"I'm busy."

"Mr. Lexington here was kind enough to offer me five minutes of his lunch appointment with you."

Caine shot him a furious look. "Did he?"

Henry smiled. "I'm a gentleman that way."

"Henry, get out," Caine said, the words quiet but forceful.

"Well, I made—"

"Now."

Clearly Henry knew something I didn't, because unlike me he didn't appear at all afraid of Caine. "Of course." He chuckled and then winked at me in a way that worked for him even more than the debonair smile. "Good luck."

I waited until the door had closed behind Henry before I took in a deep breath and braced myself to interact with Caine. I noted his eyes flickered up quickly from my legs to my face.

I shivered under that Prince of Darkness stare of his.

"In two seconds you'll be following him out of the door."

You can do this. Make him hear you, Lex. "Throw me out and I will come back quicker than a boomerang."

"I daresay a boomerang won't fare too well against a locked door, Miss Holland."

"Lock the door and I'll find other, more creative ways to torment you. I have nothing left to lose at this point."

Caine heaved an irritated sigh. "You have one minute. Use it wisely."

God, he really was an arrogant SOB. I pushed down my irritation, reminding myself who he was and what he'd been through. "Two things. First, I lost my job."

His response to that was to shrug and relax against his desk. He crossed his arms over his chest and then one ankle over the other and hit me with an insouciant "So?"

"So . . . it's because of what happened at the shoot."

"Then I suggest you act more professionally in the future. Now I have lunch to attend to . . ." He gestured to the door.

"Look." I held up my hands in something akin to surrender. "I apologize. That's the second thing. I apologize sincerely—"

"Fucking say it and I will throw you out," he warned.

"For ambushing you," I hurried to finish.

He relaxed only somewhat.

"I shouldn't have done that. I had no idea we were doing a photo shoot with you. I showed up on-set and you were there and I'm in a weird place and I acted emotionally and it was really unfair to you."

Caine merely blinked at my rambling.

"So I'm sorry," I finished.

"Fine." He stood up, his eyes moving over my shoulder, not concealing his impatience.

I took that "fine" as an acceptance of my apology and forged ahead again. "But the punishment doesn't fit the crime."

I was treated to another heavy sigh from him. "Tell me again why I should care if the daughter of the man who gave my mother the cocaine that killed her no longer has a job."

I flinched. "My father's actions were not mine."

"Same blood runs in your veins."

Any hope I had of battling my irritation with his arrogance went flying out the window. "Oh? Cocaine addict, are you?"

I regretted the words as soon as they were out of my mouth.

"Get out." The words were said with barely leashed fury.

"Okay, okay," I hurried to defuse that land mine. "That was a shitty thing to say. I'm really sorry. But you're presuming to know who I am because of who my father is, and that's shitty too."

There was no response.

Cautiously I took a step toward the brooding businessman. "Look, you didn't just get me fired. My boss lost *Mogul* and two other clients because of your ire. That means my boss blacklisted me. I won't get another job in the industry again unless you fix this. Just . . . let Benito do the shoot. Please."

A weighted silence fell between us as we stared at each other. I was pretty sure (or at least I hoped) Caine was silent because he was considering my request. The silence, however, just afforded me even more of a chance to soak in his rugged, dark handsomeness. Was it possible he was getting better-looking?

That was a problem for me.

My mom had always been so bowled over by my dad's looks that she felt inferior to him, like maybe she was the lucky one to be with him and not the other way around. I'd hated that and I didn't need a therapist to tell me it was the reason that I tended to date guys who were attractive but not so attractive they were intimidating. More important, my ex-boyfriends (and it wasn't like there were lots of those) all made it clear that they thought they were punching above their weight by dating me. I didn't look for that because I needed to feel more attractive than my partner. It was because I didn't want to feel inferior.

Not like Mom had.

Which was why my reaction to Caine was an anomaly. I could admit when a guy was a *hot* guy. But I was never attracted to *hot* guys, because I'd hard-wired my brain not to shoot off all the chemicals that would make me attracted to *hot* guys.

With Caine, though . . . well, my thoughts had wandered into the indecent since the moment we met (if I was honest, maybe even before then) and I could feel my skin prickling with awareness under his fierce regard.

"No."

No? "What do you mean no?"

He quirked an eyebrow at me. "It's one of the most commonly used words in the English language, Miss Holland. Shocking that someone who doesn't understand its meaning would find herself unemployable."

I ignored his sarcasm and flipped my hair over my shoulder with what I hoped was an air of defiance. "I won't take no for an answer."

Caine's already dark eyes shadowed with irritation as he said with a threatening calmness, "You'll take it and you'll get out before I personally remove you from my office."

I shivered again at the thought of him putting those big

hands of his anywhere near me. I quickly threw that thought aside and replied, "Please be fair."

The air around him thickened with anger. "Fair?" he said, his voice hoarse. "What part of you being here is fair? I'm going to ask you to leave one more time, and if you don't I *will* physically remove you."

I closed my eyes, unable to see the pain in his without wanting to hurt my own father. Because my father was a weak and irresponsible man, Caine Carraway had lost everything, and despite all the "everything" he had around him now, I wasn't convinced from what I'd seen so far that he actually had *anything*. "I'll go," I whispered. When I opened my eyes he was staring stonily at me. My stomach sank at the realization that this was it. His opinion of me hadn't changed, and I was still jobless. "I really am sorry. I just . . . I'm just stuck." And I meant that in so many ways. I grabbed the handle on his office door and had started to pull on it when his irritated sigh stopped me.

"I'll call your boss and tell him to take you back."

Relief swooshed through me as I whirled to look at him, amazed. "Really?"

He gave me his back. "Yes, but I will change my mind if you don't get out of my office in the next five seconds."

I shot out of that office in three seconds flat. I didn't get everything I came for, which was probably why as I drove home my relief was gradually outweighed by my disappointment. It occurred to me that I wished Caine could see what I saw—that we were the same in some ways. And I didn't want to be someone he hated.

However, it was clear Caine needed me to leave him alone. And I would. Even if it was the absolute last thing I wanted to do.

CHAPTER 3

The last day and a half of moping around my apartment had been torturous. With nothing but worry and time on my hands, I'd started reliving some pretty crappy memories, including that fateful day seven years ago when I found out the truth about my father and how he wasn't an absentee father who gave up his jet-setting career in order to see us every day. No, he was a poor excuse for a man who abandoned his first family and took no responsibility for the woman who overdosed in his presence. This led to thinking about my relationship with my mom and about how shit things were before she died. None of those were things I wanted to remember, so I spent most of my time going over and over my accounts trying to figure out a way to stretch the savings I had. I could get by, living in my apartment without a well-paying job, for six months. This meant eventually giving up the apartment was inevitable.

Accounting was so depressing.

I lounged, legs dangling over the arm of my big comfy

armchair that probably wouldn't fit into the kind of apartment I'd have to move to if Benito didn't hire me back, and I sipped at my Cherry Coke while Bing Crosby sang out "Brother, Can You Spare a Dime?" from my speakers.

"You sing it, Bing." I raised my glass in the air in a gesture of solidarity and nearly spilled my soda as the much louder sounds of Bruce Springsteen singing "Johnny 99" blasted from my cell.

So I liked a relevant sound track to my life.

Heart racing, hoping the name I'd see on the screen was Benito, I rolled off the chair, landed hard on my knees, bit out a curse word, and scrambled along my floor, spilling Cherry Coke on the hardwood.

Almost smacking my nose against the wall, I got up onto my feet and snatched at the phone buzzing on my kitchen counter. I frowned at the number on the screen.

I didn't recognize it.

Deflated, I answered in a pathetically sad tone, "Hello."

"Hello, this is Ethan Rogers calling from Mr. Carraway's office. Am I speaking to Miss Alexa Holland?"

My pulse started going wild again. "You are." I held my breath.

"Mr. Carraway requests that you attend a meeting with him in his office tomorrow at noon."

A meeting with Caine? What on earth— "Did he say why?"

"No, Miss Holland, he did not. May I tell him you'll be available tomorrow at noon?"

Why, oh, why, after all his protestations did Caine want to see me again? What had happened since I crashed into his office? My stomach did that nervous flippy thing again. "Um . . ." Had Benito said yes or no? Or was this about something else? What did Caine want from me?

Did it matter?

He wanted to see me again, and that was an opportunity to change his mind about me.

"Sure. I'll be there."

Ethan led me into Caine's office the next afternoon and I was surprised to find Caine not behind his desk but standing in front of the floor-to-ceiling windows staring out over High Street and Atlantic Avenue to the harbor beyond.

With his back to me, I stole that moment to fully appreciate Caine Carraway without him knowing it. So yeah, I couldn't see his face, which was the best part, but with him standing with his hands in his trouser pockets, legs braced, shoulders relaxed, the view was delicious enough for me. His height, those broad shoulders, and let's not forget that ass.

That was a mighty fine ass.

When the seconds ticked by without a response from him, I began to feel like a high school nerd waiting for the captain of the football team to pay attention to her.

I didn't like that nearly as much as the view of his ass.

"You rang?"

Caine turned his head slightly in profile. "I did."

"And I assume there was a reason?"

He faced me and I felt that flush of attraction as his eyes swept over me. "You would assume right." He sighed and strolled over to his desk, his gaze raking over me speculatively as he did so. "Do you own a suit, heels?" His scrutiny moved to my face. "Makeup?"

I looked down at my clothes. I was wearing jeans and a sweater, and no, I wasn't wearing makeup. I had good skin. I'd inherited my olive skin from my mother, and despite those darn freckles sprinkled across the crest of my nose, it was blemish free. I rarely wore foundation or blush, and because my eyes were so light and my lashes so dark, I only wore mascara when dressing up for an occasion.

I knew I wasn't glamorous, but I looked like my mom—I had her apple cheekbones, blue-green eyes, and dark hair—and my mom had been very pretty. No one had ever looked me over and considered my lack of makeup with disdain before.

I frowned. "Weird question."

Caine relaxed against his desk in much the same pose as he had used the last time he pinched his lips at me in his office. And he *was* pinching his lips and inspecting me. I felt like I was being judged and found wanting, which was insulting normally but somehow even worse coming from a guy who looked as put together as he did.

Sexy jackass.

"I couldn't change Benito's mind," Caine informed me. "That little bastard can hold a grudge."

If I weren't so deflated by his news I would have laughed. "Bu—"

"So I thought about it," he said, cutting me off, "and you can try working for me. You'll need to invest in some appropriate clothing, however."

Um . . . what? Did he just . . . ? "I'm sorry. What?"

"Benito informed me that it kills him but he just can't take you back after your behavior with a client lost him such big accounts. You're the biggest disappointment of his thirties and before you went insane you were the best PA he ever had. The disappointment of your behavior on-set, and I quote, Broke. His. Heart."

"Oh yeah, he sounds devastated."

"Despite his flair for the melodramatic, it seems he has

high standards and he has led me to believe that before you acted like an insane person you were intelligent, efficient, and hardworking."

"Insane person?" That word had been used as an adjective to describe me twice now.

He ignored me. "I need a PA. Ethan is a temp and my previous PA has decided not to return from maternity leave. I have a job opening and I'm offering it to you."

Dumbfounded.

There was no other word for how I was feeling.

How could this man go from never wanting to see me again to offering me a job that meant I was going to be in his face? *A lot.*

"But . . . I thought you didn't want me around."

Caine narrowed his eyes. "I need a PA who will fulfill all my wishes and demands immediately. That's not easy to find—most people have social lives. You, however, are desperate, and the way I see it, you owe me."

I sobered at his reminder of the past. "So what . . . you get to act out some kind of vengeance by working me into an early grave?"

"Something like that." He smirked. "It'll be a comfortable grave, though." He told me the salary and I almost passed out.

My mouth parted on a gasp. "For a PA job? Are you serious?"

I'd get to keep my apartment. I'd get to keep my car. Screw that . . . I'd be able to save enough money to afford a deposit on my apartment.

Caine's eyes glittered triumphantly at my obvious excitement. "As I said, it comes with a price." His grin was wicked and I suddenly felt a little breathless. "I'm a hard man to please. And I'm also a very busy man. You'll do what I want when I want and I won't always be nice about it. In fact, considering what your surname is, you can pretty much guarantee I won't be nice about it."

My heart thumped at the warning. "So you're saying you plan to make my life miserable?"

"If you equate hard work with misery." He considered me as I considered him, and that damnable little smirk quirked his beautiful mouth again. "So . . . just how desperate are you?"

I stared at him, this man who held up an armored shield so high in the hopes that nothing would penetrate it. But call it intuition or call it wishful thinking, I believed I could see past that shield of his—like I could feel the emotion he fought so hard to hide. And that emotion was anger. He was angry with me, whether because of my father or my sudden intrusion into his life, and this job . . . this job was his way of taking back control, of making me pay for throwing him off balance. If I took it I had no doubt he was going to do his best to test my patience to the limit. I was a pretty patient person normally. No way I could have worked with someone like Benito and not have been. But I didn't feel like myself around Caine.

Not at all.

I was defensive and scared and vulnerable.

It would be a huge risk putting myself in his control.

However, I knew it was a risk I would take. And not just because he was offering me more money than I would ever make anywhere else, nor because this job would look great on my résumé. I would take this risk because I wanted him to see I wasn't anything like my dad. I wanted Caine to see that if anything, I was like *him*.

I jutted my chin out defiantly. "I worked for Benito for six years. You don't scare me." *You terrify me.*

Caine slipped on that intimidatingly blank mask of his and pushed up off his desk. I held my breath, my skin prickling as he prowled across the room. I had to tilt my head back to meet his gaze as he came to a stop inches before me.

He smelled really, really good.

"We'll see," he murmured.

I felt that murmur between my legs.

Oh boy.

I stuck out my hand. "I accept the job."

Caine's eyes dropped to my hand. I tried not to tremble as I waited for him to decide whether or not he wanted to touch me. Swallowing my misery at his reluctance, I kept my gaze unwavering.

Finally he reached out and slid his large hand into mine.

The friction of the rougher skin of his palm against the soft skin of mine sent sparks shooting up my arm, and arousal tightened my muscles, including those in my fingers.

Surprise flared in both of our eyes.

Quite abruptly, Caine ripped his hand from mine and turned his back on me. "You start Monday," he said, his words curt as he made his way to his desk. "At six thirty. Ethan will give you the particulars of my morning schedule."

Still shaken from the sizzle that had just passed between us, I said hoarsely, "Six thirty?"

Caine glanced over his shoulder at me as he shuffled some papers on his desk. "Is that a problem?"

"It's early."

"It is." His tone brooked no denial.

Six thirty it was, then. "I'll be here."

"And dress appropriately." I bristled but nodded at the command. "And do something with your hair."

I frowned and touched a strand of it. "What do you mean?" I wore my hair long with a slight wave in it. There was nothing wrong with my hair.

Annoyed, Caine turned to face me. "This isn't a nightclub. I expect your hair and clothes to be stylish but conservative. Image is important, and from now on you represent this company. Slovenly hair and clothes do not reflect the company image."

Stylish but conservative? Slovenly hair and clothes?

I contemplated him and how pompous he could be. *You have quite the stick up your ass, don't you?*

He glowered as if he'd read my mind. "Tomorrow you'll receive employment contracts. Once you sign those I'm your boss." When I didn't answer he said, "That means you act the way I want you to act. That means you shelve the attitude and the twenty questions."

"Should I shelve those next to 'personality'?"

Caine did not look amused. In fact, the look in his eyes bordered on predatory. "That would be wise."

I gulped, suddenly wondering why I'd thought it was smart to poke the tiger. "Noted." Already I could tell this arrangement between us was not going to be easy, but I just had to remember my endgame here. "I guess I'll see you Monday, Caine."

He lowered himself into his seat without looking up at me. "Ethan will provide you with all the information you need before you leave."

"Great."

"Oh, and, Alexa?"

I froze but my pulse sped up. He'd never said my name before.

It sounded nice on his lips. Very, very nice.

"Yeah?" I whispered.

"From now on you will refer to me as Mr. Carraway and only Mr. Carraway."

Ouch. Talk about putting me in my place. "Of course." I took another step toward the door.

"And one other thing." This time I halted at his dark, dangerous tone. "You never mention your father or my mother, ever again."

My heart practically clenched at the pain I heard in his voice.

With a careful nod, I slipped out of his office, and despite the way he threw me off balance, I was more determined than ever that this was the right decision. Somehow this was where I was meant to be.

CHAPTER 4

The hot water sluiced down over me and I waited for it to wake me up. So far, nothing. In fact, I was so tired I couldn't even find the energy for first-day-on-the-job-jitters. I washed the conditioner out of my hair and stumbled from the shower.

Coffee.

I needed coffee.

I groaned and leaned back against the cool tiled wall of my bathroom and closed my eyes. I must have drifted off, because the next thing I knew I was jolted into full consciousness by the sounds of Rush's "Working Man" blaring from my cell. It took me a minute to realize I'd made it my ringtone the night before.

I sleepily made my way into my bedroom and snatched the cell up off my bedside table. "'Ello?"

"I'm just checking if you managed to haul yourself out of bed," Caine's voice rumbled down the line.

It was like a double shot of espresso, shooting through my blood and waking me up.

"Of course I am," I said, proud that I actually sounded alert. "I'll be at the office at six thirty sharp."

"I'd like a decaf latte macchiato on my desk when I get in."

Uh . . . I glanced at the clock. I had not factored in coffee-buying time. "Okay, but I'll probably be a little later, then."

"No." Caine's voice suddenly lowered in warning. "You'll get your ass in the office at six thirty with a latte or don't bother coming in at all." He hung up.

I sighed and threw my phone on the bed. Caine had warned me he was pretty much going to be an asshole, so I couldn't be surprised by this. I also didn't have time to be annoyed. If I was going to get him his damn latte and get into the office on time, I was going to have to forgo blowing out my hair. Instead I hurried around my room like a frantic person. I gave my hair a quick couple of blasts with my hair dryer and then coiled it up into a neat French knot.

The whole time I dressed I frowned, and it wasn't just because of my cranky tiredness. It was because of the stockings I'd had to pull on, and the tight, ass-cupping black pencil skirt I was wearing. Rachel had accompanied me on a shopping trip to Newbury Street that weekend so I could find "appropriate" clothing for my new job. We'd barely made it two blocks before I dropped a small fortune on stylish, expensive suits and blouses so I could fit the image of a Carraway Financial Holdings employee. This meant I was heading to work in that darn figure-hugging pencil skirt with a blue silk blouse tucked into it, a black peplum jacket to match the skirt, and black three-inch Prada heels I already owned but had rarely worn.

I'd even swiped on a little mascara.

I stared at my reflection in my full-length mirror and nodded. Stylish but conservative.

I wrinkled my nose.

I missed my boy shorts and flip-flops.

There was no more time to glower at my reflection. I had coffee to get! I jumped in my silver-blue Miata, flew through the streets, and got to International Place in less than fifteen minutes. After parking in the underground garage of our building, I ran inelegantly in my Pradas to the coffee place around the corner since the one in the courtyard of our building hadn't opened yet. When I got to the coffee place, I was surprised by the lack of a line.

And then I realized that not everyone was an obsessed businessman who started work at six thirty in the freaking morning! I glanced at my watch as I pushed into the coffeehouse.

I was fifteen minutes early.

All that panic for nothing.

Once I had Caine's latte and my own double espresso, I strode into the building, mentally preparing myself for being pushed to my limits by my unyielding new boss. I flashed the ID Ethan had set up for me on Friday at the security guard and hopped on the elevator all the way up to Carraway Financial Holdings.

There was no one in the office except a cleaner. The sense of stillness in the place initiated those first-day jitters I'd been waiting for.

I took the key out Ethan had also given me and unlocked Caine's office. It was immaculate. Not a thing out of place. It was kind of cold, in fact, and although there were a few plants in there, there was nothing personal. No photographs, no nothing. There was a painting of the Boston skyline that was pretty cool, but it was the only thing in the office that had any personality or color.

I placed his latte carefully on his desk and eyed the large L-shaped sofa by the window.

It needed cushions.

Eyeing the uncomfortable-looking sofa as I passed it, I decided a throw wouldn't go amiss either.

I finally allowed myself to relax a little as I settled at my glass desk outside his office. I looked down at it and grimaced. There'd be no hiding a tabloid magazine I wasn't supposed to be reading under this thing, then, huh? Caine was a stick-in-the-mud. Even his furniture prevented me from having fun.

Booting up my computer, I sipped at my espresso and sighed with relief.

Coffee.

Sometimes I thought it might be better than sex.

According to Rachel, I didn't know what good sex was, though, so apparently I was unqualified to make that comparison.

I was only sitting at the desk a few minutes when I heard footsteps approach. I looked up, my stomach doing that flippy thing again when Caine appeared around the corner. This morning he was wearing a light silver-gray suit that fit him to perfection and carrying a black leather briefcase. A white gold cuff link winked at his wrist as he reached up to straighten the thin dark blue tie that didn't need to be straightened.

He stopped by my desk with one eyebrow raised.

It was really appalling that any man could look that good at this time in the morning. Or anytime, for that matter.

"You made it."

"Yes, sir," I said breezily. "And your latte is on your desk."

Caine gave me a short nod, his eyes dropping to my torso. "Stand up."

I attempted not to bristle at the clipped demand and slowly rose to my feet. He waved his hand to the floor in front of him and I took that to mean he wanted me to go there.

Although blood heated my cheeks, I pretended I was completely unaffected by this demeaning crap, because I could tell by that gleam in his eyes that he wanted me to be pissed off. Once I was standing in front of him for inspection, Caine's face remained blank as he appraised my appearance. He made a circling motion with his forefinger and I spun slowly around for him.

You cannot kill your boss on the first day, you cannot kill your boss on the first day, you cannot kill your boss period . . .

I remained outwardly impassive as I stopped, turning to face him.

He gave me another short nod. "You'll do."

Are you finished making me feel like a prized poodle? That was what I really wanted to say. Instead I said, "May I get you anything?"

"I'll e-mail you what I need. Ethan went over your duties regarding calls et cetera?"

I looked over my shoulder at him as he stood waiting in the doorway of his office for an answer. "He did indeed."

"Good. If there's something you really don't know the answer to, ask, but please exhaust all other possible avenues by using common sense and a little intelligence." That haughty statement was finalized by the slamming of his office door.

"Oh boy," I muttered, and slipped back into my chair, hand reaching for my espresso.

I had a feeling this was going to be a *long* day.

And as the e-mails started pouring in from Caine, I wasn't wrong.

The tasks he wanted me to do ranged from setting up meetings, arranging business lunches, setting up conference rooms, mail, answering e-mails on his behalf including work and personal, to calling to check when his dry cleaning would be ready for collection, canceling lunch with Phoebe Billing-ham (the woman I knew from society pages he was currently dating), and running out to the store to buy food. Apparently he was out of milk and granola.

Every request was asked with curt impatience. It was only day one and I wanted to slap some manners into Caine Car-raway. It wasn't until around four o'clock when one of his company lawyers was leaving his office and I heard Caine call out, "Thank you, Arnold," that I realized my boss *did* have manners.

He just didn't think *I* was worth the effort of using them.

Getting Caine to see me for who I really was was proving more difficult than I had first thought. I was going to have to climb over his insurmountable arrogance and perverse sense of justice where I was concerned if I was ever going to convince him that we really weren't that different.

I stood openmouthed in Caine's apartment.

Holy . . .

The penthouse.

Caine had a penthouse on Arlington Street. Like in his office, there were floor-to-ceiling windows everywhere, giving him awesome views of the city. The apartment was open-plan living with a stunning state-of-the-art black-and-white kitchen with an island in the middle. White leather stools lined the front of the island.

White leather. In a kitchen.

Clearly the man either didn't eat there or was the cleanest guy in the whole wide world.

To my left was a raised platform where a stylish eight-seater dining table and chairs were set up so diners could enjoy that view. Opposite the kitchen was a reading area, and beyond that was a huge black sofa that faced a wall where a massive flat-screen television hung.

A spiral staircase behind me led up to the bedrooms. Lifting my jaw off the floor, I carefully made my way up the staircase and down the narrow, short corridor to the first bedroom on the left. Caine told me this was the master bedroom and I was to leave the dry cleaning I'd just picked up for him in there.

I felt a flush of heat at the sight of Caine's bed.

That was definitely *a bed*.

Huge, dark wood, masculine, with four posts.

Opposite it were two doors. After a quick peek inside both, I discovered my dream walk-in closet and an Italian marble bathroom.

The best part of the master suite, however, was the steps that led up to the glass window that ran along the back of the room. A sliding door led out onto a small terraced balcony where Caine could enjoy the view over Beacon Hill and beyond in privacy.

Carefully I laid his dry cleaning across his bed and made my way back out of the room. I wanted to be nosy and have a thorough look around, but I had to be back at the office with the salad he'd ordered from his favorite deli.

I did note, however, as I walked through his private space that again there was nothing overly personal in his apartment. There were no photographs of him or of friends . . . nothing that showed any personal ties to anyone.

Maybe that was normal for a bachelor, but I couldn't help feeling that prick of guilt again because in among all the nothing in Caine's everything there were no photographs of his family.

Frowning, I let myself out of his apartment, locked up,

and turned around only to almost collide with a small old woman in a vibrant fuchsia robe. She glowered up at me with her hands on her hips, her dyed black hair styled into an elegant beehive. Those narrowed bright blue eyes of hers were framed by lashes liberally brushed with mascara, and her lips, which were surprisingly full for a woman who I guessed to be in her late seventies, were painted a vivid red.

"Who the hell are you?" she asked in a thick South Boston accent.

I blinked in surprise. "Uh . . ."

"Well? You got five seconds to tell me before I call up Security."

"I'm Alexa Holland." I stuck my hand out. "Mr. Carraway's new PA."

It was her turn to blink owlishly. Slowly, as her gaze roamed over me, a smile stretched those youthful lips of hers. "So you're Alexa, huh? Oh, I heard all about you."

She had? "You have?"

"Mmm-hmm. When Caine told me he'd hired the offspring of that bastard that destroyed his family, I thought for sure he was making a big mistake." She laughed as she drank me in. "Now I get it."

"Uh . . ." I didn't.

"I'm Mrs. Flanagan. I live in the other penthouse." She gestured down the hallway past the elevator. "Come, have tea. We'll talk."

As curious as I was to chat with the flamboyant Mrs. Flanagan, who clearly knew Caine well enough to know his history, I had to be back at the office. I couldn't help grimacing in disappointment. "I'm sorry. I wish I could, but I have to get Mr. Carraway's salad to him."

Mrs. Flanagan's eyes twinkled. "Oh, no worries, sweetheart. Caine's putting you through the paces, huh? You tell him I said he's not to work you too hard. If you don't get enough sleep you won't age well. I know. Look at me. I get a solid eight hours every night and have done so for the past fifty years. I'm a walking testament to the power of beauty sleep." She waved her finger in front of my nose. "You've got natural beauty. Don't let lack of sleep waste that shit."

I burst out laughing, completely charmed by this character in front of me. "I will endeavor to get my eight hours if it means I'll look as good as you when I'm your age."

"Oh, I like you." Mrs. Flanagan chuckled. "When you come back you and I definitely need to sit down over some tea and cakes. Speaking of, tell Caine I'm making his favorite— banana cream pie—so he better stop by tonight."

Caine liked banana cream pie? I looked down at the bag in my hand that carried his salad. For three days I'd been in his employment and so far I'd discovered the man was a health nut. He visited the gym every morning before work and he only ate steamed veggies, soup, and salad.

Banana cream pie was a whole other side of him.

I grinned. "I will definitely tell him."

Dean from the main reception desk threw me a sympathetic smile as I flew past him with an out-of-puff "Hey, Dean!"

Although I hadn't had a chance to really mingle with many of Caine's other employees, and doubted I ever would with the schedule he gave me, Dean had dropped by a few times to check in with me. He was sweet and friendly, and honestly just having one person treat me like a human being helped me get through the day.

I hauled ass toward Caine's office and tried to catch my breath as I stopped at my desk to arrange his food on a plate and on a tray. I called into his office to let him know I had his salad. He told me to come in and I strode inside, thankfully no longer out of breath, to find him settled on his sofa with one ankle resting on his opposite knee as he frowned at the paperwork in his hands.

I approached with the tray and Caine looked up at me. I quickly wrenched my gaze away from his forearms. His sleeves were rolled up, displaying his corded, tan arms.

The son of a bitch had to have some kind of physical flaw. I was going to find it. I was.

"You're late." He curled his lip in annoyance.

Personality flaws, on the other hand . . . oh, I'd already found lots of those.

"Sorry, Mr. Carraway," I murmured, placing the tray on the coffee table in front of him. "I was delayed by Mrs. Flanagan." I straightened, eyeing him for a reaction.

And I got it.

Wariness had crept over him.

If I could have I would have done a fist pump in triumph.

"She wanted me to tell you that she made your favorite—banana cream pie." I grinned with faux sweet innocence. "You're to stop by tonight for a piece."

The unhappiness radiating from him would have quelled any normal person into silence—or at least wiped the stupid teasing smile off their face. But I never claimed to be normal. Nope, I was enjoying his obvious discomfort, because it meant I had found something real out about him, and I was eager to learn more about the charming Mrs. Flanagan.

"Get out of my office, Alexa."

At the growled command, I decided it was wise to choke back my chuckle and do just that. Caine's gaze burned into my back the whole time.

The next morning . . .

I braced myself as Caine marched toward my desk, his appearance dark and grim. I was so busy looking at his face I didn't notice what was in his hand until it was clattering down on top of my desk.

I stared in bewilderment at the Tupperware container. Inside it I could see a piece of pie.

I looked up at Caine in question.

He was clearly pissed off and extremely uncomfortable. "Mrs. Flanagan insisted you have a piece of pie," he said, teeth gritted.

I opened my mouth, but he cut me off with a sharp "Don't." With that he threw open his office door and slammed it shut behind him.

Caine cared enough about his elderly neighbor to follow through on her instructions despite the fact that it almost physically killed him to do so.

I opened the Tupperware box and stuck a finger in. Licking the sweet cream off it, I smiled and settled back in my chair. "Thank you, Mrs. Flanagan."

And not just for the pie.

CHAPTER 5

I left the conference room as an intern rolled in a tray decked out with pastries I'd bought. It was Friday morning and I'd survived almost an entire week working as Caine's PA. He had a conference in fifteen minutes and he wanted me to make sure that the room was set up.

I smiled at Caine's CFO's secretary, Verity, as I passed. His CFO, a Ms. Fenton, was scary. She was a little robotic—all cold and efficient and superintelligent. There was nothing motherly about her and that was why I was surprised to discover that the reason she was one of the busiest people I'd ever met was that she was also a wife and mother to two kids. Suffice to say we'd spoken fewer than five words to each other. I knew Verity a little better. She was friendly and we'd managed to chat for a brief few minutes when I was at the photocopier, but Caine had me running one errand after another, so I still hadn't gotten to know any of my colleagues at all well.

For half of yesterday I'd spent the day running around Boston trying to find a doll from a Disney movie for the daughter of some judge Caine rubbed elbows with. The guy was in the middle of a big case and didn't have time to buy his kid a birthday present, so Caine had offered up my services. The doll the kid wanted was not easy to find. In fact, it was so not easy I found it in this little independent toy store that should probably have been killed by the economy by now. By the time I got back to the office, I was a sweaty mess and Caine was pissed I'd taken so long.

I wanted to tell him that perhaps he shouldn't loan his PA out, but somehow I bit back my attitude. I wasn't so sure yet that Caine wouldn't fire me at the slightest provocation. He was not a man you trifled with.

Four and a half days I'd been working for him.

It felt longer.

As I returned to my desk my phone started ringing. It was in-house. Caine. "Sir?" I asked upon switching on the speakerphone.

"I need you to make a reservation for two at Menton for this evening at eight. Also, have a dozen red roses delivered to Phoebe Billingham, Harvard University Press, Cambridge. I want them delivered this afternoon."

Phoebe Billingham. Smart. Beautiful. Sophisticated. Wealthy. She was a copy editor for Harvard University Press and a society darling. She really was perfect for him.

I ignored the burn in my chest. "Of course. What would you like the card to say?"

"The card?"

"On the flowers."

"From Caine."

I wrinkled my nose, the romantic in me wailing in outrage. "That's it?"

Caine had apparently been dating Phoebe for eight weeks,

which was a long time in Caine's world. I wasn't surprised, though. Phoebe had it all, and she had the potential to make him happy. At the end of the day, Caine deserved nothing less.

He needed to step it up to keep her interested.

"Yes," he replied, the word edged with impatience.

"Don't you think you could be a little more romantic?"

"I'm sending her a dozen red roses and taking her to dinner at a nice restaurant. That's not romantic?"

"It's fine." It was a little generic, but whatever. "But the card could be a little more personal."

"I don't do personal." He hung up.

Exhaling, I put the phone down and contemplated the note I'd made for the roses. I knew it would be obnoxious of me to meddle, but sometimes you had to be a little obnoxious to do a lot of good. I smiled to myself and picked up the phone to order the flowers.

I gritted my teeth, channeling the most patient me possible as I tried to discuss the changes to the list of costs the interior designer Caine had hired had sent him. He'd hired her to revamp the summerhouse he'd just bought in Nantucket. The week was almost over and it would have been so much better if I could have ended it on a high note—not arguing with a cocky she-witch of a designer.

"I don't see what the problem is," she said in this nasally voice that, along with her bad attitude, made me want to punch her.

I refrained from *verbally* punching her. "The problem is you've sent over a new list of costs for this refurbishment and it's fifteen thousand dollars more than the original that Mr. Carraway signed off on."

"Style takes cash, darling."

"That's the thing. I'm going over the lists and I can't see where that extra fifteen thousand is going . . ." I suddenly became aware I wasn't alone and glanced to my right to see that Caine had come out of his office and was standing over me, eyes blazing in annoyance.

I cast him a wary look but continued to haggle with the irritant on the other end of the line.

Suddenly Caine's large hand appeared and he pressed the mute button on the phone. The jerky movement suggested I was right about him being annoyed, and I looked up at him wondering what the hell I'd done. "I can afford an extra fifteen g. Get off the phone. Now."

I tsked. "Just because you're loaded doesn't mean you should let people take advantage." I hit the mute button. "No, I'm still here," I responded to her frantic twittering. "Where was I . . . ? Oh yes, unless you want it getting around that you're an incompetent idiot trying to screw over your clients, I suggest you stick to the original budget."

"Well, I . . . How . . . I never—"

"Okeydokey, then." I hung up and looked up at my irate boss. "Why is there a vein popping out on your forehead?"

"What the hell did you put on that card?"

"Card?" I said innocently.

Caine's angry countenance ramped up to murderous. "I just got a call from Phoebe. She thanked me for the flowers, said my card was so sweet, and that she was looking forward to seeing me soon too."

So I'd known changing the message on the card with the flowers was forward of me, but I didn't think it would be that big of a deal. Apparently it was. Caine appeared to be excessively irritated and I had to admit that made me more than a little nervous. "Well . . . I just thought . . . Well, I thought it was more appropriate to sign the card with a greeting of some kind." I smiled up at him hopefully.

"Alexa," he warned.

"You know you can call me Lexie."

Caine actually growled.

"Okay," I hurried to explain, "I had them write 'Phoebe, I look forward to seeing you tonight, Caine.' And"—I almost closed my eyes in preparation for his reaction—"I may have put a little kiss at the end."

The air around him seemed to swell with annoyance. "What?"

"An *X*. You know . . . a kiss . . ." I trailed off, wishing I was back in Hawaii with a mojito.

Quite abruptly Caine put his hands on the armrests of my chair and shoved it against the desk as he bent down to level his face with mine. He was so close I could actually see the chocolate coloring in his eyes that stopped them from being entirely black, and his mouth . . . his mouth was but an inch from mine.

I held my breath from the shock of his sudden movement and his closeness.

"First of all," he said through clenched teeth, his hard stare holding mine in its grip, "do I look like a man who would ever put a kiss at the end of a message?"

I didn't have to contemplate the question long. "Not really."

"Not really." He nodded, and pushed in closer, his breath fanning my lips and causing me to swallow a gasp. "Second of all, if you ever meddle in my personal life again I will annihilate you. Understood?"

"W-well, annihilate is—it's pretty final," I stammered, "So—so yeah."

His eyes flashed. "Alexa."

I fought past my physical reaction to him in order to attempt an explanation. "I was just trying to help. I thought it would be more romantic. I'm sorry. I won't do it again."

"You weren't helping," Caine hissed. "Contrary to popular belief, I give a shit about the women I date. That means I don't want to hurt them. And one way I avoid that is by never making a woman feel like she has more of me than she actually has, because inevitably it won't work out and I don't want to be the bastard that led her on. What you did with Phoebe will make me that bastard."

That was kind of honorable in a fucked-up way.

"But why will things end?" I whispered, confused. "Phoebe Billingham is perfect for you."

Something flickered across his face and then he grew scarily still. I held my breath as we stared into each other's eyes. He was so close.

The sexy jackass smelled delicious.

For a moment I forgot where I was and who I was. Who I was to *him*. My eyes dropped to his mouth. It was right there. Right *there*.

Arousal shot through me and I glanced up quickly, afraid he'd catch sight of my desire, but to my surprise I found his eyes trained on my lips.

They parted under his stare.

Caine's gaze returned to mine. The tingling between my legs increased at the heat in his.

"Don't do it again," he said softly, his voice hoarse.

"New bully tactics, Caine?"

Caine jerked away from me at the interruption and I sucked in some much-needed air.

Standing beyond us was Henry Lexington. He looked back and forth between us, smirking.

"Henry." Caine nodded at him, seeming perfectly composed.

I was not.

I crossed my legs, willing the heat in my body away. I just knew if I touched my cheeks I'd burn my knuckles.

"I thought we had lunch plans," Henry mused, and his eyes darted past Caine to me.

"We do. Let me just grab my jacket." He disappeared into his office and Henry approached my desk.

He grinned down at me. "We meet again."

I smiled, still trying to shake off the intense moment with Caine. "I think technically I have you to thank for the job. If you hadn't gotten me in to see Mr. Carraway, I wouldn't be here."

"That's right." Henry's blue eyes twinkled with good humor as he leaned on my desk with flirtation written all over him. "So in a way you owe me. I do so like to have a beautiful woman in my debt."

"Do you have a lot of those?"

"Only one of them is interesting." He cocked his head, curious. "You *are* a mystery. Caine won't tell me where you came from or how he knows you. Naturally I'm intrigued."

I was sure he was, and I was also sure the last thing I'd ever do was reveal a part of Caine's tragic history, and frankly I was tied up in that in a way that depressed me. "We met in Hollywood."

Henry raised an eyebrow. "Hollywood?"

"Mmm-hmm. Boulevard." I sighed in exaggeration, leaning my chin on my palm in dreamy retrospection. "Oh, those were the days. I was a lowly hooker looking for a white knight, and he was a rich billionaire who didn't know how to drive a stick. I showed him how and the rest is history."

Henry frowned. "What?"

"It's the plot to *Pretty Woman*," Caine said dryly. He leaned against the door to his office with something akin to amusement on his face. He pushed off the jamb and gestured to Henry to follow him. "Did I mention my new PA is a smart-ass?"

Henry chuckled and I couldn't help grinning at him as he took my good-natured teasing on the chin. He shot me an appreciative look over his shoulder as they walked away. "Until we meet again."

I nodded and gave him a little wave, a gesture Caine caught as he looked back at me.

He scowled. "Remember what I said. No meddling."

Just like that, the positive vibe of the moment evaporated. "Of course." I threw him what I hoped seemed like a genuine smile, but it still made him shake his head in annoyance.

"How do you know the plot to *Pretty Woman*?" I heard Henry ask in amusement.

"Remember Sarah Byrne?" Caine replied.

"The record-breaking five-month relationship. Of course."

"She had a thing for Richard Gere. I paid the price."

They disappeared around the corner as Henry laughed. I was smiling right along with him. Sometimes, when Caine remembered to be a normal guy, he was more attractive than ever.

"Carraway Financial Holdings, Mr. Carraway's Office," I answered, hopefully for the last time that day. It was almost five thirty. Caine didn't usually let me leave until seven, but I was hoping since it was Friday and he had a dinner reservation that I'd get to haul my ass out of there early.

"Oh, good, I caught someone," a pleasant voice said down

the line. "I'm Barbara Kenilworth of the O'Keefe Foundation. I'm calling for Mr. Carraway."

"Mr. Carraway is unavailable at the moment," I said, which was what I was supposed to say to everyone unless Caine told me he was expecting a call from someone specific. "May I take a message?"

"Oh. Well, yes. I wanted to make Mr. Carraway aware that a few ladies on other charity committees, myself included, have noted his generosity and have nominated him for an award at the Boston Philanthropic Society Gala that takes place this coming fall." Her voice lowered as if she was confessing something to me. "Two of my friends and I were at lunch a few weeks ago and, well, we discovered quite by chance just how generous Mr. Carraway has been, and he's never asked for any acknowledgment. Well, we think such humanitarian efforts should be brought to light."

"Indeed," I murmured, absolutely spinning at this news.

Caine was *that* generous to charity organizations?

"So you'll inform him for me?"

"I will."

"Oh, you're such a dear. Ta-ta."

I hung up, confused. I hadn't read anywhere that Caine was a philanthropist. What was that all about?

I rang his office.

"Yes?" he answered almost immediately.

"Do you have a minute?"

"Is it important?"

"I think so."

"Then by all means interrupt me when I'm busy over an 'I think so.'" He hung up and I hurried into his office despite the unwelcoming go-ahead.

Caine sat behind his desk, watching me. Usually he had

some kind of blank or pissed-off look on his face when he stared at me. To my consternation, it seemed he was wary of me.

My only guess was that his sudden weirdness had to do with the heated moment we'd had earlier that afternoon. Not needing a reminder of that when I was around him, I threw the thought away and forged on. I told him all about Barbara Kenilworth.

His reaction was to let out a stream of expletives.

"Why are you annoyed?" I huffed. "This is wonderful. What you do is wonderful."

"Alexa," he huffed back. "I have a reputation for being a hard-ass, a ruthless bastard. And you know what? I get a lot further in business because of it. My donations are always based on the condition of anonymity. I make the foundations sign a goddamn nondisclosure agreement." He stood up now, and pointed toward the door. "So you phone Ms. Kenilworth back and inform her that if she doesn't retract that nomination and stop spreading rumors of my philanthropy all over fucking Boston, I will rip her a new asshole via lawsuit."

I blinked in surprise at his tirade. "Wow. That actually makes me feel better."

His eyebrows drew together. "How?"

"Well, in comparison to what poor Ms. Kenilworth is facing if she upsets you, you're an absolute prince to me. I have had no such threats of asshole ripping."

And then the impossible happened.

Caine's lips twitched and that lip twitch was followed by a low huff of laughter as he shook his head, relaxed, and sat back down. Mirth glittered in his eyes as he looked at me. "Just make the call, Alexa," he murmured, his tone actually soft for once.

I struggled not to smile in utter elation. "I'm on it."

I spun around and walked back out of the office, a triumphant grin on my face.

CHAPTER 6

Sun streamed into the bookshop/coffeehouse in Brighton, and the heat of the sun on my face and the delicious coffee in my hand and the fact that I wasn't at work meant I was feeling pretty great.

That was until my grandfather started airing his concerns, *again*, about Caine and how it was a supremely bad idea for me to be working for him.

This was our place. The coffeehouse/bookshop, I mean. It was this quiet little place I found when my friend Viv was renting an apartment in Brighton and I suggested it as the place Grandpa and I could meet without worrying about running into anyone who'd know him and let leak that he was meeting a pretty young thing in secret. If that happened, his family, aka his wife (the grandmother I'd never met), and his grandson, Matthew, and his wife, Celia (my half brother, and my sister-in-law, whom I'd also never met), would ask questions and then they'd find out that Grandpa was in touch with the black sheep of the family's illegitimate daughter and all hell would break loose. Or at least that was the way he made it sound.

Honestly his family sounded high maintenance, and having lived with my father for nine years, I knew that my assessment was probably right.

I didn't really want to meet them.

I sighed and relaxed back into my seat. "Grandpa, the job is not that bad, I promise. It could be worse. Caine made it out like it was going to be hell on earth. But here I am, enjoying some free time with my grandfather."

Grandpa smiled a smile that didn't quite reach his lovely light gray eyes. They were the same eyes as my dad's. Everything about my father was like Grandpa. They were both classically handsome and distinguished-looking. They were also very tall and broad-shouldered. They were the kind of men you paid attention to when they walked into a room. Once you started to get to know my father, that sense of power around him slowly dissipated. But not with Grandpa. I had a feeling you did not want to get on my grandpa's bad side. He was like the Clint Eastwood of high society—no matter how old he got, you still wouldn't want to mess with him.

"I know you, sweetheart." He studied me carefully. "You're looking for something out of this, and I'm worried you're not going to find it."

"Maybe." I shrugged and then surprised myself by admitting, "I'm in awe of him."

"Of Caine?"

"Yes. He didn't let it destroy him. The tragedy he endured made him determined. Now he has more success and wealth and power than the man who helped take everything from him. He never used his private pain. No one knows about it; he just tried to put it behind him and make his life better. It's not his fault if he's going after all the wrong things. Still, it's the attitude behind his actions that I respect. I'm in awe. He overcame a lot."

In full, what Caine overcame was family drama, betrayal, death, and suicide. From what I'd pieced together from my father and Grandpa, Caine was thirteen, living in South Boston with his mom, who was a saleswoman for a store in Beacon Hill, and his dad, who was a construction worker. His mom— her name was Grace—met my dad when he came in to purchase a present for his then wife. From the way he told it, Grace was a bored young mother who felt like her life was passing her by. It was easy to seduce her with his culture and money and charm. They began an affair and he got her into a wild scene. She got hooked on cocaine and one night in some crappy hotel room she overdosed while he was in the shower. Instead of helping Grace, my father panicked and got the hell out of there. Grace died. My father used his money and influence to cover things up and make sure the Holland name wasn't dragged into a scandal and that he wasn't charged for drug possession or, worse, involuntary manslaughter.

Caine's dad, Eric, wouldn't let it go, though, and my father had to tell him the truth about his affair with Eric's wife and his part in her death. He looked around the crappy apartment father and son were living in and offered Eric a lot of money to just let the whole thing go. Eric took the money. And three months after Grace OD'd, Eric donated all the blood money to charity and a few days later walked into his neighbor's house, a man who happened to be a cop, and took that cop's gun, put it in his own mouth, and pulled the trigger.

Caine was put in the system. A boys' home first and a couple of placements after that.

My father, the weak bastard, was disowned by my grandpa when he discovered the chain of events, and his first wife divorced him once he was without means. That year instead of coming for his annual visit to see me and fuck over my mom, he lied and said he couldn't live without us anymore. He then mooched off my mom for years until his nervous breakdown when I was twenty-one.

I didn't know what he was doing now that Mom was gone. The last I saw him was at her funeral, and when he tried to talk to me it took everything within me not to spit in his face.

Maybe if he'd been the hero I always thought he was when I was a kid, maybe if he'd stepped up to become a man, a provider, a decent father, I would have been able to forgive him. But he was a liar, and a lazy one at that, and he had my mom so tied up in knots she couldn't see who he really was. I lost her because of him.

So no.

I would never forgive him.

"Lexie." My grandpa pulled me out of my dark thoughts. "I don't want you falling for Caine Carraway. It's too dangerous to you. You'll get hurt. And if he hurts you"—his voice lowered to a warning rumble—"I'll have to kill him."

I leaned forward and patted my grandfather's hand in reassurance. "I'm not there to fall for him. I'm just trying to be there for him somehow. I get him—even if he doesn't realize it, I really do get him. I would like to be his friend if he'll have me. But . . . it would be nice for *him* to fall for someone. Say the woman he's currently dating—Phoebe Billingham."

Grandpa looked surprised. "Grant's daughter?"

I nodded.

"He could definitely do worse. That might be a good match."

"That's what I'm thinking." *Liar, liar, liar.* I frowned at my jealous subconscious. "But he's not very romantic around her. I'm trying to nudge him in the right direction."

"You don't nudge a man like Carraway anywhere," Grandpa warned.

My phone suddenly started vibrating on the table. I leaned forward to have a look at caller ID and frowned.

It was Caine.

On a Saturday.

"Oh man," I whined, and picked up the phone. "Mr. Carraway?"

"I need you to come into the office with lunch. We're nearing the end on the deal with Moorhouse Securities Company, so we're working overtime. I've got a lot of hungry people in here. We'll need—"

"Cai—Mr. Carraway, it's Saturday."

His sardonic tones rumbled down the line, "Observant." He then went on to rattle off a list of sandwiches and drinks.

"But . . ." I stared forlornly at my coffee. "It's Saturday."

"Ass in the office, Alexa." He hung up.

I looked glumly over at my grandpa, who had his "I told you so" face on. "So maybe he *is* trying to kill me," I grumbled as I got up to leave.

The last few weeks had involved much of the same responsibilities and overwhelming schedule as my first week at Carraway Financial Holdings. Caine was intent on ruining my social life.

It might have been worth it if I'd seen any more hints of the person he hid behind his professional demeanor. But with the exception of discovering he was a Red Sox fan and an EMC-level season ticket holder, and that Henry was his closest friend from college (and I didn't know if that even counted for much when it came to Caine), and that he liked sixties/seventies rock like Led Zeppelin and the Grateful Dead, I'd learned little else. I only knew about his musical inclinations because he left his iPod on his desk when he came into the office directly from the gym. There was a shower room off his office, and while he was in there I snuck a peek at his music selections.

I was surprised to say the least.

I had to admit I liked that he could surprise me.

I was musing over that when I was supposed to be choosing the wallpaper for the larger guest bedroom in his summerhouse. I was jolted out of those musings when he called me. I hit SPEAKERPHONE. "Yes, Mr. Carraway."

"Get in here."

I bit my tongue so I wouldn't make a snarky comment about his lack of manners and I strode into his office. "How may I help?"

Caine was perched on his desk, arms crossed over his chest, long legs stretched out, ankles crossed too. He appeared contemplative.

A few seconds ticked by.

Finally he sighed. "I need you to go to Tiffany on Copley Place. Purchase a necklace on my credit card—make it simple, elegant, and make sure there's a diamond in it. And then I need you to personally deliver it to Phoebe Billingham. You will inform her that I've enjoyed my time with her and that I wish her all the best in the future."

A weird rush of relief and disappointment came over me. I shrugged off the relief and went with the disappointment because it was much less complicated. "But . . . what happened?" I cried out, throwing my hands up in exasperation. "She's perfect."

Caine stared at me like I'd grown two heads. "It's none of your business what happened. Just do it."

I was outraged. Actually outraged. I struggled to berate him as politely as possible. "Shouldn't this be something you do yourself?"

He stood up abruptly and it took everything within me to keep my chin jutted out in defiance at his sudden change in demeanor. His expression was hard, his words clipped. "If I do it myself, that suggests to her more than I'd like to suggest. This way she gets the message loud and clear and it will, furthermore, make her feel better that she's shot of me, a guy who didn't even bother to break things off with her himself."

"You're just . . . ," I sputtered.

"I'm just?" he taunted, almost goading me to do something to mess up my job.

I held out my hand, palm up, in answer. "Card."

Satisfied, Caine pulled out his wallet.

Almost an hour and a half later, I stood in the doorway of Phoebe Billingham's office, a doorway I wished was closed for privacy, considering that her office abutted an open-plan office shared by many.

Phoebe was of average height, but nothing else was average about her. She had gorgeous, huge brown eyes, creamy, pale skin, full lips, and a cute button nose. She was also slender in a way that if she'd been taller she could have been a model. Clothes just molded perfectly to her body. Aside from how gorgeous she was, she was clearly a smart woman, and when I first made myself known to her she'd been all friendly smiles and happy to meet me.

Now those brown eyes were filled with angry tears as she glared down at the necklace. I wanted to die. I wanted the floor to swallow me and just suffocate me so I could escape this situation.

Phoebe closed the Tiffany box and looked up at me. Something I didn't like crept into her hurt gaze as she raked those eyes down my body and back up to my face. She sneered. "Oh, I understand this situation perfectly," she said, her voice carrying behind me into the open-plan office.

There was a hush in the air as the people nearest us heard the bitter anger in those words.

"Do me a favor." She thrust the necklace at me. "Tell your *boss* not to send a whore to do a man's job."

There was utter silence behind me. My cheeks burned with indignation at the insult.

It took everything within me to hold off my humiliation and cling to my compassion. Stiffly I took the box from her and marched out of there with my head held high despite the undesirable attention focused on me.

Forty minutes later I stormed through the building and straight into Caine's office without knocking.

I stumbled to a stop at the sight of him and Ms. Fenton sitting across from each other at the sofas by the window. Caine was not happy at my interruption. He heaved a sigh of exasperation. "Linda, go back to your office. I'll be there in a second to continue our discussion."

Ms. Fenton frowned at my lack of etiquette as she passed, but I could give a crap.

I'd had forty minutes to stew in my rage.

"What the hell do you think you're doing?" Caine snapped, standing up and striding over to me to do his intimidating "I'm bigger and taller and scarier than you" thing.

But I was too mad to be intimidated.

I threw the jewelry box with the necklace in it at him, and he blinked in surprise before somehow managing to catch the damn thing. "Don't you ever make me do that again."

He tensed, suddenly alert. "What happened?"

"Well, the entire office of the Harvard University Press now thinks I'm a whore."

Caine's jaw clenched and his face clouded over instantly. "What?"

I shook my head at the fact that for a smart man he could be pretty stupid. "What did you think would happen when you sent me, a woman, to dump your girlfriend? Phoebe told me to tell you—and I might add how very junior high this all is—not to send a whore to do a man's job."

His dark eyes blazed. "She called you a whore?"

"That's what I'm saying."

Caine marched to his desk and picked up his phone. A few seconds later he growled into it, "I got the message you gave Alexa . . . Yeah, well, your method of delivery was shittier than mine." If it was possible he looked even angrier at whatever she had to say. "For that you can kiss good-bye that dream position of yours on the art institute's board of directors . . . Oh, I can and I will." He hung up and threw his phone on the desk with irritation.

I stood there, unsure what to do or how to react to the fact that he was pissed on my behalf.

Caine lifted his brooding gaze to me, but he started at my feet and slowly worked his way up my body so that by the time he hit my eyes I felt like I was going to come out of my skin. "I didn't think," he murmured.

What? Was he just now realizing I was a woman who, if I may say so myself, was attractive? So I wasn't a knockout like

Phoebe Billingham, but I was still a good-looking female employee he sent over to dump her.

Not good.

"It won't happen again."

Okay, that was as close to an apology as I was going to get out of him. And it was more than I'd expected.

I nodded and we held each other's stare until I started to feel like all the air was going out of the room.

I wrenched my eyes from his and immediately felt like I could breathe again. "Would you like coffee?" I asked, my way of saying I accepted his nonapology.

"Yes." He lowered himself into his office chair, no longer meeting my eyes. "And send Linda back in."

CHAPTER 7

Caine's refrigerator depressed me. It really, *really* depressed me. Mostly because it would be almost bare if it weren't for a carton of milk, one of OJ, and three eggs.

And I'd just put the OJ and milk in there per his request.

I shut the door and looked around the beautiful kitchen. It was a Saturday and it was the fourth in a row Caine had ruined by asking me to run some errand he could run himself if he weren't trying to deliberately exasperate me. In the past, if Caine was out of groceries he'd counted on his cleaner, Donna, to run out and get those. She visited twice a week and was paid handsomely for the bonus errands. However, since I'd come along I'd gotten the grocery run. He said it was so he could stop inconveniencing Donna, but I knew it was really just so he could start inconveniencing me.

I'd spent the better part of the afternoon running around dropping off dry cleaning, picking up dry cleaning, getting groceries, and choosing a gift for Mrs. Flanagan's seventy-seventh birthday.

I got her this gorgeous emerald green and sapphire blue kimono I found in a little boutique on Charles Street, and I'd left it on his bed along with his dry cleaning. I'd also left him wrapping paper, ribbon, and Scotch tape. He was going to damn well wrap Mrs. Flanagan's birthday present himself.

What got me through the fact that I was running around doing all this personal crap for my boss was that he was a busy guy and usually in the office. But when he'd called me today I could hear Henry in the background asking him when they were going to hit the gym. He wasn't even busy and he was making me do his crap for him! It was official. Caine Carraway was a sadist.

Leaning against the counter, I took everything in. The penthouse was like something out of an interior design magazine—stunning, yes, but no personality had been injected into it yet. I was tempted to snoop and find photographs that I could buy frames for and then just stick 'em out on display and see what Caine did.

Maybe in a month's time.

It still felt too soon to enforce nesting on him.

My focus was drawn to a spot of color on the coffee table at the TV area. Curious, I wandered over and raised an eyebrow at the DVD case Caine had left out. When I picked it up I saw it was a foreign movie based on the events that took place during eighties Berlin. Hmm. I glanced over at the cabinet beneath the television. Opening a cabinet wasn't exactly snooping. Much.

I opened it and discovered something new about Caine. On one side he had a bunch of action movies, and on the other side were all foreign movies.

Action flicks and foreign movies.

Huh.

Smiling, I stood up, adding this new information to the inventory I'd unconsciously started compiling about my boss.

Okay, it was time to let myself out of his apartment while I was ahead of the game. There were still a few hours left of the afternoon. I was sure I could fit in some reading. I mean, it wasn't like I had any other plans, as my social circle had diminished greatly since I lost my job with Benito.

Not that I cared.

Nope.

I let myself out of the apartment and locked up.

Okay, I cared.

Pouting a little, I strode toward the elevator and pressed the button to go down.

I jolted at a sound behind me and I glanced over my shoulder to find Mrs. Flanagan standing in her doorway wearing a diaphanous orange caftan. She was smiling brightly. "Alexa, I'm so glad I caught you. Come in for tea."

"Uh . . ." Go home to an empty apartment or have a chat with a funny lady who seemed to know a heck of a lot about Caine? "Sure, sounds great."

Mrs. Flanagan beamed and stepped aside to let me pass. I was immediately hit with how different her penthouse was in comparison to Caine's. It was crammed with traditional, expensive furniture that would probably last for hundreds of years. Photographs cluttered every space, oil paintings every wall, and she had a thick Aubusson carpet taking up most of the floor space in the main room. The layout was like Caine's except Mrs. Flanagan's kitchen was more French country than sleek and modern, and there was a partition wall between the kitchen and the living space that gave an illusion of them being two separate rooms.

"Wow." I grinned at her. "This is amazing." And it was. I

could see her whole life in the place. My attention was caught by a black-and-white photo of a beautiful woman staring off into the distance. It looked like a head shot for an Old Hollywood actress. "Is that you?"

Mrs. Flanagan nodded, smiling. "I was Maria in *West Side Story* on Broadway."

"Really?"

She nodded. "I moved from Boston to New York when I was fourteen to work on Broadway. Met my husband, Nicky, after a show one night. He was a wealthy industrialist from Boston. We married when I was twenty-three." She gestured to a photograph of her in a beautiful wedding dress standing next to a handsome young man. "In love right up until he passed ten years ago. Still in love." She smiled sadly. "Thankfully it was enough because unfortunately babies just weren't in the stars for us."

"I'm sorry, Mrs. Flanagan."

"Don't be, sweetheart. I've had a beautiful life. I still have." She grinned and started waving me toward her dining table. "Sit, sit."

Once she'd prepared tea she returned to sit at the table with me—a table now laden with biscuits and cakes. I helped myself to both.

"So." Mrs. Flanagan poured tea into the gorgeous china cup she'd put in front of me. "Were you running errands for Caine again?"

I snorted. "When am I not?"

"Tsk. That boy." She shook her head, eyes bright with humor and affection. "He's certainly going out of his way to piss you off."

I gave a huff of laughter. "And I bet you think that's deserved."

"Well, you did ambush him at a photo shoot and once again in his office."

My suspicions were correct: Caine told the old bird everything! Intrigued, I leaned forward. "How did you and Caine become friends?"

"Caine, is it?" She threw me a cheeky smile.

"Mr. Carraway," I corrected myself, holding her steady gaze and refusing to give anything away.

She chortled. "You can call him Caine, sweetheart. He's not a god."

"Do you think you could tell him that? Because I don't think he knows."

Mrs. Flanagan threw her head back in laughter. "Oh, Caine was right. You are a smart-ass."

I wrinkled my nose. "I can't help it. He brings it out in me."

"Well, I can see how that might happen, what with him trying to piss you off every chance he gets even though he says he's not." She shook her head. "I don't know what to do with that boy."

"I can take it," I assured her. "I get it."

"You do?" She raised an eyebrow. "Because I don't think you do. I don't even think Caine gets it yet."

"It's about our history. About my father and his mother." I was suddenly suspicious. "I thought you knew all this."

"Oh, I know all about that, and I know it's not your fault, so get that out of your head right now."

"I know it's not my fault, but I get why it's hard for Caine to separate me from it," I admitted. "He's been through so much because of my father and what he did to destroy Caine's family. I guess it would make me feel better if I could see Caine happy. He deserves to be happy, even when he is being a grumpy, relentless, unbending pain in the ass." I took a sip of tea. "Did you meet Phoebe?"

Mrs. Flanagan seemed amused by the question. "Oh no. I've never met any of Caine's lady friends. But Caine told me about her."

"She was perfect for him. He just dumped her," I huffed. "I do not understand that man."

"Well, from what I heard she was all *wrong* for him."

Shocked, intrigued, I leaned forward. "What did you hear?"

She laughed at my curiosity. "Phoebe was intimidated by him. She downplayed her intelligence around him. Drove him nuts." She leaned forward, her eyes boring into mine with a fierceness I didn't quite understand. "What Caine needs is a woman who is not easily intimidated, persistent, and pretty much okay with bulldozing her way into his life. That's how I struck up my friendship with him. I wouldn't let him take no for an answer, and now that boy is the closest thing I have to a grandson and I'm the closest thing he has to a grandmother."

Uneasiness moved through me. "Maybe he wouldn't want us talking, then. Especially about private stuff."

"Isn't that why you're here?" She gave me a knowing look. "You're digging for some reason. Otherwise you wouldn't be spending your Saturday afternoon with your boss's kooky neighbor lady."

I gave her a sad smile. "Maybe I have nowhere else to be."

Mrs. F looked concerned. "Okay, if that's true, why *haven't* you got anywhere else to be?"

"My social circle grew smaller when I lost my former job. My friends from college all have kids now and . . ." I shrugged. "You know how it is."

"Alexa, you're a gorgeous, funny young woman. You should either be able to strike up friendships with other charming women or have a man on your arm showing you a good time at the weekend."

A man on my arm. Right. "I haven't had one of those in eighteen months and haven't even been interested in looking since my mom passed."

She reached across the table and covered my hand with hers. "I'm sorry about your loss, sweetheart. Caine told me about it after he looked into you."

What the hell? "Caine looked into me?"

"Yeah. After the photo shoot. Found out your mom had just passed. Boating accident, was it? How are you coping with all that? You okay? It must be tough trying to deal with her loss now that you're having to deal with Caine."

To my surprise everything rushed up within me at Mrs. F's genuine sympathy. It was like she really wanted to know, and I guess I hadn't realized until that moment how much I needed someone to care. "You know I haven't been able to talk about it because no one knows the truth about what my father did. The only one who does is Grandpa, and he rarely talks about it. He doesn't want to."

She squeezed my hand. "Well, I know the truth. You can tell me."

I smiled gratefully and put my other hand over hers. "Thanks, Mrs. F."

She smiled encouragingly.

"I guess . . ." I exhaled. "It's been rough because of all the resentment I carried toward Mom." I went on to tell Mrs. F all about how much I hero-worshipped my absentee father as a kid, and how I clung to that for as long as I could and when I couldn't anymore I just pretended. "But he shot that to hell when he told us the entire truth. It was Thanksgiving. I was home from college. He sat us down, and he cried as he told us about Caine's mom. And all his secrets came out because of that. I found out I had been illegitimate, that he'd had a wife and son that I knew nothing about, that my mom was just his piece on the side until he had nowhere else to go after his father turned him away. I was disgusted, betrayed, ashamed. Mom was just quiet. Of course she'd known all about the other family, but she knew nothing of Caine's mother or how he'd let her die, or even how that was the real reason he'd come back to her. I asked Mom what she was going to do, if she would leave him over it, and she told me she didn't know. She was shaken up and I had hoped that maybe it would be enough to make her see him for who he really was. My mom spent my entire life giving that man everything he wanted, and he never once tried to give back. I couldn't pretend that wasn't true anymore.

"So after a while, after I realized that he felt guilty but not repentant, I told him I didn't forgive him. I returned to college . . . and unfortunately Mom went back to him." I looked up from our hands, tears stinging my eyes as that familiar hurt clawed at my gut. "She put him before me from that moment on. It was always my fault that there was a rift. Never his. I saw her only a couple of times over the last few years, and there was this wall between us we couldn't breach." I swiped at the tears sliding down my cheeks. "And then one day she went out on her friend's boat and a storm hit and that was it. She went overboard and by the time they found her body she was gone. She's gone and I never made it right. But neither did she." *And it hurts.*

"Oh, sweetheart," Mrs. F sighed. "I'm so sorry."

"I . . . I keep remembering when I was a kid and it was just the two of us. She was my whole world, you know. I've never loved anyone the way that I loved her back then. And now I'm just so goddamn mad at her. And I guess when I walked onto that photo shoot weeks ago and saw Caine, it was an opportunity to focus on something, anything, but the fact that my mom is dead and the most powerful feeling I have toward her is anger. I'm just scared that forgiveness and acceptance might never come."

Without another word, Mrs. F got up from her seat and came around to me to pull me into her arms, and for the first time since Mom died, I really and truly let it all out.

A bunch of tissues and two more cups of tea later, I smiled gratefully at Mrs. F. "This is going to sound weird, but thank you."

"For what, sweetheart?"

"For listening." I shrugged. "I feel lighter somehow, like it helped just to admit my anger out loud. I tried to talk to Grandpa about it a while ago, but he just got so mad and then he let slip Caine's name and everything else was shoved to the side at that revelation."

"I'm sorry you didn't have a good shoulder to cry on at the time." Mrs. F actually looked mad about it. "But you can come to me anytime, sweetie. Everybody needs somebody."

"Very true. I'm glad Caine has you."

Curiosity entered her gaze. "You really do want him to be happy, don't you?"

The way she asked it made me wary, like my answer held more meaning than I wanted it to. Finally, though, I nodded.

"Good. Maybe with two of us on the job we'll get it done." She glanced over at the clock. "Oh, look at that, it's dinnertime. And I know the number for a great Chinese. Join me? I have wine."

I laughed. "I would love that."

"Fabulous." She stood up. "Oh, and, Alexa?"

"Yeah."

"You're allowed to be mad at your mom, sweetheart."

Before I could swallow past the sudden lump in my throat long enough to thank her, Mrs. F strode away, caftan fluttering behind her, into the hall. I heard her on the phone before she appeared less than a minute later clutching her cell and a menu.

She thrust the menu at me. "Choose what you want. Caine's already told me what he wants."

Um . . . "Caine?"

"Yeah." She grinned impishly. "He just finished a squash game at the gym and is hungry, so he's going to be joining us."

I did not have a good feeling about this.

I narrowed my eyes on Mrs. F. "He doesn't know I'm here, does he?"

"Nope." She pointed at the menu. "Now choose."

Looking down at the menu, I wondered if I should choose something with peanuts in it and then fake a peanut allergy so I could escape the situation I now found myself in. Then again . . . it would be a chance to see Caine interact with Mrs. F. I sighed and decided to face his wrath in order to appease my curiosity. "I'll have the moo shu pork, and a little less matchmaking from you." I handed her the menu and she burst out laughing. "Mrs. F," I warned, "you know with our history it's never going to happen."

"Call me Effie, dear. And yeah, I thought that too, about your history, I mean," she admitted, "but you and Caine don't get what this is all about. He thinks he gets it and you think you get it, but really that's not why."

I stared dumbly at her. "That made no sense."

"It made sense to me."

Panic transformed into nervous flutters in my stomach. "Please don't do this."

Effie patted my shoulder in reassurance. "I would never do anything to make either one of you uncomfortable or upset, but from what I've learned from both of you, you're both dancing around each other and you haven't really learned a thing about each other that means something. A little time together outside of work will do you both good."

"He's very scary," I pointed out.

She snorted. "To you maybe. To me he's a sweet, sweet boy."

My jaw almost dropped at the double use of that adjective. "Sweet? Caine? No, I don't think so."

She smiled almost smugly to herself. "You'll see."

The minute I heard Effie's door open, my pulse stopped for a second, and when it restarted it was suddenly going a hundred miles an hour. Effie grinned at me and looked over my shoulder as heavy footsteps drew into the main room from the hall.

They suddenly stopped.

"Effie?"

Huh, so it wasn't just my name Caine used that warning tone with.

I glanced over my shoulder at him and gave him a little wave. "Hey, boss."

I was so glad I got the words out before I took in his appearance, because my mouth went dry and my brain stopped processing actual words. Caine was wearing a white T-shirt that sculpted his body. I could see the superb strength in his shoulders and arms. To make matters worse, he was wearing a faded pair of blue-wash jeans that hung on his hips in the most delicious way.

Caine Carraway in a business suit was gorgeous. Caine Carraway out of a suit was sexy as hell.

He also seemed human and normal to me for the first time ever.

Or he would have if he'd stopped scowling at me.

"Caine, come and sit down. Alexa's joining us for dinner."

He looked from Effie to me and then back to Effie. "Is that right?" he muttered.

The buzzer from reception sounded in the apartment before anyone could say anything else.

"That'll be dinner," Effie said.

"I'll get it." Caine strode away, tension stiffening his shoulders.

Once he'd left, I said to Effie, "He's not happy."

The older woman just grinned at me.

Caine returned with the takeout, and without saying a word he walked into the kitchen and surprised me by plating up the food and serving it to us. Effie didn't seem at all shocked by this.

As he correctly guessed that the moo shu pork was mine and placed the plate in front of me he must have felt my burning, questioning stare because he asked quietly, "What?"

"You just did something for me. Me. Another person."

That familiar scowl returned to his face. "I put food on a plate. Shut it and eat." He sat down and began digging in to his own sweet and sour chicken and rice.

"Caine, be nice to Alexa," Effie said, "or you won't get a piece of the lemon meringue pie I made earlier."

"There's lemon meringue pie?" Caine and I asked in unison. We shot a look of displeasure at each other.

Effie laughed.

Suddenly my moo shu pork became very interesting to me.

"How was your day?" Effie asked Caine.

His reply was to give me a wary look as he lifted another spoonful of rice into his mouth.

I almost rolled my eyes. I'd never met a person so concerned about his privacy, and so concerned about keeping me in my place. "Right now I'm not your PA. You can even pretend I'm human."

Caine looked at Effie but pointed his fork at me. "See? Smart-ass."

"I think she's hilarious." Effie raised her glass of water to me and I smiled in thanks.

"You would," Caine grumbled in this adorably boyish way that caused a little flutter in my chest.

In order to rid myself of the feeling, I just remembered the start to my day. "Well, if you're not going to talk about your obviously very busy day, I'll talk about mine and how my boss had me running all over Boston doing personal errands for him on a Saturday."

Once more Caine surprised me by substituting a glower for a smirk. "Sounds like you need to get yourself a social life."

"I see no point in that, considering you'll just endeavor to ruin it."

His eyes flicked to me and I saw amusement glittering in them.

The fluttering lowered to my belly and then lower still.

Oh boy.

Hoping my attraction wasn't obvious, I glanced guiltily over at Effie, who was staring at us both with something akin to glee on her face.

Damn it.

Sensing my scrutiny, Effie smoothed her expression and addressed Caine. "I'm going to have to get that idiot carpenter out—the railing in my walk-in has come down again."

"Don't." Caine shook his head. "He's clearly incompetent. I'll have a look at it after dinner."

What? I blinked rapidly. "Did you just . . . You do DIY?"

"When necessary."

"And you're good at it?"

His answer was to stop eating and look across the table at me with no small amount of wickedness gleaming in his eyes. "I've always been good with my hands."

My breath caught.

Heat and tingles of arousal shot through my core.

I was trapped in his gaze and the only way I knew I'd be able to breathe again was by escaping. Somehow I forced my eyes down to my plate and exhaled. "I have no response to that," I said, nonplussed.

When he didn't respond I looked back up at him.

Caine was grinning. "You're having an off day?"

He must have known the effect he could have on a woman when he did the whole smoldering thing. *Sexy jackass.* "I'm just tired after all the errand running I did around town today."

"If that tired you out we need to get your stamina up. You should have been in the gym with me and Henry."

I wrinkled my nose. "Um, no. The gym and I parted ways a long time ago. I'm in a relationship with Pilates and we're very happy together."

"Dancing," Effie said, "now, that's exercise and it's fun. I've never seen the attraction in sitting in some smelly gym lifting weights."

"Hear, hear," I muttered.

"And then of course there's sex. Lots and lots of sex."

Caine's fork clattered to his plate. He looked vaguely ill.

The snort I was trying to hold back bubbled up out of me and then Effie started cackling with laughter. It was infectious. I couldn't stop my own from joining hers.

Caine looked from her to me, his lips pinched together. Finally he settled his irritation on me. "I *will* eat all of the lemon meringue pie," he warned.

The thought cut off my laughter. "You can't. Effie won't let you."

"Christ." He shook his head. "You're on a first-name basis? I'm fucked."

Effie chuckled, wiping tears from the corners of her eyes. "Let me go get that pie."

His eyes followed her as she disappeared into the kitchen and then he turned his attention to me. He leaned across the table and lowered his voice. "Look, I'm not sure I like you spending time with Effie. She's like family to me. I don't want my business life mixing with my personal."

Some might call me stupid to make myself vulnerable to Caine, but I'd just had one of the best afternoons in a really long time and that was because of Effie. I didn't want to lose that just when I'd found it. "I really like her," I said quietly. "I can talk to her."

Caine's eyebrows drew together, but not in annoyance. There was curiosity in him. Finally he made me feel less stupid about my honesty. "Okay. Just no talking about me."

I smiled and crossed my fingers under the table. "Deal."

By the time we'd finished the most delicious lemon meringue pie I'd ever tasted in my life and Caine stood up to clear the table and load the dishwasher, I'd lost count of the many times he'd surprised me that night.

"Effie, you're running out of detergent for the dish-washer," Caine called through to us. This was followed up a few seconds later with "And milk. And eggs."

"I used the last up on the pie," she called back before taking a sip of the fresh tea she'd brewed.

"I'll run out tomorrow morning and get you some more. Do you need anything else?"

My jaw practically hit the table.

Effie chuckled at me. "I'm in the mood for an omelet tomorrow. Can you get me some cheese, red and green peppers, and spring onions?"

"Just write down what you need and I'll get it," he said, wandering back over to us.

I was choking on my words.

Caine took one look at me and his eyes glinted with mischief.

I stood up abruptly. "I'm going to leave now." *Before I commit homicide!*

He grinned evilly as Effie stood up, still laughing.

"It was lovely having you, Lexie. You sure are fun."

Ignoring the devil, I looked at my wisecracking angel. "Thanks, Effie. I had a wonderful time. I hope we can do it again sometime."

"Oh, sweetie, you come by anytime you want." She rounded the table and enfolded me in a surprisingly strong hug.

"I'll walk you to your car," Caine said as Effie pulled back.

"You don't have to," I said, still pissed at him for making me do shit he was perfectly capable of doing himself and clearly was used to doing for himself.

"Alexa." He used the old familiar warning tone. "You knew what the job was when you took it."

And wasn't that the truth? I exhaled heavily, trying to let go of my annoyance. I nodded and then gave Effie a small wave, grabbed my bag, and followed Caine to the door.

We were silent as we stepped into the elevator. Caine pressed the button for the underground parking garage.

"I saw the kimono," he said as we neared the garage level. "It's perfect for Effie."

Yes, I'd definitely lost count of the many times he had surprised me this evening. "Was that almost a 'good job'?"

We stepped out of the elevator into the coolness of the garage. Caine threw me a quelling look as he led me to my car. "Don't ruin it by being a smart-ass."

I grinned. "I don't think it's possible to ruin an almost 'good job.' A good job, yes, not an almost."

We stopped at the car and Caine did so with a weary sigh. "Fine. You did a good job." He leveled me with that heavy, dark gaze of his. "You are doing a good job."

And there he went, shocking me again.

A smile prodded my lips.

There was a whole other side to Caine, and Effie Flanagan, a seventy-seven-year-old Broadway actress, brought it out in him. He was relaxed, he was funny, and he could even be . . . yes . . . sweet. Just like Effie said.

A wary aspect had entered Caine's eyes, as if he was waiting for me to say something cheeky that would piss him off.

"Thank you."

The wariness disappeared and he gave me a little nod of acknowledgment that was so much hotter than it should have been.

"I'd better get back to Effie. I promised to fix that railing."

"So you did." I smiled and opened my car door.

"Good night, Alexa."

"Good night, Mr. Carraway."

Caine responded with a stiff smile and then he slowly retreated and strode off.

I got in my car and drove out of there, wondering why the hell I couldn't let this go, why I had to push my way into his life, just so I didn't have to deal with my own. I wasn't sure about anything anymore. The only thing I was starting to predict was that if I did by some miracle find a way to make Caine see who I really was, I was almost positive that I wasn't going to come out of it unscathed.

CHAPTER 8

My prediction started coming true almost immediately. That Monday when I returned to work, Caine was back to his usual charming, clipped, and cool self. It was like Saturday had never happened. I had to admit it hurt.

And I really didn't want to feel that way.

He made it easier to turn the hurt into irritation when he complained that his latte was a soy latte (it definitely was not) and told me that I needed to stop stapling paperwork together and learn how to use a paper clip.

I'd learn how to use a paper clip all right, but only after I used the staple one last time to shut him up permanently. Yeah, I said it!

"Said what?" Caine snapped.

That was when I realized I'd let the latter half of the conversation with myself slip out of my mouth. "Uh . . ." I stared down at him, trying to think fast. "That you're so right." I reached out and grabbed the paperwork from him. "I'll just go remove the staples for you."

I thought that was a pretty crappy start to the day. However, it wasn't until lunchtime when things really started to go bad.

I was in the middle of typing up my squiggly notes from Caine's meetings that morning when I heard Henry call out my name. He was striding down the hall toward me and when he came to a stop, he perched himself on the edge of my desk and gave me a soft smile. "Good afternoon, beautiful."

Over the last few weeks I'd come to like Henry. He was the opposite of Caine. He was all friendly and flirtatious and laid-back. Henry worked for his father's offshore bank, traveled a lot, and overall seemed to enjoy life way more than Caine did. He oozed charm and contentment, and I had to admit he did a lot to soothe my Caine-related wounded pride and self-esteem.

I relaxed back in my chair and smiled up at him, pleased to see him. "Good afternoon, handsome. How was your weekend?"

"Not as interesting as yours. I heard you dined with the queen."

I laughed. "Effie? Yeah, she's awesome."

Henry threw his head back in laughter. "Effie? Mrs. Flanagan lets you call her by her first name. I'm sure Caine was delighted by that."

I rolled my eyes. "What's the big deal?"

"Believe it or not, Mrs. Flanagan is a hard nut to crack. She and I are *not* on a first-name basis and she's spent the last five years denying me access to her baking." He pouted comically. "I'm not a big fan of rejection."

Amused, I tsked. "There must be a reason for her rejection."

"She says I'm a ne'er-do-well, and until I settle down and act like a real man she wants nothing to do with me."

"That's not fair. I'd say Mr. Carraway is as much of a ne'er-do-well as you."

"Thank you!" He nodded in agreement. "That is my argument exactly." He leaned closer. "Maybe you could put in a good word since she's taken such a shine to you."

"I'll do my best."

Henry smiled and stood up. "Have I told you recently how happy I am that Caine hired you?"

"No, but it would be helpful if you tell *him* that." I pressed the call button to Caine's office.

"What?" he grumped on the loudspeaker, and Henry grinned at my answering grimace.

"Mr. Lexington is here to see you."

"Send him in."

I gestured to the door. "His Majesty awaits."

He nodded. "Thank you, beautiful."

The heavy door shut behind him and yet I heard Henry ask, "Someone in a mood?"

The speakerphone. Caine had left it on. I opened my mouth to tell him when he returned with "I don't remember the last time I was in a good mood. Oh, right . . . the pre-Alexa days."

My mouth shut, my skin hot and prickling with hurt, embarrassment, and annoyance. It was one thing for him to be grouchy and insulting to my face, but to talk about me with other people. Not nice.

"Oh, well, you must be an idiot, then," Henry responded cheerily. "I find her delightful. In fact, I find Alexa so delightful I'm asking her to the Andersons' Anniversary Ball on Saturday."

I clamped a hand over my mouth to smother my gasp. Caine had had me arrange appointments so he could get a new tux for the Andersons' ball. Richard Anderson was a well-known media magnate. He and his wife, Cerise, were leaders of Boston society. Cerise was on every board of directors for charities and the arts in the city. It was their fortieth wedding anniversary on Saturday and they were throwing a party fit for royalty. Everyone who was anyone in Boston had been invited.

Henry wanted to take me as his date?

"Don't even think about it," Caine bit out.

"Is it because she's a PA? Do you think she's beneath us? Because I have to say, considering your humble background, that's pretty shitty of you."

It *was* pretty shitty of him.

You tell him, Henry!

"It's not that." Caine's voice sounded tight, strained. "It's because you can't keep your dick in your pants. I won't have you and that wandering dick anywhere near Lexie."

I sank back in my chair.

Lexie?

Lexie?

What the hell?

I heard Henry harrumph. "You sound jealous . . ."

Was he jealous? My belly flipped at that thought.

"I'm not jealous." Caine sounded like he was sneering at the thought. "Despite her smart mouth she's the best PA I've ever had. I won't have her chased off because you like her legs."

Best PA?

Best PA?

"Not just her legs. I'm quite taken with the whole package. She's gorgeous, she's funny, she's smart. I won't be bored out of my mind all night. Anyway, you're taking Marina Lansbury. I'm not going as some juvenile third wheel."

Marina Lansbury?

My belly flipped again, this time the sensation unpleasant.

"Henry, you're a Lexington. You can ask any woman in Boston to be your date and she'll say yes. You're not asking Lexie on an evening out with us. It's crossing the line."

Like, say . . . thinking of me as "Lexie" behind my back? What was that all about?

"Oh, get the stick out of your ass, Caine."

I was really starting to like Henry more and more.

"Shit, Henry, surely you can do better than Lexie."

That burned.

I blinked back the sting of tears and clicked the speaker off. That was what I got for eavesdropping.

The burn in my chest wouldn't dissipate and I had to really struggle to hold back the urge to cry. I couldn't believe how much it hurt.

I was such an idiot. Caine was never going to see me as anything more than Alistair Holland's daughter.

The door to the office opened and Henry and Caine stepped out. I avoided Caine's eyes but gave Henry what I hoped wasn't a wobbly smile.

Henry took my smile as an invitation and perched himself on the corner of my desk again. I shot a look at Caine, who stood behind him, waiting impatiently.

More than impatiently.

If he could have flayed Henry's back with his eyes, he would have.

"Alexa." Henry drew my attention back to him. "I'm sure you've heard about the Andersons' Anniversary Ball on Saturday. I know it's a little late notice, but I'd be honored if you'd say yes to being my date to the party."

I didn't even have to think about it. I gave him one of my

own flirty little smiles that made his eyes dance. "Yes. I would love to."

Caine walked away and Henry glanced over his shoulder to watch his friend's departure.

"Everything okay?" I said innocently.

Henry gave me a reassuring smile. "Everything's wonderful. If you give me your address I'll pick up you up at eight."

I took the fact that Caine gave me a nod of acknowledgment when he returned from lunch as a good thing, so later that afternoon I dared to be bold. We were returning from a business meeting with the CEO of a flailing investment company.

We were quiet in the car as it took us back to the office.

As always, the tension between us was thick.

I sought to break it . . . or make it worse. It was a toss-up. "I was hoping I could take a late lunch tomorrow so I can buy a dress for the Andersons' ball on Saturday."

I watched as Caine stiffened and then he stared at me with an infuriating imperiousness. "A late lunch? For a dress?"

"It's about time I spent some of that money I'm making running around after you." I smiled sweetly.

His eyes raked down my body and they took their time drinking me in on the climb back up.

I flushed, squirming. "Well?"

He looked away, returning his gaze outside the window at the city passing us by. "Move the meeting with Peter from Risk Management tomorrow and I'll accompany you."

What? No. He was joking, right? "Are you kidding?"

"No." He drew the word out with impatience. "You'll still be representing me and my company on Saturday. I have to make sure you don't dress . . . inappropriately."

My blood started to heat. "Inappropriately?" I said through clenched teeth.

"I don't have to look in your wardrobe to know it's filled with shorts and tank tops that show too much cleavage."

Ugh! "Let's not forget the fancy-ass work clothes you make me squeeze into on a daily basis," I snapped, forgetting I was talking to my boss.

He glared at me. "They're the only appropriate things in your wardrobe. You've made my point for me. I'm taking you dress shopping."

Like hell! "No offense, sir, but I am not going dress shopping with you. It's supposed to be fun, and I'm sure you understand that having my boss there detracts from the fun."

Caine sighed and straightened the cuffs on his suit jacket. "Shopping is never fun."

"Look, you . . ." I couldn't even find a word perfect enough to describe his jackassery. "I am an intelligent woman and just because I like comfortable clothes doesn't mean I don't know how to dress at a formal event."

"Alexa." He curled his lip. "This isn't prom night back home. This is Boston society."

I threw him a disgusted look, feeling triumphant when he flinched. The car drew to a stop in the parking garage and I opened my door. Before I got out, I remembered his words to Henry earlier. I turned back to him. "You know, I understood when I took this job that you weren't going to make it easy on me, but not once in all the hard work have I actively disliked you. Until today." I shook my head, disappointed in him, so much more than I ever thought I could be. "You're from Southie. Now you're part of high society. But instead of embracing where you come from and mixing that with where you are—something that gives you a better perspective than *all* of them—you've become this elitist snob." I shot out of the car before he could reply and I marched up to the office without him.

Then I sat at my desk stewing in my outrage.

Ten minutes later I heard his footsteps down the hall. When he turned the corner and headed toward me, I braced myself to be fired. His shadow fell over me as he stopped by my desk and I forced myself to look up at him.

Caine's face was carefully blank. "You may take the extra hour tomorrow. Alone."

Shocked that he hadn't canned my ass, but still hurt by his perception of me, I nodded and returned my attention to my computer screen.

He hovered for a few seconds longer, but I couldn't look at him.

Eventually he moved away, slamming his office door behind him.

It would suffice to say that things between my boss and me were more than a little chilly for the rest of the week. He'd even curbed how much running around he had me doing because it meant he didn't have to interact with me as much.

I refused to be upset over it, however. So he didn't want me there at his fancy-ass party with his fancy-ass people. He thought I was beneath him. I decided not to give a shit.

At least . . . well, I tried to convince myself not to give a shit. I wasn't too successful at that, although Henry did help a little. He sent flowers to the office on Friday, and the card said he was looking forward to spending Saturday evening with me. It was the first time a guy had done that for me, and I had to admit that being on the receiving end of the delivery was way more romantic than I'd expected.

Plus, it really made me gleeful how annoyed Caine got every time he passed my desk and saw the flowers. If I didn't know it was impossible, I would have suspected he was jealous.

By the time Saturday evening rolled around, my smug rebelliousness had been crushed by my nerves. I'd been to a few parties attended by celebrities when I worked for Benito, but nothing like this event. A society event was a whole different ball game. It was a complex social arena, and much more intimidating than anything I was used to. So when Caine made the dig about prom night, he wasn't far off it.

There was also the fact that I liked Henry but I wasn't attracted to him. Guilt niggled at me for using him to irritate my boss. A boss who begrudged my presence at the ball.

To conquer my nerves I concentrated on looking my best. My dress was gorgeous and I looked good, even if I had to say so myself because there was no one else around to give me the confidence boost. That depressed me. So I stood in front of my mirror, took a selfie, and sent it to Rachel.

A minute later she texted back: *OMG, I'd fuck you!!!*

There. That made me feel better.

Standing by my window, I looked down onto the tree-lined street and sipped at a glass of wine. I sucked in my breath, trying to fight down the nerves.

I almost succeeded until the black limo pulled up out front and Henry ducked out of it and strode quickly up my stoop. The buzzer went and I let him into the building. I waited a few seconds after he knocked on my door before grabbing the pashmina and the little clutch that matched my dress.

When I opened the door, Henry's lips parted in surprise. His gaze drifted over me slowly, taking in everything, and when they finally returned to my face, there was a heat in his eyes that made me feel both anxious and flattered.

"Wow." He shook his head, smiling as though dazed. "You look . . . wow."

The "wow" was for the amazingly fantastic olive green dress I'd found for a bargain on the sales rack of a small boutique on Charles Street. The material was a vibrant silk that felt wonderful against my skin in the muggy Boston summer air. It had a halter neckline and a low-cut back with a slit up to my knee on the right side of the dress.

Overall it was not demure, it was not conservative, but it was still classy as hell and sexy to boot. It was going to piss Caine off and I was going to love every minute. I'd made an appointment at the hair salon that afternoon, and after experimenting with different looks we decided to go with an elegant updo, leaving a few wavy strands loose.

"Thank you." I took Henry's proffered arm. "You look very handsome." And he did in his sharp, immaculately fitted tux.

He grinned at me. "If I look good it's because I've got you on my arm."

I laughed and shook my head. "You know your charm only has a very superficial effect on me."

Henry chuckled. "That works for me."

The Andersons' mansion was in Weston and as soon as the limo joined the line of cars on the massive circular driveway, my nerves began to multiply a hundredfold. The redbrick mansion with its white trim was the biggest house I'd ever seen in real life. It seemed to engulf us, casting us into shadow as the driver held the door open and Henry helped me out after him.

He patted my hand, seeming to sense my nerves. "It's just a house."

"That swallowed ten other houses," I said.

Henry laughed. "Come on. I've seen you paste on a serene smile when Caine is trying your patience, so I know you can fake it with the best of them. You've just got to pretend you belong here. It's how Caine does it, and no one ever questions him."

There was truth in that and it actually helped calm my nerves. I gave him a grateful smile. "Thanks."

"Ready to dazzle them?" He held out his arm.

"Let's do this."

We were greeted at the mammoth double entrance doors by big brooding men in black suits wearing earpieces. Henry handed over his invitation and the men waved us through. I tried not to gulp as we walked into a large oval-shaped entrance that seemed to have been built entirely of marble. We followed the guests down a small group of stairs at the end leading us into a huge entrance area. Oversized pocket doors had been opened on our right, leading directly into a ballroom.

An actual ballroom.

"Someone should tell them they have a ballroom in their house and that it's roughly half the length of the entire mansion."

Henry's body shook with amusement as he led me into the gargantuan room. "I think they might already know about it."

"True. It's kind of like having Godzilla living with you. It's not like you're not going to notice that baby." I took in the high arched ceiling and the stunning chandeliers that hung from it. Long tables draped in pale gold tablecloths were lined with hors d'oeuvres and glasses of champagne. A champagne fountain sat proudly in the middle of the center table. The room was decorated with simple elegance, but everywhere seemed to sparkle. Classical musicians were seated way, way down at the other end of the room where four sets of French doors led out into the garden. "Or in this case drape it in white gold and silver and fill it up with five-hundred-dollar bottles of champa . . ." I trailed off when I realized that some of the elegantly dressed guests were staring at us.

"Your fingernails are biting into my arm."

"Because people are staring," I whispered, and my pulse picked up speed.

"That's because—and I'm trying very hard not to sound like a conceited ass—you're with me, a Lexington, and more important, you're stunning and they're all wondering where I found you."

I eyed him suspiciously. "You better not tell them Hollywood Boulevard."

He laughed. "Damn, ruin my fun, why don't you?"

Relaxing at his good humor, I let my gaze drift over his shoulder, and what (or whom, rather) I saw made me stiffen with surprise. Uneasiness quickly followed the surprise.

My grandfather was here.

With my grandmother.

Shit!

Why did I not think? I'd been so harassed this week and so caught up in my own crap that I hadn't spoken to Grandpa and I'd completely, stupidly, so, so stupidly, forgotten that these were his people. Of course he'd be at one of the biggest society events of the year.

Oh God.

Where was my brain?

Oh yeah, Caine had turned it to mush.

"Alexa." Henry tugged on my hand, pulling my focus back to him. He was frowning. "You okay?"

"Uh, yeah—"

"Henry, Alexa," Caine's voice interrupted. He'd come to a halt, standing only a few feet from us. Even through my panic I still felt the impact of him. He wore a tux cut similarly to the one Henry was wearing, but the effect it had on me was entirely different. My gaze drifted over his outrageous handsomeness, and the yearning inside me overwhelmed and depressed me. When our eyes met, his gave nothing away.

There was no "wow" from him.

So much for the expensive dress.

"This is Marina Lansbury." Caine touched his hand to the lower back of the brunette he was with. She was as tall as me but curvier in a way that was alluring and sexy. Some might say without the makeup Marina was almost plain, but that body of hers, in that figure-hugging black dress, made you forget all about that. She looked amazing. "Marina, you remember Henry Lexington."

She smiled politely and held out her hand to shake Henry's. When I shook her hand her gaze was assessing in a competitive way she just couldn't hide.

I mentally grimaced.

Clearly she was one of those women—the kind who viewed other women as competitors no matter what. Those kinds of women were exhausting. I thought I'd left them behind in college.

"And this is my PA, Alexa Hol—"

"Hall." I quickly cut off Caine, holding out my hand. Marina reluctantly shook it.

I ignored Caine's questioning look. I couldn't introduce

myself tonight as a Holland. All hell would break loose for Grandpa.

I had not thought this through.

"Well." Caine gently pressed Marina to the left. "Just wanted to say hello. We're going to get a drink. We'll talk later."

Once they were out of earshot, Henry sighed. "It's not like him to disappear with his date like that. He usually sticks close to me. He likes to keep me around to smooth things over when rich people say things that annoy him."

I raised an eyebrow. "That actually happens?"

Henry nodded. "Caine doesn't have the patience for ignorance and snobbery."

"Yeah, well, he has a funny way of showing that."

Henry touched my lower back and began walking us toward the champagne. "You have a habit of bringing out his worst side." He grinned at me. "I find it highly entertaining."

I laughed, shaking my head at his nonsense. "You need to grow up, Henry."

"And why would I do that?"

The hours passed and Henry charmed and entertained me. He introduced me to people and they were genuinely interested to learn I was Caine's PA. No one looked or talked down to me, and I used my experience from years of dealing with celebrities on the job to converse with them like I wasn't intimidated. I was cool, appropriately witty but inoffensive, and I bounced well off Henry, who everyone seemed to love.

Henry was convinced Caine was deliberately avoiding us, and it aroused his suspicion. He just didn't get what it was about me that Caine so abjectly disapproved of.

I wasn't about to enlighten him.

After returning from the ladies' suite (yes, *suite*), I'd only taken a few steps back inside the ballroom when I saw my grandfather and grandmother walking straight toward me.

I halted, not knowing what to do.

Grandpa was in the middle of talking to my grandmother when he glanced over casually and then froze when his eyes locked with mine. They drew closer.

I held my breath.

"I don't know what was in that vol-au-vent, Edward, but my stomach is unsettled," I heard my grandmother complain as they approached.

"Adele," Grandpa said, voice weary, eyes still on me, "you just had it fifteen minutes ago. I doubt it could have taken much effect already."

"I know what I know. A brandy will relax it."

"I'm sure it will," he replied sardonically, dragging his gaze from mine. "Dick's in his study hiding out. He'll have some."

They walked right by me, his shoulder almost brushing mine.

I stared after him, my chest burning with hurt, even though I understood why he had to pretend he didn't know me.

I got it. I did.

But fuck, that killed.

I blinked back the sting of tears and spun around, only to draw to an abrupt halt.

Caine stood before me, staring down at me in question. "I understand now why you introduced yourself as Hall. I think you forgot to mention that you're not on speaking terms with the rest of the Hollands."

I shifted uneasily, glancing around to make sure there was no one close enough to overhear. "I am with my grandfather, but he can't acknowledge me publicly. No one in the family knows he and I are in contact. It would cause problems."

Caine looked past me to where my grandparents had departed. "Yet another reason you shouldn't be here."

His rejection on top of my grandfather's was too much. I took a step toward him and I saw something flicker in his gaze. I wanted to hiss and insult him and make him feel as bad as I felt right then . . . but as I stared up into those dark eyes I slumped with disappointment.

I shook my head, words failing me, and I pushed past him, hurrying to Henry's side.

"You okay?" Henry frowned when I reached him.

My cheeks flushed with anger and wounded pride. "I'm fine."

"Do you want to get some air?"

No, I wouldn't be chased from the ballroom by Caine's insensitivity and determination to make me feel unwelcome. "Let's just dance, okay?"

Henry led me onto the dance floor and expertly maneuvered me into the slow dance. He held me close but not too close, and I knew without a doubt that Henry and I were just friends. When a guy danced with you and held you, you were supposed to feel tingles and butterflies and go all melty inside. I just felt comfortable with Henry. I guess that was nice in its own way.

"He has spent most of the night scowling and brooding and ignoring his date," Henry murmured suddenly, obviously talking about Caine. "Last time I saw Marina she was flirting with Governor Cox."

I wrinkled my nose. "Isn't he married?" And why, oh, why, would you flirt with Governor Cox when Caine Carraway was your date?

"Yup, but his wife is flirting with Mitchell Montgomery."

"The toilet paper guy?"

"The one and only. Although we have a different name for him in our circle."

"And that would be?"

"The Asswipe."

I burst out giggling at the hilariously childish moniker. "How fitting."

Henry grinned. "What it lacks in sophistication it makes up for in entertainment."

I leaned into him, laughing harder.

"Sorry to interrupt." Suddenly Caine was there, towering over us both. He fairly bristled with impatience. "I need Alexa."

"What for?" My momentary amusement was gone.

"That was Arnold. He's got a colleague in Sydney on the phone, and it's important I take this conference call. We need to get to the office."

"We?" I shook my head. "Do you really need me for this?"

He bent his head toward mine, thunderclouds in his eyes. "I will need coffee and assistance for whatever else might be needed this evening. That's what I pay you to do. To *assist* me."

I could not believe it!

Was he kidding me with this crap?

I glanced back at Henry to apologize, only to find him wearing this weird, triumphant little smirk on his face. He quickly smoothed his expression. "I'm sorry to have to leave you," I said, eyeing him in confusion.

He further confused me by shrugging nonchalantly. "When work calls you've got to go."

I decided to ignore his weirdness for now. I could only

deal with one puzzling man at a time. "Thank you for under-standing." I kissed his smooth cheek. "And for a lovely evening."

He gave my hip a squeeze. "You're very welcome, beauti-ful. Thanks for classing up the place."

I laughed, my amusement dying another quick death when the impatient Caine whirled around and strode through the dance floor. I gathered my own worn-out patience before hurrying after him.

CHAPTER 9

The atmosphere between us was fraught to say the least as the limo driver took us back into Boston, heading for the financial district.

Caine obviously wasn't in the mood to chat and I definitely wasn't either after the way he'd treated me this entire week. His behavior had gone from being overbearingly bossy to downright insulting.

We made it to the office without uttering a word to each other. I tried to keep up with his long strides, but I was struggling in my heels and long dress.

I drew to a halt outside Caine's office. The entire floor was empty.

No Arnold.

Nobody.

Caine unlocked his door, flicking on lights as he strode inside his office. I followed him in.

He turned and looked at me blankly. "It appears I missed it. I'll take you home."

Uh . . . what? I held my hand up, palm facing out to stop him. I gestured around the room, my agitation mounting. "Where is Arnold? Where is this conference call?"

He shrugged. "Obviously I missed it and Arnold locked up."

"Without calling you?" I asked, incredulous.

He shrugged again. "Let me take you home."

"Did you lie? Did you lie to get me out of that party?"

"I don't lie," Caine said, sounding affronted. "I manipulate. It's how I got rich. Now let me take you home."

No. We weren't going anywhere until I got to the bottom of this. It felt like I had fire in my blood, I was that angry with him. Suddenly I didn't care if he fired me. "You *lied* to get me out of a party and away from my date. Are you that much of a snob?"

"It wasn't about that," he snapped, his eyes sparking with his ire. "I didn't want you there and I made that clear. When I want something a certain way I get it. I thought I'd also made that clear by now."

"You son of a bitch!" I shouted, losing all cool. "All week you've made me feel like I'm nothing, like I'm worthless. And now this crap!"

"What the hell are you talking about?"

"Monday afternoon. Henry came to your office and you forgot to switch off the speakerphone."

The air around him crackled dangerously. "You were eavesdropping?"

I flushed. "I was going to tell you, but then I heard . . . Henry started talking about me and it's only natural to listen in to a conversation about yourself," I argued. "And you were beyond insulting."

His expression cleared. "Is that why you said yes to Henry? To piss me off?"

"I said yes because he was complimentary. And yes, I have to admit to getting some satisfaction out of irritating you since it was so clear you think I'm beneath you."

His nostrils flared. "Bullshit."

I blinked rapidly at the denial. "Seriously? You've been treating me badly all week. Not to mention how you were tonight? You're not a stupid man, Caine, so you had to know I was hurt when my grandfather chose to ignore me, and you just dug the knife in deeper. You're never going to see me for me, are you?" I clenched my hands into fists. "You're just going to wound me and humiliate me. You're determined to make me pay for what *he* did." At his silence my anger increased. "Aren't you!" I yelled.

Suddenly my back hit the wall behind me as Caine moved me there, caging me in as he crowded me against it, his hands pressed to the wall above my head. Emotion blazed from his eyes. "I don't think you're beneath me," he hissed.

The surprise of finding myself barricaded in by him had knocked my attitude down a few levels. "Then why were you cruel?" I whispered.

Remorse flickered in his eyes. "I didn't mean . . . I just didn't want you there. With him."

And the shocks just kept coming.

I sucked in my breath and then slowly exhaled. *It isn't possible* . . . I didn't think so, but . . . I took in the aspect of his dark gaze that hinted at another emotion besides anger. "You're jealous?"

The muscle in Caine's jaw flexed.

My heart started to slam against my ribs and I couldn't seem to get control of my rapidly increasing breathing. With our eyes locked, our bodies touching, the heat around us blazing off the charts, I forgot where we were. I forgot everything but him.

"Cai—"

He crushed his mouth over mine, swallowing my gasp of shock and excitement. His cologne, the heat of his skin, and the taste of him, hot and sharp . . . it all overwhelmed me as he gripped the back of my neck with one hand and slid the other down my stomach . . . He smoothed it down my hip and under my thigh.

Realizing his intent, I kissed him back harder and clung to him, my fingers digging into his back, as he tugged my thigh up so he could press deeper between my legs. My lips parted on a whimper of lust and triumph. Caine growled. The sound caused a ripple of arousal in my lower belly and I pushed into him.

His hand tightened around my neck and he groaned again, the vibration of it causing more heat to shoot through me, tugging at my nipples, melting through my belly, and exploding between my legs in a burst of needy tingles. His kiss grew more demanding, long, drugging kisses that muddled my head and took me with him to somewhere else entirely. We were panting and pulling at each other's mouths like we couldn't get deep enough. Caine crushed me harder against the wall, grinding his erection against me. My belly squeezed again, and it occurred to me I'd never been this turned on from just kissing someone in my life.

It was him.

I slid my hands up his back and over his shoulders, my fingers sinking into his hair as I silently begged for more, for harder, for deeper . . . for everything.

From him.

Caine released his hold on my neck only to trail his fingers along my collarbone. As he skimmed his fingertips slowly over the silk of my dress, shivers cascaded down my spine, giving me goose bumps and causing my nipples to peak against the fabric of my dress. His thumb brushed lightly over my breast and stilled at the evidence of my arousal.

He broke the kiss, pulling back only an inch to gaze into my eyes. His lashes were low-lidded with lust as he studied me. I held his heated gaze, my lips swollen and stinging, my whole body taut with need.

Caine slowly lowered my leg and for a few awful seconds I wondered if that was it.

"Take off the dress."

His voice was thick with need, but still there was authority in it—bossiness.

Turned out in the right situation, Caine being bossy was less annoying and actually very, very hot.

Slowly, I let go of him, and still holding his gaze, I reached behind my neck for the crystal clasp on the halter.

Caine took a few steps back, allowing cool air to rush in around me.

I'd undressed for boyfriends before. It wasn't something I'd ever been shy about, because unlike most of my friends I didn't really have any body hang-ups. But it was different standing in front of Caine, preparing to bare myself to him. For some reason it didn't just feel like I was taking off a dress. It felt like I was letting him see me naked.

And there was a difference.

I hesitated, my fingers fumbling on the clasp.

Caine saw it. His answer was to tug at the bow tie around his neck. I watched him as he removed it and then he began to shrug out of his jacket. As he started unbuttoning his shirt, he said in a low, deep voice that made me pop the clasp, "I fantasize about fucking you in this office a hundred times a day."

His confession made me breathless.

I'd wondered if he was attracted to me, but I never thought he'd admit it or act on it.

But to know he was as attracted to me as I was to him . . . well, that made me brave again.

I pulled the halter of the dress down and watched Caine's eyes grow impossibly black with heat as I bared my breasts to him. My nipples pebbled under the kiss of the cool air, and gaining my confidence, I tugged down the dress and shimmied out of it. I lifted it up off the floor and draped it across the back of the sofa. Caine's gaze devoured every inch of me.

I was left in only my jewelry, my underwear and my heels.

I curled my fingers into my panties.

"Stop." Caine took a step toward me and I let my own gaze eat him up. His shirt was completely unbuttoned, revealing a sliver of his tan skin and hard abs. "Leave them on. Sit on my desk." He moved aside of it, leaving me a clear path.

He could hear how breathless I was when I asked, "Are you this bossy with all your women?"

Caine grinned, a wicked full-on smile that made my heart palpitate. "No, you just bring it out in me."

I smiled back. "You're saying you have a thing for bossing me around?"

"Just like you have a thing for being a smart-ass. Now sit on my desk and spread your legs."

My whole body zinged with anticipation and I released a hitched breath.

Caine's eyes gleamed at my response.

Straightening my shoulders, I walked toward his desk and him, my breasts bouncing with the movement, and I was more than smug about the fact that Caine's arousal was straining to break free of his zipper. I slipped past him and lowered my ass to his desk. I shivered at the coolness of it against my skin as I settled my weight on it and spread my legs.

The air in the room fairly crackled as Caine approached me. His fingertips trailed over the tops of my thighs as he moved in between my legs and bent to brush his lips over mine. I clung to his waist and captured his mouth again before he could pull back.

Soon the kiss was out of control, wild and hurried, as I pushed his shirt out of the way and smoothed my hands over every ripple and hard muscle on his torso, and he touched me everywhere.

Abruptly Caine pulled back, panting. "No, you don't," he murmured against my mouth.

"No, I don't what?" I said, confused by being suddenly wrenched from his lips. God, the man could kiss like no one could. "I want your tongue back."

"And you'll get it." He pulled away only to tug his shirt off impatiently.

I grew hotter at the sight of him half-naked and turned on. His strong shoulders, muscled biceps, and hard, sculpted six-pack . . . All he needed was a trickle of sweat running down those washboard abs and he would be a diet soda ad. I licked my lips and Caine groaned.

"Do you know how sexy you are?"

A burn, the exact opposite of the burn that had been stinging in my chest all week, flared out near my heart. "I do now," I replied softly.

Because I did.

I had never felt more so in my life than in that moment under Caine Carraway's needy, heated gaze. I'd never felt more wanted.

And from a man I thought would never want me.

Tonight was blowing my mind in more ways than one.

Caine lowered himself to the floor and curled his hands behind my knees, tugging me gently until my ass was practically hanging off the desk.

My head fell back in a groan as he began pressing soft, teasing kisses along my inner right thigh. I jerked at the touch of his mouth against my sex. He blew the lace of my panties against me and I shuddered.

"These are soaked." Caine curled a finger around them, brushing my labia. "Let's get rid of them."

"Uh-huh." I was barely coherent.

Suddenly the panties were gone and Caine was pressing my thighs apart again. "You're so fucking beautiful," he said reverently, his breath puffing against me.

"Please." I slid my fingers in his hair, staring down at him in torment. "Please."

His eyes blazed up at me. "You want me?"

He even had to ask?

"From the moment I saw you," I admitted.

Those eyes flared with triumph and then his mouth was finally on me.

"Oh God," I whimpered, leaning back on my hands as he licked at me, his tongue flicking and tormenting my clit. "Caine, please."

I could it feel it building, the muscles in my thighs trembling and tightening.

And then two fingers pushed inside me.

He sucked and licked at me and slid his fingers in and out of me. I was heading for the cliff edge. I stiffened and then fell over, crying out his name as my inner muscles clamped around his fingers in a hard climax.

Caine stood up, only to lean down into me, wrapping his

arms around my waist so he could gather me against him. I lifted my legs around his hips and clung to him as he kissed me, his tongue moving against mine in hard, quick strokes—the kiss was so desperate it was almost punishing.

I loved it.

I loved the taste of him and me on his tongue.

Caine broke the kiss, his hot lips trailing down my neck. I arched my back, anticipating his needs, and thrust my breasts up for his claim.

Claim he did.

Quickly the gloriously languid aftermath of my climax was decimated by the heat he fanned in me again. He cupped and stroked and kissed my breasts, learning every inch of them. And then he wrapped his mouth around my nipple and tugged, sucked, and licked it until it was so swollen it was tender. He moved on to the other until my legs were climbing his hips, and I was writhing against his erection, desperate for him to take me.

"Caine," I pleaded. "Come inside me."

He kissed me, one hand under my ass urging me up against his erection as he rubbed it between my legs, the friction of the material of his trousers against my sex building me toward climax again. I gasped against his kiss as his other hand moved into my hair, his fingers plucking at the pins that held it in place. A few seconds later it came tumbling down around my shoulders and Caine's hand was gone.

I heard a zipper go down and then he was hot and throbbing and hard against me.

Caine reluctantly tore his lips from mine and panted against my mouth. "You're on the pill, right?"

The question was almost pleading.

I nodded and looked down, feeling a sudden roar of fire

lick up from my heels, shooting through my whole body, at the sight of him. It was big. It was thick.

I licked my lips.

"Fuck, Lexie," Caine breathed against my mouth.

I kissed him, my tongue flicking against his lips. I took the silken heat of him in my hands and squeezed and Caine kissed me harder, gasping and panting, as I stroked him with one hand and dug my fingers into his ass with the other, urging him to me.

I guided his tip to my entrance and smoothed my hand up his rigid stomach.

With our lips still touching, our eyes met and held.

Caine gripped my hips and pushed inside.

My eyes fluttered closed at the satisfying burn that quickly evaporated under the relief of being completely filled.

"Lexie, open your eyes," Caine demanded hoarsely.

I opened my eyes and held his fierce gaze.

"Keep your eyes open." He thrust in deeper. "Fuck," he whispered, "keep your eyes open."

He tilted my hips up farther as he slid in and out of me slowly. I trembled against him as he took pleasure in taking his time, and like earlier, I couldn't remember ever feeling more naked. It was holding his gaze, him demanding that I held it as he moved inside me. It intensified whatever this connection was between us. There was no denying this was us—him inside me.

"You feel amazing," he grunted against my lips.

I moved against his thrusts, my heart racing out of all control. "So do you."

"Lexie." His grip tightened, his eyes blazing into mine. "Lexie."

"Caine," I whimpered back as he thrust at just the right angle to brush my clit with his movements.

"Fuck." He started pumping harder, faster.

It began to build again and I was shuddering against him in little jerks as it did so.

"Come for me, Lexie," Caine commanded, his voice gruff with need. "Come around me."

That soft, hard demand was a trigger.

I cried out his name again, my fingers digging into his skin as I clenched around his driving cock, and I lost his gaze as my eyes practically rolled into the back of my head.

As I melted around him, Caine held me to him as his rhythm increased. A few seconds later, his face pressed against my neck, he stiffened and groaned my name. His hips jerked against mine and I felt the release of his climax inside me.

I held on to him as we tried to catch our breath. My skin was slick against his, my breasts crushed against his chest, and we were as close to each other as we could get. I squeezed my thighs around his hips, glorying in this delicious aftermath.

Then . . . his muscles grew taut beneath my hands.

Uneasiness crept over me.

Call it intuition, call it whatever you want, I just knew I wasn't going to like what happened next.

CHAPTER 10

Only seconds before, Caine had been determined to maintain eye contact. Now he was avoiding it. He'd gently pulled out of me, grabbed tissues off his desk, cleaned up, and put his pants back on.

All the while I sat there naked on the desk, watching him put the wall back up between us. My stomach felt sick. "Caine?"

Instead of answering me he ran a hand through his hair as he glanced around the room for his shirt. He found it and shrugged it on.

"Something's wrong," I said. Clearly there was something wrong. One minute we'd been going at it like lust-starved teenagers and now he wouldn't even look at me.

"Caine."

Finally he glanced up from buttoning his shirt. He was guarded as he avoided looking anywhere but at my face. I crossed my leg over the other and leaned back on my palms, thrusting my breasts out in defiance. That instantly distracted him. He clenched his jaw as his gaze roamed over me.

"Well?"

Eyes blazing he glared at me. "This was a mistake."

Even though I knew it was coming, it still hurt like hell. "A mistake?"

"Yes. We crossed the line."

"I see. We're back to that again." I stared at him in disappointment but refused to budge. We were not leaving this office until I'd removed the stick from his ass, something that apparently only sex could do.

Well, if I had to, I had to.

My eyes greedily took in his handsome face.

It wasn't like it was a hardship or anything.

I smirked at the heat in his eyes. At least I knew he wanted me physically. That made it easier to keep pretending that I was completely comfortable sitting cross-legged and naked on his desk. "We should talk."

"You," he snapped, reaching over to grab my dress off the sofa, "should get dressed." He held it out to me.

I took it from him, but I had no intention of actually getting dressed while my nakedness did so much to throw him off balance. We stared defiantly at each other.

"Alexa, get dressed."

No more Lexie for me, huh? Another sharp pain sliced across my chest. I hid it from him. "We're back to Alexa, I see."

Apparently Caine was done with being impatient and was now moving on to annoyed. "Look, we were attracted to each other, we got it out of our systems, and now we need to go back to being boss and employee. And from this point on we're maintaining a strictly professional—" He cut off to scowl as I uncrossed my legs only to cross them again in the opposite direction. He looked away. "Strictly professional relationship," he finished, his voice thick. "Now get dressed."

Realizing I wasn't going to get anywhere with him until I conceded this one thing, I slipped gracefully off the table. "I need to clean up."

Without looking at me he pointed to the bathroom off his office. "You know where it is."

Shrugging on as much confidence as I could muster, I strode into the bathroom, my dress trailing from my hand, and I was satisfied to feel the burn of his gaze on my back as I went.

The truth was my heart was racing as I cleaned up and slipped my dress back on. I'd left my panties out in the office, but I was too shaken up to go back out there for them. As I stared into the mirror, seeing my flushed cheeks and bright eyes and post-sex hair, I was flooded with the sensation of being with Caine all over again. I could still smell him. Taste him. *Feel* him.

I'd just had the best sex of my life with a man with whom I shared off-the-charts chemistry. What was between us wasn't average or everyday. It was extraordinary.

And he was acting like it meant nothing.

The sickness in my stomach intensified and when I looked back in the mirror I could see the flush draining from my cheeks.

I'd never felt like this about any man.

This was lust. This was what all those books and films were always going on about. This wasn't the sexual attraction I'd felt for other men. This was full-blown desire.

Yet—I closed my eyes, remembering the way he'd held my gaze as he moved inside me—it could be more between us. If we tried, who knew where extraordinary could take us?

More scared than I had ever been in my life, I threw my shoulders back with determination and walked out into the office to face Caine.

He was shrugging on his jacket and I saw his relief that I'd put my dress back on.

My belly flipped at the sight of him all rumpled and sexy. Why, oh, why, out of all the men in the world did Caine Carraway have to be the one to make me feel this way?

I stopped a few feet before him and he narrowed his gaze, as if he sensed what was coming.

"You're afraid to let me in."

He shot me a warning look. "Alexa."

I forged ahead. "But I know something all those other women who have tried and failed with you don't. I know you're a good man. Real in a way they've never had the chance to see. I know that because I saw it when you were with Effie. I saw who you really are. I see who you are because . . . we're not so different, you and I. We both deserve happiness."

For a moment Caine just stared at me and a little bubble of hope floated around inside me. When he took a step backward, extremely guarded, that little bubble just went *pop*. "Happiness? This coming from the daughter of the guy who destroyed my family?"

All the air went out of the room.

It was like he'd punched me in the chest.

And he wasn't finished. "I don't know what this is you're trying to do, but you and I are not the same." He took another step back from me. "And I am not for you. I'm not your white knight. I'm just the guy who wanted to fuck you."

I flinched under the sting of his words. Words that humiliated me. I'd idiotically allowed myself to be vulnerable with a man who'd already proven he had no qualms hurting my feelings.

My God, I was such a stupid, stupid fool. Worse. I was . . . some kind of masochist!

I was my mother.

I tried to pull my feelings back inside me so he couldn't see how he'd cut me up into slices. However, I knew it was too late when he said my name in a gentle, remorseful tone. He wore guilt and regret on his face.

"I'm sorry," he whispered. "I didn't mean . . . I shouldn't have said that." He ran his hands through his hair, looking appalled that he had, and frustrated by my effect on him. "I'm just not the guy you're looking for. I'm not ever going to be that man. Trust me."

How could I have allowed myself to forget who I was to him? That was what I'd done here.

Oh God. He must have felt terrible for having sex with me. A *Holland*. Warily I looked over at him. Did he want to wash me off? Forget I happened? I sucked in a breath at the painful thought.

He sighed. "Let's just put this behind us and go back to being the pain-in-the-ass boss and the smart-ass PA."

I stared at him, bewildered by the suggestion. He really thought I could be around him after this?

No. I was done.

What my family did to his had damaged him. The kinship I felt between us . . . I didn't know if it was real or just something I had imagined to life out of the seeds of my loneliness, but I did know that Caine was determined never to feel the connection.

"I shouldn't have come to you for help," I said. "You're right. This was all a mistake. You can consider this my two weeks' notice. After it's up, you'll never have to see me again."

I knew Caine well enough to know that the emotion that flashed in his eyes that he tried so hard to bank was anger. I didn't know how to interpret that reaction, though, and frankly I was raw, mortified, and completely done with the whole mess we'd made. I didn't want to overanalyze a flash of emotion from him.

"I'll call a cab."

"No." He shook his head. "I'll have the driver drop you off at your place."

I did not want to spend another twenty minutes stuck in a car with him. "I said I'll call a cab."

Caine was visibly pissed as he took a menacing step toward me. "For the next two weeks you're still my employee. If I say I'll take you home, I'm taking you the fuck home and it's final."

It was the most silent and uncomfortable car ride in the history of car rides.

After showering the smell of him off my body, I climbed into bed, hugged my pillow like a five-year-old, and then cried all over it. The sun was just starting to filter through my curtains when I eventually nodded off to sleep.

It was with tear-crusted eyes I woke only a few hours later to the sounds of Gloria Gaynor's "I Will Survive."

I'd changed my ringtone before I'd gotten into bed.

"M'ullo," I said into my duvet after grabbing the phone off my bedside table.

"Lexie?"

At the sound of Grandpa's voice I groaned and pushed myself up into a sitting position. "Morning."

"You sound like hell."

"No comment."

"Look, I'm calling to apologize for last night. I wish you'd told me you were going to be attending Dick and Cerise's anniversary. If I'd known I would have come up with an excuse not to go so I didn't have to put you in that position. Christ," he said regretfully, "the look on your face, sweetheart, well, it made me . . . I felt like shit all night."

I felt a pang of remorse for my resentful thoughts when he'd ignored me. I understood the situation. I couldn't start pretending I didn't whenever it suited me. "It's okay, Grandpa. I understand. I even introduced myself as Alexa Hall all night so people wouldn't ask questions."

"I know." There was a smile in his voice. "You made quite an impression. You looked beautiful. I just wish this family wasn't full of malicious drama queens. If they were more understanding, this could all be out in the open. Anyway, I hope you didn't disappear because of me."

I flushed at the real reason. "Uh, no. Caine had a work thing."

My grandfather was silent for a few seconds. "You slept with him, didn't you?"

"How—" I lifted my jaw back up off my duvet. "How the heck did you know that?"

"Because he ignored his date all night as he prowled around the room like a jungle cat hunting my granddaughter. I thought at one point he might actually kill Henry Lexington."

A thrill coursed through me at the thought of Caine's jealousy. "He was watching me all night?"

"What do you think everyone was talking about?"

"Oh my God," I muttered as a realization hit me. I remembered that weird little triumphant smirk on Henry's face when Caine interrupted our dance. "Henry knew. He asked me to the party to push Caine's buttons."

"That sounds like a Lexington." Grandpa's voice lowered. "So, was this part of the plan?"

"I'm not sure I'm comfortable discussing this with my grandfather."

"I'm not sure I'm comfortable with my granddaughter dating a known womanizer."

The ache from last night returned. "Don't worry about that. I don't even qualify as a date. It was a onetime thing."

"I'm going to kill him," Grandpa immediately growled over the phone.

There was every chance he might actually consider something stupid like that. I put on my sternest voice. "You'll do no such thing. It was my mistake. I stupidly forgot who I was to him and I thought there was something there that wasn't . . . I gave him my two weeks' notice."

Grandpa heaved a sigh. "Lexie, I'm sorry."

"Don't be. I did this to myself."

"Well, you make sure he gives you a good recommendation."

I smiled sadly. "I will." I glanced at the clock. It was early yet, which meant many hours to kill. "For now I'm going to buy myself something to make me feel better before I start job-hunting."

"Okay. You call me if you need me, sweetheart."

For some reason that made me tear up.

I thought of how stupid I'd felt after putting myself out there to Caine and being rejected. But I also felt kind of free. For the last few weeks I'd had our attraction hanging over me and subconsciously I knew I'd been building it up in my head into something more than it was. Now, though, I had my answers and I could move on.

Being honest had been scary and it hurt, but at least I wasn't a coward.

It was time to keep living life that way. I sucked in my

breath, exhaled, and then said something I'd never said to a man since I was fourteen years old and I finally realized the truth about my dad. "I love you, Grandpa."

Shocked silence echoed down the line.

And then came his warm, hoarse reply, "I love you too, Lexie."

CHAPTER 11

I knew things were *not* going to return to a state of normality for the next two weeks when I was late into the office on Monday. A flustered mess, I'd hurried into work after sleeping past my alarm and came up short at the sight of Caine sitting behind his desk.

The desk we'd had sex on.

I flushed, remembering every second in vivid detail.

I could tell Caine knew exactly what I was thinking and he shifted uncomfortably as I handed him his latte.

The fact that he didn't call me out on being late said it all.

I couldn't get out of his office fast enough, and we spent the next few hours avoiding contact with each other. I knew we weren't going to get away with that for the entire two weeks, but I could tell we were both going to try our darnedest.

"You look pensive."

My head jerked up from the e-mail I was reading and I stared into Henry's handsome face in surprise. "Henry? What are you doing here?"

He smiled. "It's Monday. Lunchtime. The usual."

"It's that time already?"

"You really were lost in concentration, huh?"

I smiled weakly. "Doing my best."

Henry perched on the edge of my desk. "I also wanted to check in on you after Caine hauled you away from the party on Saturday night."

"I'm fine."

He frowned. "That was the least-fine-sounding 'fine' I've ever heard."

Instead of answering I called through to Caine.

"Yes?" Even this was asked quietly, cautiously.

I glowered at the phone. I never thought I'd see the day when I wished for Caine's impatient grumpiness. "Mr. Lexington is here to see you."

"Send him in."

Thankfully Henry seemed more amused than upset by my obvious brush-off. He threw me a look and wandered into Caine's office. From that moment on I couldn't think about work. I couldn't think about anything but what they were talking about. Would Caine tell Henry that I had sex with him? And how would Henry react? After deducing that Henry was either playing matchmaker or just messing with his friend by asking me out in the first place, I didn't think Henry would be too affected by the news of my sexual escapade with his friend.

Either Caine didn't say anything, or Henry wasn't upset, because when he stepped out of the office with my boss he was laughing about something. My gaze moved to Caine, who stopped at the sight of me and scowled. "I'll be out for lunch. If there's anything urgent have it forwarded to my cell."

Why was he telling me something I already knew?

"I know how to do my job, sir," I said, smiling through clenched teeth.

"Did I say you didn't?"

I saw Henry's eyebrows draw together as he watched our interaction.

"Well, when you instruct me to do something I already know to do, you're implying I don't know my job." I shrugged, crossing my arms over my chest.

"Are you going to be this sensitive for the next two weeks? Because I'd like to prepare myself."

"Oh, why don't you—"

"Children, children." Henry stepped in between us. "What is going on here? I thought after Saturday—"

"You thought what?" Caine and I snapped in unison, and then glowered at each other.

It seemed we both suspected Henry of messing with us.

Henry at least had the good grace to appear sheepish. "Nothing," he lied with a shrug. "I'm just wondering why there's all the extra antagonism between you."

Caine shot me a warning look, and I knew instantly Caine hadn't said a word to Henry about what had happened between us and he didn't want me to mention it either. He addressed Henry. "Alexa quit this morning. She handed in her two-week notice."

"Why?" Henry looked genuinely put out by the news.

Oh, great. So I was the bad guy. I harrumphed. "Call it an 'unacceptable working environment.'"

"What? No." He gave me a charming smile as though it would change my mind. "There's got to be something we can work out."

"Nope." I stood up and grabbed my purse. "Don't have time. I'm going out for lunch."

"Not while I'm out for lunch," Caine reminded me. "You can have your lunch at your desk. Like always."

"I feel like eating now. Outside."

"You'll eat at your desk when it's your lunch break."

I narrowed my eyes. "I just decided this is my lunch break and I'm taking it outside."

He took a step toward me, eyes flinty with warning. "You start acting like a child and I will make the next two weeks an absolute misery for you."

I sighed and said, infusing boredom into my voice, "Is that before or after you huff and puff and blow my house down?" And while he stared at me, speechless I strode past him and a chuckling Henry. I strolled right on out of there with a triumphant swing in my hips.

Round one to me.

Upon reflection while I sat in a café by myself and nibbled on a sandwich I didn't really want to eat because I felt sick, I decided I *was* acting like a child. Okay, so Caine had hurt me and he continued to hurt me by acting like nothing happened between us, but I was a grown woman and I knew what I was getting into when I allowed Caine Carraway to have his wicked way with me.

We were both at fault for that, and the next two weeks would go a whole lot faster if I pretended to be polite.

So that was my intention.

Honestly.

Yet when Caine returned from lunch he was in a foul mood. I was going to promise him that I'd be civil to him from now on, but he didn't even give me a chance to speak before he slammed inside his office.

My mood plummeted with his about half an hour later when the phone rang.

"Carraway Financial Holdings, Mr. Carraway's office."

"This is Marina Lansbury for Caine." Her husky, impatient voice made me stiffen. "Put me through."

The burn of jealousy radiated out of my chest, and my cheeks flushed. "Just one second," I managed. I put her on hold and called through to Caine with no little amount of trepidation.

"What?" he snapped.

Okay, so maybe I didn't miss his impatient grumpiness after all.

"I have Marina Lansbury on the line for you."

"Put her through."

My pulse started racing.

Put her through?

Why?

Why would he speak to her during working hours?

"Alexa?"

"Just one second," I choked out, and then I patched her through to him.

For the next few minutes I glared at the telephone. Was he seriously going to date that sneering she-wolf?

I shook my head in exasperation. "It's not your business," I whispered heatedly to myself.

"Alexa," Caine's voice crackled on the speakerphone. "Come into my office, please."

Bracing myself, I got up and walked sedately inside. He was sitting behind his desk, reading something on his computer. At my appearance he merely afforded me a quick glance before turning back to the screen. "You rang?"

"I need you to book a table at Menton for two at eight tomorrow evening. I heard through the grapevine they might be fully booked, so if you can't get Menton, here's a list of acceptable alternatives." He pushed a notepad toward me.

That burn returned with a vengeance and I stared at him incredulously. He wanted me to make a date for him? Was he shitting me?

"Alexa?" Caine finally looked at me, his eyebrow quirked in question.

I gave him a slow saccharine smile as I put my palms to his desk and leaned over so our faces were only inches apart. His eyes narrowed at my nearness, but he held still. "You know what, Mr. Carraway?" I said with faux sweetness. "You can book your own table."

Anger sparked in his eyes as I stepped back and spun around on my heel. Whatever he might think, as much as I'd put up with his crap as a diligent employee, I was not a woman he could walk all over.

"The table is for me and Jack Pendergast. You know, the president of Atwater Venture Capital."

Oh.

I halted.

Oh, bulls.

I sheepishly looked over my shoulder. "Oops?"

To my surprise Caine smirked. "Even I'm not that big enough a bastard to ask you to arrange a date for me two days after we . . ." His eyes flicked to the top of his desk.

"Had sex on that desk?" I finished helpfully.

The muscle in Caine's jaw flexed as he nodded.

I sighed, feeling silly for overreacting. Still . . . anyone could have made the same mistake. It wasn't like Caine was known for being Mr. Sensitive around me. "Well, I suppose it's good to know I didn't fuck a complete asshole." And on that note I walked out of his office.

Okay. Maybe I wasn't done being mad at him.

My speakerphone crackled. "Alexa."

I rolled my eyes. "What?"

"Why don't you run out and pick me up a latte? Don't come back until you've cooled off."

I clenched my teeth and started to count to ten.

"Alexa?"

"You are extremely condescending."

"And you are extremely annoying. Now get gone."

I sighed, feeling like my skin was too tight, like my emotions were being smooshed and suffocated and thus in their desperation to breathe and be heard they were making me act like a crazy person. For some reason I found myself admitting, "I'm not usually like this."

"I know," he said. "Let's just try to get through the next two weeks. All right?"

And that was when I realized why I was acting like a woman scorned. It wasn't just because we had sex and he was acting like it meant nothing. It was because he seemed completely okay with the fact that in two weeks' time we'd never see each other again.

"Yeah," I said, trying to mute the sadness in my words. "I can do that."

It occurred to me that evening as I changed my ringtone to Ray Charles's "Hit the Road Jack," that leaving Caine meant leaving Effie. And just when I'd found her.

This only fueled my heightened emotions, and despite my best efforts I barely caught a wink of sleep that night. As I lay in bed in the wee hours of the morning, I refused to be this sad, nonsleeping little person because of a man. If I couldn't sleep, then I was hauling my ass out of bed. After hitting the shower, I perused my wardrobe for the outfit that screamed *I am woman, hear me roar.*

I decided on my most figure-hugging black pencil skirt, my four-inch Prada black platform pumps, and a tight blush-colored silk blouse with little cap sleeves. I left a few buttons undone, hinting at my cleavage. I topped it off by wearing my hair slicked back in a high-fashion ponytail that made my eyes look feline and exotic.

I even wore a touch of makeup.

I nodded at my reflection. Sometimes uptight clothes could be smoking hot. I wanted Caine Carraway to be as off balance as I was. He'd admitted he'd fantasized about screwing me in his office, and yes, we'd played that little fantasy out already, but there was no harm in trying to push his buttons. Just in case.

By the time I made it into the office, I was more than half an hour earlier than I usually was. To my surprise, Caine's office door was unlocked. I was just musing over that and what could have made Caine so absentminded as to leave his office open when I wandered inside and abruptly drew to a halt.

The lights were on and there were clothes scattered on his sofa.

What was that noise?

I glanced over at the bathroom door and my eyes widened as it opened. Steam poured out as Caine appeared.

Wearing nothing but a towel around his waist.

Holy crap.

Caine froze at the sight of me. Our eyes locked.

I knew if I dropped my gaze I'd see little water droplets coursing down his rock-hard abs.

Why did he have to be so beautiful?

"You're early," he complained.

He shifted uncomfortably and a wave of satisfaction rolled

over me. So he wasn't completely unaffected at the thought of being practically naked in a room alone with me. I decided to fan the flames. Very deliberately I let my eyes roam over him.

I wanted to lick him.

Yearning shot through me.

When my eyes returned to his I was gratified to find an answering heat in them.

"You're early too." My voice was husky from my wicked thoughts.

He caught my tone and his eyes dipped to my mouth.

Feeling smug, I gave him my back and very deliberately bent over his desk so I could place his latte by his computer. "Your coffee," I said, feeling the heat of his gaze singeing my ass. Without looking back I stood away from the desk and headed toward the door.

"Alexa," he said in warning.

I half turned, my eyes round with mock innocence. I couldn't maintain it when I saw that he was aroused under his towel.

My lower belly flipped in response, followed by a burst of tingles between my legs.

"Quit it," he demanded.

"I'm not doing anything. After all . . ." I grinned wickedly, my gaze dropping pointedly to his hard-on. "I'm out of your system, right?"

Caine shot me a filthy look but didn't say anything. What could he say? Having successfully tormented him, I smirked and left him alone in his office. As soon as I closed the door behind me, I sank against it. My legs were trembling.

I had to get myself together.

That took me a while, considering that I spent the next thirty minutes fantasizing a different ending to that scene—it mostly consisted in Caine screwing me hard against his office door.

I wanted the two weeks' notice to be over. Now.

Perhaps I should have walked out.

But then . . . then he'd know he had really gotten to me and I had to leave this situation behind with at least some of my pride intact.

"Alexa, come into my office, please," Caine's voice came over the speakerphone a few hours later. Maybe he was going to ask me to leave. That way I could get out of this without it looking like I was the one who had caved.

I sighed. I guessed that was wishful thinking, and as soon as I got inside his office I knew I was right.

"You want us to what?" I croaked in disbelief.

"Business trip," he repeated impatiently. "Seattle. This Thursday. I wouldn't normally go, but they've asked to speak to me in person. I need you with me."

"Do you think the two of us going on a business trip together is wise?"

Caine replied with a cool look. "I'm not a teenager, Alexa. Whatever you think you might have won this morning, you're wrong. No woman leads me around by my dick. I promise you I can manage to keep my hands off you if that's what you're asking."

Why was I attracted to this jackass again?

I grimaced. He didn't know it, but he'd just made it a whole lot easier for me to walk away from him at the end of the two weeks.

"Can you handle it?"

"Oh, trust me," I said, "being around you right now is like a constant cold shower."

His lips pinched with annoyance. "I've e-mailed you the details. I'll need you to arrange flights and accommodation."

"Done." I walked out calmly and just as calmly settled back into my seat.

That was when the calmness left me.

Seattle? With Caine? In a hotel?

I'd either kill him or screw him again.

"Fuck."

"Alexa, the speakerphone is on," Caine's amused voice sounded from my desk.

Oh, balls.

One of us was definitely not making it out of Seattle in one piece.

CHAPTER 12

Caine took it easy on me for the next few days. He didn't have me running around doing crappy personal errands. It was his way of extending his hand in a truce and I offered him my hand in return by curbing my smart-ass responses to his requests.

That didn't mean I wasn't battling a kaleidoscope of butterflies swarming in my belly on Thursday morning. I'd barely slept and I was stumbling around my apartment trying to make sure I had everything I needed in my overnight bag.

I was just chugging a huge mug of coffee when I saw the black street car pull up outside my building. My mug clattered to the counter as I watched the driver open the back passenger door. Caine stepped out and stared up at the building with a pensive mien. I eyed him hungrily.

He hadn't shaved in a few days and it looked good on him.

As did the four-thousand-dollar Savile Row suit he'd had commissioned along with a number of others while he was in London. It was a slim fit. It was stylish. It was pure class. And the man wearing it looked like pure class too. Sometimes, when he wasn't being a jackass, he even *was* pure class.

I wrenched my gaze from his as he started making his way up the front stoop. My overnight bag was on the couch spilling open.

Toiletries. I needed my toiletries.

My doorbell rang and for one confused moment I stood there wondering how on earth Caine had gotten into the building. I hurried to the door and threw it open with the question on my face.

"Your neighbor let me in," he explained immediately.

I frowned at my neighbor's lack of thought to security. "You could be a serial killer."

He shrugged and stepped forward, forcing me to move back to allow him inside. "I guess I don't look like one."

"It was Evelyn who let you in, right?" She was a single career woman much like myself except she was man-crazy and had a different one sneaking out of her apartment every weekend.

"Young, blond?"

I nodded in consternation. "She's going to get me murdered in my sleep one of these days."

Caine just nodded absentmindedly and strode into the center of the open living area. He gazed around, taking absolutely everything in.

"I'll, uh . . . just be a moment." I disappeared into the bathroom, grabbing my toiletries bag and my cell phone charger from the side of my bed. When I returned to the living room, Caine was standing in front of one of my windows. I stuffed my things into my overnight bag and zipped it up.

While I did this, Caine turned around, his eyes traveling up to the ceiling and down and then into the kitchen.

Bemused by his curiosity, I said, "What is it?"

He looked back at me. "This is where you live."

I couldn't work out his tone or what he meant by the statement, so I just sighed and grabbed my bag. "I'm ready to go."

Caine strode toward me and reached for the bag.

"What are you doing?" I pulled it back from him. "I can carry my own bag."

"You have to at least allow me the pretense of being a gentleman." His large hand wrapped around the strap and he gently tugged it out of my grip.

Following him out, I grumbled, "I hope you're not going to pretend the entire trip."

"And why not?"

"Well, I've built up a resistance to your ungentlemanliness. My immune system can't handle politeness from you. I might go into shock and die." It wasn't entirely true. In public he was every inch the gentleman. In private not so much. I locked up my apartment and found Caine smirking behind me.

I paused, surprised by the humor in his eyes.

"Ungentlemanliness?" he teased. "I dare you to say that five times fast."

I eyed him warily. "I mean it. Quit it."

His reply was to shrug and lead me out to the car in silence. And it seemed he was set to grant me my request. The car ride to the airport was awkward and quiet and I really just wanted to be able to put more than a couple of feet between us.

Upon arrival at the airport, I said to Caine, "I'll meet you on the other side."

His eyebrows drew together. "What are you talking about?"

I handed him the boarding pass I'd printed off. "You're

flying first class. That means you go through first-class security and get to wait in the first-class lounge."

"And what are you?" he asked, snatching my boarding pass from my hand. "Economy? Are you kidding?" he huffed impatiently, and grabbed my bag. Before I could say a word he strode off.

"What are you doing?" I hurried to catch up with him in my stupid heels as he marched to the fast-lane check-in and right up to the check-in clerk.

"We need to upgrade my employee's ticket to first class. Is that possible?" He slid my boarding pass across the desk to her.

"What are you doing?" I repeated. "I don't need a first-class seat. I never sat in first class with Benito."

"That's because your former boss is a tightfisted bastard. My employees don't sit in the cheap seats." He threw me a glare that said, *Now, shut up.*

Once my ticket was upgraded, Caine tersely ushered me toward the first-class lounge. He dropped our bags at the bar. "I need a drink. Do you need a drink?"

I definitely needed a drink. "A mimosa, please." I slipped onto a stool beside him and we waited in uncomfortable silence as the bartender poured my drink and got a draft beer for Caine.

A beer.

That was not what I was expecting at all.

For some crazy reason the fact that Caine was drinking a beer in his fancy-ass suit in the first-class lounge made me smile.

Feeling my stare, he glanced at me. "What?"

I looked away and lifted my glass to my lips. "Nothing," I muttered.

"Lexie?" I jerked in surprise at hearing my name called from behind me and spun around on my stool. My eyes moved up the tall, fit, stylishly attired body standing inches from me until they stopped on the familiar handsome face of Antoine Faucheux.

"Oh my gosh, Antoine." I hopped off the stool to hug him and felt his strong arms wrap around me.

He gave me a squeeze and kissed me once on both cheeks. His dark brown eyes glittered happily into mine.

Antoine was the men's fashion buyer at Le Bon Marche in Paris. We'd known each other for four years because of my work with Benito. Mostly we met up while I was in Paris with Benito, but the last time I'd seen him was in New York when he came over for fashion week. He'd even propositioned me the first time we hung out, but I was in a relationship at the time, and the next time we met he was in a relationship, and so on and so forth. It was a shame. Definitely a missed opportunity.

He shot a look over my shoulder and I tensed, remembering we had an audience. I glanced back at Caine, whose hard appearance didn't exactly compel a person to be friendly, but my mother had raised me to be well mannered. "Antoine, this is my boss, Caine Carraway. Mr. Carraway, this is a friend of mine, Antoine Faucheux."

Antoine held out a hand with a polite smile. "It's nice to meet you," he said in his gorgeous accent.

Caine stared at his hand and for a moment I worried he wasn't going to shake it. I breathed a sigh of relief when he did.

Antoine immediately focused on me. "It's so good to see you. I'm over here visiting a friend and I met up with Benito. I was shocked when he told me he fired you. What an idiot."

He tilted his head and gave me his sexy low-lidded stare I liked so much. "I've never seen anyone anticipate someone's needs the way you did Benito's. You know he's having a terrible time without you."

I grinned, feeling smug. "Good."

Antoine laughed and then shot another glance behind me at Caine. "It looks like you're doing fine."

It did look like that, and I had no intention of telling Antoine the truth. Instead I gave him a noncommittal smile and a shrug.

"Well"—he pouted a little and it would have looked ridiculous on any man but him—"I have to catch my flight to Paris. It was a short trip this time, but next time I'm in Boston, or New York even, we should catch up." He lowered his voice and gave me a knowing look. "Noelle and I broke up and I heard you're not seeing anyone, yes?"

Oh, balls.

Heat radiated from behind me and I knew Caine had heard and interpreted Antoine's comment. It wasn't like it was hard to understand.

I never thought I'd want to run my way out of the hot boy sandwich I was in the middle of, but if the floor had opened up in front of me I'd have dived right into the gaping hole to escape the utterly awful awkwardness.

"True," I murmured.

"And of course if you're ever in Paris . . ." He leaned down and kissed me on my cheeks again, this time more slowly. His hand rested on my waist. "The new job suits you. You look beautiful."

And if we'd had this encounter a few weeks ago, I'd be putty in his sexy-as-sin French hands.

Unfortunately my mind was muddled enough by the

brooding businessman whose stare was burning holes into my skull. "Thank you," I replied. "I'll hopefully see you soon."

Antoine smiled and then gave Caine a nod of acknowledgment before he left.

I gathered myself before sliding back onto the stool beside Caine and his foreboding expression.

I sucked in my breath and waited.

Just as I was beginning to think he wasn't going to comment and I could relax, he finished his beer and scowled at me. "I presume you realize he wants to fuck you."

I wrinkled my nose in distaste at his crudeness. "You really took my word for it on the whole not-pretending-to-be-a-gentleman thing, huh?"

He ignored me. "The question is, do *you* want to fuck *him*?"

Oh no. He did not get to be angry or jealous. And yes, okay, maybe I felt a little thrill course through me at the idea that he was jealous of Antoine, but at the same time it was unfair and confusing! Caine had already made it clear that what he got from me on Saturday night was all he was willing to take. He was not messing with my head now.

My answer to him was to slide off the stool with my drink. I sauntered casually across the room, as far as I could get from him, and settled in a seat with my mimosa and magazine.

I was glad we had an aisle between us in first class, because I was more likely to punch Caine than speak to him. Six hours later when the plane landed in Seattle, I was much calmer and actually managed to be civil to him as we made our way out of the airport to find our chauffeur waiting for us.

We were staying at the Fairmont Olympic and I tried not to gape as we wandered inside. I'd stayed at nice hotels before, but Benito favored extremely modern hotels. The Fairmont was old-school beautiful with its high ceiling and grand twin staircase at the end of the reception hall. Plush, expensive traditional chairs and sofas furnished the hall, and giant crystal chandeliers hung from the ceiling, casting light over all the gleaming chestnut wood.

"Checking in under Carraway," Caine said as a greeting to the young woman behind the desk.

She smiled and began typing on her computer. "Mr. Caine Carraway and a Ms. Alexa Holland. We have you booked for a deluxe executive suite, and a standard Fairmont room for Ms. Holland."

Caine exhaled wearily and shot me a displeased look. "Again?"

I knew what he meant without having to ask. "I'm your PA. I'm perfectly happy with a standard room."

He ignored me. "Can you upgrade the Fairmont room to a suite?"

The girl did a quick check and gave Caine an apologetic thin-lipped smile. "We only have a deluxe room available."

"That'll do."

After we'd checked in and were walking toward the elevator, I said, "You really didn't have to do that."

"I'm not repeating myself," he muttered impatiently.

"Right, appearances," I muttered back.

Caine walked me to my room even though his was a couple of floors above mine. Once inside my perfectly lovely deluxe room, I spun around to face him. He lowered my bag to the floor by the television cabinet. "The dinner with Farrah Rochdale and Lewis Sheen is in the hotel restaurant," I reminded him. "At seven o' clock."

He gave me a tight nod and started to back out of the room. "I'll collect you at six fifty."

A few seconds later he was gone and I could breathe properly again. I sank onto the beautiful bed and kicked off my heels. As I stared at the door, a feeling of melancholy began to bring me down. I fought to keep it at bay.

I just had to make it through dinner this evening and then tomorrow we were on that plane back to Boston. It was safer somehow in Boston. I could hold it together. Here, in close quarters with him, I was constantly reminded of the possibility between us, and Caine's stubborn-ass refusal to see what might have been.

Promptly at six fifty I opened my hotel room door to Caine and I had to quickly look at my feet to hide my reaction to his appearance. He'd shaved off his scruff—the clean-shaven look was as hot as the unshaven look—and he was dressed in a light gray slim-fit three-piece suit.

"Ready?"

I nodded and closed the door behind me, following him as he started walking down the hall. He made no comment on my appearance and I tried not to let that sting.

Of course it did.

I'd dressed carefully in a simple but sexy little black dress. It had a high neck, it was sleeveless, and it came to a few inches above my knee. It also hugged my body like a second skin. I'd whipped out the Louboutins I'd gotten for free at a magazine shoot a couple of years ago. For once I left my hair loose and wavy. It wasn't Caine's preferred style, but I was feeling rebellious.

In the restaurant we were led over to a table where a thirtysomething woman and her fortysomething colleague sat. Farrah Rochdale was CEO of Rochdale Financial Management, and Lewis Sheen was her CFO. The company had started up two generations before, but when it had finally made it into Farrah's hands it was struggling to draw in new clientele despite having helped some of the country's fastest-growing businesses in the past. Caine's company came along to save a company they believed could do well again. They brought Rochdale under their umbrella and injected money and influence into the business. It was now thriving as one of the West Coast's foremost financial management groups as part of Carraway Holdings.

However, Farrah had requested a face-to-face meeting with Caine to discuss something of importance that would affect the company.

I didn't know what to expect of the meeting or what was going on. I just knew I hadn't expected Farrah Rochdale to be so young or attractive. She and Lewis stood up at our approach and I noted how tall she was. Her auburn hair was twisted up in a stylish knot and she was dressed in a gorgeous lilac wraparound dress that showcased her phenomenal figure. Farrah stepped forward to receive a familiar kiss on the cheek from Caine before he offered his hand to her CFO.

"This is my PA, Alexa," he introduced me, and I shook Farrah's hand first, feeling the burn of her curiosity on my face.

With much relief I let go of her hand and turned to Lewis. He smiled and took my hand, but instead of shaking it he brought it to his lips in an old-fashioned gesture that I found charming.

"Shall we sit?" Caine pulled my seat out for me and Lewis gently released my hand.

I wasn't surprised by Caine's gentlemanly gesture. We were in public and one of the many things Caine did that was pure class was that he always pulled out my chair for me at business meetings. Moreover, he waited until I was seated before he sat, and if I stood up to leave for any reason he always stood up too.

Lewis followed suit with his CEO's chair, and once Farrah and I were seated, the guys settled down beside us. I sat directly across from Farrah and had Caine on my left and Lewis on my right, and I could feel Farrah's gaze on me as I looked at my menu.

It wasn't until after we'd ordered that Caine relaxed back in his chair and asked Farrah, "So, what's the problem?"

She released a heavy sigh. "I want to step down."

Caine frowned. "Why on earth would you do that?"

"Caine." Farrah sat forward, her tone suggesting familiarity between them, "You know I never wanted to take over my family's company."

I found myself scrutinizing Caine's response to her and felt a burn of discomfort in my chest at his own familiarity with her. "And yet you fought so hard for it?"

There was definitely something there between them.

I couldn't put my finger on it, yet I just knew. It was in the way they looked at each other. In their soft tones.

She smiled. "I didn't want the company, but I also didn't want my grandfather's legacy to die. My own father worked himself into an early grave for the company. I couldn't just let it all be for nothing. But now it's time for me to move on."

Caine was silent upon this declaration. The starters arrived before he could say anything and we'd just begun eating when he stopped. "You realize that my board of directors will have strong opinions on who your successor should be?"

Farrah rewarded him with an intimate smile and I swallowed past a lump of jealousy in my throat. Yup. They'd definitely been together. "Yes, which is why I asked you here. The company is called *Carraway* Financial Holdings. You have a strong influence, and I know you'll take my recommendation to heart."

Caine gave nothing away. He flicked a glance at Lewis Sheen. "You want Lewis to take over."

Farrah smiled at her CFO. "He knows the company better than anyone. He knows where we were and where we're going."

"And I care what happens to the company," Lewis added. "Which is a rare commodity in an employee of modern business."

Caine stared at him a few moments. "I agree."

Farrah and Lewis seemed to deflate with relief. "Thank you, Caine."

"Don't thank me yet. I can only do so much."

She smiled gratefully at him. "I know exactly what you're capable of."

I tried to act normally after that, but it was hard. My skin felt like it was on fire and I just wanted to be anywhere but sitting at that table with Caine and his ex-lover.

They discussed Lewis's possible takeover for a while until the conversation turned to what Farrah intended to move on to, and while she told Caine about the job offer she'd received in the finance department of a major fashion line in New York, Lewis attempted to engage me in conversation. I tried my best to concentrate, but it was difficult when I wanted to be as far from the table as possible.

After we'd finished eating and Caine, Farrah, and I had ordered coffees, Lewis stood up. "I apologize, but I promised my wife I wouldn't be late home tonight." He smiled down at me. "It was a pleasure to meet you, Alexa." He held out his hand to Caine. "As always, a delight, Mr. Carraway. Thank you so much for taking the time to meet with us, and for appreciating what I can bring to the table." He nodded at Farrah. "We'll talk soon."

We bade him good-bye and I sank deeper into my chair, wishing I had an excuse to leave too. I did not want to be the third wheel in this situation.

However, Farrah seemed to have forgotten my existence. I didn't think it was deliberate. I think she was just that smitten with Caine.

She hogged the conversation, turning it personal as she brought up a number of dinner parties they'd attended together. Although Caine was his usual difficult-to-read self, he did seem marginally more relaxed around her and I almost hated her for that. The only thing that made watching her stroke his arm and laugh about the good old times together was the fact that she didn't make Caine laugh and he rarely smiled.

That would have killed me if she'd managed that feat.

The flirting, though, was enough to do some serious damage. The truth was I didn't even know why I was there in the first place. Caine didn't need me here for this and he certainly didn't need me there to witness him flirt with a woman who was obviously an old flame.

I didn't want to watch them rekindle something.

My stomach was sick. I wanted a stiff drink, far away from him.

I stood up abruptly and a bewildered Caine got to his feet too. "If you'll excuse me I think I'll call it a night."

He frowned but nodded.

I nodded at Farrah. "It was a pleasure to meet you." *Fucking lie!*

She bestowed upon me a vague smile. "You too."

Without sparing Caine another glance, I walked out of the restaurant and headed through the hotel to the bar. I found an empty stool at the bar and settled in.

The young bartender smiled at me. "What can I get you, madam?"

Ugh, when did I become a "madam"? Just one more thing a drink would help me forget about. "Glenlivet on the rocks."

The bartender didn't even blink at my order and he was back a few seconds later with the drink. I took a sip, letting the heat of the scotch slide down my throat and spread out across my chest. I instantly felt a little more relaxed.

For a while I sat there, nursing my scotch and playing around with my cell. Rachel had sent me a picture of Maisy sitting on her husband Jeff's back. Jeff was flat out on his stomach on the floor, and his hands had been tied behind his back.

Your kid worries me, I texted in return.

A few seconds later my cell pinged. *I know, right? It's hilarious.*

I grimaced and shoved my phone in my purse. To Rachel, Maisy was hilarious. To the rest of us she was a demon child.

"Can I get you another?"

Surprised by the closeness of the voice, I felt my body give a little jerk. A young guy in a suit was sliding onto the stool beside me. I took him in, feeling a little buzzed. He was attractive and there was a sparkle of good humor in his eyes that I liked.

What the hell?

"You may."

He grinned. "What'll it be?" I told him, and his grin widened. "Scotch?"

I smiled unhappily. "I'm drowning my sorrows."

The guy waved down the bartender and ordered two whiskies. When his attention returned to me, he said, "Why is a pretty thing like you drowning your sorrows?"

I made a face.

He laughed. "What?"

"Pretty thing? Really?"

"I just say it like I see it." He held out his hand. "I'm Barry."

I took his hand. "Alexa."

"So, Alexa, I'll ask again . . . why are you drowning your sorrows?"

Wrapping my hand around the glass of scotch the bartender put in front of me, I tilted my head in a coy gesture. "Guess."

"Hmm . . . career troubles?"

I snapped my fingers and pointed to him. "Bingo."

Barry smiled and leaned closer. "Well, why don't we see how long it takes me to make you forget about your troubles?"

"What the hell? I've got nothing to lose. Give it your best shot, Barry."

And he did.

We talked about music and movies, and I argued fervently in favor of the Red Sox while he argued for the Mariners, and we did it in a flirty, suggestive way that soothed the wounds to my feminine vanity. We didn't discuss anything serious and for a little while it was wonderful to be buzzed, relaxed, and admired.

I didn't know how long we'd been sitting there, but my second scotch was nearly finished and I was thinking it was time for another when Barry suddenly slid his hand along my thigh.

"Why don't we take this up to your room?"

Looking down at his hand on my leg, I had to admit that there was a part of me that actually thought about it. I wanted to forget what it felt like to feel Caine all around me, and surely the old adage was true—the best way to get over someone was to get under someone new. With the scotch hot in my blood, that suddenly sounded like very good advice.

"Or better yet, why don't you remove your hand before I break it?"

The breath went out of my body at the menacing voice.

I stared up at Caine, who towered over us, his dark gaze scorching Barry.

Barry flushed and started a stumbling slide from his stool. "Sorry," he mumbled.

He scampered off before I could do anything to stop him. Not that I wanted to now—there was nothing more unattractive than a scaredy-cat. Although . . . taking in the look on Caine's face, I couldn't imagine many men wouldn't find him intimidating. "What was that?"

The muscle was working overtime in his clenched jaw. It took him a few seconds to manage to utter the words, "That was me stopping you from making a drunken mistake. A mistake you'll regret in the morning." His warm hand wrapped around my elbow and he gently guided me off the stool. "Let's get you to your room."

I jerked out of his hold, infuriated by his high-handedness. "What? You're done ignoring me while you flirt with Farrah Rochdale so you thought you'd come spoil my fun?"

Caine's features hardened, but he didn't answer. Instead he gripped my elbow again and began striding through the bar.

There was nothing I could do. If I attempted to stop him

I'd just make a scene, and despite what he thought, I was buzzed, not drunk.

He manhandled me into the elevator. "I wasn't ignoring you. You were ignoring me."

The elevator began to rise. "Oh yes, of course. How silly of me. I was the one to blame when you were flirting with another woman right in front of me merely days after we had sex."

"Not that it's any of your business, but Farrah and I are just old friends. I never mix business with pleasure."

I shot him a look. "I know from personal experience that's not true."

Color appeared high on his cheekbones. "Usua—"

The abrupt halt of the elevator and its doors opening cut him off. I hurried out, hoping he wouldn't follow.

I had no such luck. Caine caught up to me and grabbed my arm again.

"I'm perfectly capable of making it to my room."

Instead of listening to me, he took my purse out of my hand and raked through it for the room key.

"I'm not drunk," I insisted.

"So that was a sober decision to flirt with that asshole?" he asked, his voice tight, as we stopped at my door.

I huffed and waited for him to open it. To my dismay he pushed his way in first, holding the door open for me.

"You can leave." I glowered at him and strode inside.

I bent down to tug off my shoes, whirling and almost falling when I heard the door shut behind me.

Caine stood watching me.

"You can leave," I repeated

He just stared at me in that intense, overwhelming way of his.

"What?" I snapped. "What now?"

"I'm sorry if I hurt you tonight," he said, and for some reason his apology only fanned the flames of my anger. "You don't deserve that."

Whether it was the alcohol or a buildup of tension from the past few weeks of ignoring our chemistry, my self-control slipped. The hurt and fury just exploded out of me. "You know what? You're right. I deserve better. I've deserved better my whole life, but I never got it. Neither did my mother." I let all my pain blaze out at him and he stood there, frozen by my words. "But my mom refused to ask for better. I won't make that same mistake.

"From the moment my father told me what he did to your mom, to your family, I cut him out of my life." I watched how this information made Caine's eyes glitter, arrested on my face. "I used to think he was some kind of hero," I whispered. "Some kind of fairy-tale prince who came around on my birthday and showered me with gifts and made my mom really happy. Then suddenly he was there all the time. I thought he'd finally come to save us. And I kept thinking of him like that until I was a teenager, until I was old enough to see how spoiled and lazy and entitled he was. How he made my mom cry more than he made her laugh. But I pretended." I gave a huff of bitter laughter as I remembered the way I'd stuck my head in the sand.

"I kept pretending right up until seven years ago when he confessed his sins. I hated him for what he did to your mother. I hated him for lying to me all those years, for having a family I knew nothing about, for coming to us because we were all he had left, his only recourse. I left home. But I couldn't let it go until I knew everything. So I went back and I asked my father your mother's name, your name, but he wouldn't tell me. I decided I didn't need to know your name. I just needed my father to apologize to you, to prove he really was remorseful and that whatever he was going through wasn't just about him, but about the people he hurt. But he refused. So I told him I didn't want anything to do with him ever again, and I never went back.

"I lost my mom because of him. She refused to walk away from him and she blamed me for the rift. Now I can't fix the relationship I helped break, because she's dead, she's gone . . . And all I've got left in this world is a grandfather who's too ashamed to acknowledge me and a boss who gets a kick out of treating me like shit." My voice hardened. "Well, no more. I am done with this game. Because I am not my father and I would never hurt people the way he did. I wanted you to see that. I wanted you to see me. To see . . . to see that I *get* it. I've never deserved your contempt. And I won't put up with it anymore." I gestured, weary of it all, to the door. "Just get out, Caine."

I was too angry to see the change in his expression, to hear the softness when he said my name.

"Caine, get out."

"Lexie, I never knew any of that."

"Because you never bothered to ask!" I yelled. "And now it doesn't matter. When we get back to Boston, I'm done. Screw the two weeks. This is over now." I whipped around, walking away from him toward the bathroom, hoping by the time I got out of there he'd be gone.

But I didn't even make it inside.

I heard the quick footsteps behind me seconds before I was yanked around and crushed against him.

He whispered my name before his head dipped and his lips came down on mine.

CHAPTER 13

I kissed him back.

The truth was, even when he pissed me off I wanted him.

And that made me even angrier.

My emotions fed into the kiss as I wound my arms around his neck and curled my fingers into his hair. Our tongues stroked in desperation as Caine felt the heat of my anger and caught fire.

His thumbs brushed against my cheeks, seeming to swipe invisible tear tracks away.

I pushed at his jacket and he dropped his arms so he could shrug out of it. We didn't break the kiss, our mouths pulling at each other's.

Caine started moving me back in the direction of the bed and our lips didn't part until he lifted me and then dropped me on my back across the middle of the mattress.

I stared up at him, panting, my whole body aflame. He kept me trapped in his gaze as he unbuttoned his waistcoat and shirt.

How could it be that a moment ago I was ready to walk away from this man for good, and now all I could think about was getting him inside me? "This is insane," I whispered. "What are we doing?"

He tugged off his shirt and threw it behind him. He then immediately sought out the side zipper on my dress. "Taking what we both want." He tugged the zipper down and I shivered.

"It doesn't matter that I'm drunk?"

Caine smirked and took hold of the hem of my dress. Slowly he pushed it up past my thighs, up over my stomach, my breasts, and I raised my arms above my head so he could pull it off. His eyes devoured me, raking me over as I lay under him in my black lace bra and panties.

My gaze dropped to the thick arousal stretching the fabric of his pants.

When I looked up our eyes met.

"A minute ago you were just buzzed, not drunk," he reminded me, amusement lacing the words.

I raised an eyebrow. "Buzzed or drunk, a gentleman wouldn't take advantage."

"Well, you're in luck." He grazed his knuckles over my stomach, his eyes following his fingers as they trailed along the edge of my underwear. My stomach rippled and his gaze went black with heat. "We both know I'm no gentleman."

My nipples peaked against my bra at the dark arousal in his voice. "I thought I was out of your system."

His hand flattened on my stomach and he smoothed it upward slowly, heading between my breasts. "And we both know that was a lie." He unclipped the front clasp on my bra and eased it off.

The cool air rushed over my breasts and they swelled under his perusal. My breath hitched as he stroked them softly, his thumbs brushing over my nipples. Caine held my gaze as he gently, slowly, torturously teased my breasts. "You're so fucking beautiful."

I think I stopped breathing.

"I can't stop thinking about being inside you." He leaned over, his erection pushing insistently against my belly, and his lips whispered over mine, "It's like heaven inside you." His features were taut as he squeezed my breasts. "I almost want to punish you a little for making me feel like this."

I sucked in air as I fought for some equilibrium. "And here I thought a woman couldn't lead you around by your dick," I attempted to tease him, but my words were hoarse with need.

He slid his body down, pushing my thighs open, and thrust his cock against me. I groaned, feeling a flush of heat move up my stomach from between my legs. "No woman can," he maintained. "But you certainly have a habit of making me feel like a teenage boy peeping into the girls' locker room."

I chuckled throatily and Caine grinned. He nudged against me again. "I like that."

"Like what?"

In answer he kissed me and I wrapped my arms around his back, trying to draw him closer. His lips moved down my chin, trailing in soft caresses along my throat and breasts. As much as I wanted his mouth all over me, I was desperate to explore him. I'd wanted to touch and kiss every inch of Caine for a long time, but since I walked in on him in nothing but that towel earlier in the week, I'd dreamt about having him at my mercy.

I pushed up, throwing all my weight behind the maneuver, and flipped him on his back.

He gazed up at me, eyebrows drawn together.

I straddled him, rubbing against his hard-on while I trailed my fingers lightly down his abs. His stomach tightened under my touch, and there was an answering throb between my legs. At least with sex we were *equally* in each other's power. It evened the playing field, and I had to admit I got off on that. "You had your turn last time. Now it's mine."

Caine's eyes glittered and he clasped my hips in his hands. "Have at it, sweetheart."

Sweetheart.

I liked that.

I kissed him, wet and deep, as I pumped my hips against his erection. He tried to take over the kiss, his fist tightening in my hair, but I broke away from his lips and started kissing my way down his throat.

I nuzzled against him, inhaling the smell of his cologne that I loved so much.

While my lips journeyed down his chest, his hands were stroking me—caressing my back, my breasts, my sides, my stomach, and coasting down to cup and stroke my ass.

I licked his nipple and felt his cock jerk against my stomach.

Hiding my triumphant smile, I licked and caressed him. As I felt his patience strain, my mouth continued on its downward path, tasting every inch of his sculpted stomach.

I pulled back to unbutton his pants.

Caine's every muscle was taut as I shuffled off the bed to yank his pants down. I stood, taking a moment to drink him in in his designer boxer briefs.

He looked like a brooding, sex-starved underwear model sprawled across my bed.

My nipples tightened.

"Fuck," Caine whispered, staring up at me with something akin to awe on his face.

He didn't have to say anything. His eyes said it all.

He had a way of making me feel like the sexiest woman alive.

Before I could make my next move, Caine hooked his fingers into his boxer briefs and pushed them down, his erection springing out.

I took over, pulling them off and discarding them on the floor. Panting now, I crawled back onto the bed, and over his body, coming to a stop at his cock.

Without a word I lowered my head and took him into my mouth.

His exultant groan echoed around the room.

I wrapped my hand around the base of his hard-on and fisted him while I sucked. I found my rhythm quickly, growing more and more turned on as Caine's pleasure intensified. His chest heaved, his thighs taut as his hips pumped upward, thrusting his dick in and out of my mouth and fist.

"Lexie," he gasped, and I squeezed my thighs together, desperate for my own relief. "Stop."

His fingers brushed my arm.

"Lexie."

But I couldn't. I wanted him to lose control completely. I needed him to.

Suddenly I was jerked up and over him so I was straddling him.

"You had your turn," he growled, dipping his fingers beneath my panties. His eyes flashed. "So wet."

I pressed down on his fingers as they slid easily inside my

slick heat. "I get off on making you lose that tight control of yours," I admitted, my words soft.

"Is that right?" He increased the strokes of his fingers inside me, pushing me toward climax.

I was so turned on I knew it wouldn't take him long to get me there.

"Works both ways . . . I'll make you lose control first."

I dislodged his fingers and pushed my panties down, leaning on my side so I could slip them down my legs. Once they were gone, I straddled him again and wrapped my hands around his cock, bringing it to my center. "I accept that challenge," I gasped as I eased him inside me. My head fell back, my eyes closing as I savored the feel of him filling me.

He grabbed my hips, his fingers biting into my skin, and my eyes flew open at his touch. Our gazes held as I began to ride him.

My entire focus was on him, on us, on our pleasure. There was nothing else but his eyes staring into mine, the feel of his heated skin under my hands, his hands gripping my hips, guiding me up and down him, the sounds of my pants, his groans, the smell of sex in the air . . .

The tension coiled tighter and tighter inside me and there was nothing on my mind but chasing ecstasy. My rhythm changed and I slammed down harder.

"Lexie," Caine gasped, his grip almost bruising now. "Fuck, Lexie."

"Yes, yes, yes, ye—"

The breath rushed out of me as I found myself unceremoniously flipped onto my back. Caine pinned my hands at the sides of my head and pulled out of me.

"What are you doing?" I moaned in frustration, pressing

my thighs against his hips in hopes of drawing him back to me.

He brushed his mouth over mine, flicking his tongue teasingly against my lips. He pressed sweet kisses along my jaw to my ear and whispered, "Just reminding you who's boss."

My frustration transformed to indignation and I tried to pull my hands loose. "Are you kidding me?"

His body shook against mine and when he raised his head I saw he was laughing.

I narrowed my eyes and unsuccessfully attempted to loosen his hold on my hands. "You really are a control freak."

"It's all part of my charm." He kissed me, this time trying to push inside, but I clamped my lips closed, furious with him. Apparently I didn't appreciate the burn of an unfulfilled climax. "Lexie," he murmured, his tone coaxing, "open your mouth."

I shook my head adamantly.

Caine smiled and pulled back. "You really are the most stubborn woman I've ever met." He moved his hips, bringing his erection back against my wet center. I sucked in a gasp of pleasure. "It makes me want to tame you with no hope of success."

That penetrated and I found myself smirking. "You like me stubborn, huh?"

He released one of my hands so he could cup me between my legs. I moaned as his thumb pressed down on my swollen clit. "I wouldn't have you any other way, Alexa Holland."

I gasped at his use of my surname, the blatant acknowledgment of who I was. The sound of my shock was swallowed in his deep, passionate kiss that told me he no longer cared who my family was. He wanted me.

Me.

I curled my fingers in his hair, kissing him back with everything I had, but as his thumb continued to circle my clit I could only focus on the pleasure building in my core. Caine took over the kiss while I sighed and panted and murmured his name into his mouth as my hips pushed up against his touch.

My fingers tightened in his hair. "Caine," I gasped, and my thighs trembled.

One more press.

His thumb slicked over me and took me right over the edge.

As my whole body was taken over by the powerful orgasm, Caine took my free hand and pinned it again. I cried out as he slammed inside me, my inner muscles clamping around him while he thrust deep.

"Lexie," he groaned, his eyes flashing with satisfaction.

I echoed that satisfaction, my body feeling fluid and languorous beneath his as he moved inside me. He pumped harder into me, his fingers lacing with mine and holding me down so I was completely at his mercy. To my amazement I began to feel pressure growing inside me again, a burn of pleasure-pain.

I moved my hips against his thrusts and set him ablaze.

He let go of my hands and got onto his knees, gripping my thighs, opening them wider. And then he pounded into me. I could feel his cock kissing my womb.

"Take me, Lexie," he growled, his words guttural, broken.

I could do nothing but that.

And it was incredible to watch as his pumping hips stuttered, the muscles in his neck corded, and his teeth gritted. His climax tore through him.

"Christ." His chest heaved and he let go of his bruising grip on my thighs to collapse over me. His body melted against mine as he tucked his face into the crook of my neck.

Our chests moved against each other's as we tried to catch our breath, and Caine's warm hand coasted down my left side and then curled around the back of my thigh. He gently pulled on it and I understood what he was asking for.

I wrapped my legs around his waist and my arms around his back and held him to me for a long while.

CHAPTER 14

Perhaps it was the light streaming in from the curtains that hadn't been closed all the way, or maybe it was just that somewhere in my subconscious I could feel the heat of his gaze on my face.

Whatever it was that woke me, I did so to discover Caine lying beside me on his side, his head resting on his hand and his eyes on me.

He'd been watching me sleep.

Memories of last night flooded me. After our first round we'd drifted to sleep for a little while, but I woke up in the dark of night to find him beside me and I'd instigated an energetic round two.

Sated, we'd fallen asleep right after it.

It was the best sleep ever, after the most wonderful sex ever, but now we were awake in the light of day. I didn't know what it meant that Caine had stayed in bed with me until morning. I didn't know what it meant that he'd watched me sleep.

My stomach flipped as I realized that I was about to find out for sure.

"Hey," I greeted him, my voice soft, uncertain.

Caine reached out with his other hand and stroked his thumb along my cheekbone. "Hey."

The fact that he wasn't bolting out the door suggested that this might turn out to be a good morning after all. But I wanted to know for sure. "You look pensive."

"I've been lying here thinking about the way I've treated you." He frowned. "I don't like guilt, Lexie. I try to avoid it."

His perturbed countenance made me snort. "You have your moments."

"I've made you work your ass off."

"True."

His eyes grew black. "I put you in a shit position with Phoebe."

"Also true."

"I was insulting because I didn't want to admit I was attracted to you."

Wow. Okay. I had not expected him to freely admit that. The fact that he could apologize caused the warm, mushy feeling in my chest to expand. "And now?" I held my breath, waiting in hope for a positive answer.

Caine's eyes dipped to follow his fingers as they whispered across my collarbone and down over the rise of my breasts. I shivered under his touch and he looked up at my face. "I held who your family is against you when I shouldn't have. You can't help where you come from. Just like I can't."

I stared up at him, relieved he'd finally realized the truth in that.

His lips curled at the corners in this sexy smirk. "You

know you're the only one who dares to yell at me. I'm not sure I like it."

I assessed him and the amused arousal in his expression. I grinned. "I don't think you hate it."

Instead of smiling at my retort, Caine grew suddenly serious. "You were right last night, you know. You deserve better. That's why . . . I have something I need to tell you."

My stomach dropped. "You do?"

"I don't want to hurt you, but you need to know the truth about your father and grandfather."

The look in his eyes told me I did not want to know whatever it was he had to tell me. "Caine . . . ," I whispered.

"Edward was the one who paid off my dad. Not Alistair. Your grandfather gave my dad the blood money to keep my mom's death and your dad's involvement in it quiet."

I felt like the bed had disappeared beneath me and I'd just smacked into the floor. Hard. I stared at Caine as I attempted to process what he'd just told me.

My grandfather, the one person I thought I could rely on, was a part of the ugly family history. He'd tried to cover up my father's sins? Why? It wasn't for my dad obviously, because he'd gone on to disinherit him. It was to protect the Holland name. To protect their place in society. I felt sick.

If Grandpa was capable of that. . . . then what kind of man was he really?

Memories of his soft words, his tenderness flooded me. The man I knew was so at odds with the man Caine was telling me he was. And if Grandpa was the one who'd paid Eric off, then that meant my father wasn't as terrible as I thought. He was still terrible . . . but he wasn't the only catalyst for Eric's suicide.

Oh my God.

"Are you sure? How do you know?"

Caine's eyes were hard. "Because I was there when he did it."

"Oh my God." My chest ached so badly.

"Lexie?"

I looked up into Caine's troubled gaze and realized something. Caine had just told me the last thing I wanted to hear . . . If it had been anyone else, if they had kept this from me and then blurted it out in a moment when I was vulnerable, I might have held it against them. But not Caine. In fact, my concern was not only for myself but for him too, and that was when I realized that what I felt for him was real. "You must hate them so much."

"Hate is giving them too much power."

In that moment his strength washed over me, and the hurt, the pain I was feeling at his revelation was diminished a little by the fact that he was here with me, and the look in his eyes was tender. "You're the one real thing in my life right now," I said upon the sudden realization. "You should know I don't want to let that go."

He brushed the tips of his fingers across my cheek and said, "I'm not the guy you're looking for, Lexie. I'm never going to be that guy."

That hope I was feeling unhooked itself from my chest and plummeted into my stomach, causing a flurry of nervous ripples in it. "What are you saying?"

Regret clouded his gaze. "You're looking for something special even if you won't admit it. And me? I can't compromise, I can't change, and I can't do forever. It's just not in me." He caressed my arm with his knuckles and there was the heated purr of a growl in the back of his throat as he continued. "But I don't want this to end just yet either. We like each other. We want each other."

I looked up at him, surprised. I'd thought we were about to discuss my departure from his life, not—

"And the sex is . . ." He grinned wickedly. "I don't know about you, but I'd really like to explore that some more."

My body tingled just at the thought of it, but I didn't know how to respond. I already knew I was emotionally invested in Caine. Sex wouldn't be enough for me. Would it?

"I'm selfish enough to ask for more time with you, Alexa. We could enjoy this together for however long it's good, and then we would walk away when it was time to end it—no harm, no foul."

Looking up into his handsome face, I wondered how on earth I was supposed to respond to such a suggestion. As Caine looked at me I caught the warmth in his gaze while he waited for my answer. He'd never looked at me that way before. There was something in that look. Something . . . more.

No.

It was a dangerous idea.

Yet . . . wasn't it worth a try?

The worst could happen, of course. I could fall for him and he could still want to walk away from me at the end of it all.

But Effie said Caine needed a woman who was bullheaded and persistent. I had no hope of changing how he felt about me, about us, if I wasn't there to do it. He said he was selfish, but I'd seen another side of him with Effie. Caine could be a sweet, good guy. He just didn't realize it.

I felt guilty before I even opened my mouth because I knew I was about to agree to have an affair when the truth was I was angling for more.

"Okay." I gave him a tremulous smile that strengthened under his answering grin.

And as he kissed me I tried to quiet my guilt. After all, my little white lie was told for the greater good. It would all work out in the end if Caine and I both found the happiness we were searching for.

Or so I hoped.

One minute we were kissing and then the next Caine was up and out of bed getting dressed.

I leaned up on my elbows, watching the muscles in his arms flex as he pulled on his pants. He looked over at me as he reached for his shirt. Obviously noting the confusion on my face, he explained, "We have a flight to catch. I need to shower."

Right. "So do I." I watched in disappointment as he buttoned up the shirt, hiding his gorgeous abs from me. "We could shower together, save us some time."

He threw me a look. "Somehow I think we won't save time doing that."

I smiled at the thought. "Yeah, probably not." Heaving a sigh, I swung my legs out of bed. "Fine. I'll meet you in the lobby in an hour."

Caine nodded, grabbed his jacket, and started toward the door.

I stared after him, more than a little nonplussed that he was leaving without giving me a kiss. Of course, I'd just agreed to a no-strings-attached affair with him, so I guessed I shouldn't hold out for silly little important things like affection.

Not that Caine struck me as the type. And I'd bet all my money he wasn't into PDA either.

Suddenly a thought crossed my mind. "Caine."

His hand was on the door when he glanced back at me. "Yes?"

"Maybe we should keep what's happening here between us a secret."

He frowned. "Why?"

"Because you're not exactly low profile and I don't want anyone in Boston to find out who I am, because then the rest of the Hollands will find out who I am. I don't want that."

"Don't you mean your grandfather doesn't want that?"

I flinched at the mention of Grandpa. I knew, after Caine's revelation about him, that I shouldn't care, but it wasn't so easy. I couldn't just flip off my emotions. Only fifteen minutes ago I'd loved and trusted Edward Holland. I was gutted, shocked by the truth about him, but I was also confused as to how I was supposed to feel about him now. I lowered my gaze and shrugged. "Same thing."

"Is it?"

I got off the bed and reached for the robe that was draped over the nearby chair. Caine watched me with great interest as I pulled it on to cover my nakedness. "Look," I said, "I don't know what to do about my grandfather now, but I do know I don't want anything to do with the rest of the family. If that means keeping who I am a secret, then fine. Can you just do this for me?"

He contemplated the request for a moment and then gave me a sharp nod. "Fine. We'll keep it a secret."

"Thank you." I smiled gratefully and I could have sworn Caine's eyes warmed in response.

"I'll probably end up telling Effie, however," he said with an air of weary inevitability. "That woman is like a blood-hound when it comes to sniffing out secrets."

I chuckled and nodded. "That's okay."

Caine gave me a small smile in return, just the tiniest of little lip quirks, and it warmed me.

And then he was gone.

My answering smile slipped from my lips and I stared after him, forlorn. I already wanted more from him and we were only five minutes into our casual fling.

Once we landed back in Boston, the driver took us to the office instead of home. Caine had a meeting with the board of directors and he couldn't miss it.

I discovered quite quickly that everything between us was the same as before except that it wasn't. Although our working relationship had the same efficient rhythm to it, things were definitely more pleasant between us. Caine was naturally quite abrupt in manner, but his grumpy impatience with me was gone.

Then there was the tension between us.

It had always been there.

But now it was actually intensified—the air between us thick with knowing and sparking with electric chemistry.

We did a good job of ignoring it in public. On the plane we ate lunch and discussed business, and when we got back into the office we each pretended we didn't know what sex sounds the other made. I caught up on my work while Caine met with the board of directors. Every now and then I'd find myself drifting off, thinking of my grandfather and his betrayal. I'd push those ugly thoughts aside, replacing them with memories of the night before and the absolutely sensual adventure my boss took me on.

I smirked.

My boss.

That was kind of naughty.

I grinned even harder.

I'd never done anything naughty before.

I laughed quietly to myself.

"What's funny?"

I glanced up, taken by surprise at the sudden appearance of Caine. He approached my desk, eyes alight with humor. I spun around to face him in my chair and grinned back. "I could tell you, but I won't."

Encroaching on my personal space, he stopped so his knees were almost touching my legs and I had to arch my neck to look up at his face. His eyes washed over mine before roaming lower. They lingered a little longer than appropriate on my legs before traveling upward. "I'm going to be here a little late tonight, but you should head home. I'll have my driver take you."

This was different too. Usually Caine delighted in cutting into my personal time. "Are you sure you don't need me?"

His eyelids lowered slightly in an unconscious smolder that sent off a rush of tingles between my legs. "Not just now. But I'll come by your place when I'm finished up here."

"My place?"

"Mmm." He put his hands on my armrests and leaned into me so our mouths were about an inch apart. His hot breath whispered across my lips. "I'll text you when I'm on my way."

My whole body tightened at the thought of what he'd do to me once he got to my apartment. I sounded a little breathless when I replied, "Shouldn't you wait to be invited first?"

His eyes narrowed. "Lexie, may I come to your apartment tonight so I can fuck your brains out?"

Lust whooshed in my lower belly.

I lifted my gaze from his mouth to his eyes and a smile tickled my lips. "I suppose that would be okay."

That was when he grinned at me—a full-on grin that made my heart flutter and turned me into a puddle of warm mush.

I was still staring at his office door in wonder minutes after he'd disappeared inside it.

Sun poured in through my windows, illuminating Caine as he sat at my breakfast bar, sipping coffee and reading the Saturday paper. I tried to keep my attention on the omelet I was making for us, but I found I was easily distracted by the fact that Caine was sitting, casual as you please, in my apartment waiting on breakfast.

The night before, I'd waited with those darn butterflies in my stomach for Caine to finish up his work and come to me. I killed time by calling Rachel and updating her on the situation. She thought it was exciting and announced she wanted absolutely every detail so she could live vicariously through me. Grandpa called not long after my conversation with Rach. I'd thought when I heard from him I would be able to confront him about the blood money he'd offered Caine's dad. But I found the words stuck low in my throat, painful and resistant. I told myself that when I finally saw him in person, we'd discuss it. It wasn't a conversation I could just start up over the phone. Yet the truth was . . . I was scared. I wanted Grandpa to have a reason that made sense for what he did, but I knew that he couldn't. I knew no reason would be good enough, and I wasn't quite ready to face the reality that he wasn't the man I thought he was. So when he asked me if I'd found a new job I told him Caine and I had worked it out and

I was going to remain in his employ. Somehow Grandpa read between the lines and he was not happy. But that didn't bother me like it would have yesterday. Who was he to be disappointed in me, after all?

After the phone call with my grandfather I pushed him to the back of my mind in favor of overanalyzing this thing with Caine. I went over and over whether I was doing the right thing. I swung back and forth, reaching for my cell to call Caine and tell him not to come to me. But I couldn't do it. I couldn't do it because I wasn't ready to give him up.

Just before midnight I let Caine into my building and opened the door to him. I was wearing a tiny silk camisole and matching shorts.

The tiredness in the back of his eyes faded when he took me in. He'd stepped into the apartment, kicked the door shut behind him, pressed me back against the wall, and slid his hands up to my waist. His lips brushed mine. "I was wrong. This is what you should wear to work."

My laughter had been swallowed up in his deep, hot kiss.

Sex this time had been slower, headier, as Caine took his time getting to know my body and allowing me to get to know his. We'd only drifted to sleep a few hours before dawn, but Caine was an early riser. In every way. And that meant I was awake early too, although I wasn't complaining. An orgasm was a nice way to say hello to the day.

And now here I was.

Making him breakfast in my kitchen like we did this all the time.

I put his omelet down in front of him and slid onto the stool opposite him to dig into mine.

"Thank you," he said before cutting into it.

"You're welcome."

We ate in silence and I realized that Caine seemed perfectly happy for us to remain in silence.

I frowned.

Suddenly the whole kitchen scenario didn't give me the warm fuzzies.

When Caine said he wanted this to be an affair, he literally meant sex. Just sex. And the occasional quiet breakfast, obviously.

Hmm.

I wanted to get to know him better, but how did I go about drawing him into conversations that actually meant something?

Well, first you need to get him talking. About anything.

"Why my apartment?" I blurted out.

When Caine looked up from the paper, confusion wrinkled his brow. "What?"

"Why did you come to me? I could have come to you. Is it because of Effie?"

"No." Caine shook his head and returned to his paper. "I just like your apartment."

Surprised, I was quiet a moment. I gazed around at my apartment, trying to work out what it was about it that Caine liked. It couldn't have been more different from his place. "Why?" I said.

He shrugged and kept eating. He frowned at something he read and turned the page.

Okay, that wasn't an answer, and it looked like I wasn't going to get one.

I decided not to push it and take the fact that he'd admitted he liked my apartment as a score for the day.

We sat in silence until we'd finished breakfast, and when he was done Caine thanked me again, leaned over the counter to kiss me, and then left. There was no arranging to spend the day together, no word of meeting up at night. Nothing.

I stared glumly at our empty plates.

But at least I'd gotten a kiss good-bye this time.

CHAPTER 15

Sex followed by the quiet breakfast foreshadowed what was to come. Saturday night Caine didn't come over to my place. He called the next day and said if I was around he'd come over that night.

And he did.

We had mind-blowing sex in my living room and then he left.

Monday through Thursday that was pretty much our lives. We worked together under the pretense of complete professionalism. I went home around six thirty and Caine came over around ten thirty. We fucked and then he went back to his apartment.

There was nothing romantic about it. Yeah, it was hot and that heat only seemed to be getting hotter, but Caine's walls were still high and impenetrable and I had no clue how to break them down.

I was failing miserably.

But then two things happened that gave me a spark of

hope. The first was that Caine had an art gala to attend that Friday evening that was being hosted by the wife of one of his board of directors. As soon as I arranged for one of his tuxes to be pressed, I was on tenterhooks, worrying about the person he would invite to go with him. I couldn't attend because we'd decided to keep our relationship private. However, we also hadn't discussed whether we were going to be exclusive during our affair. I was more than gratified, then, when Caine told me that he was going to the event solo. Still, I wished I'd had the courage to ask him about exclusivity so I could know for certain one way or another.

Come Friday the second thing happened to give me my answer . . .

The stationery room was about to pay witness to my printer-induced rage.

I'd spent the last twenty-five minutes fiddling around with the digital computer screen on the damn thing, trying to work out why on earth it wouldn't print.

"Argh!" I smacked the side of it. "What is wrong with you?"

"This is just a guess but I'm thinking it's the tall lady physically abusing it."

Recognizing the voice, I cut Henry a look out of the corners of my eyes. He was lounging against the doorframe, grinning at me. "I should warn you that I am this close to committing printercide, and if that doesn't calm me down I'm moving on to homicide. Closest person gets it."

Henry chuckled and ignored my warning by walking casually into the room. "Let me have a look."

I stepped back, doubtful. "I'm not sure there's any point."

"I'm offended," he said, not sounding the least bit as he

leaned in to look at the screen. "You think a Lexington doesn't need to know such provincial things as fixing a malfunctioning printer?"

"Well, yeah."

He chuckled and started flicking through the screen. He hit a button and suddenly the printer whirred to life.

My jaw almost hit the floor. "How did—but how . . . ?"

Henry reached for my letter as it printed out. He handed it to me with no small amount of smugness. "You look like you're going to cry."

I took the papers from him and nodded. "I feel like I might. I've been in here for twenty-five minutes. They were the longest twenty-five minutes of my life. And then you walk in, spend two seconds with the thing, and just fix it. Voila. Like it's nothing."

"Oh, poor baby." Henry laughed and put his arm around my shoulder, leading me out of the room toward my desk. "You should have called."

"How was I to know that Henry Lexington is fluent in Printer?"

"Ah, well, there are a lot of things about me you'd learn if you gave it the time."

I rolled my eyes at his flirting, more than used to it by now.

"Where have you been?" Caine stepped out of his office door, stopping us in our tracks. Displeasure registered on his face when he took in the sight of Henry with his arm around me. I gently extricated myself from his friend's grasp.

"The printer wouldn't work." I waved the letter at him.

"For thirty minutes?" he snapped.

I frowned at his tone. I thought we were past him talking to me like that. "Yes," I snapped back. "For thirty minutes. I don't do printers. Luckily Henry came along and fixed it."

Caine's eyes narrowed as they swung back to his friend, who stood watching us carefully. "Oh, did he?"

Henry raised an eyebrow at the predatory tone. "Do you have a problem with that?"

Instead of answering his question, Caine continued to glare at him. "I'll meet you in the lobby."

They stared at each other for a few seconds and then Henry said to me, "Always a pleasure, Lexie."

I smiled at him, refusing to be cowed by Caine's temper. "Henry," I murmured, and gave him a little wave as he left.

"My office," Caine bit out. "Now."

Scowling at his back, I followed him inside and shut the door. "What is your problem?"

He whipped around, his face like granite. "My problem? *My* problem?"

"Well, mine isn't that I have a hearing problem," I huffed. "No need to repeat yourself."

"Alexa," he warned.

"Don't you 'Alexa' me." My hands flew to my hips. "I was going about my job minding my own business when suddenly I found myself hurtled back into the past where my boss talks to me like I'm garbage under his shoe."

"And I stepped out of my office to find out why my PA wasn't answering my calls to discover it was because she was too busy flirting with my best friend, who had his hands all over her."

I froze at the realization that Caine was still jealous.

Exultation rushed through me and it took all of my self-control not to grin in triumph. Caine was still jealous of Henry and me? Even though there was nothing going on between us. That had to signify something, right? A person wasn't jealous and possessive over someone he didn't care about. Right?

"There's nothing between me and Henry," I assured him. "He flirts. It's meaningless."

Caine glowered. "You don't need to flirt back."

"I wasn't."

"You were. And I don't want you to do it again."

I took a tentative step toward him. "I would never do anything to encourage your best friend, Caine. You must know that."

Regret instantly flashed in his eyes. "I'm sorry. I know you wouldn't . . ." He shrugged. "It's just . . . I just . . . Not Henry, okay?"

Sensing how important it was for him to hear the words, I nodded. "I won't flirt with Henry. I promise."

Appearing altogether uncomfortable with the whole thing now, Caine gave me a sharp nod and reached for his phone, avoiding eye contact. "I'd better go meet him."

Catching Caine in a vulnerable moment was surprising, but it gave me that hope about our no-strings messed-up-affair. I also thought it was an opportunity to clear up something. "Caine?"

"Hmm?"

"I know this is just sex . . ."

He stiffened at the sudden turn in conversation and glanced over his shoulder at me. "Alexa—"

"But maybe we should discuss if this affair is exclusive or not."

"Exclusive." His voice was terse, like he was pissed I'd even had to ask. And then it seemed to occur to him that he'd answered the question emotionally. "I'll see you after lunch," he muttered, and strode past me.

I jumped at the sound of his office door slamming shut behind him.

How was I supposed to interpret that? On the one hand his seeming possessiveness could be construed as a step forward to him admitting that he had feelings for me. On the other hand, he'd raced out of here like I'd suggested we wear a vial of each other's blood around our necks.

Having an affair with Caine Carraway was not only deliciously physically exhausting, but not so deliciously emotionally exhausting too.

That night my uncertainty won.

Caine didn't come to me after the gala. In fact, I had no word from him at all that night or the next morning.

I did not have a good feeling about that.

"Go get him." Effie nodded at Caine's door.

I grimaced. "He's going to be pissed I just showed up like this."

And by "like this" I meant it was Saturday afternoon and I'd decided I was done playing this Caine's way. We weren't getting anywhere playing the game by his rules, so I'd decided to start acting like a grown woman. If I wanted to see Caine, there was nothing to stop me from going to see him. I didn't have to work around his schedule. No, sirree, I did not.

The whole acting like a grown woman thing deserted me when I got to the building and suddenly feared Caine outright rejecting me by refusing to allow me up to the penthouse.

So I'd called up to Effie instead and explained the situation.

As Caine had warned me, Effie knew we were having an affair. She was also smart enough to know I was angling for more and she also liked me enough to want me for Caine.

Effie was on my side.

It was a small comfort, but one nonetheless.

Effie sighed at my less than inspiring performance of "a woman on a mission to win her man." "You don't know that. Now knock on the goddamn door before I do it for you."

Realizing she would do just that, I pressed the buzzer. As soon as I did, Effie hurried back to her penthouse. She could certainly move for an old lady.

I was still staring after her in amusement when Caine's door opened.

My head jerked forward and my gaze raked over him. He was unshaven, unkempt, and wearing a black Def Leppard T-shirt and well-worn jeans.

Yum.

"Hey." I gave him a small wave.

In return he frowned at me but stepped aside to let me in. "What are you doing here?"

His tone was definitely less than welcoming.

I imagined a dozen metal sheets of armor flying across the room and clipping on around my body like Iron Man. I was going to need all the protection I could get to defend against the sting of Caine's possible rejection. And considering his tone, that rejection was becoming more and more of a possibility.

"I just thought I'd stop by." I shrugged. My gaze moved to his breakfast bar. It was covered in paperwork.

He'd been working.

"And you never thought to call first?" He stood in front of me with his legs braced and his arms folded over his chest.

Yes, there was absolutely nothing about him that said *welcome*.

I tried not to flinch. "It's okay for you to drop by my place unannounced, but it's not okay for me to do the same thing?"

"Not when you're here looking for something." His eyes narrowed. "What, you didn't hear from me, so you presume the worst? Did you think you'd come over here unannounced and catch me fucking someone else?"

My eyes grew round at the accusation. It seemed to come from nowhere. "Excuse me?" I huffed. "First of all, if that *had* been my intention I would have come around unannounced in the morning when I would have had a better chance of catching you fucking someone else. And second of all, don't put whatever jealous, stalkerish, creepy shit that other women have done to you on me. I came around for coffee or sex. Possibly both. Now I'm not in the mood for either." I threw him a disgusted look and made to stride past him.

Caine wrapped a hand around my upper arm, halting me.

I looked up at him warily.

"I don't mean to be a bastard, okay? I'm just busy today." He nodded in the direction of his work.

I pulled gently at my arm, but Caine wouldn't release me.

He tugged me closer, his eyes warmer. "I really want to fuck you and make you some coffee afterward, but unfortunately I have to get this work done today. There's tonight, though." Wickedness glinted in his eyes. "I could come to your place."

Although my body instantly liquefied at his suggestion, I found some small satisfaction in being able to turn him down. "I can't tonight. I made plans with an old work colleague." And I wasn't lying just to be peevish. Sofie had lost her internship from Benito and had called me looking for sympathy from someone who understood. I'd offered to take her out on the town to take her mind off it for a few hours. "We're going dancing."

Caine's grip tightened imperceptibly. "To a nightclub?"

I gently extricated myself, not sure why the fact that I was going dancing was a cause for concern. "Possibly several."

Caine stepped back from me. He was shutting down.

I sighed heavily. This visit had not gone at all to plan. "So we'll talk tomorrow?"

"Sure."

He was turning away, about to head back to his paperwork, quite ready to forget my existence already, when the impulse to pull him out from whatever wall he'd just slammed up took over me. I placed a hand on his arm and went up on tiptoes to press a soft kiss to the corner of his mouth. As I pulled back I smiled into his now-arrested face. "Bye, Caine."

Before I could move away I found myself tugged against him. I let out a little gasp of surprise seconds before his mouth fell on mine.

He wrapped his arms tight around me and kissed me with a passion that flooded molten heat into my blood. I held on for dear life, returning the deep kiss with my own.

It grew hotter and wetter as he crushed me as tight against him as he could. I could feel his hard-on digging into me. My skin flushed into a greater blaze.

When Caine eventually lifted his lips from mine and gently released me, I was too lost in a lust-filled fog to say anything.

The kiss had come out of nowhere.

"We'll talk later," Caine said, his words thick with arousal.

"Later," I croaked, smoothing my hair with trembling fingers.

Satisfaction gleamed in his eyes.

The waitress placed another mojito in front of me and gave me a knowing grin. "From the cute blond in the navy suit by the bar." She nodded in the bar's direction.

I glanced over and caught sight of a good-looking guy in said navy suit. As soon as my gaze hit him he smiled and raised his glass to me.

"Ooh, he *is* cute," Sofie said, nudging my elbow with hers.

I pushed the drink toward the waitress. "Sorry. Can you take this back?"

She smiled and removed the mojito from our table. "Gotcha."

"What are you doing?" Sofie narrowed her eyes on me as the waitress walked away. "You just turned that cute guy down. Why? I thought you hadn't gotten laid in, like, a year and a half."

I frowned at that calculation, counting back to when I'd last been in a relationship. To my shock I discovered Sofie was right. Before Caine the last guy I'd slept with had been my boyfriend Pete. We'd only dated for three months and the relationship naturally fizzled out because neither of us was that into it.

But yeah, that was eighteen months ago.

The last time I had sex, however, was of course a totally different story.

I sipped the mojito I'd paid for and avoided Sofie's eyes, pretending to innocently inspect the bar. We were at Brick & Mortar in Cambridge and as always it was packed.

"It *was* a year and a half ago, right?" Sofie sounded suspicious.

"Mmm-hmm."

She grabbed my arm, forcing me around to look at her. "Oh my God. Who are you sleeping with? You have to tell me! It will totally take my mind off the fact that I just lost my internship. Please, please, pretty please."

"All right, all right," I huffed. "I met someone at work, but I can't tell you his name because there's this whole employee fraternization thing, and plus, you know, we're not serious. It's just sex."

Sofie's eyes were round. "I've never done casual sex before. Is it hot?"

I wouldn't know. There was nothing casual about sex with Caine despite his silent protestations that what was between us was the epitome of casual. "Uh, sure."

"Wow. Getting engaged young is a good thing, but at the same time I feel like I'm missing out on loads." She lifted her hand and stared at her simple but pretty engagement ring.

I grabbed her hand and gave it a squeeze. "Trust me, you're not."

She smiled. "So you can't even give me a clue who it is?"

"Nope."

Her eyebrows drew together in concentration. "The only person I even know that works there is the man himself, Caine Carraway, but I know it's not him because he kind of hates you."

I flinched on the inside but somehow managed to give a small smile. "Yeah, boy, does he ever."

"So you're really going to turn down hot guys all night? Because you're having a casual fling with someone? I mean . . ." Sofie looked around. "I'm getting married but I'd still like to dance with someone. Dancing is okay as long as the guy doesn't get handsy."

I grinned. "Okay, you find us two nonhandsy guys to dance with and you're on."

I hugged Sofie good-bye in the taxi, but she wasn't done.

"I had so much fun!" she cried. "I missed you so much, Lex. We gotta do this like more. Like a lot more. 'Cause I love you, Lexie."

I smiled at her drunken affection. "Love you too, babe."

Relief moved through me when her fiancé, Joe, opened the driver's door. Although I was tipsy, Sofie was smashed. I'd forgotten what a lightweight she was. After we'd danced the night away in a few bars in Cambridge, changing dance partners when they got too "handsy," I'd tumbled Sofie into a taxi and had the driver drop her off first even though she lived in Southie. My worry had been that I'd have to carry her into her apartment, but Joe had obviously been keeping an eye out for us.

"Joe!" Sofie cried, her whole face lighting up at the tall, handsome redhead. "I love you, Joe."

"I love you too, Sofie. I'll love you even more if you keep it down." He reached for her, helping her out. He shot me a smile. "Thanks for bringing her home, Alexa. What do I owe you for the cab?"

I shook my head. "It's on me."

He smiled gratefully. "On us next time, okay?"

"Sure."

"Bye."

"Night."

"Bye, Lexie!" Sofie shouted, and I laughed as Joe tried unsuccessfully to shush her and half carry her into the house.

As the driver drove back toward my place, I contemplated directing him to Arlington Street. I was still wide-awake and Caine had suggested we get together tonight.

I chewed my lip, thinking it over.

Eventually I decided against it, wishing it could be easier between us, wishing we could trust each other enough not to feel so insecure around each other. For all I knew, Caine didn't even feel that way. I was probably projecting my neurosis onto him.

He'd been so busy that day that he'd more than likely passed out surrounded by paperwork. I decided he'd be even less amused than he had been earlier if I showed up unannounced again.

It was a shock, then, when I stepped out of the cab and found Caine sitting on my stoop.

I stared at him as the cabdriver pulled away, taken aback to see Caine sitting there in a sweater and jeans, his phone dangling between his hands. He looked like an ordinary guy. A very hot, ordinary guy, obviously, but gone was the impressive, intimidating businessman. Right then Caine was just a guy waiting on his girl.

Except . . . I wasn't really his.

"Did you have fun?" he asked quietly in the hush of the very early morning.

"I danced a bit," I replied, my voice as soft.

He nodded and looked away, staring off into the distance. "Alone?"

I stared at his handsome profile, trying to work out what was going on here. "No," I admitted.

After a few seconds he looked at me. "May I come up to your apartment?"

In answer I strode toward him, my heels clicking loudly on the sidewalk. Caine stood up as I approached and he held out his hand to help me up the stoop.

I curled my fingers around his, shivering at the slide of skin against skin.

We were silent as I let us into the building, and we were silent as we climbed the stairs to the first floor. We were silent as we walked into my apartment and I locked the door behind us, and we were silent as I threw my purse on the sofa and kicked off my shoes.

No words passed between us at all as Caine reached for me.

The only noise that filled my apartment was the rustling of clothes, the panting of breaths against lips, and our groans as Caine took me hard on the floor of my living room. We were so frantic to have each other that we couldn't even make it to the sofa, never mind the bedroom.

I was nearing climax when he pinned my hands above my head and stopped thrusting into me.

"Caine?" I gasped, the first word spoken between us since the stoop.

Fierceness tightened his features along with his impending orgasm. Something primal glittered in his gaze, something thrilling but terrifying that I'd never seen there before. "Say you're mine. Right here, right now, you're mine," he growled.

I pushed my hips against his, desperate for him to move again. I was so close. So, so, so close. I whimpered, "Caine."

"Say it." He almost slid all the way out of me. "Say you're mine."

"I'm yours, I'm yours," I agreed, barely cognizant of what I was agreeing to. "Please."

He crushed his mouth over mine and started to pump harder into me.

It wasn't until long after, after we came in unison, after he picked me up and carried me to bed, and after I woke up in the early hours of the morning to discover he'd left, that I realized what Caine had asked of me.

And if he hadn't snuck out on me and ignored my call a few hours later, I would have said his caveman request was a turning point.

Maybe it still was.

Or maybe it had him running scared instead.

CHAPTER 16

I didn't hear from Caine on Sunday at all.

Whether it was the mixed signals—the back–and–forth "I want you, I don't want you" shit—or the fact that I'd gotten my period, the truth was I was feeling highly emotional about the state of our "relationship." I even avoided calls from Rachel and I definitely avoided my grandfather's calls. I knew if I picked up the phone to him that I'd just spew my accusations at him, and I was still wary of the fallout of that confrontation. Until I sorted my feelings out about his part in Caine's father's death, I couldn't talk to him. Instead I did what I'd been good at doing since I discovered the truth—I pushed it to the back of my mind. Instead I thought about Caine and wondered if it was silly and possibly dangerous to my heart to keep seeing him when so far he was showing no signs of wanting to deepen the connection between us.

By the time I walked into work on Monday, my feelings were hurt. Again. I was unsure whether I should let things continue between us. I'd never thought I was a particularly sensitive person, but I guessed Caine had a way of getting under my skin.

I didn't know what to expect from him when I got into the office, and what I got was Caine being his usual self. He wasn't cold or impatient, but he wasn't overly warm either. He was professional and cordial.

Such blah little words.

I, on the other hand . . . Well, I was distant.

It wasn't like I'd had any intention of going into work and deliberately throwing a very obvious wall up between us. It just naturally happened. I walked into his office, took in his handsome face, and felt this horrible, jagged melancholy overwhelm me.

The only way not to feel like that was to have as little interaction with him as possible until I had the feeling under control.

"Here are the photocopies you needed," I said after knocking on Caine's door.

He waved me in. "Thanks."

I placed them on his desk, feeling his eyes on my face. "Do you need anything else?"

"May I have another coffee?" he said, his question quiet.

"Of course." I began to walk away, but he stopped me, calling out my name. "Yes?" I whipped around to face him.

Caine stared at me, his mood seeming contemplative. "Did you have a good Sunday?"

I was surprised by the question. And honestly I didn't like it. It was a question that reminded me I'd woken up alone, thus ensuring that the rest of my Sunday would be utter crap. There was nothing quite like a guy sneaking out on you after sex to diminish your confidence. "It was fine."

"Did you do anything nice?"

I wept like a dumb-ass little girl when I woke up alone, and then I spent the rest of the day curled up on the sofa feeling bloated, fat, and tired, as is normal on the first day of my period. I also ate a ton of chocolate. But that part was nice. "I did." I moved to walk out and he called my name *again.*

I looked back at him, exuding calm and patience. "Yes?"

"So, what did you do?"

"I hung out. Let me get that coffee for you."

Upon my returning with his coffee, Caine halted me again by wrapping his hand around my wrist as I placed his coffee on his desk. He seemed troubled.

"Is everything okay, Lexie?" His fingers tightened their grip.

"Everything is fine." I shrugged and gently pried my hand from his hold.

"You would tell me otherwise?"

"Of course." At that bald-faced lie I walked out, but I could feel Caine watching me the whole time.

By the time I got back to my desk, I exhaled, letting go of all the air I'd been holding in in his presence.

It was pretty easy to avoid Caine after that, because he was busy with a couple of conference calls. I was buried with work, which took my mind off how I was feeling. Part of me felt more in control being distant with Caine, but there was another part of me that wished my period would fuck off so I could return to my more rational, easygoing self. I had to keep reminding myself that as far as Caine was concerned this was just sex, and I'd agreed with him. Just sex meant emotional distance and I needed to get used to that.

For at least an hour I wasn't really thinking about the state of things between me and Caine, but that all changed when Security called up to announce a Darcy Hale had arrived hoping to catch a moment with my boss. I had never heard of her, but when I checked in with Caine he recognized the name and told me to let her up.

When the tall, elegant blonde sashayed down the corridor toward me, it took everything within me not to narrow my eyes in suspicion. Everything about her was sophisticated, from her wide-tailored dove gray trousers and cream silk camisole, to the stylish black Gucci sunglasses sitting perched on top of her head. Her blond hair was pulled back sleekly in a high-fashion ponytail that accentuated her sharp bone structure.

She looked like a model.

I had every suspicion she *was* a model.

She gave me a cool smile as she approached my desk. "Darcy Hale for Caine Carraway."

"Of course." I gave her a strained smile and felt my gut tighten unpleasantly. "One moment." After I called through to Caine I relayed to her that he would be just a few moments.

"That's fine." She shrugged elegantly. "I was just passing by and thought I'd pop in, so I would have understood if he couldn't see me." She gave me a sly smile. "Looks like I made an impression, however."

I wanted to yank on her ponytail like a five-year-old. "And you met Mr. Carraway . . . ?"

"On Friday at an art gala. My father is president of an investment company that sits proudly under the Carraway Holdings banner." She smiled and this time it was surprisingly wolfish. "We had quite the meeting of minds."

And what the hell did that mean?

Caine came out of his office to welcome Darcy inside

with a gentlemanly suaveness I did not like. I looked away, catching sight of him gazing in my direction a few moments before he closed the door behind him and Darcy.

I fumed at my computer screen.

Hadn't he said before he left for that damn gala that we were exclusive?

What the hell was going on? And what exactly did he get up to with that feline woman who was barely even a woman? She looked about eighteen!

To my relief Darcy left the building only ten minutes later. I was not relieved, however, by the fact that she looked far too pleased with herself for my liking when she did so. She'd only turned the corner at the top of the corridor, disappearing from my sight, when Caine called me into his office.

Somehow I managed to remain perfectly serene. "Yes?" I asked, stopping in the doorway.

Caine's face instantly clouded over. "For God's sake come into the office."

I wanted to snap something back at him but decided he didn't deserve any kind of passion from me if he was messing around with Blondie behind my back. I took a few steps into his office.

"Shut the door and come here."

I did as he said, but for some reason this made him even madder.

"What's wrong with you?" he snapped.

I frowned. "Nothing is wrong with me."

"Bullshit." He stood up abruptly, rounding his desk. I braced as he came toward me. "You've been cold with me all morning."

"I'm tired, that's all."

He leaned into me and hissed, "More bullshit."

"Stop saying *bullshit*," I growled.

Light flared in his eyes. "There she is."

"What? You're trying to goad me into reacting to you now? Are you bored?"

"I'm pissed." He curled his arm around my waist and hauled me up against him, ignoring my attempts to pull away. "You're acting strange and I want to know why."

I ceased my struggling and looked him directly in the eyes. "I'm fine."

His lips pressed together as he gazed at me for a few seconds. His gaze was searching, as though he could find whatever answers he needed if he just looked hard enough. "I would say it was about Darcy Hale, but you were acting distant before she even got here."

"She did say you two had, and I quote, a meeting of minds on Friday." I cocked my head to the side. "That must have been some meeting for her to drag her skinny ass all the way up here to see you."

Caine stopped scowling to smirk in a really arrogant way that annoyed me enough to restart my attempts to get out of his arms. He easily fought my struggles and won. "I gave her my time because of who her father is. I can't outright insult her. But trust me, her skinny ass does nothing for me. Neither does her narcissism. Anyway"—his hands slid down my back to *my* less than skinny ass—"I'm far too distracted getting my fill of you."

Are you sure about that? That wasn't quite so clear on Sunday morning.

My doubt must have registered on my face, because Caine pressed a kiss to my jaw before brushing his mouth across my ear. "In fact, I'm in the mood for a little appetizer." He pressed lazy, sweet kisses down my throat and then up again until he reached my other ear. "I want you naked right now and I want my mouth on you." He leaned back to read my face. His eyes were ablaze with hunger. "Do you want my mouth on you?"

I so, so wanted his mouth on me.

"We can't. I got my period yesterday."

To my surprise Caine let his disappointment show. He squeezed my waist. "That's a shame. But I guess we'll have something to look forward to in . . . ?"

"The end of the week." I tried to extricate myself from his embrace, but Caine wasn't having it.

He stopped me, giving me a gentle shake. "Are you going to tell me what's going on with you? I don't like this." His voice had lowered dangerously.

What? Was I supposed to be afraid? "Seriously? Mr. Distant doesn't like distance?"

His arms instantly dropped and he stepped back. "Are you playing games with me?"

"No." I sighed and threw my hands up in the air. "I don't know what I'm doing. I came in this morning, took one look at you, and decided it would do me a world of good to put a little bit of distance between us because . . ."

He frowned, edging closer again. "Because?"

"Because . . ." *Just say it. Be honest. Or at least somewhat honest.* "I don't know where I am with you. You can't have it both ways, Caine. You can't be distant with me, sneak out because sex got a little intense, ignore me, and then get pissed at me when I react in turn."

He looked away. "This is just sex, Lexie," he said through clenched teeth.

"I know that." Boy, did I know that. "But that doesn't mean we can't react the way we want to, be who we are . . . I feel like you're constantly pushing and pulling because you're uncomfortable with how things go down between us some-times." I stepped toward him tentatively. "I just want you to be you. No pressure. And I'll be me. I feel like you're trying so hard to prove that this is just sex that it's making this even more complicated. I want to uncomplicate it."

"How?"

I gave a huff of resigned laughter. "For whatever reason I like you, Caine. I'd quite like it when we're not having sex if we could be friends. No expectations, I promise." *Just hope.*

He raised his eyebrows, looking adorably confused. "Friends?"

"Mmm." I smirked. "You know . . . friends."

"With benefits?"

"Exactly."

After a few seconds of silence, Caine finally gave me a hesitant nod. "Friends."

I smiled. "I should warn you, though, that I'm a smart-ass to my friends."

"Oh, well, then I guess we've been friends since you first walked through my door." As he rounded his desk to his chair, he threw me a grin that sent my heart racing off in a gallop.

My whole being lit up at Caine's sudden transformation. Before, he'd been on edge because of my mood, but now he was relaxed in a way I rarely saw from him.

Yes. No expectations . . . but God, I had a lot of hope.

CHAPTER 17

"What's your favorite color?"

I heard the whisper of Caine's movement against my pillow as he turned his head to look at me. "My what?" he said, bemused.

After a few days of no sex and some major anticipation, I'd given Caine the all-clear for resumption of the fun stuff that Thursday morning. He'd appeared at my apartment a few hours after work and we'd gone at each other as though we hadn't had each other in years.

Relaxed, I lay beside him on my bed, my arms flung above my head in postcoital satisfaction, and decided it was time to ease him into the whole getting-to-know-each-other thing. "What's your favorite color?" I repeated.

"What's *your* favorite color?"

I looked at him and saw his mouth was curled up at the corners in amusement. I liked this side of him, this playful, boyish side that peeked out at me sometimes. "Purple. Now yours?"

"I don't have a favorite color."

I frowned. "Everyone has a favorite color."

"I don't."

"You must at least have a color that you're partial to more than other colors."

He grunted. "Wouldn't that be the same thing as having a favorite color?"

I stopped and resaid it in my head. I giggled at the realization he was right.

Caine gave a huff of laughter, but I wasn't quite ready to let him off the hook. I rolled to my side to face him, resting my head in my hand. "Okay, let your mind go blank."

His gaze moved over my naked chest. "Can't do that, I'm afraid."

I rolled my eyes. "Try."

"Okay." He gave a long-suffering sigh. "Now what?"

"What is the first color that comes to mind?"

"Yellow," Caine blurted out, and then immediately scowled for some unknown reason.

"Yellow?" I grinned. "That's definitely a surprising color, but we'll go with it. Your favorite color is yellow. What's your favorite movie? And don't say you don't have one, because I've seen your DVD collection."

Caine raised an eyebrow. "Has someone been snooping?"

"No."

If anything his eyebrows rose to greater heights.

"Fine," I huffed. "I snooped in your DVD cabinet."

To my surprise and gratitude he didn't say anything else about that. Instead he said, "*Seven Samurai.*"

I attempted to mask my shock that he'd offered the answer so easily. "What's it about?"

I watched, fascinated, as Caine moved onto his side so we

were facing each other. There was interest and light in his eyes. "It's this Japanese movie made in the fifties and it's about these seven down-on-their luck samurai who are hired by this poor farming village to defend them against marauders. The battles scenes are some of the best in cinematic history—for its time it just . . . It's fantastic. It's real, though—it's got grit and heart. It's a great movie."

I brushed my fingers along his forearm. "Do you have it?"

"I do."

"Maybe we can watch it sometime."

Caine's gaze roamed over my face. "I think you'll like it."

I took that as a yes to us watching the movie together and hid a smile. "Favorite band?"

"You didn't tell me what your favorite movie was."

"That's easy. *Gone With the Wind*. Although I could slap Scarlett silly for most of the movie. I mean, who would ever choose Ashley over Rhett?"

Sensing I wanted an actual answer, Caine shrugged. "I'm not sure."

"No one, that's who. Ashley is this Byronic limp noodle and Rhett is dark and challenging and all man. There's no competition. Scarlett was a nincompoop."

Caine's lips twitched. "A nincompoop?"

"Yes! It would be like me choosing to have Dean in this bed instead of you."

His amusement fled. "Who's Dean?"

I choked on a laugh. "Dean. Your main receptionist. You know, the guy that sits at that big glass desk and directs people where to go."

"Oh, that Dean." Caine appeared adorably confused. "I thought he was gay."

"My point exactly."

"Ashley wasn't gay," Caine argued. "He was a gentleman."

"Whatever he was, he was boring and spineless." I flopped over onto my back. "Women are attracted to men who can take charge of a situation."

"Not all women."

I glanced up at him. "Speaking from experience there, are you?"

He sighed. "I've been known to intimidate some women."

"You? Intimidating?" I teased. "No."

Caine laughed and reached for me, sliding one arm across my belly so he could pull me into him. "And some women need to learn to be more intimidated by me."

I giggled, wrapping my arms around him as he rolled so he was braced over me. "It's not going to happen."

He nodded, contemplating me. "I'm getting that."

"I think you like it."

Instead of answering in the affirmative, Caine brushed his thumbs across my cheekbones. "Favorite band?"

I smiled, glad he was so cool with sharing, even if it was just trivial stuff. "The Killers."

"Nice choice."

I warmed under his approval. "You?"

"Led Zeppelin."

I trailed my fingertips over his muscular back in a lazy, familiar way that felt altogether much too good. "Favorite city outside of Boston?"

"Sydney. You?"

"Prague."

Caine stilled under my touch. "A very nice choice."

"I really want to visit Budapest, though. All the places I visited were with Benito, and none of them were the one place I wanted to see."

"I've been to Budapest." He bent his head to sweetly brush his lips against mine. "You'd love it."

I *loved* this. I loved that he was no longer fighting to keep who he was from me. Right now we were two friends getting to know each other. While we were naked.

"Why do you like my apartment?" I suddenly blurted out.

Caine studied me a moment, seeming to drink in every aspect of my face. "Because it's got charm. There's no flash— it's got a timeless, simple beauty about it. A lot like its owner."

His compliment seeped into me, warming through to the very tips of my fingers. "I think that's the nicest thing anyone has ever said to me," I whispered.

Caine smiled. "You think that's the nicest thing anyone's ever said to you?"

"Yeah."

"See. No flash. Just beauty."

I narrowed my eyes in thought. "You secretly like my tank tops and short shorts, don't you?"

He grinned in answer before swallowing my laughter in a deep, drugging kiss.

My greatest issue with our relationship was coming to terms with the fact that even if Caine allowed me those small moments of intimacy, he had no intention of changing his mind about what we were doing together. I'd developed a bad habit of building my hopes up only for Caine to remind me that this was still a friends-with-benefits situation.

Only a day after we'd spent the morning laughing and talking and playing, I was brought back down to earth with a bump. I'd felt close to him in those moments, but the next day everything was back to the way it had been before. I didn't blame Caine. He didn't know I kept changing the rules in my head. I was frustrated, however, by my lack of progress and I needed to regroup, to find another way to get through to him, and so far I'd come up with nothing.

We made no plans to meet that weekend and I considered dropping in on Effie for her unique perspective until a phone call with Rachel that Friday afternoon.

Caine was out to lunch and I was at my desk, nibbling at a salad. I hadn't exactly had the best appetite these last few days.

"Lexie, come on," Rachel huffed in her annoyance. I'd just told her about my failed attempt at getting closer to Caine. "Maybe it's time to call it quits on this guy before you get hurt."

I ignored that. "I've been trying to come up with a new tactic, but I realized something this morning. No more tactics. Maybe honesty would work best."

"No way." I could sense her rolling her eyes. "Unless you want things to definitely end between you . . . and I'm not exactly averse to that anymore."

"You need to make up your mind. Do you find me screwing my boss sexy or stupid? Choose one." She kept flitting between the two, which was not good when it came to needing advice.

"Right now it's stupid. I think it's ti— Maisy, Ted is not a toy!" She cursed, and I heard the phone drop. A minute later she was back with a breathless "Sorry about that."

"Who is Ted and do I want to know what the devil child was doing to him?"

"You know I'm going to start taking your comments about my kid seriously one of these days."

"I wish you would."

Rachel snorted. "Ted is our puppy."

My eyes widened in horror. "You gave the kid a puppy?"

"He loves her. It's so adorable."

I was one hundred percent sure that poor puppy did *not* love Maisy. I was certain that poor puppy was terrified of Maisy. "What was she doing to him? And be careful what you say, because I am not afraid to call Animal Protection on your ass."

"Oh, stop it. She was just cuddling him a little too hard. I was there. I'm keeping an eye on her. Don't you trust me?"

Um . . . "I've seen what you've let that kid do to your husband."

"But that's just Jeff. I would never let Maisy hurt an animal. *Not* that she would mean to . . . She's just overly exuberant. I've got my eye on Ted, though. Don't you worr—hey, you changed the subject," Rachel snapped. "Ditch the loser boss."

My silence made her sigh heavily.

"Rach—"

"Okay, whatever, but at least promise me you'll keep Saturday night free, because I have an extra ticket to the Red Sox game and these tickets are fucking awesome. Jeff got them from work. Get this, field box forty-three, row four, behind home freaking plate."

I chewed my bottom lip in thought. Those *were* great seats, but there was every chance Caine would be at that game. He couldn't make it to every one, but he did try and with Saturday's game set against the Yankees, there was a more than huge chance he would be there.

"I didn't hear the 'hell yeah' I was expecting. Come on," Rachel pleaded. "We haven't hung out in ages and yeah, Jeff will be there, but we've got a babysitter, so Maisy won't be."

That did sweeten the idea a little more.

And even if Caine was there he would be up on EMC level and no way would he spot me in a crowd of thousands. Wait.

If he did, so what? I was allowed to go to a game. He didn't have a say in what I did in my free time. "Do not go down that path," I warned myself.

"What path? What path am I going down?"

"Not you, Rach. And yes, I will go to the game."

"Yay! Okay, Jeff and I will meet you at the entrance at six thirty. Do not eat before the game. I intend to buy copious amounts of junk food and beer and you will join me so I don't feel so bad about it."

I grinned, suddenly feeling a whole lot better now that I had concrete plans for the weekend that didn't involve Caine. "Hot dogs are on me."

There was a mixture of guilt and mischievousness in Rachel's eyes as I walked toward her and Jeff. They stood outside the busy entrance to Fenway Park and they were not alone.

Crushing my irritation with them, I managed a smile of hello as I approached.

Rachel's eyes bugged out and I caught her silent *Please don't kill me* message.

But I wanted to. I really, really wanted to.

They'd brought another guy with them.

A date.

For me.

I hadn't bothered to tell Caine what my plans were for the weekend because he hadn't asked. After I'd gotten off the phone with Rachel, Caine returned from lunch and perched his ass on the corner of my desk.

"How's it going?" he said, seeming genuinely interested

"Fine." I tilted my head to the side and smiled. "You?"

His eyes warmed for the first time in days. "I'm fine." He looked away. "I've been really busy and I know we haven't . . ."

I put my hand on his thigh. "Don't worry about it. I knew going into this that you're a busy guy."

"Right." His fingertips brushed over the hand that rested intimately on him. "I don't know when I'll be free. Perhaps Sunday?"

I shrugged, like it didn't hurt me that I was that far down on his list of priorities. "Call me when you're free and we'll see if I am and then we'll go from there."

Caine smirked. "You're being very amenable."

I squeezed his thigh. "I'm just giving you what you want."

He frowned at that, suggesting he didn't like my response, but eventually he nodded. He shot a look over his shoulder to make sure the coast was clear and then he leaned in to press a soft kiss to my lips. His soft kiss suddenly turned hard and he gripped the nape of my neck as his tongue slipped into my mouth. The kiss ignited into something hungry and arousing, and it took me a moment to remember where we were. I pulled back, panting.

Running a hand through his hair, looking consternated by the kiss, Caine stood up, gave me a disconcerted half smile, and disappeared into his office.

I stared at his closed door, wondering when I had become such a good actress.

The reality was I shouldn't feel bad that I'd allowed myself to be duped into a blind date, but as I shook the hand of Jeff's work colleague, Charlie, I felt like I was doing something wrong by allowing this to play out. Caine and I had agreed to be exclusive.

Charlie was tall and he was attractive in a guy-next-door kind of way that was really appealing. He had a great smile and if I hadn't been currently trying to win over Caine Carraway's heart, I would have been happy to be set up with Charlie.

The guys went through Security first and Rachel clung to my arm as we followed after them. "Please don't be mad at me," she whispered. "Charlie saw your picture in the wedding photo on Jeff's desk and asked about you. Jeff doesn't know anything about Crazy Boss Guy, and when he suggested it I thought it might be good for you."

I kept smiling because Charlie was throwing me looks over his shoulder every now and then, but I was pissed. "You don't get to make those decisions. Caine is probably at this game."

"So what?" she snapped.

I looked away, drinking in the sight of all the vendors underneath the bleachers, and inhaling the smell of fast food, popcorn, and beer. People sat in benches outside the vendors eating and laughing. There wasn't anything quite like the atmosphere at Fenway, and I realized that one of the reasons I loved coming here was that it gave me that feeling family was supposed to give me—that warmth, that unity. It was a sweet place to be on game night.

"You're mad."

"Yes," I admitted. "Caine and I may be—"

"Nothing. You and Caine are nothing."

"Not true." I scowled. "We're exclusive."

She sighed. "Look, even if he's here, so are at least twenty thousand other people. I'm pretty sure there's a snowball's chance in hell he'll see you, considering he's probably up on EMC level."

My expression confirmed her suspicion.

"Good. Now that that's out of the way, come and let Charlie buy you a beer and a hot dog."

Under silent protest I went with her.

Charlie smiled his cute smile and waved to the nearest hot dog vendor. "Can I buy you dinner?"

Guilt slammed through me. This was so a date. I couldn't even pretend it wasn't. *Bad, Lexie, bad, bad, Lexie.* I glanced over my shoulder, certain that at any moment Caine would appear and make me feel even worse. "You know what?" I gave Charlie a friendly smile (there would be no flirting or encouraging of the flirting!) "Why don't we just take our seats? The vendor guys run up and down the field box every few minutes. We'll just grab them then."

"Sounds like a plan."

We started walking back the way we came, turning right under the bleachers toward our field box. Rachel and Jeff settled back, giving Charlie space with me. I could have punched them both.

"So . . . Rachel says you're a personal assistant?" He stuffed his hands in his pockets and threw me a coaxing smile.

There was something about his manner that suggested he was nervous.

Great.

I felt even worse.

"Uh, yeah." I was not getting into that. "What do you do?" Jeff worked in advertising, but I knew from listening to him that there were a lot of different job positions in the agency.

"I'm with the art department."

"Oh, that's great. I always wished I'd spent more time on art at school. I enjoyed drawing, but that's as far as my skills go."

"You're creative?"

I thought about it. "I don't think I'm creative per se. Organized. Very organized. And I think I have a good eye. You know, I always wanted to be an events planner and combine the two."

He shrugged. "So why don't you?"

"Don't I what?"

"Be an events planner."

I laughed. "Like it's that simple."

"All you have to do is get that one great client to give you a shot, and a glowing reference could kick-start your company."

I stared at him incredulously. "I don't think it's that easy."

Charlie smiled. "I don't think you know if it's that easy. You've never tried to give it a shot."

"Because I'm a personal assistant. I organize things for one person."

"Caine Carraway." He nodded and just hearing the name sent another shard of guilt stabbing into my gut. "If you can organize the life of someone as prominent as Carraway, you can organize a party or two."

"We just met and you're already giving me career advice. How did that happen?"

"Sorry." He shot me a sheepish look and flicked his silky brown hair out of his blue eyes. *So cute.* It was a definite shame we hadn't met months ago. "I have a tendency to do that. I should have been a guidance counselor."

"It's okay," I reassured him. "I'm used to getting advice about my career." Or at least I'd grown used to hearing all about it from Grandpa and Rachel since I started working with Caine.

Charlie's gaze questioned my enigmatic comment, but before he could say anything Rachel bounced in between us like an excited teenager. "This way!"

I chuckled and threw Jeff a look.

He shrugged. "She gets like this when we have a babysitter." He grinned and strode after her up the concrete slope into the light of the bleacher stands.

"After you." Charlie gestured.

I blinked against the late-afternoon sun, and then spotted

Rach and Jeff heading left toward the field box. I didn't wait for Charlie to catch up before taking off after them. I wanted to be clear in the most diplomatic and least cruel way possible that this date was a nonstarter.

When I took my seat beside Jeff, I ignored the sight of a bunch of people getting their picture taken at home plate with the Red Sox mascot, Wally the Green Monster, and waited for Charlie to take his seat beside me. He got settled in, smiled at me, and let his eyes drift down over my legs. I was wearing a Red Sox girly-fit T-shirt and jean shorts.

Practically my entire body was blushing by the time he was done checking me out.

And that was when I decided the least cruel way was the most honest way.

I leaned into him and Charlie smiled and ducked his head toward me so he could hear me over the crowds and the guy talking into the mic about a charity foundation. "I didn't know about tonight."

He frowned. "About me?"

"Yeah. Rach didn't tell me." I could feel Jeff stiffen beside me as he overheard.

Charlie grimaced. "Is it a problem?"

I gave him an apologetic look. "I'm kind of seeing some-one . . . I mean it's . . . I don't know what it is but—"

He held up a hand and gave me a disappointed smile. "I get it. Really, it's no problem."

"I'm sorry."

"You have nothing to be sorry about," he assured me. I smiled gratefully at him. Such a seemingly sweet guy. What the hell was I doing? "You've still got to let me buy you some-thing to eat, though. No strings?"

"You know what . . . ? I think we should make Rachel do that."

"I concur," Jeff agreed beside me, and I looked at him to see he was not happy. Apparently Rachel hadn't told Jeff I didn't know about the setup either.

"I couldn't," Charlie insisted. "My mother would kill me if I let a woman buy her own dinner."

I chuckled. "Isn't that a little outdated?"

"Probably." He grinned. "But she's terrifying, so I do what she says."

I nudged him with my arm. "Okay, then, I'll have a hot dog, please."

"*Hot dogs! Hot dogs! Get your hot dogs!*" a burly guy in a yellow vendor's shirt bellowed from behind us, skipping down the steps with his hot case of dogs held above his head.

We burst out laughing. "Nice timing," Charlie said, and lifted a hand to catch the guy's attention as he turned at the bottom of the box.

Two hot dogs and a cold beer later, we were thirty minutes into the game and the Red Sox were killing it. The electric atmosphere of the crowded park fed into me and like always made me forget even the slow moments in the game.

"I have to get one of those shirts!" Rachel reached across Jeff to slap my knee. "The replica baseball shirts."

"Why don't you try the team store?"

"I want a girly one, though. My breasts will get lost in the guy's one."

I couldn't remember seeing a feminine style of the shirt in the store. "Online?" I suggested.

Instead of answering, Rachel looked over my shoulder

and her eyebrows rose. I glanced back to see what had distracted her.

A tall, well-built older man in a Red Park Security shirt was staring down at me with this deeply disturbing blank mien. "Alexa Holland?"

I ignored Charlie's curious gaze on my face and wondered what the heck I'd done wrong. "Um . . . yes," I was almost afraid to admit.

"Mr. Carraway requests your presence in his suite on the EMC level."

Holy . . .

I blanched.

How the hell had he spotted me in this crowd?

As if he could read my mind, the security guy pointed up behind me. I looked up over my shoulder. Caine's suite was right above me.

Of course it was.

I sighed.

"You don't have to go, Lex," Rachel shouted over the noise.

I threw her a look. "Yes, I do." If he'd seen me with Charlie I could only imagine what he was thinking. After telling them I'd catch up with them later, I followed the security guy out of the field box. I stewed over what kind of reception I was about to get, and what would bother me more—Caine not trusting me or his indifference.

As soon as the security guy swung open the door to Caine's suite, I was taken aback to see Caine was not alone. Effie and Henry were there, among familiar faces from work. Effie came hurrying over to hug me close, and the guilt I'd been feeling dissipated under my anger.

He'd invited all these people to watch the game and he hadn't invited me.

Not until he'd seen me there with someone else.

"You look hot, kid." Effie grinned up at me.

I smiled, pushing my ire back down. "As do you."

She made a "pfft" noise at me as Henry stepped up to say hello. He looked different wearing his Red Sox shirt and jeans. More approachable. Gorgeous. "I got banana cream pie," he announced, and I laughed. I'd managed to talk Effie into easing up on Henry.

Effie rolled her eyes, but she was smiling as she engaged an older couple in conversation.

People waved who recognized me and I smiled politely back, letting Henry edge me closer to Caine. He was standing on the balcony, his back to me as he watched the game. He looked remote out there, even surrounded by so many people.

My anger drifted away.

He liked it this way. He liked to be alone even with so many others around him.

But I was beginning to think he was unable to be alone around me . . . and I realized then that was why he'd never invited me to share the game.

Until he'd seen me there. With someone else.

"Better go say hi to the boss." Henry winked at me.

Although Caine hadn't told a soul about our relationship, I knew Henry had very definite suspicions that something was going on between us. Other than Effie, he was the closest thing Caine had to family. And he was a smart man. He knew Caine well enough to note changes in his schedule, his demeanor, and his attitude with me.

Feeling butterflies flutter to life in my belly, I strode out onto the balcony and settled in beside Caine, keeping a few inches of space between us. I glanced up at his profile, hating the way those butterflies went crazy just at the mere sight of his face. "Hey."

"Who are they?"

I flinched at the coolness of his tone. "Friends. A college friend and her husband and his colleague."

"You didn't think it was important to mention you'd be at the game tonight?"

His words were quiet, but I could feel the tension emanating from him, and my own frustration and irritation started to build again. "You didn't tell me you were coming to the game."

"I have season tickets. You know this."

"You don't always go to the game," I argued softly.

"I don't care that you came to the game." He finally looked at me, anger in his dark eyes. "I care about the guy who is all over you."

I should have been thrilled by his jealousy, but I wasn't. Not anymore. I was sick of the uncertainty between us. "Rachel set up a blind date and didn't tell me. I told him right away that I'm . . . seeing someone."

"I don't think he got the memo."

"And you can tell that from up here?"

Caine suddenly leaned into me, clearly forgetting where we were and that we had an audience. "I saw you weren't doing much to dissuade him."

I looked pointedly over my shoulder, silently reminding him where we were.

He pulled back, his jaw clenched as he stared forward again.

I edged close enough to him so he would hear me without anyone else overhearing. "I wasn't encouraging him, and honestly this whole possessive bullshit is pissing me off."

Caine threw me a cutting look, but I refused to be intimidated. "I'm not the only one who gets jealous," he reminded me.

"No, you're not. And do you know why we're acting like crazy people? Because you're not willing to give the whole 'friends' part of our deal a real shot. There is uncertainty between us because you keep throwing up this wall." I looked over my shoulder again, double-checking that no one was near us. My gaze returned to meet his. No more games. No more tactics. Honesty. It was all I had left. "This isn't just sex, Caine. This is an affair." I held my hand up to stop his coming protest. "I'm not suggesting permanency. I'm suggesting that you admit that there's a difference in what we're doing here. We aren't two people who just have sex now and then. There are feelings here whether we want to admit it or not. I'm not asking for forever. I'm asking you to stop pushing me away. I'm asking you to be real with me for however long this lasts."

His eyes blazed. "And if I don't?"

My knees trembled. "Then I think we should end it."

He exhaled and looked away again.

Time to be even braver. "I don't want to end it. I don't think you do either."

"And what makes you think that?" he drawled lazily, and I almost believed his indifference.

Almost.

"We're not done with each other."

After a few seconds Caine looked at me again and I saw the heat and longing in his eyes. "No, we're not." We held each other's gaze for a few moments and that burn of desire started to pool low in my belly. "So, what exactly do you suggest, Lexie?"

I smiled slowly. "Spend the day with me."

He blinked in surprise. "Spend the day with you?"

"Anywhere I choose. Spend the day with me and just be my friend for a few hours. Afterward I promise to bang your brains out." I grinned.

Caine considered my suggestion and then chuckled before looking back out at the game. "Deal."

CHAPTER 18

My toes sank into the sand and a gentle breeze from the ocean cooled my cheeks against the hot summer sun.

"Was this what you had in mind?" Caine broke the silence, throwing me a small smile.

I returned that smile. "Maybe."

True to his word, Caine had given me Sunday. All of Sunday. To be friends. To hang out. I'd chosen Good Harbor Beach in Rockport as our hangout destination. Although Caine was surprised by my choice, I think he was secretly pleased. He owned a dark blue Vanquish Volante that he only drove around the city when he didn't need his company driver, which wasn't often. Good Harbor was a little over an hour away, which gave him the excuse to stretch the Aston Martin's sleek lines.

I had to admit it was fun riding shotgun.

When we'd arrived Caine had parked near the beach, oblivious of the men and women who were drooling over his car as we got out of it. He was too intent on me. I think he was trying to understand what I really wanted from him.

Standing on the beach, his shoes and socks dangling from one hand while his other arm rested lightly around my waist, he said, "Why Good Harbor?"

I shivered at the question, feeling the breeze cool my body even more as it slid across my arms. "I like it here. The only vacation I ever remember taking when it was just Mom and me was here." I looked out at the water, pain slicing through me at the memories. It was funny, but for once I welcomed that pain over the frustrated anguish that wrecked me when I remembered my life with my mother in my adult years. "Back then my whole world revolved around her." I glanced up at him, wondering how he'd react if I mentioned my father. Deciding today was a day for pushing all limits, I stepped into the quagmire that was our shared history. "My father visited on my birthday every year and he stayed a few days. I thought there was no one quite like him, and my mum helped create that idea. She filled my head with all these romantic notions about him. He was like a fairy-tale character, a relief from real life. My mom . . . well, she was the real deal. My entire happiness depended on her.

"We didn't have a lot, but it didn't matter because she made me feel safe and loved. We had more than we should have, though."

"Your father?" Caine deduced.

I looked up at him, searching his face for a reaction to our conversation. He seemed contemplative, not agitated like I'd half expected him to be. "Yes. He gave my mom money."

"And Good Harbor? Your mother lived in Connecticut. I find it more than coincidental that your only vacation with her was in Good Harbor . . . near your father."

I smirked unhappily. "She grew up in Boston, so this place was familiar to her, but . . . yeah, my father showed up toward the end of our vacation. Before he turned up, my mom and I spent every day on the beach." I smiled. "It was heaven. We goofed around and just hung out. My mom never spoke to me like I was a little kid, you know. She had actual conversations with me.

"Her parents died when she was a baby and her aunt raised her in Boston. She told me this story about when she was a little girl. One summer her aunt took her to Good Harbor. My mom told me that her aunt had to take her home from the beach and she refused to go back. When I asked why, she said that there was a little boy there and he kept jabbing this stick into an injured seagull. My mom got really upset and so her aunt asked the little boy why he was tormenting the bird. And he said that a seagull had swooped down and taken his last piece of fried dough the day before. He'd found this injured one and decided it just might be the offending seagull. So while it was hurt, he was exacting his little-boy vengeance. My mom said to the little boy that he should forgive and let the poor creature alone, and his answer was to jab at it even harder. My mom burst into tears and her aunt took her away. Mom refused to go back to the beach.

"I don't even know why she told me that story . . . but I remember it sticking with me for a while." I blinked back the burn of tears. "Now I can't seem to get it out of my head."

We walked along the shore in silence for a few seconds and then the heat of Caine's skin met the coolness of mine as he laced our fingers together and clasped my hand in his. I didn't say a word to acknowledge the gesture. I just held on.

"She was a sweet person," I said. "A good person. But around my dad she changed. Our vacation at Good Harbor ended abruptly after my father showed up. Everything was okay the first day—more than okay, it was exhilarating like always. But the next day he was suddenly gone and my mom wouldn't stop crying. She packed us up and cut the vacation short. It was kind of a theme as the years wore on."

"Do you forgive her? For abandoning you for him?"

"I don't know. She stopped being the mom I had when I was a kid. She put him before me."

"She was human. She was flawed, Lexie. It doesn't mean she didn't love you." He squeezed my hand. "Perhaps you should stop poking that seagull."

My step faltered.

Caine smiled kindly. "She's gone. It's done. The only one you're hurting here is you, baby."

I blinked back more tears and squeezed his hand in return. "How did you get so wise?" I gave a halfhearted teasing laugh.

"I've always been very wise." He tugged me gently back into step with him. "My mom was the same around my dad."

It took every ounce of self-control I had not to trip in surprise at him mentioning his mother. As far as I was aware, this was a completely taboo subject. I kept utterly quiet, hoping he'd continue.

"My mom was a different person around my dad," he admitted somberly. "It was like she was trying to be who she thought he wanted her to be."

Tentatively I asked, "What she did . . . the choices that she made . . . did they shock you?"

"Yeah." He stared out at the water as we walked and I studied his profile, looking for any signs that he was upset. But he seemed perfectly calm. "I was just a kid. I had no idea she was that selfish. It was just like you with your mom. You thought she was a superhero, right? Until you grew up. For me . . . I just happened to have the truth knocked into me a bit young." He looked at me. "Do you want to know how I get through?"

I held my breath and nodded. I was transfixed. Awed. Gratified.

Caine was confiding in me.

"I concentrate on all the good things. Because people aren't just one thing. Your mom wasn't just weak and selfish and neither was mine. Your mom wasn't unhappy all the time and neither was mine. There were times when my mother was more alive than anyone I ever met.

"She was obsessed with the color yellow. Wore it nearly every day, even if it was just a ribbon in her hair. And she had a ton of yellow ribbons." He smiled softly, his gaze reflective. "She kept them in this cheap little jewelry box I won at a school fair.

"And she made everything an event. Even Sunday morning breakfast. She had this yellow dress . . . like a fifties dress. Dad and I would get up in the morning and there she was, in that dress, smiling as she made baked goods for breakfast. Not eggs and bacon, none of that. It was cakes and pastries and muffins. Because me and Dad had a sweet tooth."

I fought back the tears at the thought of Caine's happy childhood with a mother who sounded vivacious and caring.

"Dad was always saying how beautiful she was. How I had the most beautiful mom in the world. And I'd feel proud walking down the street with her. I'd feel proud as she walked me into school, because I had the most beautiful mom in the world.

"And she loved me," he said, his eyes now filled with pain when he looked at me. "It took me a while after it all to remember that, but she loved me. It was always all about me as a kid. But looking back, I realized she would hold parts of herself back around my dad. It was just little things. Like, she used to sing all the time when he wasn't there, but she wouldn't sing around him. She was quieter. She deferred to him in everything, even things I'd seen her cope with on her own, understand by herself. And it was because he needed her to be that way; he needed to feel *needed*.

"But when she was with me she was take-charge. She knew what we were doing, where we were going. And she wanted a lot for me. That's what I remember the most. She would tell me nearly every day how much she wanted me to have everything. Everything she never had." He threw me a rueful smile that caused an ache in my chest near my heart. "She named me after some guy in a romance novel. She said his name made him sound like *somebody*, and she wanted me to be *somebody* when I grew up."

"Is that why you've worked so hard to be somebody?"

He didn't answer me. Instead he said, "Maybe you need to remember the best in your mom to forgive her, to move on."

"How do you do that?" Since we'd already walked into territory I never thought we would, I decided to continue being brave. "I mean you're obviously still furious and unforgiving over what my family—my father, my grandfather—did to your family. But you seem at peace with what your mother did."

He frowned. "I'm not at peace with it. You can't be at peace with something like that, just like I won't ever be at peace with the fact that my father took his own life knowing it would leave me with no one. But I have to consider everything that they were both going through at the time, and I have to somehow find a way to move on knowing that I wasn't enough to save either of them from their mistakes. So I remember the good stuff and most days it gets me through it. Not every day, but most days. I don't believe you can make a firm decision to just forgive. Sometimes forgiveness can be won back, but there's no one left around to earn that from me. So it's about trying every day to be okay, to let it go. It takes work. There are days when it's impossible to do that, and one of those times was the day you walked onto that set. I was pissed because you were trying to apologize for something that a simple 'sorry' can't undo. It's fucked, but it's true."

I nodded, understanding. "So you *want* to forgive your parents?"

"Honestly?"

"Yes."

"I really do."

"But . . ." I tugged on his hand, needing to know—perhaps hoping he would have the answers to help me. "After everything they took from you. Why?"

Caine stopped and faced me. There was a hard aspect in his gaze that I didn't like. "I want to forgive them because . . . I know how easy it is to fall down a path you never meant to take. I know what it's like to have done things I'm not proud of."

"I don't believe that. You could never have done the shameful things they did."

At that Caine scowled and began to walk away again, this time no longer holding my hand.

Not understanding his reaction, I hurried to catch up. "Do you think I should forgive my father and grandfather?"

"I don't know that either," he said quietly. "I just know that kind of bitterness can eat you up from the inside out." He softened. "You've got too much going for you to let that happen."

I smiled, feeling an overwhelming amount of emotion for him surge up inside me. "You amaze me. You know that, right?"

Apparently, somehow, in all the hard subjects we'd just touched on, that was the wrong thing to say.

An uncomfortable silence swelled between us.

And I pushed. "You don't think you're amazing?"

He looked at me sternly. "No. And I don't want you to either."

"Caine—"

"It's not about pushing you away," he interrupted, anger in his eyes. "It's about making sure you don't start seeing something in me that doesn't exist." He shook his head and looked away. "You wanted friendship between us? Well, the truth is you *are* my friend, Lexie. And I don't like disappointing my friends. So don't pretend I'm a man I'm not."

What Caine didn't realize was that he couldn't disappoint me. We'd had a more than rocky start, a more than complicated history, but I was still standing by his side, and I wanted to keep standing by his side, because I didn't think he even realized how good a man he was.

My whole life I'd been terrified of making the same mistake as my mother—of falling for a man who wasn't worthy without even realizing I was wasting my heart on him. Because of that fear I'd never truly let myself fall.

But Caine Carraway was not Alistair Holland.

Caine was ambitious and hardworking. He was strong and stubborn and ruthless, but he was also this contradiction. He could be kind and compassionate and generous.

And even if I didn't understand him sometimes, even if I didn't agree with him on occasion, I would never, ever be disappointed in him.

However, I knew him well enough to recognize that look in his eyes. That obstinate glint. So for once I let it go.

"I'm buying you ice cream." I held out my hand for him.

Caine gave me a dubious look.

I grinned and urged him to take my proffered hand. "You've never tasted ice cream like Luigi's."

Sighing, Caine laced his fingers through mine. "Did you ever really grow up, Lexie?"

I shot him a saucy look. "I did in all the places that matter."

Like always, triumph rushed through me at the sound of his answering laughter.

CHAPTER 19

What happened between Caine and me next took me by surprise. There was definitely an intimacy between us that hadn't been there before, but instead of us relaxing into it, a new kind of tension sprang up between us. There was a desperation in our interactions—sex between us became almost an addiction, an obsession. It was wild and passionate as we tried to quell this tension that couldn't be quelled.

"Are you sure it's a good idea for me to be there tomorrow night?" I was perched on Caine's desk, my legs crossed at the ankles. There was a possibility I was sitting on important paperwork, but Caine hadn't said a word.

He was too busy staring at my legs.

"Caine?"

His gaze roamed up my body and I shivered at the heat in his eyes. "I told you this party is mostly business. We're there to rub elbows with clients and potential clients. No one will question the fact that I brought my PA." He suddenly grinned and it was wickedly sexy. "Although they might question my motives in hiring one that looks like you."

"Henry's already suspicious."

He shrugged. "Henry doesn't know a thing."

Hmm, I wasn't so sure. "And what about my name?"

"We already introduced you as Alexa Hall at the last party."

"And you don't think anyone is eventually going to find out that's not my name? Everyone in the company knows my surname, Caine."

"Fine." He sighed. "We just won't mention your surname. We'll introduce you as Alexa. Not to be a dick or anything, but no one there will really care what my PA's surname is."

Arrogant SOB. "Ouch."

He slid his hand along the inside of my thigh in a comforting gesture that mostly just turned me on. "The truth is these people, *my* people, they're self-important, self-involved, and all they care about is who has the most influence."

"Which doesn't include the PAs." His expression gave me my answer. "You know, I was thinking about a career move. Like . . . moving into the events management business . . ."

Caine smiled softly. "You'd be good at that."

Gratitude rushed through me. "You really think so?"

He nodded. "I know so. But give me plenty of warning." His fingers moved higher up my thigh and his voice thickened. "You're the best PA I've ever had. It'll take time to replace you."

As he touched me I let my head fall back and I savored the physical rush of being with him, but somewhere in the back of my mind his words twisted into something ugly.

Something real I didn't want to face.

Caine would eventually replace me.

. . .

I should have known attending the party with Caine was a bad idea. The only other person I knew there was Henry, and he'd brought a date and was much more interested in seducing his date than doing anything to promote "friendship" with other businessmen at the party.

The party was hosted by investment guru Brendan Ulster and his wife, Lacey. Caine said their circle took turns to throw these kinds of bashes throughout the year, and this year it was hosted under the pretense of an apartment warming, as the Ulsters had just purchased a top-floor apartment across the Common from Caine on Beacon Street.

The place was beautiful.

The people . . . well, not so much.

Among the men, Caine was a man's man, the kind of guy that other men looked up to and admired. Among the women, Caine was that elusive catch. If the men weren't attempting to engage Caine in business conversation, they were trying to engage me in flirtation. It was exhausting fending them off, my irritation increasing as so many of them looked at me as if I were easy pickings. I was of course just the PA. And I had the distinct impression that they thought I was the kind of woman who would do anything to be near a powerful man.

They weren't the only reason I was annoyed. The night had started out well—Caine was attentive and funny as he made dry remarks about some of the snootier people we met. However, as the evening wore on, he began to treat me with a familiar aloofness that was driving me insane. I had no idea what had happened in the space of an hour, but I was biding my time until the end of the party to let him have it.

"You've been noticeably absent from society lately, Caine," some woman whose name I couldn't remember purred to him as she cut me off from his side by insinuating herself between us. She ran a perfectly manicured nail along his shoulder and pressed her breasts against his arm. "There are rumors that you're hiding some kind of forbidden dalliance."

Forbidden dalliance? I rolled my eyes. *Who talks like that?*

Caine extricated himself from her and looked away in boredom. "There are always rumors, Kitty."

She fluffed her hair, seeming perturbed by Caine's aloofness with her.

Yeah, I could relate.

"True." She shrugged. "People talk. Well . . ." She stared at him a moment, waiting for him to pay her some attention. When he didn't she finally glanced at me questioningly. I merely raised an eyebrow at her. She gave a little huff. "Well, if you'll excuse me . . ." She sashayed away from us, her elegant figure wrapped up tight in a pale gold dress.

"The women around here certainly like you," I noted dryly, wishing I didn't feel that curl of jealousy in my belly. I'd never been a jealous woman until Caine, and I didn't particularly like that he provoked that aspect of my personality. I did my best to keep it under wraps, using humor to hide behind.

Caine didn't reply.

"You know, you might have them fooled, but you don't fool me."

He slanted a look at me out of the corner of his eye and I could tell he sensed the dark undercurrent of my mood. "Is that right?" he murmured.

"Mmm. They all whisper behind your back that you're dangerous, ruthless, exciting, giggling like titillated morons. But I know something they don't."

Turning fully now to face me, Caine practically dared, "And what's that?"

Melancholy coiled around my heart like an iron fist. "You seem dangerous because you *are* dangerous. You walk among them like a surly tiger, and they're all just prey caught in your paws. They're so busy looking up at you, *ooh*ing and *aah*ing over how beautiful you are, they have no idea that you're mere seconds from eating them. That you're just going to chew them up and spit them out." I looked away, taking a sip of my drink and willing my hands not to shake as I did so.

The tension we'd felt between us all week seemed to expand into this suffocating thing that wrapped around us, shutting everyone else out.

Finally I found the courage to look at him.

He was staring out at the crowd, seemingly bored. Only the tightness of his jaw gave away his irritation.

A grim-faced gentleman nodded at him from across the room and Caine lifted his drink in acknowledgment.

"Who's that?" I said curiously, trying to draw focus away from the bad mood between us.

"Leonard Kipling. Pharmaceuticals giant."

"You know everyone, don't you? I didn't think Kipling was the kind of man you wanted to get into bed with."

"He's powerful. I don't rule out anyone with his kind of influence. Who knows where the future may take me, or if there'll come a day when an acquaintance with him will benefit us both?"

I eyed the stranger, noting that behind his grim expression was actually the handsome face of a fit man. He looked to be in his late forties. A number of women were shooting him come-hither looks. "Is he married?"

"Divorced," Caine replied, his tone cool with affected ennui. "Why? Thinking of asking him to replace me when we're done fucking?"

The ugly suggestion hit me from left field. I stilled, shocked by the hurtful insinuation.

I couldn't even look at him.

It was true that in the beginning of our acquaintance Caine had been cutting sometimes, but he'd never been outright disrespectful. He'd never sought to be deliberately cruel. Only once . . . when he was on the defensive.

But never since then.

And never had he made what we were doing feel so cheap . . . Never had he made me feel so inconsequential.

"Alexa . . . ," he murmured.

I edged slightly away from him, taking a long gulp of my champagne. Thankfully more people I didn't recognize came over to talk to Caine and he was distracted while I attempted to regain control of my emotions.

In order to continue at his side for the rest of the evening, I switched off my emotions. I was polite to everyone, even to him, but I was coolly distant. Funnily enough, I sensed my indifference caused some intrigue among some of the guests.

Like I cared.

I cared nothing for them.

I wanted to be away from them and away from this man beside me who was suddenly a callous stranger.

"I appear to have lost my date," Henry said as he approached us, and the latest gaggle of admirers around my boss departed.

"Did you try the bar?" Caine said.

"Yes." Henry grinned at him, unperturbed by his mocking. "And before you ask I also tried the restroom." He slanted a look at me and instantly frowned. "Everything all right, Lexie?"

"I'm fine," I muttered before finishing off the last of my champagne. I'd been nursing it for an hour.

"Another glass?" Caine asked, and I was gratified to note the uncertainty in his query.

"No, thank you," I replied, full of demure politeness.

"Is it just me or is it chillier on this side of the room?" Henry quirked an eyebrow at Caine.

"Not just you." Caine's gaze burned into me as I studiously avoided it.

"Okay, then. Well . . . since I'm not interrupting any scintillating conversation over here, Caine, I was speaking to Kipling earlier. He mentioned some business that may interest you."

"Lead the way . . ." I noted him starting to follow Henry out of the corner of my eye and then stopping. "Alexa, are you coming?"

I still didn't look at him. I couldn't. "Yes. I just need to use the restroom."

The tension between us rose to new levels as he waited for me to look at him. I didn't. Finally Caine said, "We'll be right over there."

As I watched him walk away, I let the ache I was holding down inside me unfurl.

I was done. I wouldn't let any man talk to me the way he did.

Every time I thought we were going somewhere, he proved me wrong, and my frustration at the ups and downs in our relationship was at boiling point. It was time to leave before I let my anger erupt in public.

Instead of heading to the restrooms, I made for the exit, my breathing harsh in my ears as I attempted to manage the pain and fury. That meant I didn't hear the footsteps behind me as I marched down the narrow corridor toward the front door.

A strong hand gripped my arm and I let out a soft cry as I found myself jerked into an alcove opposite the front door. I pressed back into it as Caine's cologne tingled my nose and senses when he leaned into me. He rested his hands on the wall at either side of my head, caging me in.

"Get out of my way."

"Lexie—"

I glowered up at him. "I said get the hell out of my way."

Caine cursed. "Lexie," he said, his voice hoarse, "I'm sorry."

Not wanting to crumble in my resolve, I looked over his shoulder, avoiding his dark, liquid gaze. "I'm tired and you have a party to get back to."

"Don't do this," he growled, pressing his fingers against my jaw and gently forcing my gaze back to his. "I fucked up . . . but don't shut me out."

After his behavior tonight he had the audacity to ask that of me? "Are you kidding me?"

He briefly closed his eyes, and there was remorse written all over his face. "Jesus, Lex, I should never have said what I said. As soon as the words were out of my mouth . . ." He lowered his head and I found my eyes caught in his. "You are the last person in the world I want to hurt."

My mouth trembled with emotion and I fought the burn of tears. "Then why?"

Caine looked at his feet and when a few seconds passed without an answer I huffed in annoyance and pushed at his chest. "Get out of my way."

"No." He lifted his head, eyes heated. "I fucked up and I'm apologizing. Let's leave it at that."

Anger curled in my gut. "Get. Out. Of. My. Way."

His jaw clenched. "Lexie—"

"If you say my name one more time I'm going to scream bloody murder. Just get out of my way, *Mr. Carraway.*"

He narrowed his eyes. "Alexa—"

"Why?" I pushed up from the wall, pressing my body against his, turning the tables on him, trapping *him.* "Why? What happened? We were fine when we got here and then suddenly you started acting like I'm the enemy again. Or worse . . . like I'm a Holland whore you can pass off to someone else when you get bored w—"

"Wrong." He pushed me back into the wall, his features harsh, his words guttural with feeling. "I'm a jealous bastard who watched man after man flirt with you and I can't stand the thought of you being with one of them. I said something I didn't mean because of it." His chest heaved with emotion.

I sucked in a breath at his confession.

We stared at each other in thickening silence.

"Fine," I whispered. "But don't ever speak to me like that again."

I saw a measure of edginess leak out of him at my response. "I won't," he promised softly. "I'm sorry. I'm not . . ." He shook his head, seemingly as frustrated with his feelings as I was with my own.

And that was when I realized what the problem was between us, where that tension sprang from, where the animosity had a place to fester and grow from . . .

Friendship, intimacy—it hadn't made us any less uncertain of each other because of the temporary nature of our relationship. Other couples, *normal* couples, could admit how they really felt . . . but admitting anything more than we already had meant setting ourselves up for an even bigger fall.

And yet . . . I couldn't help myself.

The words just spilled out of me. "I only want *you*, you know."

Caine's chest shuddered beneath my hand and then suddenly I was in arms. His kiss wasn't gentle or apologetic. It was wild. His lips pressed hard against my lips, his tongue licking and stroking mine in a wet, deep kiss that I felt between my legs. I clung to him, kissing him back just as passionately, my fingers curling into his hair as I bit playfully at his lip. He groaned into my mouth and shoved me hard against the wall—

A throat cleared behind us and we both froze.

Slowly, Caine broke our kiss but kept his arms wrapped protectively around me as we both looked over his shoulder.

Henry stood smirking at us. "I guess you're making up after a lovers' quarrel? Am I right? I'm right, aren't I?"

I pinched my mouth closed to stop from laughing at his boyish good humor.

Caine, however, had grown taut against me. "You breathe a word of this and I'll knock your fucking head off." There was a hint of his old Southie accent in the words.

Henry laughed, but he had the good sense to agree. He pointed to his own mouth. "As silent as the grave." His chuckles trailed behind him as he wandered back toward the party.

Caine relaxed against me, his eyes still filled with heat. "Let me take you back to my place." He smoothed his hand over my hip. "Let me apologize properly."

"What about Kipling?"

"You're more important." His confession was so quiet I almost didn't hear him, didn't believe him.

But hear him I did.

And God help me but I wanted to believe him.

Hope bloomed through my whole body. Caine might not

have admitted what I had with words, but his reaction was all the confirmation I needed.

He only wanted me too.

"Then we better leave now, because you have a lot of apologizing to do."

I stared at Caine's luxurious bed with its masculine wooden bed frame and majestic four posts. I'd seen this bed on numerous occasions when I stopped by his apartment to drop off his dry cleaning.

I'd fantasized about what it would be like to lie down on it and have Caine's body cover mine.

Up until now that had remained a fantasy.

We'd never stayed at Caine's. Our affair had until this point taken place at my apartment (and occasionally the office).

For some reason a flutter of nerves woke in my belly as I stood in his bedroom. We'd had sex more times than I could count, but as the heat of him pressed against my back, as his fingertips coasted lightly over my bare arm and his breath whispered across the back of my neck, it all seemed new and even more thrilling.

The fabric of my dress tightened across my chest for a moment at the gentle tug on it. Caine slowly pulled the zipper down. My breasts swelled and my nipples peaked with anticipation.

I covered his hands with my own as together we leisurely removed my dress. I stepped out of it, goose bumps rising all over me as I stood in nothing but lingerie and heels. Caine gripped my hips, gently pulling me back against him so I could feel the hard, rigid length of his arousal against my bottom.

He swept my hair off one side of my neck, and his hot lips brushed my ear. "You're driving me crazy," he confessed, and the words elicited a groan of pleasure from me as I ground my ass against his erection. "It's never enough . . . never enough . . ." He trailed light kisses down my neck.

"Caine." Desire bolted through me, slickening the heat between my thighs.

His hands moved back to my hips, and cool air whispered between us as he stepped back a little to allow himself room to explore.

And explore he did.

With light strokes he memorized me with his touch. It was like an erotic massage, the tantalizing gentleness of his hands only increasing my anticipation and arousal.

His heat blazed against my back, his hard-on prodding my ass again as he removed my bra and cupped my naked breasts in his hands.

I sighed, rested my head against his shoulder, and arched into his touch. Ripples of desire undulated low in my belly as he played with my breasts, sculpting and kneading them, stroking and pinching my nipples into hard buds. I thrust into his touch, his name falling from my lips in breathless whispers while he pumped his hips in rhythm with my own movements.

"Your mouth," he growled in my ear.

I turned my head at his demand and my lips instantly met his. Wrapping my arm around his neck, I opened my mouth, inviting his tongue inside. He kissed me with deep, slow abandon. I gasped as he pinched both my nipples, causing another wave of lust to ripple through my lower belly. His growl of satisfaction rumbled into my mouth and he released my breast to coast his hand down my stomach and over my panties. He rubbed his fingers over them, his hold on me tightening when he discovered they were soaked with my arousal.

He pulled back from our kiss, his eyes low lidded with his own longing. He pressed his fingers against my clit, causing the lace of my panties to catch in delicious friction against it.

"Oh God." I slipped my hand over his, guiding him.

"So beautiful," he said, watching my face as his fingers moved under the panties. My hips jerked against him at the feel of his thumb directly on my clit.

"Caine," I whimpered, my hips moving against his touch.

My eyes drifted closed as the pressure inside me began to build.

"Look at me," he demanded.

I opened my eyes and stared up at him in a daze.

Suddenly I shattered. "Caine!" I cried out softly.

The floor fell away from my feet as Caine lifted me up into his arms and carried me to his bed. My languid muscles gave way to his wishes and when he settled me on it I fell back against the covers, my arms above my head, panting my satisfaction.

Somehow I found the strength to tilt my hips up when Caine began removing my panties. He threw them on the floor beside the rest of my clothes and then curled his hands around my ankles. His thumbs caressed my skin as we stared at each other in potent silence.

I dropped my gaze to the huge erection straining against the fabric of his Armani pants, and I unconsciously licked my lips.

His fingers sensually caressed my ankles before taking a leisurely, seductive path up my calves. When he reached my knees he pressed down and then outward, forcing my legs open.

I felt decadently shameful as I lay open to his perusal.

For no other man would I have let myself be so vulnerable.

But for Caine I was sexy, sinful . . . seductive.

I shifted a little, thrusting my breasts out.

His eyes flared as his hands skimmed down the insides of my thighs. "Will it ever be enough?" he said, his voice thick with hunger.

"I don't know." I sighed in rapture as he stroked my breasts, his thumbs dragging over my sensitive nipples. "Do you ever want it to be?"

He leaned down, his familiar scent causing another squeeze of desire in my belly. His lips brushed over mine and he pulled back to whisper, "I'd spend my last hours inside you if I could."

Emotion broke through the desire and I closed my eyes to hold back the overwhelming feeling of euphoria that moved through me.

As if he felt it too and didn't know how to deal with it, Caine kissed me, this kiss much rougher than the last. He only let go of my mouth to trail kisses down my throat and over my chest.

My thighs tightened against his hips when his lips closed around my nipple. He sucked deep, hard, a pleasurable pain rushing through me as he moved against me. As he had done with his hands, he began to play my breasts with his hot mouth until I was on the brink of coming undone all over again.

"Caine," I pleaded, my fingers digging into his back. "Undress."

He looked up, his gaze dark. "Not yet."

And that was when he shifted lower. His lips traveled

down my belly to between my legs. I melted into the mattress in anticipation as he nuzzled his mouth against my sex. He licked my clit, pressed his tongue down on it, and sensation blew through me. "Oh God!" I arched back on the bed, my inner thighs trembling.

That coil inside my belly was unfurling, pulling apart until the tension within me grew tauter, more electric, screaming for release—

"Yes!" I cried loudly as the tension reached its apex. Lights sparked behind my eyes as I came in overwhelming, hard pulses.

While I lay panting, warmth rushed through my limbs to the tips of my fingers and toes. I vaguely felt the bed move. When I could finally pry my eyes open, I saw Caine undressing quickly.

There was a fierceness, a harsh quality of craving in him that thrilled me. I stared at him in awe.

The men who had come before him had always made me feel attractive . . . but not one of them had ever made me feel necessary. Vital. Not like Caine. Like if he didn't have me this very second the world would come crashing down around him.

He put a knee on the bed, his cock thick and throbbing between his legs. His hands curled behind my knees and I let out a little mewl of surprise as he pulled me roughly to him. Angling my hips, gripping tight to my thighs, he held my legs open as he kneeled between them and gazed down at me.

My breath stuttered at the heat of him nudging against me. Eased by my arousal, he pushed inside me, his lashes fluttering as my inner muscles clamped around his length.

With a tenderness that made the air whoosh out of my lungs, Caine caught his rhythm. He watched himself sliding inside me and his chest moved up and down in shallow breaths as his excitement increased. His grip on my legs suddenly tightened and he braced on his knees. Caine began to power in and out of me with harder, deeper thrusts that dragged across my clit and stirred me all over again.

"Come for me, Lexie," he demanded, fucking me harder now, his teeth gritted together as he held his own climax at bay. "Come around me. Fuck, you feel so good . . ." His words trailed off as the climax started to take him, and seeing the need in his face was the last jarring smash against the growing pressure inside me.

I split apart, and my inner muscles rippled around him.

"Jesus." His eyes widened at the deep, hard tug of my orgasm on his, and he froze for a second before his hips jerked against me in a long release.

My legs flopped to the bed as he let go of them to collapse over me. Somehow I found the strength to wrap my arms around him and hold him close. The throb of his cock pulsed inside me and an aftershock of arousal moved through me. "Wow," I whispered, still picturing the look on his face when he came.

It was the hardest he'd ever come with me, and it was the sexiest thing I'd ever seen.

I smiled languorously, feeling smug.

"Yeah." He exhaled slowly, easing up off me but holding on to me so that when he rolled onto his back I was pressed against his side and my head rested on his chest.

"So, that was pretty intense," I whispered.

Caine drew circles on my arm with his fingertips. "Yeah," he repeated, sounding staggered.

I laughed softly. "We were both pretty worked up."

"Yeah," he repeated again.

"I don't think this is a night I'll forget anytime soon."

A second later I was on my back. Caine leaned over me and gazed down at me with determination. "No, it's fucking not," he said thickly. "And it's not over yet."

My eyes widened. "I don't know if I can take much more."

He kissed me gently, the gesture at odds with his rough vow. "I'm not stopping until we've had each other in every way we can."

CHAPTER 20

Light pricked at my eyelids in an unwelcome sensation as I stirred to wakefulness. I groaned, turning my head on the squishy pillow that was much softer than my own.

Where was I?

The night before suddenly hit me in image after image, memory after memory, and my eyes popped open. The fog cleared from them as I took in Caine's bedroom. My hair rustled on his pillow as I looked at him.

He lay on his stomach, facing toward me in sleep.

A little sigh of happiness escaped me at the sight of his face. He looked so peaceful and relaxed.

A smile tugged at my lips.

More like he was exhausted.

True to his vow, Caine had kept us up practically all night and had given me a record-breaking six orgasms.

I was spent.

I was—I looked past him to the clock radio—up way too early.

We'd only fallen asleep a few hours ago.

My instinct was to roll into Caine and fall back asleep curled up next to him. However, I wasn't sure it was wise—Caine and I didn't wake up together often. If we did Caine got us up out of bed quickly because he had work to do. Mostly, though, I woke up and Caine was gone. It would be so easy to let all my fears plague me up out of that bed and his apartment. But then we'd be back where were before, and after all the ups and downs we'd taken to get to this point, it would be a crying shame to let a little fear fuck it all up.

So instead of creeping out of Caine's bed and treating him to his own medicine, I shimmied into him. I slid my arm over his back, rested my head on his shoulder, and closed my eyes.

"Lexie."

The low voice rumbled in my ear, eased its way into my consciousness, and gently woke me.

"Baby," Caine whispered.

I smiled.

It wasn't the most original endearment in the world, but I had to admit to feeling a thrill shoot through me every time he called me "baby."

He chuckled. "I can see that smile of yours, so I know you're awake."

With lazy slowness I opened my eyes.

Caine's face hovered above mine, amusement visible in the little crinkles around his eyes. "Good morning."

I groaned. "Why is it morning? We only went to sleep a few hours ago."

His lips twitched at my grumpiness. "I'm well aware."

I closed my eyes at his masculine satisfaction. "You can

thump on your chest with smug pride later. For now let me sleep."

"I would." He squeezed my waist. "But Effie's downstairs and she's making us breakfast."

"What?" I slammed upright and Caine pulled back just in time before my forehead cracked against his. I noted he was wearing a T-shirt and sweatpants. "How long have you been awake?"

"Since Effie let herself into the apartment and I had to move fast to stop her from coming in here."

I blanched at the thought. "She has a key."

He snorted. "It's Effie—what do you think?"

"I think she has a key and a spare," I muttered.

Caine's eyes were bright with mirth and my grumpiness dissipated at the sight. "I thought you loved Effie."

"I do." I rubbed the sleep out of my eyes. "I'd love her more, though, if she'd let me sleep a few more hours."

"Her breakfast will make the tiredness worth it," he promised, and grabbed my hand to gently haul me up. I winced and he instantly stopped. "You okay? Did I hurt you?"

Not exactly.

I slid gently off the bed. "I'm feeling a little sore, that's all."

He frowned, understanding. "Oh."

Sensing where his thoughts had gone, I patted his arm in reassurance as I passed him. "It was worth every twinge, believe me."

His arm shot out, sliding around my waist to stop me. I looked up at him in question. He still looked concerned. "You're sure you're okay? I got a little carried away last night."

I grinned. I could still feel the throbbing between my legs as a reminder. "I know. I was there. And trust me . . . you can get carried away like that with me anytime."

Caine's hand tightened on my waist.

"Last night was amazing," I insisted.

The tension leaked out of him and a smirk pulled at his lips. "Yeah, it was," he agreed, his voice deep with satisfaction.

"Are you two kids coming down for breakfast or what?" Effie shouted from downstairs.

My eyes widened. "She has quite the pair of lungs on her for an old bird."

Caine tapped his ear. "She also has superhuman hearing, so I'd cool it with the 'old bird' comments."

"Right." I pressed my lips together and looked around the room at my discarded clothes. An uncomfortable thought hit me. "I have nothing appropriate to wear."

In answer Caine wandered into his walk-in. He came out a few seconds later and thrust a Red Sox T-shirt at me.

I stared at it, aghast. "A T-shirt. You want me to wear a T-shirt."

With an impatient huff Caine rolled it up and then none too gently yanked it over my head. "It's just Effie."

Annoyed, I pushed my arms through the sleeves and jerked it down over my body. With my being tall, it only reached the tops of my thighs. I shot him a look. "Are you kidding me?"

He crossed his arms over his chest, seemingly pleased with himself. "It's very sexy."

Ignoring the familiar thrill that shot through me at his appreciative gaze, I retorted, "Yeah, and that would be fine if I were just having breakfast with you. But I'm not. I'm having breakfast with your pseudograndmother."

"And she's the least grandmotherly person I know."

"Not true," I argued. "She bakes and cooks."

"Well, if that's the qualification, every top male chef in

the city is a grandmother." He shrugged and moved past me. "Come on, I'm starving."

"Don't you have a pair of sweatpants I could borrow?"

He glanced back over his shoulder at me, his eyes hungrily roaming over my legs. "Nope."

There was no freaking way I was going down to breakfast with Effie half-naked! Knowing exactly what his game was, I put my hands on my waist and cocked my hip. "Do you really want to chance getting turned on in Effie's company?"

He stopped with a grunt and faced me with an arrogant quirk of his right eyebrow. "I'm a grown man, Lexie. As gorgeous as you are I think I can control my libido for a few hours."

I tapped my chin in mocking retrospection. "I'm sure I've heard that somewhere before . . ."

"Lex—"

"But if you're sure you'll be fine . . ." I shrugged and lowered myself onto the fat armchair in the corner of the room. I slowly crossed my legs and the T-shirt rode up to the tops of my thighs, almost to crotch level. "I mean it's just a little skin. And if I have to bend down"—I stood back up to demonstrate and the shirt rode up, revealing my ass in the high-cut panties—"it certainly won't remind you of the way you bent me over your bed last night and had your wicked—"

"Fine," Caine snapped, a telltale flush visible on his cheekbones. "I'll find you some damn sweatpants."

I grinned at his back as he wandered back into the walkin. "A wise decision, Mr. Carraway."

"Lexie, good to see you, sweetheart," Effie greeted me warmly as I walked toward her wearing the Red Sox T-shirt and sweatpants that were held up at the waist with one of Caine's ties. She wrapped her strong arms around me, enveloping me in her familiar sweet scent of vanilla and sugar.

"You too." I gave her a squeeze and stepped back, my eyes automatically going to the dining table. It was covered with food. There were pancakes, maple syrup, eggs over easy, bacon, muffins . . .

My belly suddenly let out a hungry little rumble.

"Effie, this looks amazing as always." Caine kissed her papery cheek and then immediately homed in on the table.

As he settled in at the head of it, I shot Effie an amused smile. "I guess I should learn to cook."

She grinned back at me. "Somehow I think you're doing just fine without it, but if you want a teacher I could show you some of my recipes."

"I'd love that." I followed her to the table and we settled at either side of Caine, across from each other. Feeling suddenly ravenous, I dug in with as much enthusiasm as Caine did. Effie's pancakes practically melted in my mouth, they were so fluffy, her bacon was crisp and full of flavor, and her eggs were just how I liked them. I dipped my toast into egg yolk. "Your husband must have been a very happy man, Effie."

She swallowed a piece of bacon and nodded, her eyes glinting. "Oh, very. We had a good life together. A great life."

"You met at the theater, right?"

"There's more to it than that." She smiled mysteriously.

I was curious, but I didn't want to intrude where I wasn't welcome. "That sounds intriguing."

Effie's whole face lit up. "You want to hear it?"

"Uh, *yeah*."

Caine chuckled at Effie's delight as she leaned over her plate and began her story. "It was 1960 and I was about to turn twenty-three. I was playing Maria in *West Side Story*. I was also completely infatuated with my asshole of a director, Albert Reis. Of course I didn't think he was an asshole at the time." She gave me a girlish smile. "I was sunk deep in my crush, but Reis wasn't interested. So, one night after the show when this handsome, wealthy industrialist from my hometown stopped by my dressing room to pay his regards, I agreed to go on a date with him. Nicky was fun and sweet and he was a real gentleman with me, but I took him for granted. I kept him on a string, all the while hoping the enigmatic and artistic Reis would finally pay me some attention.

"I forgot Nicky got wealthy for a reason. He was smart—a perceptive cookie, my Nicky. He realized I was infatuated with Reis and he broke things off with me." She appeared sheepish as she remembered the moment. "He was really mad at me. Told me to go to hell. I was shaken up by it. I didn't want to hurt him . . . but I didn't realize until he went back to Boston and was in all the society papers for philandering around that I was shaken up because I actually had feelings for him."

My breakfast forgotten, I rested my chin on my hand and whispered, "So, what did you do?"

"I found out when his next trip to New York was and I cornered him at his favorite restaurant. I told him I wanted him back."

"That was brave."

"Maybe. It was also fruitless. Nicky told me he wasn't some toy I could just set aside and then pick up as soon as another girl reached for it."

"Oh boy."

"Exactly. I had to work my butt off to get him back. I made sure I was at all the same parties and I made certain sure that he knew I was there for him."

I grinned. "You wore him down."

Effie surprised me by shaking her head as she dimmed with regret. "I really hurt him. He'd fallen in love with me, you see, and I broke his heart. I'd lost his trust. He wasn't sure of my affections anymore, and the fact that I was a damn good actress didn't help him believe me when I said I was for real. Plus . . . I was never very good at making myself really vulnerable. So he doubted my sincerity.

"Anyway, he started dating this one girl in particular and, well . . . that hurt. A lot. They were together for only a few weeks, but everyone kept telling me how serious she was about him. One night we were at the same party and rumors met my ears that he was planning on proposing to this girl. Well, I couldn't hide how I felt. I was so used to being able to turn on a smile even when I was sad, but not then. I had to get out of there. Our friends and acquaintances realized what was going on and it was a spectacle for them, you know. Word made it to Nicky about my reaction and he was concerned enough to come after me." She rolled her eyes, as if mocking the drama that had played out between her and her late husband. "Finding me in floods of tears finally got through his thick noggin and he believed me when I told him I loved him." Her grin was wicked. "Of course his passionate reaction to that news meant we had to get married, if you know what I mean."

Caine groaned beside me. "Effie, a monkey would know what you mean. No sex talk. It's disturbing."

She just laughed. "Anyway, the moral of my story is that sometimes you've got to let yourself be vulnerable even when it's the scariest thing in the world. You can reap the rewards— I'll tell you that." Her pointed look toward Caine did not go unmissed, and he braced himself.

I squirmed uncomfortably.

I knew Effie's advice was well-meaning, but there was a time and a place to push the boundaries between me and Caine, and too much too soon would have him running in the opposite direction. Deciding to pretend I missed her point, I pushed my plate back. These breakfasts were the only real time I imagined Caine got to spend with Effie, especially with me taking up what little free time he had. I decided to give them privacy. "Well, I'm stuffed. I'm going to have a shower."

Effie smiled gratefully at me and Caine's own expression was warm, tender almost. It took everything within me to restrain myself from caressing his cheek as I passed him.

Slowly, Lexie. Slowly but surely, I reminded myself.

When I wandered back downstairs after my shower, the table was cleared and Effie was nowhere to be seen.

Caine approached me and I stilled at the predatory look in his eye. "Where's Effie?"

"She had a book club meeting to get to. She told me to tell you she'll see you soon."

"Oka . . ." The word died on my lips as Caine drew to a stop in front of me and felt under the Red Sox T-shirt for his tie. He yanked on it and the sweatpants instantly began sliding down my hips. With satisfaction etched into his features, Caine forced the pants down my legs and then bent down to his haunches to pull them off. I stared at him, confused, as he stood back up.

"The T-shirt looks better on its own," he explained.

His actions suggested I was sticking around the apartment for the day. "Aren't you busy?"

"Probably, but let's pretend I'm not."

Delighted, I grinned up at him. "So you want to hang out? Like normal people?"

"Neither of us will ever be normal, but we can certainly hang out."

"What do you want to do?"

"I don't know." He looked around his apartment. "I've never just . . . hung out before."

"Hmm." Sensing I needed to take control of the situation, I stepped past him and stared over at the TV corner. "We could watch a movie." That was something that normal couples did. In fact, it sounded so normal I had butterflies of excitement fluttering around in my belly.

In answer Caine strode across the room and opened his DVD cabinet. "What do you feel like watching?"

I made my way over there and bent down beside him. Eyeing the movies, I felt overwhelmed not only by the choices but by the fact that this was happening. I was spending the day with Caine, dressed only in his T-shirt, and he was prioritizing me over work just as he had done last night. Surely that was *huge*. I bit my lip to contain my giddiness and began looking through his foreign movies.

After selecting one about World War II, Caine set up the movie and then flopped down on his sofa so he was stretched out along it on his side. My initial instinct was to gaze down at him uncertainly, as he'd never really invited casual affection before.

But I was over uncertainty.

I'd decided I was over that this morning and I was sticking to it.

Decision made, I curled up on my side in front of him and relaxed when his arm snaked around my waist to pull me closer.

For the first fifteen minutes of the movie I found it difficult to concentrate on anything but the fact that I was cuddling on the sofa watching a movie with Caine. My awareness of him was heightened even more than usual—his hard body pressed close to mine, the steady, slight rise and fall of his chest against my back, the clean fresh scent of his skin and the hint of his cologne . . .

Eventually, however, I relaxed completely and allowed the film to draw me in. I was enjoying the fraught story and the coziness of the situation, but was beginning to realize where the plot was going and what it would eventually lead to. Somewhat familiar with foreign movies, I knew they could be more sexually explicit than our homegrown fare, and I wondered how I'd deal with watching a sex scene with Caine when the two of us were still so hyperaware of each other.

Sure enough, a sex scene began and I found my breath catching at the highly sensual acts unfolding before us. Caine strained slightly behind me as the cries of pleasure filled the room while the hero put his mouth between the heroine's legs.

Ripples of desire moved through me, shooting electric tingles between my own legs. My nipples hardened as I watched the lovemaking on-screen while surrounded by Caine.

Slowly I reached for his hand that rested on my hip and I drew it down over my thigh and back up under the T-shirt.

His breath hitched behind me as I guided his fingers underneath my panties; all the while my eyes were glued to the screen.

His erection pressed against me. "I thought you were sore," he whispered, the words heavy with lust.

"It's a good kind of sore," I managed to whisper back.

In answer Caine rubbed his fingers over my clit.

Our breathing grew louder, shallower, as the couple on-screen fucked at the same time Caine's magical touch took me toward orgasm. I cried out, coming around his fingers as the guy on-screen thrust into the heroine.

Quite abruptly I found myself on my back as Caine braced himself over me and yanked my panties off with rough need. I gasped, thrilled by the harsh lust hardening his features, and a renewed rush of desire swept over me as he shoved down his sweatpants enough to free himself.

And then he was inside me, pushing into me with a deep need that I matched as I lifted my hips against his thrusts. Lying beneath him, my fingers digging into his gorgeous ass as he moved inside me, I wondered at this madness between us, and if this base demand for each other would ever calm.

With a cry of satisfaction, Caine shuddered against me as he came.

I wrapped my legs around his waist, my arms around his back, and felt that his T-shirt was damp from exertion.

He nuzzled my neck, pressing soft kisses there as his breathing returned to normal. When he pulled back, it was only to look at me; he made no move to remove himself. His gaze moved over my face, drinking me in. "Maybe we could stay like this forever." His words were rumbly and deeply satisfied.

They made my inner muscles squeeze his cock and I saw he felt it in the flutter of his dark lashes and in the softening of his mouth.

"I don't think we could have much interaction with other people if we stayed like this." *On second thought* . . . "So it's not actually a bad idea."

Caine was amused. "I definitely like the sound of that. Although we would need to eat. I don't feel comfortable asking Effie to bring us food while we're like this."

I giggled. "Yeah, that's not going to happen. We could ask my friend Rachel. Nothing fazes her."

"I'm pretty sure this would faze her."

"Oh no, it really wouldn't. Rachel has no boundaries. This is a woman who once called a ten-year-old an asshole. To his face. In front of his mother."

Caine gave a bark of laughter. "A ten-year-old?"

"To be fair he *was* acting like an asshole."

Shaking with amusement, Caine wrapped his arms around me so that when he moved back onto his side he was taking me with him. "Is Rachel looking for a job? I'm always open to hiring no-bullshitters."

"I know." I pressed my face into his warm chest. "You hired me."

His hand slid over my naked bottom and squeezed me gently. "I had other motives for hiring you."

Surprised, I arched my neck so I could look into his eyes. "Are you saying you hired me because you were attracted to me?"

"I didn't think so at the time," he admitted, looking boyishly rueful. "But looking back on it, yeah. When you walked onto the photo shoot—before you told me who you were and all that shit went down—I took one look at you and decided I was going to fuck you."

I laughed and hit his chest playfully. "How romantic of you. And presumptuous."

He shrugged, his own grin teasing. "Presumptuous, huh?"

I thought about the fact that he was still inside me and I sighed in defeat. "You are so arrogant."

"Pot, meet Kettle."

Shocked that he thought so, I whispered, "I'm not arrogant."

"Baby, you wouldn't let just anybody near you, and I'm not just talking guys. I'm talking friends, family, too. You place a high value on your friendship and on your body. And you should."

"Self-worth is not arrogance."

He eyed me contemplatively. "Are you good in bed?"

After last night he even had to ask? "Uh . . . yeah."

He smiled. "Are you good at your job?"

"Hell yeah."

"If you wanted a man, do you think he would fuck you?"

I thought about it, about my history with men, and how (with the exception of Caine) I was the one who called the shots. "Probably. Not all."

"But most."

I shrugged.

"See? Arrogant."

"Confident," I argued, but I could see what he was getting at. "Okay. So you're confident . . . with a touch of arrogance." Bemused, I stared at the ceiling in thought. "I never thought of myself as arrogant before."

Caine's fingers brushed along my jaw, bringing my gaze back to his. "Arrogance can be obnoxious when it's not earned. But if you're good at something and you know it, then it's fake and a waste of time to pretend that you're not."

I found myself smiling at his logic. "You know, some people are good at something and they don't realize how good they are at it. It's called being humble and modest."

He shook his head, grinning as he pushed me onto my back. "I'm neither of those things. It sounds boring."

My answering laughter was caught between his hungry lips.

CHAPTER 21

The sight of Henry perched on my desk caused me to hesitate a little as I returned from the copy room. I knew even before noting that curious smile of his that he would want to know what was going on between Caine and me.

But it wasn't up to me to discuss my boss's personal life with his friends (even if I happened to *be* his personal life), and after spending an absolutely amazing day with Caine all day yesterday, I didn't want to ruin the newfound intimacy between us.

I slowed to a stop in front of Henry and gave him a knowing look. "Mr. Lexington."

He grinned. "Lexie." He cocked his head to the side in thought. "You know, if you'd been smart about it and chosen this guy"—he pointed to himself—"your name could eventually have been Lexie Lexington."

I snorted. "All I'd need were cowboy boots and a broken heart and I'd be a country singer."

Henry's eyebrows drew together. "Huh. You're right." He chuckled. "And a very beautiful one at that."

"Henry, stop flirting with me."

"I'm just waiting to see if Mr. Carraway comes bursting out of the doors to tell me to stay away from you. He's awfully possessive of his PA."

Sighing, I nudged him off my desk. "Why don't you stop with the joking around and just say what it is you want to say?"

He eyed me carefully. "Caine is a good friend. I knew something was going on between you two from the start, and although he's never been the most forthcoming guy, he was weirdly cagey about you. And I wasn't joking about the whole possessive thing. You have no idea how many times he bit my head off when I mentioned how attractive you are. It came as no surprise to me to find you two going at each other on Saturday night."

I crossed my arms over my chest. "I didn't think it *would* be a surprise to you. I knew what you were up to the night of the Andersons' ball. Really, Henry, you should consider leaving banking for matchmaking."

He smirked. "So you two are together. No surprise. To anyone. You have to know most of his staff has been speculating about you two since the beginning."

Uncomfortable at the thought, I frowned. "You didn't tell anyone, did you?"

"No." He stepped toward me. "Which brings me to my point. Why is it a secret? I know Caine well enough to know he could give a fuck if anyone knew he was sleeping with his PA, so that's not the reason for the secrecy."

And there it was. The question I'd seen burning in his eyes the moment I saw him perched on my desk. "Henry, if Caine wants to tell you his business, he will. Ask. And see. What you don't do is ask me. I'll never betray his confidence."

Henry studied me a moment, all humor and teasing leaving him. "You care about him," he murmured.

I didn't reply. There was no need. I'd worked out a while ago that Henry Lexington was more perceptive than he let on.

"Lexie," he said, his voice low, concerned, "Caine isn't . . . No matter how he feels for you . . . don't expect . . ."

My heart was pounding in my chest. "Don't expect what?"

"Just . . ." He reached up to clasp my shoulder in a comforting gesture. "You're a good person, and I'm glad you've got his back . . . but I don't want you to get hurt."

Uneasiness settled over me, and I fought desperately to push it back. Henry's opinions were based on what *he* knew of Caine, but he didn't know how his friend acted around me.

He didn't know that this weekend was a breakthrough for us.

I held on to my confidence, letting it bite back at the uncertainty. "I won't," I promised.

"I'm still not sure it's a good idea for us to be seen together here." I glanced warily around us.

It was a warm Thursday afternoon and Caine and I had been in Beacon Hill for a brunch meeting. To my surprise he'd suggested we stick around during our lunch hour, some of which we passed with a stroll through the public gardens. We walked over the bridge, watching tour guides pedal by on the swan boats.

"I think as long as we don't start groping each other, we'll be fine," Caine said.

My eyes flew to his face at the irritation in his words. Sure enough, the telltale sign of his annoyance was in the twitch of muscles in his jaw.

It had been nearly a week since the party and I'd never felt closer to Caine. However, this was the first sign he'd shown me that hiding our relationship bothered him.

I kept my silence, not sure how to address the issue since there was really nothing we could do about it. Of course, I knew we couldn't go on like this forever, but until I had some sure sign from Caine of the permanency of our relationship, I saw no point in taking on the headache of trying to work out how to deal with my father's family.

Just *thinking* about it gave me a headache. I sighed and stepped off the path, the grass tickling the exposed parts of my feet as I wandered down to the lake edge to watch the ducks and geese. A squirrel, completely unconcerned by my presence, shot by my feet and scurried up a nearby weeping willow tree. I tilted my face up to the sun and closed my eyes.

A few seconds later Caine's arm brushed mine.

"What are you thinking?" he said.

"How peaceful it is in here. How uncomplicated." I opened my eyes to meet his curious gaze. "People jogging, people sunbathing, people doing yoga, strolling, sleeping, relaxing. The worries get left outside on the street. They pick them back up as soon as they walk out of here."

"And what are you worried about?"

Honestly, everything, I thought. *You, me, my grandfather, my job*. None of it was weighed down by the solidity of any security. Not one thing was permanent. Not me and Caine, and certainly not my position in his company, because if we ended, then my career ended. And my grandfather . . . My relationship with him was as uncertain as it was secretive. I could leave Boston and it would be like our days together had never happened.

I tried to shake off the sudden melancholy, wondering how I could go from being so happy to so scared within the span of five minutes.

I gave Caine a small smile. "Nothing."

His gaze sharpened, as though he didn't believe me. He moved toward me and just as he did I felt a wet plop hit my head.

My eyes widened as Caine's flew to my hair. "No," I said in denial.

His lips twitched. "Yes."

Horrified, I gave a little hysterical laugh. "Please tell me . . . a bird did not just shit on my head."

Caine gave a bark of laughter.

"Caine!" I watched him give in to his amusement, and if it hadn't been for the smelly bird poop in my hair, I would have been delighted to see him laugh. However, this was not amusing! I grimaced, raising a hand to my hair but afraid to touch it to discover where the mess had occurred. "It's not funny." I slapped him across the arm and that just made him laugh harder. "You choose now to be immature? I have bird shit in my hair!"

"Stop it," he breathed, wiping tears of laughter from his eyes. He choked on his mirth, taking a step toward me. "Keep saying that and I won't be able to stop laughing."

"It's not funny." I wrinkled my nose. "It's vile."

He smiled, his gaze going to the mess. "You were just so serious and then . . ."

"Bird poop," I finished. He choked again and I held up my hand in warning. "Don't even. I have to go back to the office.

I can't go with—" I cut myself off, not wanting to set his hilarity off again by using the phrase *bird shit*.

Suddenly the humor of it hit me.

Caine Carraway laughed like a schoolboy over bird poop. Who knew?

As he watched my lips twitch, Caine's demeanor warmed with tenderness. "We'll head up to my apartment . . ." He looked around, his gaze arrested on something. "For now . . ."

Confused, I watched him stride back over the path and stop at a bench where two college-age kids were sitting. He said something to them and then pulled out his wallet. I watched as he handed them money and in return they handed him their water bottles.

Warmth flooded my chest as Caine came back to me. "How much did those cost?" I eyed the bottles.

"Ten bucks." He shrugged. "But they'll wash it out so you don't have to walk to my apartment with bird shit in your hair."

"My hero."

He threw me a warning look that did nothing to dispel my secret giddiness. "Just lower your head."

I did as he said, smiling all the while as he very carefully poured the water into my hair and gently worked the bird poop out. A few minutes later, he squeezed the excess water out of my hair and eased my head back. My gaze appreciative, I dug in my purse and pulled out the mini hand gel I kept in there.

"Thanks." He took it, slathering the stuff over his hands.

"No, thank *you*." I gazed upward to his apartment building, visible on Arlington. "Do we have time for me to shampoo?"

"We'll make time. It's not every day my PA gets crapped on."

Our eyes met and that warmth flooded through my whole body now as we grinned at each other.

Just like that . . . all my earlier worries were crushed by the return of my hope.

Usually when I stepped foot onto the redbrick-paved, tree-lined sidewalk of Charles Street, I was in my element. It was my favorite street in Boston with its quaint gas lamps, antique stores, restaurants, and boutiques. There was something fresh in the air there, and much like the gardens, it was like wandering into a little oasis from city life.

Yet the content calm I usually felt walking down Charles Street was gone.

Two weeks had passed since the weekend I'd spent with Caine, and although he seemed done with throwing up walls between us, he also seemed done with keeping us a secret. Something I hadn't agreed on.

I glanced around the street, busy because our gorgeous summer was still going strong and it was a Saturday. This was also Caine's neighborhood, which meant we were more likely to run into someone we knew here. Someone who would wonder what Caine was doing dressed in jeans and a T-shirt wandering down the street with his PA by his side. I, also, was not dressed for work, having reverted to my shorts, tank top, and flip-flops.

It was Caine's idea to spend the day shopping. It was Henry's mother's birthday next week and he needed to buy her something. It was not my idea to accompany him, but when Caine wanted something he could be pretty persuasive . . . with his mouth. And okay, his tongue.

I squirmed, remembering his method of persuasion in the bed this morning.

I really needed some willpower.

I wondered if it was for sale on Charles Street.

"If someone sees us, they see us." Caine sighed, obviously annoyed.

Clearly my anxiety had not gone unnoticed. "We're playing a dangerous game here," I argued.

"Really?" He stopped to peer down into the basement store window where ladies' clothing was displayed. "I thought we were walking down a fucking street."

Oh, he was cursing. He was pissed.

"Caine—"

"That would look good on you." He changed the subject, jerking his chin down toward the teal dress. It had a conservative cut, but the material was extremely clingy. Classy but sexy.

"However, it would not look good on my credit card statement."

In answer, Caine slipped his hand into mine, causing me to look around quickly to see if anyone was watching. He didn't seem to notice my wariness because he was too busy leading me down the stairs into the boutique.

"What are you doing?" I said.

"You're trying the dress on."

I frowned, confused by his actions. Was he just trying to ignore the argument that had been about to brew between us? "No, I'm not."

The willowy saleswoman approached us with a gleam in her dark eyes as she took in the sight of Caine. A few weeks ago the modellike young thing with her sculpted cheekbones, perfect Afro, and silky coffee skin would have caused a sharp streak of possessiveness to bolt through me. Not now. Sure, I still felt a thrill go through me that I was the one who'd just rolled out of bed with him, but the jealousy that had come from a lack of reassurance was muted now. It was manageable. And I realized that Caine hadn't gone at all caveman on me these last few weeks either.

Progress.

So when he pointed to the dress and said, "Size six," I humored him.

Thirty seconds later I found myself stuffed into a tiny dressing room.

I spun the tag over on the dress and balked at the price.

Yeah, there was no way I was buying this freaking dress no matter how good it looked on me.

I huffed and yanked my tank top off.

"You look so familiar to me," I heard the saleswoman say to Caine.

I practically rolled my eyes at the purr in her words.

Caine didn't reply.

I smirked.

Certainty.

The word made me relax as I thought about it. I wouldn't feel that certainty if I didn't feel sure of Caine's feelings for me. Although we hadn't discussed changing the terms of our affair, there had also been no more mention of it coming to an end. We didn't want it to end. *I* didn't want it to end. Ever.

I froze middressing.

I was falling in love with him.

"Do you work around here?" the salesgirl tried again.

"Close by," he said, and then the privacy curtain moved a little, jolting me out of my breathless realization. "Are you done?"

I sought to sound normal and not at all overwhelmed by a life-altering recognition of my feelings. I cleared my throat.

"Unless the dress is supposed to be worn with my boobs hanging out, no."

"Smart-ass," he muttered, but I could hear his amusement in the word. Just as I tugged the dress up, Caine slipped inside the dressing room, taking up way too much space.

I stared up into his face, suddenly impatient for the right time to tell him how I felt.

I'd never been in love before. When was the right time to say it?

Caine was too busy checking me out in the dress to deduce that my thoughts had gotten mushy. "You look beautiful."

I flushed with pleasure and smoothed my hands down the gorgeous material of the dress. "Thank you."

He reached for me, coasting his own hands down my waist until they settled on my hips. He gave me a little tug until I was pressed up against him. "You're getting this dress."

I ran my hands up his arms and gently let him down regarding any fantasies he was creating about me in this dress. "No, I'm not. The price tag . . . it's extortion."

"Who said you're buying?" He made a move toward the curtain, but I tightened my hold on him.

"Caine, no." I shook my head adamantly. "You are not—"

He shrugged out of my grasp with an imperious rise of his right eyebrow and then disappeared out of the dressing room.

"Caine," I hissed.

Cursing under my breath, I began to remove the dress, my hands stilling when I heard him say to the salesgirl, "We'll take it."

I huffed and shrugged back into my own clothes. By the time I got out of the changing room, it was too late. He'd bought the dress. I kept my silence as we walked out of the store, my new dress inside the paper bag dangling from my wrist, but as soon as we were back up onto street level, I stopped.

Caine glanced over at me and sighed at whatever he saw on my face. "What?"

"Why did you do that when I asked you not to?"

"Because you looked good in it and I wanted to buy you it." He sighed again. "Lexie, I've never bought you anything before."

"So?"

"So last week you bought me a movie and a book just because you thought I might like them."

I was still confused. "So?"

"So the week before that you bought me a bunch of cushions and shit I don't need for my apartment and for my office."

I grinned. I had done that. I'd finally felt confident that I could introduce a little "nesting" into his life. "That sounds less like a gift, and more like an annoyance."

Caine gave a huff of laughter. "True. But it was still a gift. And you did it just because. The dress? It's just because." His eyes suddenly smoldered and I melted under them. "And because I'd like to fuck you in it."

A delicious shiver rippled over me at the thought. "So it's a gift for the both of us?"

"Yeah. One that will hopefully keep on giving."

I laughed and moved to lean into him, completely forgetting where we were.

"Alexa?"

The familiar voice stopped me. My pulse raced as I spun around to face my grandfather.

Although we'd spoken on the phone, we hadn't seen each

other in weeks. Caine's revelation held me back from arranging a tête-à-tête with my grandfather. Not too long ago I'd cherished them. But after discovering the truth, I dreaded meeting up with Grandpa. So I put it off again and again. I suspected my grandfather was blaming my relationship with Caine for my distance with him. It had only increased his disapproval. Seeing the look on Grandpa's face when his gaze darted beyond me to Caine, I knew that disapproval hadn't lessened any. I'd always thought his feelings were born from concern, but now I was questioning everything. Was Grandpa really worried for me or was he just worried that somehow my closeness with Caine was going to unleash the secrets we'd all buried?

"Gran—" The word was abruptly cut off at the sudden appearance of my grandmother as she came striding out of the jewelry store next to us. I tried to hide my reaction, pretending all the while that my heart wasn't banging away in my chest.

Adele Holland's face hinted at what must have been her youthful beauty. Her style and perfectly coiffed ash blond hair and tip-tilted crystal blue eyes were still very attractive. She looked at her husband and then at me and scowled in confusion. Caine edged behind me, drawing her gaze, and that was when understanding paled her features.

Of course she knew who Caine was. I watched as she surmised that *he* was the reason for the awkward tension in the air.

"Edward?" she whispered in question, looking anxious and scared, and much less of the dragon lady everyone said she was.

"Well, we should be going." Grandpa cleared his throat

and gave us a jerky nod. "Mr. Carraway, miss." He took my grandmother's arm and led her past us.

I stared at the spot he'd just been standing in, and ignored that ache that split through me. It always woke that insidious little whisper that taunted me. *Not loved enough by your father, your mother, your grandfather . . . or by Caine.*

I felt alone. Alone, unloved, and with no one to trust.

"Alexa?"

I glanced up at Caine to see his eyes were shadowed with anger.

At the sight of it I shook off my hurt and gave him a fake smile.

That only made him madder.

Without a word he started stalking down the street in the opposite direction my grandparents had taken. I started after him, my steps slower.

And then quite abruptly Caine whipped around and marched back toward me. Features etched with determination, he yanked me roughly to him and crushed his mouth down over mine. I made a noise of surprise in the back of my throat before my instincts took over. I couldn't help sinking into his kiss.

When he finally let me go we were both breathing hard. Caine smoothed his thumb over my cheek, his eyes still dark with passion and anger. "*I* could give a fuck who saw that."

My answer was to wrap my arms around him, and to my pleasure, Caine held me tightly.

Standing there on Charles Street, being hugged by him, I was choked by emotion. Not only had I realized today that I loved Caine; I also finally understood why he hated keeping us a secret.

He knew what his revelation about my grandfather had

done to me, and he knew what it did to me that Grandpa couldn't acknowledge me in public. And I think he knew that I was questioning Grandpa's love for me.

And Caine did not want to be the guy who treated me to the same.

He wasn't ashamed to be with me, to know me, to want me in his life.

My arms tightened around him.

Maybe, God, just maybe . . . I wasn't the only one falling in love.

CHAPTER 22

"You look gorgeous. Let me take a photo of the two of you together." Effie held up her iPhone and began snapping away before Caine or I could protest.

Laughter bubbled between my lips as I glanced up at Caine. He was wearing his "I'm holding on to my patience only because it's Effie" expression. Lately he wore that expression a lot around his neighbor. "Do you think she thinks we're going to the prom?" I muttered, teasing him.

He shot me a look. "Make it stop."

"Caine, stop scowling," Effie chastised from across the room.

I snorted, grabbed his arm, and grinned for the camera.

Effie was chuckling so hard I doubted any of those photos would be blur free.

"You're both hilarious." Caine extricated himself from my grasp, shooting us a warning look we both knew he didn't mean. I think secretly he liked the two of us teasing him. "I'm going to call down for the car." He strode out of the room, his shoulders lined with tension.

Okay, so maybe *tonight* he wasn't enjoying the teasing.

We were both dressed in formal wear—Caine in his beautiful black Ralph Lauren tuxedo, and I was wearing a Jenny Packham dress I'd made the mistake of showing to Effie two weeks ago, who had then showed it to Caine, who had then bought it for me.

I'd attempted to argue with him about it. I didn't want him thinking I needed or expected him to buy me expensive gifts. However, as I'd discovered earlier with the flights and the hotel situation in Seattle, Caine didn't argue about money.

He said his piece and then he switched off.

Which was seriously annoying.

But less so when a beautiful dress showed up on my doorstep.

So kill me, I could be shallow sometimes. I'd worked with a media photographer for years, mostly in fashion. I'd been exposed to the most beautiful pieces of clothes ever designed and had a real appreciation for the artistry in it. We were talking about a Jenny Packham. The pale green gown had a timeless quality about it—its sleek silhouette was a perfect match for my tall physique. It had delicate silver and crystal beading in a beltlike design around my middle, a plunging neckline that still somehow managed to be classy, and along the bottom line of the dress the fabric was shot through with silver.

I felt like a princess.

Caine was not acting like a white knight tonight, however.

The last few weeks together had been spectacular. A whirlwind of passion, intimacy, laughter . . . I'd never been happier. And I thought Caine felt the same way, but he was broody tonight, and I had to wonder if it was because of our earlier discussion.

Tonight we were attending the Vanessa Van Hay Delaney Benefit for Alzheimer's. It was hosted by Michelle and Edgar Delaney, the children of Vanessa Delaney, a woman who'd been a pillar of Boston society for over fifty years before she was diagnosed with Alzheimer's. She passed away a few years after her diagnosis, and ever since, every year, the Delaneys hosted their benefit to fund finding a cure for Alzheimer's. Only Boston's very elite were invited to come share their philanthropy, and it was one of the few cases where Caine didn't mind that anyone knew he'd donated money to a charity, because anyone with any power or influence in the city was there doing the same thing.

His reputation would remain intact.

This was the first event I'd be attending as his "date," and we both had discussed how people would speculate. We had no intention of announcing that I was his *actual* date, especially with there being media people at the event, but I was sure to draw curiosity being on Caine's arm. I'd asked that we not confirm our relationship until I had a chance to hash *everything* out with my grandfather. In fact, I hadn't wanted to attend the event at all, but Caine was growing increasingly frustrated by the secrecy surrounding us. It made him feel like we were doing something to be ashamed of. So I'd agreed to go with him under the stipulation that I was there as his PA until I'd had a chance to confront my grandfather and then warn him there was a possibility of his family finding out about me. Caine hadn't been happy about the compromise, but he did agree to it.

Now I had to wonder at the reason for his broodiness. He'd been so insistent about me going to the event with him. Now he was acting like he'd rather I didn't attend.

"Hmm." Effie shoved her iPhone back into the pocket of her kimono. "Someone's in a mood tonight."

I grimaced. "Yay for me."

She laughed. "It'll be fine. Just promise him a good time when you get back from the party and it'll cheer him right up."

"Ugh, Effie, he's like your grandkid."

"He's a man. A man's a man."

I shook my head at her open-minded attitude, and wondered how she'd ever survived the fifties as a teenager.

"Let's go," Caine called from the hallway.

Effie and I walked out of the penthouse after him and he gave Effie a kiss on the cheek. "Night, Effie."

"Night, sweetheart." She patted him affectionately on the cheek. "Enjoy yourself, handsome. If you don't when you've got the most gorgeous woman in the room on your arm, then there's something wrong with you."

He gave her a small, almost tired smile and nodded in her direction.

I hugged her and we walked her down the hall to her penthouse. As we stepped into the elevator, she gave me a knowing wink from her doorway. I grinned but immediately sobered at the imperious, questioning look Caine shot me. The elevator doors closed.

"What was the wink about?" he said.

"Oh, Effie thought I would improve your mood by assuring you that there was something to look forward to when we got back from the party."

He groaned. "Sex advice from Effie. That's just wrong."

"That's what I said." I shrugged nonchalantly. "But I'm also one step ahead of her, so I didn't need the advice."

Caine raised an eyebrow. "Oh?"

I gave him a slow, wicked smile. "I'm not wearing any underwear."

The elevator doors opened before he could wipe the surprise off his face and I chuckled in triumph as I walked past him and out into the garage where a driver was waiting for us.

"I could kill you."

I smiled smugly. "You have two minutes to think of anything but me."

Caine cut me a smoldering look. "Difficult to do when you're sitting next to me not wearing any underwear."

We were in the car and we were only minutes from the Delaneys' house. Taking pity on him, I tried to help. "Hummus. Rom coms. That tsking sound that Linda makes all the time—"

"That's not how it works. You're supposed to make me think of things that don't turn me on, not things that I generally don't like."

"Yeesh. You are moody tonight." I sighed. "Fine. Henry and Effie making sweet, sweet love."

Caine's features were frozen as the car pulled to a stop. "That was just mean."

"But it worked, right?"

"Hell yes, it worked. Now I'll be disturbed for the rest of the evening."

The Delaneys' home was much like the Andersons' mansion—over-the-top wealth that intimidated the heck out of you. However, at least I'd gotten the shock and awe over with at the Andersons', and as Caine led me inside with a hand on my lower back, gently guiding me, I didn't feel as uncomfortable as last time. Perhaps it was because Caine was with me now, and I never felt more safe than I did when I was with him.

"Alexa, looking more beautiful than ever," Henry said as he approached us in the main ballroom. Elegant dinner tables had been set up all around one half of the room. At the other end of the room, there was a stage. What seemed to be a small orchestra was set up offside on the left, and there was a dance floor in front of the stage.

Henry drew my gaze from the general splendor of the ballroom to him and his voluptuous and somehow familiar redheaded date. "Henry," I murmured as he kissed both my cheeks. His hand rested on my waist as he did so, but I knew there was nothing in the gesture.

However, when I pulled back I could see the storm clouds gathering in the eyes of an already wired Caine.

The past few weeks had proven my theory correct, and Caine had been noticeably more laid-back when I was around the opposite sex.

Henry was a completely different matter. The man was a natural flirt, and I understood he didn't mean anything by it. But his flirting with me bothered Caine. His laughing with me bothered Caine. His touching me bothered Caine, and his being anywhere in my general vicinity bothered Caine.

This bothered *me*.

Henry was Caine's closest friend. I did not want to cause problems between the two of them. I had the suspicion that the problem had existed between them before I arrived on the scene. There was a story behind Caine's weirdness and I was more than curious to find out what that story was. I just hadn't found the right time to mention it yet.

Catching the look on Caine's face, Henry practically rolled his eyes and backed off. He put his arm around his date and nudged her forward. "Caine, Lexie, this is Nadia Ray. She's a local weather girl."

Recognition hit me. Nadia Ray had caused quite a stir a few months ago when she appeared on our televisions. The ratings at WCVB had gone through the roof since she joined the weather team. "It's nice to meet you," I said as Caine gave her a clipped nod in greeting.

She smiled a little nervously, and I wondered if she was feeling like a fish out of water. I knew that feeling well. "This place is insane, right?" I said, bugging my eyes out humorously.

Nadia gave a huff of relieved laughter. "It's not what I'm used to."

"I hear you." I nodded, scanning the room. My eyes fell on a waiter who was serving appetizers. "But the mini crab rolls at these things are usually to die for."

"Nowhere near as good as the crab rolls we used to get at this little deli on campus at Wharton." Henry closed his eyes in exaggerated blissful reflection. "Oh, those were the days."

I smirked. "Crab rolls. That's what you remember most about business school?"

"I didn't say that." His eyes popped open as he grinned. "The women were also very memorable."

"Oh, so it was the *crabs* you remember most?"

He snorted. "I wasn't that bad. Okay . . . I was almost that bad."

"How did you put up with him? Or were you even worse than him?" I said to Caine.

Caine didn't join in on our teasing. If anything he looked more uncomfortable than ever.

And I knew why. I sighed in exasperation. "Caine never talks about Wharton. It's like he's wiped it from existence."

Henry sobered as he and Caine shared a dark look I didn't understand. Uneasiness moved through me, but before I could say anything Caine beat me to it.

"We'll get you a crab roll in a minute," Caine said, returning to our earlier conversation. "First we have to go over and say hello to the Delaneys."

He was already physically guiding me in that direction before I could protest. I shot Nadia and Henry an apologetic smile over my shoulder and then hissed, "That was rude."

His fingers curled into my dress. "Excuse me?"

"I think it would have been nice for us to hang out with them a little longer. Nadia is clearly not comfortable being here, and since I know what that feels like, it might have been nice to spend time with her."

"We're here on business."

"I thought we were here because it's a charity event."

"We're here because if the Delaneys invite you to an event, you go. They own a third of the real estate in Boston, Philadelphia, and nearly all of Providence. That's a lot of money, and I'm in the business of making money, so I don't ignore them. So yes, it's business."

I was stiff against him as we neared the host and hostess. "I wish I knew what was wrong with you tonight."

Caine didn't reply. He just pasted on a polite mask and introduced me to people who peered at me speculatively and then turned their attention elsewhere.

I sighed inwardly, my eyes searching for a waiter.

I needed a drink if I was going to survive this crowd *and* Mr. Moody.

While Caine was busy talking with one of his board of directors, Henry's father and some investment guy I'd never met before, I managed to subtly back away from the group so I could rescue Nadia, who Henry had abandoned beside the ballroom entrance for whatever reason.

"You look like you need this," I said as I approached and offered her a fresh glass of champagne.

Nadia smiled gratefully, a gorgeous smile that along with her figure had gone a long way to making her the most popular weather girl in Massachusetts history. "Thank you. Henry was pulled away by some catty society girl and there really was no polite way for him to get out of it."

"Henry's a catch around these parts." I smiled sympathetically. "The women that have grown up in his circles think of him as theirs."

"I'm getting that."

"Honestly, I think they bore him," I reassured her.

"Well, I'm from Beacon Falls, Connecticut, which is a slightly different crowd of people. Definitely not boring." She grinned dryly.

My mouth fell open. "I'm from Chester."

"No way." She chuckled. "We grew up, like . . . what? An hour from each other?"

"It's a small world."

From there we launched into conversation, talking about growing up in Connecticut, about college, about Boston, and our favorite places in the city. What I liked about her was that she didn't ask me about my relationship with Caine, just as I didn't pry about hers with Henry. Nadia didn't even comment when the stunning Phoebe Billingham floated by in Chanel Couture and threw me a look that would have felled a mountain lion.

That was awkward.

What was not awkward was conversation with Nadia. We clicked, and in the back of my mind I was already cursing Henry for introducing me to her, knowing that our friendship probably wouldn't last, given his reputation with women.

Nadia and I could have chatted all night with each other, and I was pretty sure we would have if Henry hadn't come back to claim his date.

"I'm sorry to interrupt, ladies." Henry reached out and gently tugged Nadia toward him. "My father is finally free from the bigwigs and I want to introduce you to him."

Nadia paled. "Your father?" She shot me a pleading look, but there was nothing I could do but offer her a bolstering smile as Henry dragged her away.

"Finally," a familiar voice grumbled behind me as a hand wrapped around my wrist and jerked me backward.

I stumbled out into the hallway to face my very anxious grandfather. "Grandpa?" I looked around, but the hallway was nearly empty, only occupied by staff and security.

Without a word Grandpa spun on his heel and started walking. I hesitated a moment, unsure if I should follow him. That sharp ache of betrayal knifed across my chest as I watched his departing back.

That was when I realized I was fed up with living with the uncertainty I felt about him. I hurried to follow him, keeping up as he took a corner and strode down a much narrower hallway. He stopped at large sliding doors and pushed them open. "Inside," he said quietly, darting in.

I found myself in a beautiful study. Books lined the walls on intricately carved dark wooden shelving. An equally stunning library desk sat in the corner, a burgundy leather armchair chair behind it. A sofa with cashmere throws strewn stylishly over it sat before a grand fireplace.

The doors slid shut behind me.

Dressed in a superbly cut tux and sporting a new and very distinguished short beard, Edward Holland looked every inch the respectable gentleman. I wasn't so sure anymore that it wasn't all just a facade.

He scowled at me in disapproval. "Your grandmother and I arrived only fifteen minutes ago and already someone has speculated in our presence about your relationship with Caine. What the hell were you thinking coming here as his date?"

My cheeks burned. I felt like a scolded child. "We haven't said I'm his date."

"Oh, well, that makes it okay, then."

"Don't." I shook my head stubbornly. "Obviously now is not the time to discuss this, but we do *need* to discuss it. Caine isn't comfortable hiding our relationship anymore and neither am I. To be with him I'm going to have to be a part of this community, and people are going to question my connection to the Hollands. We don't have to decide right away whether we lie to everyone or not . . . but it is time you stop lying to your wife."

"I never wanted you to be a part of this. I didn't want these people, my people, to hurt you." He gazed at me in concern. "You and Caine have grown serious, then?"

"Yes." I took a step toward him. "I know this is huge, and I know you'll need time to think it over and prepare yourself. I just wanted you to know that with the way things are progressing, it may not be too long before questions are asked and I'd like to know how to answer those. I believe you'll have to discuss that with my grandmother before a decision can be made."

He ran a hand through his short hair. "This is going to be a bloody mess," he muttered quietly.

All this secrecy just so he didn't have to put up with drama.

That was when I snapped. "I know, you know. He told me."

Grandpa frowned. "What are you talking about?"

As much as I hated to acknowledge that the only family I had left had done something terrible, Grandpa's actions with Eric were despicable, and I needed to know why he did it. I found the courage to ask something that had plagued me for the last few weeks. "Why did you do it?" I said, my words soft, tentative. "Why did you cover it up?"

Understanding slackened Grandpa's features seconds before regret darkened his eyes. "I was protecting my family," he said softly, his defeated expression suggesting he knew how weak an excuse that was. "It wasn't until afterward, when I discovered Caine's father had . . . Well, the guilt and the shame . . . I couldn't rid myself of it. The only way I knew to alleviate it was to exact some kind of justice for Caine. My only way to do that without hurting the rest of the family was to disinherit and disown my son. Losing his money and status." Grandpa shook his head. "That hurt Alistair more than anything else could."

"Why didn't you tell me about your involvement in the cover-up?"

"Because I didn't want you to look at me the way you're looking at me right now."

"I don't know how else to look at you. I don't know if I can believe anything about you anymore. Honestly I don't even know if you love me."

"Alexa, of course—"

I moved past him, sliding the doors open and cutting him off because suddenly I knew I wasn't ready to hear his answer. I wasn't ready to believe it. "I have to get back before Caine wonders where I am."

Striding toward the ballroom, I willed my heart rate to slow down, but it wouldn't. My hands trembled as I returned to the ballroom, and this had everything to do with the strange sense of foreboding that had come over me.

It never occurred to me until I faced my grandfather that there was a huge possibility that I'd have to give Grandpa up once the truth came out. I didn't know how to forgive him just yet . . . And even if I did I couldn't imagine his family would want him to have anything more to do with me, and I was starting to think that perhaps the whole reason the idea of revealing the truth upset him was that he knew he'd have to choose . . .

I stopped, staring dazedly around the room.

. . . and he would choose *them* over *me*.

Like always I'd be second best.

Needing Caine, I scoured the room for him, but I couldn't see him.

"He left the room with Regina Mason."

I glanced over my shoulder at Phoebe, who was standing with one arm wrapped around her waist while she casually sipped her champagne. I would have expected there to be spite in her eyes, but to my surprise there was only begrudged sympathy.

I stiffened at the sympathy. "Left?"

She nodded her pretty head toward where I'd just come in.

I decided not to mention that it was slightly stalkerish of her to be watching Caine, and instead nodded my thanks and headed back out into the hall. They were nowhere to be seen, which meant searching. I decided to start by checking the rooms on the right off the large entrance hall.

My heart was beating faster now for a different reason.

Stop. You're being silly. Caine would never . . . There will be a rational explanation.

Hearing the rumbling murmurs of a male voice down the corridor, I walked quietly along it, trying to calm my trembling. As I neared a door I recognized the baritones as Caine's. But I didn't recognize the female voice.

"After all these years that's really quite disappointing," she said as I approached.

I stopped in the doorway and peered through the narrow opening into what looked like a cozy sitting room.

All the air seemed to go out of my lungs.

Caine was standing by the window and an attractive woman was pressed against him. He held her by her upper arms as she stroked his chest with her fingertips. "Regina," he murmured.

Uncertainty froze me as I waited to see how this situation would unfold.

"You're really saying no to me." She pouted her surgically enhanced lips at him. My eyes narrowed on her unnaturally smooth face. This woman was much older than I'd first thought. Who the hell was she?

Get your hands off him!

I prepared to barge in.

Caine gently pressed her away, but his features were hard. For the first time I noticed how hostile he was. Extremely so. "I really am."

She raised an eyebrow at him as she smoothed her hair back off her face. "You know that's pretty risky."

He scowled dangerously. "Don't play games with me, Regina. I will ruin you."

As if she suddenly realized who she was dealing with, Regina gave him a tight smile. "No need to get vicious, Caine."

Watching the muscle flex in Caine's jaw, I decided enough was enough. I didn't know who this woman was or what was going on, but I wasn't leaving them to this cozy little argument. I pushed the door open and they both looked around with sharp jerks of their heads.

Caine's eyes narrowed on me.

Regina smiled smugly.

I met her smugness with a steely stare of my own. "If you'll excuse us," I said with all the imperiousness I could muster.

Taking the hint, she moved to pass me, her beautiful sapphire gown swishing around her legs as she did so. She flashed me a catty smile, one that was tight more out of physical limitations than from emotion.

The door closed behind her and I looked at Caine in question. "What was that all about?"

Instead of answering me he glowered in outrage. "Were you fucking spying on me?"

I flinched at the nastiness in his tone. "No, I was not. I had an altercation with my grandfather and I needed you. Phoebe told me you'd gone this way."

I thought my explanation would cool his temper, but to my surprise his fury seemed only to be increasing. Far beyond what the situation warranted. I watched him pace the floor like a tormented bull, surprised that smoke wasn't billowing out of his nostrils.

That uneasiness I'd been feeling transformed into dread, a heavy, sinking dread in the pit of my stomach. "Caine, what's going on?" I said quietly. "Who was she?"

"It was nothing." He stopped suddenly and I saw it happen. I saw him closing down, shutting me out. "Let's go back to the party."

"No." I stumbled in front of the door, blocking the exit. "You're going to tell me what's going on here."

"None of your business, Alexa."

"See, that's where you're wrong. I'm pretty sure you'd want to know if I was locked away in a room with some guy while he held me in his arms."

His dark eyes flashed. "You're misconstruing the situation, and I don't have the time or the patience to deal with your unwarranted jealousy this evening."

Outrage burned in my blood. "Don't you dare speak to me like that. What the hell is wrong with you? You've been acting like a caustic bastard all night."

"Caustic bastard." He sneered. "Not very ladylike, Alexa."

"Don't." I gritted my teeth. "Don't act like this. Please."

Something in my face made his soften infinitesimally. "Not here," he finally said. "This isn't the time or the place. Let's just go back out there."

"Later, then?"

"Lexie." He moved toward me and wrapped a hand around my arm. Not sure what he was doing, I allowed him to gently tug me forward.

To my annoyance he released me only to walk out the door.

That horrible sense of foreboding was back.

CHAPTER 23

My fingernails bit into my palms as the driver pulled the car down my street.

"My apartment?" I whispered.

There was no reply from Caine.

I sucked in a huge breath, trying to ease the tightness compressing my chest.

After hours of strained conversation I should have been relieved by silence. A person might believe that silence took less energy than forced communication, but the bristling tension radiating from Caine suggested he was exerting great control to remain reticent.

The dinner at the benefit had gone by in a blur of false niceties and banal discussions that went in one ear and out the other. Singers and dancers had entertained and yet I could barely remember the pretty turn of a ballerina's pirouette. I'd ignored the concerned looks from Henry and Nadia while Caine had sat next to me only engaging in conversation with me when prodded. No one else seemed to notice his terseness, because he was universally known for it, but Henry was aware there was something wrong with his friend.

I was more than aware.

His attitude made me feel like my skin had caught on fire. It burned and itched as I tried to claw my way outside myself— outside this downward-spiraling evening into hell. Somehow I knew what was coming. My instincts were screaming at me to find some way to turn everything around. And then there was that little part of me that hoped my gut instinct was wrong.

Yet, as soon as Caine's driver turned down onto my street instead of taking us to Caine's apartment, that hope slipped out of my hands.

"Caine?" I looked at him as the car drew to a stop, wondering why that person with the coldly blank mien had come back after all these weeks. I didn't like him. I much preferred the man who'd broken through his icy facade.

Where was *he*?

And why after that strange interaction with that Regina woman had he disappeared?

"I'll walk you up," Caine said in a monotone.

The driver opened my door and I got out, murmuring my thanks. I waited, shivering in the cool air of the early morning. Instead of coming to a stop beside me, Caine marched right by me and took the stoop two stairs at a time.

Now trembling more than shivering, I moved as quickly as I could in my heels and dress, and fought the quickly rising wave of nausea inside me.

"Keys?" He held out a hand to me.

I gazed up at him.

Still blank. Still ice.

Looking away, I dug into my purse and produced the

keys. They were snatched out of my hand before I could say or do anything and Caine let us into my building.

I followed him upstairs, my heels clacking obnoxiously loud on the stairwell. Any noise in the face of his dispassionate taciturnity seemed obnoxious, if only because I was so hyperaware that to *him* it was obnoxious.

This was a man who wanted to be done with me as quickly and quietly as possible.

My dignity warred with my outrage.

I reached my front door to find Caine had opened it but was still standing out in my hallway. He gestured for me to go inside.

Indignation narrowed my eyes. "You first."

Still blank. Still ice. "I'm tired. We'll talk later."

"You first or I'll follow you back outside."

"Don't be childish." Again with the monotone.

Earlier his overreaction, his fury, had pissed me off. Now I'd give anything to have it back. "You first," I insisted.

With a long-suffering sigh Caine walked into the apartment. Bolstering myself for what was to come, I exhaled shakily and followed him in. I closed the door quietly behind me and strode down my hall and into my living room.

Caine stood staring out the window, reminding me of the first time he'd been in my place. Pain lanced across my chest. The silence between us was unbearable. It felt thick and cold and dangerous. Like if I slammed my fist against the air in front of me it would shatter and tear my skin.

I drew in a ragged breath. The noise caught Caine's ear and he glanced at me. The moonlight illuminated his face, allowing me to see that his expression had not changed.

"Who was she?" I said.

He turned around. "It doesn't matter."

"I think it does matter. If this conversation is going where I think it's going, it matters a whole lot."

"And where do you think this is going?"

"Oh no. I'm not making it that easy for you. If you want to do it, you do it yourself."

"The agreement was that this would end."

"I think we moved past that agreement a while ago."

"Since when?"

"Don't. Don't pretend like you aren't as deep in this as I am."

"We're not deep in this, Lexie. This was just . . . It was an affair. As agreed. And now it's over."

Even though I'd known it was coming, nothing prepared me for the loss I felt. My knees actually buckled and I pressed a hand to the top of my armchair for support.

My reaction caused the first flicker of emotion on Caine's face since the Delaneys'.

"It wasn't just an affair," I whispered.

"Of course it was." Monotone. *Again.*

It was like listening to someone touch polystyrene. I gritted my teeth in reaction. "Why is Mr. Cold Carraway back?" I wondered out loud, flinching at the bitterness I heard in my voice. "What secrets are you hiding? They must be big to bring this guy back. I thought I got rid of him weeks ago."

"I don't know what you're talking about. I'm only one man."

"No, you're not." I shook my head adamantly and took a step toward him. "I didn't fall in love with that man I met on a photo shoot. Or the man who was my boss for weeks."

"Alex—"

"I fell in love with Caine Carraway. I fell in the love with the man who teases me, laughs with me, listens to me, and respects me. A man who wakes me up every morning by making love to me, and then kisses me good night every evening after fucking the life out of me—like he can never get enough. No man has ever been as deep inside me as this man, in every way. And because of that when he looks at me he sees *me* like no one ever has before. That first man judged me, mistreated me. Caine Carraway did not. He made me feel safe for the first time in my whole life. I want him back. I love *him*. I want him back," I pleaded.

He wouldn't look at me. He gave me his profile, staring into my kitchen.

"Caine?"

When he finally met my gaze his eyes were blazing with emotions, all so tightly knit I knew he was in turmoil. He was angry, he was distraught, he was desperate, and he was guilty, all in equal measure.

"You don't love me." He shook his head. His voice sounded like sandpaper rasping against stone. "You can't because you don't know who I am. I never really let you."

We stared at each other and the tension between us pulled, like each of us was holding the end of a long piece of piano wire. One more tug and . . .

"Liar," I bit out finally, feeling a volcano of ugliness erupting from the pit of my stomach.

"You don't have to give me two weeks' notice. Just give me a few days to find a replacement and I'll release you from your contract."

"Coward."

His expression dulled again and he started toward me. "I'm not sticking around for this."

The smell of his cologne wrapped around me as he brushed past me, and that along with the heat of his body flooded me with memories of our time together. I'd never felt pain like it in my life. "That's right," I said, the words sounding as empty as Caine's. "Don't choose me. I've come to expect nothing less."

He hesitated a moment, his shoulders hunching up a little.

I took a tentative step toward him and whispered, "I hope your secrets keep you warm at night."

And then just like that, he shrugged whatever emotion he'd been feeling off and marched out of my apartment for the last time.

In the dark I stumbled in disbelief to my sofa, momentarily numb.

I heard the sound of his car pulling away from my street and driving off into the distance. My belly-deep sob rose to chase after it.

CHAPTER 24

"You have four new messages."

I stared stonily at my answering machine. If it were up to me I'd be ignoring the little bastard, but the blinking red light on it lit up the dark when I switched off my bedroom light. If I wanted to pretend I was going to get some sleep tonight, I was going to have to listen to the messages or delete them so the blinking would cease.

It had not been a good day.

My face was swollen and puffy. I hadn't eaten a thing. I drank two glasses of wine I'd then puked up, and because I hadn't eaten anything it was just red liquid that came back up, and that had made me want to vomit again.

My cell had rung, the chorus of Alanis Morrisette's "You Oughta Know" flooding my apartment at least a dozen times, so I'd put it on silent. That didn't work, because people just called the apartment instead and left messages on the answering machine.

If I listened to the messages I had no doubt in my mind that they would make me feel worse.

And yet I'd discovered that worse than the pain of watching the man I loved walk out on me was the cruel, grasping, cloying pain of that abysmal little thing called hope. It clung to me. It whispered in my ear.

There's still time.

He could change his mind.

When you walk into work tomorrow he'll take one look at you and he'll want you back.

I hated that hope. I hated that it made me feel so weak and broken by him. Like without him, without that hope, I'd never, ever quite be the same again.

I hated that he had that power over me.

And I hated that that stupid hope had me thinking that perhaps one of the four messages was from Caine.

He could have called to change his mind.

Sighing impatiently at my pitifulness, I stabbed a finger at the button to listen to my messages.

"You received a message today at nine oh seven . . . Lexie, it's me," my grandfather's deep voice rumbled into the room. "I hate the way we left it last night, sweetheart. Call me. We need to talk . . ." Upon listening to the irritating answer service lady's options, I deleted the message, needing to be numb from the pain he'd caused me too.

"You received a message today at ten forty-four . . . Lexie. It's Effie. What has happened? Caine wouldn't let me into his apartment this morning. He was a snippy little shit and he's never like that with me. He says he's changing the locks. What's going on? Call me right away."

The ache in my chest intensified at the panic in Effie's voice. Caine was shutting her out too. I squeezed my eyes closed, rubbing at the throb of pain behind them. What on earth had I walked in on last night? What secret was he hiding that had set him off?

I sighed and pressed the button again.

"You received a message today at two twenty . . . Hey, it's me," Rachel greeted. "I'm just calling to see how the ball went last night. I still can't believe you attend balls. Wait. Was it a ball? Or a gala? Or do you just call it a party? What is the difference and does anyone whose head isn't up their ass actually give a fuck? Did you wear the Jenny Packham, you lucky bitch? Please tell me that hot Neanderthal didn't rip it off your body and ruin a three-thousand-dollar dress. On second thought, don't tell me anything. If my jealousy increases over a certain level, I will have to end our friendship. Anyway, gorgeous, call me. I want the delicious details . . ."

Tears clogged my throat and I stubbornly swallowed them down. I'd cried enough tears today to fill a very deep well.

I was done.

I had to get a grip on myself so I could face Caine tomorrow with some goddamn dignity.

Bracing myself, I pressed the button again . . . a little breathless with anticipation.

"You received a message today at three oh two . . . Lexie." Effie's voice dashed my hope that I'd hear from Caine. "I just wanted you to know that Caine cooled down and he dropped by to see me . . . He told me what happened, sweetheart. I'm so sorry. I can't tell you how sorry. I've tried reasoning with him, but I . . . I think he's hiding something. Just . . . don't give up on him. When he goes Mr. Big Chill on me I know he's feeling things deeper than usual. It's his way of coping. I . . . Please don't give up on him . . ."

The familiar sharp stinging in my nose declared the arrival of my tears before I could halt them. The sound of Effie begging me to help someone we loved killed me. Because I wanted to . . . God, I wanted to if it meant Caine would come back to me . . .

But . . . he hadn't left a message.

There was this huge part of me that was hurt beyond repair . . . a huge part of me that was so tired of coming in last with the people I loved. A huge part of me that was sick of doing all the saving.

And I realized that more than anything right now I needed to take care of me. My whole life was up in the air . . . because of him.

I had a heart to heal and a career to fix.

I didn't know if I had it in me quite yet to fight some more for Caine.

CHAPTER 25

The look on Caine's face as he approached my desk the next morning tore apart any remnants of that hope I'd been holding on to. Although he wasn't cold, he was carefully polite.

I stood up from behind my desk as he came to a stop and there was a part of me that took pleasure at the sight of the dark circles under his eyes. His features were drawn tight with tiredness. He was still beautiful but now in an unkempt way I wished wasn't so appealing.

It was nice to know that he was affected by our breakup. However, it didn't change anything, and I could see that in the way he carefully nodded his greeting to me. "I've been in touch with an agency. They're sending a temp out on Wednesday."

Panic gripped me.

We had only today and tomorrow left together.

It made me react without thinking. "Whatever it is you're hiding, it won't change how I feel about you."

Last-ditch effort.

He stared me directly in the eye. "I'm sorry I hurt you. I am. But this is done now." He took a step back. "Of course I'll see to it that you get a month's pay and you can use me as a reference."

"Tell me you don't love me," I said quietly to his retreating back.

He froze at his door and then a few seconds later glanced over his shoulder at me. "I don't."

I slumped back into my chair as he slammed inside his office.

The hope shattered, slicing me to ribbons.

So this is what this feels like.

"Your schedule is on my computer, as are all your contacts, and notes from recent meetings that are relevant to matters that are still in progress." I put a USB drive on his desk. "I've put them all on there for you because it'll be better for your new PA to start with fresh information. If he or she has those notes it'll confuse him or her, and that could be inconvenient for you. I kept notebooks on my daily duties along with instructions, as well as your personal preferences. There's everything from standard e-mail and invite responses to your favorite dry cleaner."

I looked up from my notepad and locked eyes with a contemplative Caine.

"Thank you, Alexa. That's extremely helpful."

The careful politeness between us made me want to scream, but somehow I managed to curb that instinct, along with my inclination toward smart-assery. I wanted to end things between us with dignity. Not sarcastic shrewishness.

"You're welcome."

He looked down at the papers in front of his desk. "Do

you have any prospects for a job? I can put you in touch with the temp agency I use."

"No, thank you," I said quietly. "I think I'm going to take some time to reevaluate my career."

"That sounds like a plan."

I just managed to stop myself from rolling my eyes. How could it be that I'd had sex with this man on his desk (more than once), and now we were acting like two complete strangers?

That horrendous ache seemed to have taken up residence in every part of my body and it threatened to overpower me. I shook it off. "We have a meeting with Jeremy Ruger in forty minutes," I reminded him.

His gaze sharpened. "Ruger is obnoxious. You don't have to go to that."

I knew Ruger was obnoxious. He was also the CFO at Winton Investments, a company that had gone from being small potatoes to a major player in the financial district in the last two years since Ruger took control of the company's finances.

When Linda, Caine's CFO, had surprised him by announcing she was pregnant again and she and her husband had decided he should go back to work and she'd take some time to be with the kids, Caine started his search for a new CFO.

We'd met Ruger at the party on Saturday night, and financial genius he might be, but he was also a grubby little sleazebag who spent most of the night chasing attractive wait staff.

I didn't have to go the meeting. The truth was I probably never needed to go to more than half the lunches and meetings Caine attended. But I suspected, like his peers who also always had someone with them, he brought me along to relax the atmosphere. He always said people who were relaxed were more amenable to persuasion.

"I always come with you," I reminded him. "And honestly I want to be in on this. I have to see what's so special about this guy that you would put up with his crass jokes."

I thought Caine might protest at my being there because it would mean more time spent in my company, but he didn't.

We were leaving the building at lunchtime rush hour, and since the meeting was at a restaurant on Congress Street, we were walking there. In those crowds it would be easier to pretend that it was natural that we weren't talking to each other.

It didn't start off great. We greeted colleagues who were packing up to go out for lunch and they chatted to us as we headed for the elevator. When Caine awkwardly guided me into the crowded box, I flinched at the feel of his hand on my lower back. He must have felt me tense, because he removed his hand with whiplike speed, as though he'd just dipped it in invisible fire.

We stood together, our bodies touching because there was no way of avoiding it, and I gritted my teeth against the tension between us. Caine and I practically dove out of there when the elevator doors opened and we refused to look at each other.

Taking the main exit, Caine held the door open for me and I muttered my thanks, stepping out into the dreary day. I walked into the busy sidewalk by our building and realized I was alone. Caine had been delayed at the door, talking to someone I didn't recognize. It was a big company—I couldn't keep tabs on who absolutely everyone was.

Someone bumped into my shoulder and I stumbled back, attempting to move out of the way of the oncoming traffic of pedestrians. I looked over at Caine, saw he was on his way back to me, and stepped out onto the main sidewalk again.

The blur of a body in black brushed right up against me.

This sharp agonizing burn tore through my gut, the pain radiating throughout every nerve in my body.

Stunned, I was incapable of processing anything but the pain.

"Alexa?"

The voice penetrated and I blinked, the unfocused vision of Caine's concerned face appearing before me.

Along with the pain I suddenly became aware of this wet warmth leaking on my belly. I looked down, my hands trembling as they sought out the problem.

I felt the blood before I saw it.

"Lex—what the . . ." I heard Caine's voice.

My legs buckled, my vision flickering out.

"Lexie!"

His panicked features blinked in and out of the darkness.

"We need an ambulance! Call nine-one-one!"

The darkness swam toward me.

"Lexie, baby, hold on. Fuck, hold on."

To what? I thought before I floated away from the agony toward safety.

CHAPTER 26

There was tightness around my legs. I couldn't move them freely and it felt like I was suffocating—too warm, needing air.

I kicked and the covers around them began to give way.

"Hey, hey," a deep, soothing voice said in my ear, "Careful."

Caine?

The beeping sound in the distance suddenly grew louder as I forced my eyes open. I blinked against the brightness of the unfamiliar room. I was in a bed. One much smaller than my own.

At the foot of it stood my grandfather. "Grandpa?" I croaked, and then pressed my tongue against the roof of my mouth. It was so dry.

Grandpa's hands curled around my foot. He looked tired. Disheveled. Not at all himself. "You're going to be okay, sweetheart."

"Lexie."

I moved my head to the side and found Caine sitting at my bedside. He held my hand between both of his and he was leaning in so close his face was inches from mine. He looked exhausted too.

I was confused. "What's going on?"

Caine frowned. "You don't remember? You're in the hospital."

The hospital?

I frowned and glanced up behind me at the origin of the beeping. I saw the monitors and the IV drip that pierced my arm and it finally hit me that I was in a hospital bed. "Hospital?" I repeated.

The memories came back in an avalanche of images.

The dark blur. The pain. The blood.

Waking up on the gurney as I was wheeled into the ER. Caine's anxious face. His shirt covered in my blood. His hand refusing to let mine go as the paramedics tried to calm me down.

The sight of the ER doctor rushing toward me was the last thing I remembered.

The beeping on the machine escalated in rhythm as my heart rate picked up.

"I had better go tell the doctor she's awake," Grandpa said before disappearing out of the private room. As he passed the door I noted the huge guy in a tight T-shirt and jeans standing outside with his hands behind his back, alert to the world around him. A gun holder was strapped across his back. He was armed?

Understanding only the basics of what had happened to me, I felt fear and panic starting to crawl inside me. I looked back at Caine, whose grip on my hand had tightened. "Someone stabbed me."

I remembered the black blur of the body that had brushed me before the pain hit me in the gut.

Why? Why would someone attack me?

Anger blazed in Caine's eyes as he replied thickly, "Yes. I

didn't even see it happen. When I came over to you, you looked up at me with this strange, pained look on your face. Your eyes weren't focusing. You were pale. And then I looked down and I saw the blood spreading across your shirt. You passed out. We got you here and you woke up for a bit in the ER, but then you were out again. A surgeon arrived and he didn't think anything major had been hit. He had you taken to the OR to explore the area. Thankfully he was right. The knife didn't hit any major organs or arteries. They stitched you up and we got you a private room. They said you'll have to stay in the hospital for a few days."

All of that of course was great to hear, considering the fact that someone had put a knife in my belly . . . but I was more interested in what Caine wasn't saying. "Why would someone do this?" I moved to push myself up, but a sharp burn shot down my stomach and I cried out in pain.

"Jesus, Lexie," Caine scolded, "you just got stabbed. Try not to move."

I glowered at him. "I forgot about my wound, okay?" I winced at the ghost of pain. "I won't again anytime soon."

"Alexa, you're awake." I looked up at the sound of the rich, smooth voice and found it belonged to a pleasant-looking young man. "I'm your surgeon, Dr. Fredericks." He looked so young I was kind of anxious about the fact that he'd been poking around my knife wound.

"Hey."

He smiled at my weak greeting and came closer, followed by my grandfather. "When you were admitted to the ER, I took you up to the OR to explore your wound and make sure that no major organs . . ."

I listened as he repeated pretty much everything Caine had already told me.

"So I'm okay?" I said when he was finished.

"Yes. You're going to be okay. I recommend that we keep you in the hospital under observation for a few days just to make sure you're fighting off any possible infection, and then we can send you home. You're looking at a recovery time of four to six weeks. Your nurse will be in soon to discuss antibiotics, pain management, and the routine for dressing the wound." He looked between Caine and me and obviously drew his own conclusions when he said, "I'm glad you've got someone to help you. As much as I want you to be gently exercising throughout your recovery, the first week or so is difficult. You'll need someone to help you get around."

I lowered my gaze at the doctor's misunderstanding, and wondered how the hell I was going to cope on my own for the next six weeks. "Thank you, Doctor."

"You're welcome. We gave you something for the pain, but if you need anything just use your call button. Angela, your nurse, will be in soon."

The door closed behind him and I pulled my hand out of Caine's grasp. "Now that that's done, would one of you like to tell me why there's a huge guy guarding my door? I'm thinking it's got something to do with being stabbed, but I've been wrong in the past in situations like these. Oh, wait. I've never been a situation like this before."

"Lexie." Caine's warning only pissed me off more.

"Don't."

"I'm asking you to keep calm so I don't fucking lose it," he snapped, pushing up out of his chair with agitated energy.

"Please, Alexa," Grandpa said soothingly. "It took a lot to calm him down while you were out."

Guilt pricked me. I glanced up at Caine from under my lashes. He was worried about me too. "Sorry. I just . . . I half want to know whatever it is you guys know and I half really don't."

Caine shared a look with my grandfather, then sat back down beside me. "We looked at footage from security cameras outside the building, and I have friends in the police department, so we've got them moving fast on this. They looked at footage from traffic cameras in the area. Both show you were approached by a man dressed in a black hoodie and jeans. He brushes by you, pauses a moment, and then hurries away like all he did was stumble into you. He had his hood up the whole time. We followed him using the traffic cameras, but we lost him at Faneuil Hall. The police are looking for him, but there are no leads so far."

"We'll be looking to see if anyone has a grudge against Caine," Grandpa spoke up. "But we also need to know of anyone in your past that might have a grudge against you."

I was paralyzed by disbelief. "No. I can't think. No one who . . . This was . . . You think this was premeditated?" I was outraged and hurt in so many ways. "Why would . . ."

The hardness in Caine's eyes dissipated and he took my hand in his again. "I don't know. But I promise you I will do everything to find out. For now I've got private security guarding your hospital room, and when you're released I'm taking you back to my apartment where you can be protected."

Horror racked me. "Are you saying . . . are you saying this person might try to hurt me again?"

Their silence was answer enough.

I suddenly felt stifled by my fear in a way I'd never encountered before. I felt hunted, trapped, by the idea that some person was out there waiting for his next opportunity to attack me. I'd never feared walking out of my door, stepping out on my street before, but now the very thought of standing anywhere out in the open caused me this bone-deep terror.

My chest wheezed as I tried to draw breath.

I couldn't breathe.

I can't breathe.

Black dots speckled my vision and my skin felt suddenly clammy and too tight.

"Lexie." Caine's hand tightened on mine as his other smoothed my hair back from my face. "Deep breaths, Lex." He took in a deep breath and let go of it slowly.

I concentrated on his face and on mimicking him.

The panic began to ease its death grip on me.

My limbs felt limp, and I was more exhausted than ever. "Why is this happening?" I whispered as I closed my eyes.

A few seconds later warm lips brushed against my forehead. "I'm not going to let anything happen to you."

I relaxed a little more upon Caine's hoarse vow and felt the darkness of sleep reach for me.

"I'll have to tell Adele everything," I heard Grandpa's voice in the distance. "I'd like to help in any way I can. I don't want to leave Alexa to deal with this alone."

"She's not alone. She's got me," Caine said. His voice sounded much colder now.

"Yes, but for how long?"

"Don't you dare . . . You have no right to even be here. I'll take care of Lex. You just go back to keeping the peace in your family, Edward. Lexie knows where your priorities lie. It would be hypocritical to change your mind now."

"This coming from you? I watched you on Saturday night and I can see the way she is with you now. You've left her."

"I never stopped being her friend. Now, the last thing she needs is us arguing, and frankly there's only one Holland in this room I can stand, so why don't you do what you're good at and leave, and let me take care of her?"

"She's my granddaughter, my family. I'm going home to tell Adele about her, and I'm going to bring her to the hospital to see her granddaughter, and by God, no one, including you and your security guards, is going to stand in our way."

I tried to stay awake to hear Caine's reply, but the darkness was much too warm and inviting . . .

CHAPTER 27

The hospital threw Caine out. They had a strict visiting hour policy and although he'd somehow managed to arrange it with them and the police to keep the two big, burly security guys stationed outside my door, the hospital wouldn't budge on allowing him to stay. The fact that we'd broken up had temporarily fled my mind and I didn't want him to leave. When I woke up my grandfather was gone and the police were waiting to talk to me. Caine sat by my side the whole time as I recounted what I could remember. None of it was very useful since I hadn't seen the guy's face.

"He smelled a little," I recalled. "Like stale sweat."

The police left with grim faces and Caine's hand was gripping mine so hard I had to ask him to ease up on me. I knew my attack had shaken him up, and I had to admit that took a little of the sting out of his rejection. He didn't love me, but he at least cared about me, and that was enough right then. Because right then I was scared, and he was the only thing that made me feel safe.

I didn't want him to leave.

I could tell he didn't want to leave me.

So, even though I didn't think I owed it to him, I gave him a reassuring smile and told him I'd be fine.

"I'm tired anyway. I'll just be sleeping. And you do have Stallone and Schwarzenegger stationed outside my door."

"I'll be back in the morning." He reluctantly shrugged on his jacket and leaned down as if to press a kiss to my forehead. He hesitated and instead of brushing his mouth across my temple, he bent lower and brushed his lips across mine. "Get some rest."

Dazed, I nodded and watched him leave, all the while wondering what the hell that had been about.

The next morning I woke up before visiting hours in pain. Angela, my nurse, gave me Percocet and told me to stop wriggling around so much if I could help it. I couldn't help it. I'd had approximately three hours of sleep. I'd woken up at every little noise and then had almost suffocated as I subconsciously held my breath while I attempted to hear over the sound of blood rushing through my ears.

I'd remind myself I had my own commandos outside and then I'd doze off again, only to be woken up by the sharp, burning pain in my belly.

Restless sleep did not go hand in hand with a knife wound.

Caine showed up at morning visiting hours and he came brandishing pastries and coffee. He snuck them to me, and I swore if he had wanted to, I'd have married him right there and then.

"Thank you." I threw him a soft smile in gratitude.

"You sleep okay?"

"Fine. You?"

"Fine."

We were both lying. He looked exhausted and I could only imagine I looked like shit.

"I have a few things I need to do, but Effie said she's dropping by this afternoon. I called Rachel and let her know what happened. She said she'd be here soon. I'll drop by again this evening."

"Thank you," I repeated. "You really don't have to take care of me, you know."

He looked instantly annoyed.

"Not that I'm not grateful," I hurried to assure him.

"There's a possibility that the person who did this did it to get to me." He stood up abruptly and started shrugging into his jacket. "I'm going to get to the bottom of it."

All I'd been thinking about was who the possible culprit was. I knew my father was capable of some pretty shitty things, and that mixed with how I'd treated him for the last seven years, plus not knowing what my mother's death might have done to him . . . but it was ridiculous. I shook the thought off right away, disturbed that I'd even considered it. It plagued me that I'd considered it. So I desperately tried to think of who else it might have been. And although I hated to think that Caine was right, something occurred to me. "What about that woman you were talking to on Saturday night? She sounded like she was threatening you."

Caine frowned. "I'm almost positive it wasn't her, but I'm looking into it."

"We should tell the police about it."

"No," he snapped.

I blanched, feeling that ugly suspicion that I'd felt on Saturday night coil in my stomach. "Why not?"

"Just . . . trust me. Please." He stared me down until I nodded my uncertain agreement. "I'm doing everything in my power to find out what was behind your attack, whether it was random or has something to do with me. I won't stop until I uncover the truth. You can believe that."

"So you're taking care of me out of guilt?"

"I'm taking care of you because it's the right thing to do."

I narrowed my gaze on him. He'd gone all "preknifed Alexa" on me. "Wow, that makes me feel so special."

Caine sighed. "The smart-ass is back," he muttered. "Someone's feeling better."

"Yes, some mystery assailant did a drive-by slicing on my belly. I'm positively perky."

He cut me a dark look.

I huffed, "You're allowed to be concerned about me, you know. I'm not going to take your concern as an avowal of love."

We glared at each other for a few seconds and then Caine gradually softened. "Sorry. I'm being an ass. Of course I'm concerned. I'm taking care of you because I'm concerned, no other reason."

Grateful at his admission, I reassured him, even though it hurt my heart to do so. "As your friend, and nothing more, I appreciate it and understand where it's coming from. I'm not expecting anything to change because I got stabbed in the gut."

"Would you stop saying that?" He gritted his teeth. "I keep seeing it every time you say it."

"Sorry."

He sighed again, but his lips had curled up at the corners, so I knew he wasn't irritated anymore. "I'll be back tonight."

As soon as he walked out the door, I slumped against my pillows and felt tears burn my eyes. I hated to admit it to myself, but the truth was, after his behavior yesterday, I'd let that hope sneak back in again. I'd hoped that his tenderness, his affection, his irate reaction to what had been done to me meant that he finally realized how he felt about me.

God, I was such an idiot.

"When Caine called I was so freaking worried." Rachel slumped on my bed beside me. "And then I stepped out of my door and saw this." She slapped the tabloid newspaper on my knee.

A photograph of Caine and me occupied the lower half of the front page with the headline CARRAWAY'S PA ATTACKED OUTSIDE CARRAWAY FINANCIAL HOLDINGS.

"Oh my God."

"Oh, it gets worse."

I pulled the paper up toward me and began to read out loud, "'Yesterday afternoon, busy workers in the financial district were horrified during lunchtime rush hour to witness Caine Carraway's PA, Alexa Holland, loaded into an ambulance. Although there was no actual witness to the event itself, it has since been reported that Miss Holland, who is pictured above with Mr. Carraway at the Delaneys' Alzheimer's Benefit on Saturday evening, was brutally stabbed outside Two International Place. Miss Holland is said to be in recovery while the police search for the attacker.

"'It is not clear whether Miss Holland was the victim of a targeted attack, or was just simply in the wrong place at the wrong time, but what is clear is that Mr. Carraway, of Carraway Financial Holdings, is pulling out all the stops to bring justice to his employee. An insider reports that he has hired private security to watch over Miss Holland while she's in the hospital, and that he is working diligently with the police in tracking the culprit. Questions are being asked not only about the nature of the relationship between the beautiful PA and the wealthy CEO, but also of the mysterious secrecy revolving around Miss Holland's family. Our investigator reports that Miss Holland is in fact the daughter of Alistair Holl . . .'" I trailed off, sucking in a breath.

"Go on," Rachel urged.

"'. . . the daughter of Alistair Holland, the son of Diamond heir and entrepreneur Edward Holland, who famously and mysteriously disinherited his firstborn almost twenty years ago. Alistair Holland divorced his wife, Patricia Estelle Holland, leaving behind her and their son, Matthew, while he went on to settle down in Connecticut, where he married Julie Brown, the mother of his daughter, Alexa Holland. Edward Holland and his family have not publicly acknowledged Miss Holland despite the fact that she's been a resident of Boston for the last seven years. Edward Holland was not available to comment.'"

I looked up at Rachel, who was staring at me with something akin to hurt on her face. "Rach," I whispered.

"Look. I don't want to take away from the fact that you've been stabbed and I'm really scared and upset for you right now, but I can't believe you didn't tell me who your family is. I mean I knew your dad was a bastard, but I didn't know he was also the son of one of Boston's oldest and wealthiest families."

"It wasn't . . ." I worried my lip, wondering if my grandfather had gotten to my grandmother with the news before the tabloids. I remembered what he'd said to Caine before I drifted off, and his fierce vow went a little way toward soothing the hurt he'd caused me. Not all. I still didn't know how to forgive him, but it meant something to me that he was finally looking out for me and not his family name. I'd been waiting on him appearing with my grandmother when Rachel showed up. Did this front-page news mean he wouldn't show? "That side of my family . . . There are a lot of bitter feelings there, and the fact is that my dad had an affair with my mother and kept her on the side for years. When my grandfather disinherited him, his wife divorced him and he came crawling to us. I never knew any of that until seven years ago."

"Wait . . ." Rachel frowned. "Why did your grandfather disinherit him?"

I sucked in a breath at the question, thinking of its ugly answer. "That's not my story to tell, Rach."

Thankfully she let it go. "So . . . you're saying that you didn't tell any of them that you've been in Boston this whole time."

"My grandpa knows," I admitted sheepishly. "We spend time together in secret."

"Wow." She threw me a sympathetic look. "Your life is really complicated."

"Oh, you have no idea."

She grabbed my hand and gave it a squeeze. "I want you to know I'm here for you. I get why you couldn't talk about any of this, but now you can. No one should have to deal with this shit alone. I love you, Lex. I had a heart attack when Caine called to tell me what had happened to you. You're my family. Okay?"

My nose stung with tears. This time good tears. "Thanks, Rach. Love you too."

Rachel stuck around for a little longer, distracting me from the current scary status of my life by gossiping about her neighbors and her neighbors' kids. Although it was a little unfair of her to complain about anyone else's terrifying children, considering Maisy, I let her babble on because in her own way Rachel was almost soothing. She brought normality to me in that hospital room, and I needed that so much right then.

My friend was barely out the door when my grandfather showed up. Alone.

I looked beyond him expectantly, but the door to my room closed behind him.

Grandpa strode to my side, grabbed my hand, and squeezed it. "I told Adele last night, sweetheart, but she's . . . She needs time. And with the news hitting the papers . . ."

I tried to pull my hand free. "I get it."

Grandpa held on. "What you don't get is that I love you and I will always love you. I made a mistake, Alexa, a terrible mistake that I have regretted ever since that night. I tried in my own way to see it right, but it can never be made right. I'm sorry. I'm sorry I hurt you and that you feel betrayed. But more than anything I'm sorry this horrible act of mine ever made you question my love for you."

Tears burned in my eyes. "I just feel really alone."

"Never think that. It took me too long, but I'm here now. You're not alone."

"It's not that simple."

"It will take time. I can wait."

And he started waiting right then, as I sat in silence and began the process of trying to forgive him.

A while later, just as Grandpa and I had begun to talk a little, Angela came in looking flustered. She scowled back at Don, one of my security guys, as the door closed behind her. "They really are obnoxious," she told me. "I've got a short, frantic little guy outside claiming to be a friend of yours. Says his name is Benito."

Holy hell.

I wondered if getting stabbed warranted forgiveness.

"Show him in."

Angela pushed open my hospital door. "He's allowed in, jackass," she snapped at Don as she passed him.

I chuckled and then immediately winced at the pain from my wound. I guessed laughter was out for a while, then.

Benito marched into the room and slammed to a stop at the sight of me. It was like watching him walk into a brick wall. He paled as his big round eyes took in the scene before him. "Oh, dear God." He hurried to my side and snatched up my hand. "Alexa . . . I had to come as soon as I heard."

I gave him a somewhat confused smile. "It's nice to see you, Benito." *What are you doing here?*

He looked at my grandfather, his eyebrows raised. I so did not want to get into that with Benito.

Grandpa cleared his throat and stood up. "I'll let you have privacy with your friend." He bent down and pressed a sweet kiss to my temple. "I'll be back tomorrow."

I nodded carefully and watched him leave. I had to admit I felt a certain relief in having decided to try to mend the breach between us.

Benito squeezed my hand. "Edward Holland is your grandfather?"

"We're not discussing that. At all," I warned him.

He let go of my hand to pull the chair up beside the bed, the feet screeching across the floor in a way that didn't even seem to compute with him. I gritted my teeth against the noise and waited for him to explain his presence.

"I feel just awful," he launched in, gesticulating wildly. "You wouldn't be in this hospital bed if I hadn't fired you."

I snorted. "And you drew this conclusion . . . how?"

"I was working on a shoot in New York yesterday. You would have been with me, nowhere near International Place."

Ah. I got it now. He was under the impression that this was not a targeted attack. I, however, was still convinced I might have been assaulted because of Caine's mysterious secrets. "We don't know that," I assured him. "We're not sure what's going on here."

"All I know is that I'm a shit for firing you. I've been racked with guilt all morning. I came to apologize."

The truth was I didn't regret Benito firing me. What he did actually changed my life. Okay, so right now that wasn't for the better, but the months before the attack had been the most amazing of my life. And although things were shitty now, at least I was reevaluating my future. If Benito hadn't fired me I would still be working alongside him, existing on the perimeter of someone else's career.

"You don't have to do that."

"Let me," he snapped impatiently.

"Fine," I sighed. "Apology accepted."

He narrowed his eyes. "You could be a little more gracious about it."

I raised an eyebrow in answer.

"Right." He winced, his eyes dropping to my stomach. "How is it?" His hands fluttered over the area as if he was afraid any minute now I was about to go all Warrant Officer Ripley on him.

"Gestating."

"What?" He squinted in confusion.

"Nothing," I murmured.

"I've missed your weird sense of humor, Alexa." He patted my hand condescendingly.

Frankly I didn't think I had a weird sense of humor—it was just that Benito didn't have any kind of sense of humor.

"There was another reason I came to see you."

"Oh?" *Please do not offer me my job back.* It would be very difficult to say no, and I knew the best thing for me was to start afresh.

"Antoine Faucheux called me a few days ago."

Interest piqued, I urged him to go on.

"Apparently his sister, Renée, is looking for a new events planner in her events management company. In Paris. It's a very successful company—it deals in society weddings, launch parties . . . Antoine is going to suggest you to his sister, and he called me to ask me to forgive you long enough to write you a glowing reference."

I stared dumbly at him, processing.

A job. In Paris. In events management?

Was this real?

Benito grimaced. "You're not saying anything."

"I'm trying to get my head around it. You just told me someone might offer me my dream job the day after some psycho stuck a knife in me. It's all a little overwhelming."

"Of course, dear." He patted my hand again, this time staring at me as if he were worried I was about to start shouting for Nurse Ratched.

I'd forgotten how trying Benito could be. "Are you going to give me a reference?"

"What kind of monster would I be if I didn't?"

"That's a yes, right?"

He rolled his eyes. "Yes."

"Wow." This changed everything. I could start over in Paris. I wouldn't have to put up with my grandmother's more than likely rejection and the rest of the Hollands' reaction to my presence in their city. I'd be doing something I'd always wanted to do. I'd be living in Paris! I could escape whatever arcane hell was going on with this attacker business.

But the most alluring part of taking a job in Paris?

I wouldn't have to worry about accidentally bumping into Caine anymore. I could take my broken heart to another continent. Somehow that was reassuring. Maybe in Paris I'd have a chance to actually move on.

Whereas if I was stuck in Boston, everything would remind me of him.

"What about this?" I pointed to my belly. "Doc says recovery time varies from four to six weeks."

"Well, I'm sure you can work something out with Antoine's sister."

I smiled with sincerity. "Benito, thank you."

He grinned. "I'm forgiven?"

I laughed. "You're forgiven."

CHAPTER 28

I was being tortured.

The familiar, delicious scent of Caine's cologne tickled my nose, and other less innocent places. My arms were wrapped around his neck as he carried me, holding me close to his hard body. I stared glumly at his lips that hovered near my face, and fought the urge to kiss him.

"You know, with all your money you could have installed an elevator inside your apartment so you didn't have to carry me all the way upstairs," I grumbled, only half joking, as he laid me down on his guest bed.

His hands rested on the bed at the sides of my shoulders as he braced over me. His eyebrows drew together as he searched my face. "Did I hurt you?"

The whole moving from the hospital to Caine's apartment hadn't been the most comfortable process, but no, he hadn't hurt me. At least not physically.

"No," I mumbled, and looked away.

Caine sighed. "Are you still mad at me?"

Yes, but now for a different reason. I glared at him. Why hadn't he moved away? *Move away!* "Yes."

"I'm trying to protect you." He pulled back and I sighed in relief.

"I could have stayed with Rach. She offered."

"And put up with a crazy four-year-old who would have no consideration for the fact that you're wounded? There's a way to guarantee ripping your stitches."

Since I couldn't argue with that, I continued glowering.

He smirked at me. "I would never have guessed you'd be an irritable patient."

"Oh, I'm glad this is amusing you." I groaned as I lifted myself up into a sitting position and Caine hurried forward to help me. I stopped him by raising a palm to ward him off. I'd had enough of being manhandled by the man I was no longer allowed to handle.

While I was in the hospital, someone had outfitted Caine's guest room for me. It had always been a nice room, but now there was a television and a DVD player across from the bed, and a bookshelf stacked with books and magazines in the corner. An eReader and a laptop sat on the bedside table along with . . . knitting needles? I stared at them for a second and then raised an eyebrow at Caine.

Amused, he explained, "Effie says knitting calms the soul."

"Do I look like I knit?"

"No, but you like you're in a *snit*."

"Oh, great, I get stabbed and you get cute."

He threw me a look. "Seriously," he muttered, coming over to fluff my pillows like the perfect nursemaid, "what's crawled up your ass since leaving the hospital?"

"You." I batted his hand away from my pillows. "You, you,

you." Could he really not see this was difficult for me? "It's bad enough I have to be here to recuperate. Maybe you could just help me out a little by backing off."

He seemed stunned by my outburst ... until slowly I watched understanding dawn on his face. He stepped back from the bed. "I have to be here to help you out, Lex. There's nothing to be done about that."

I nodded and looked away, feeling utterly vulnerable that he now knew just how much it affected me to be around him. "But Effie will be here mostly?"

"Yeah."

"Good."

"I take it you don't want to watch a movie with me, then?"

An ache gripped my chest as I remembered our first movie night together.

"Maybe we could stay like this forever ..."

I pushed the memory of his words out of my head and reached for the laptop. "Not tonight."

Taking the hint, Caine moved to leave. He stopped at the doorway. "Can I get you anything before I leave you alone for the night?"

Leave me alone for the night?

The panic must have shown on my face, because he gentled. "I meant alone in this room. I'll be down the hall."

The thought of him lying down the hall from me filled me with even more frustration. I cursed my complicated feelings. I wanted him there, but I didn't want him there. How fun for me. "A glass of water."

He gave me a nod, seeming pleased to have been given a job. "Coming right up."

At his departure I exhaled slowly.

I could hear Effie in my head, urging me not to give up on

Caine, urging me to keep pushing and pushing at him until he finally gave me his secrets.

Right now I just felt too angry. I knew my anger came from the attack that left me feeling scared. I hated that I'd been made to feel like a victim. That feeling was seeping into every aspect of my life, and somehow it felt like a betrayal of myself—a weakness more than a strength—to fight for Caine when he was so resistant.

"If I don't get out of this room soon, I'm going to scream."

Effie gave me a warning look. "Scream and I will not bake you any more cakes."

"Good. I'm getting fat."

"Pfft." She drew her eyes over me. "You've been eating like a bird since you got here. The only reason you're not disappearing before my very eyes is my cakes."

"Effie," I whimpered like a child. "I need fresh air. At least let me go out on the balcony."

To be fair I had been cooped up in Caine's guest room for the last week. Effie stuck around the apartment while Caine was at work. I appreciated her help more than I could say. She was there to make sure I got in and out of the shower okay. She helped me change my dressing daily and proved herself once again pretty spry and strong for an old lady. Effie was also a great babysitter because she hung out with me, but she also hung out downstairs, giving us both space. Other than Effie I'd had Caine's cleaner, Donna, for company the two times she arrived for work. It was my first time meeting her and I was more than a little uncomfortable with the circumstances. Along with Effie and Donna, I'd had Rachel and Sofie visit when they dropped by a few times. As did Henry and Nadia. They entertained me without even meaning to. I was fascinated witnessing Henry's interaction with her. He constantly watched her—tender with her in a way I'd never seen from him before. As for Nadia, she was clearly really into him. I had my fingers crossed for them both, because I genuinely liked Nadia, and I'd come to care for Henry over the last few months. Someone had to get a happily ever after at the end of all this.

As for Grandpa, he called. Obviously it would be unfair to ask Caine if my grandfather could visit me at his apartment, so we just chatted for a little while on the phone. Grandpa was still dealing with the fallout of his family's discovering I was in Boston and that he'd been seeing me behind their backs all along. Apparently there were a lot of discussions, but none of them reached a conclusion.

I think that was his polite way of avoiding telling me that the rest of the family, including my grandmother, didn't want to have anything to do with me.

That stung. A lot. Along with Caine's rejection, it pretty much could have threatened to bring on the great depression of the twenty-first century. But I had other things to worry about. For instance, the fact that there were still no leads on my attacker.

"You're being a terrible patient. You know for your own safety we can't let you out on the balcony," Effie grumbled.

I scoffed, "We're God knows how many stories high. Surely Caine doesn't think my attacker can get to me on the balcony. I mean he'd have to have a sight gun."

Effie blanched at the thought.

My heart pounded in my chest. "No. Caine doesn't believe that's even a remote possibility. Right? I mean . . . that's . . . th-that's crazy."

"Sweetheart, it's a little far-fetched, and Caine knows

that. But right now he's paranoid about your safety. You didn't see him when he came home from the hospital that first night. He was wrecked. So you have to give him this."

"Wrecked?" I whispered, my heart beating fast for a different reason now.

"I told you to keep fighting for a reason, Lexie. You really think a man like Caine lets someone infiltrate his life as thoroughly as you have because he 'cares about you'?" It was her turn to scoff. "No. The feelings have to be a little more than lukewarm."

"He let *you* infiltrate his life," I argued.

She beamed. "Because he loves me."

"He doesn't love *me*."

"No. He's wildly and madly crazy about you. There's a difference."

"Don't," I pleaded. "He told me to my face that he doesn't love me. I don't need false hope from you."

Effie scowled. "No, you need a swift kick up the ass. I told you to push him."

"And I told you I'm still too pissed off to do anything else but be pissed off."

"You need to get over that. It's an ugly way to be."

I narrowed my eyes in indignation. "You try getting over this kind of anger. Someone put me in this bed, someone who hasn't been found yet. I'm sitting in this apartment feeling like a hunted animal. And all the while I'm being looked after by a person I love more than I've ever loved anyone and he rejected me. Please, tell me how *not* to be angry and I'll do it."

Effie leaned forward, her eyes kind. "You tell yourself that being angry and bitter and feeling hunted is giving the bastard that hurt you too much power. You shake him off, concentrate on staying safe and getting better, and force Caine to realize that he can't live without you. Instead of pushing him away—yes, he told me you barely let him near you—you get in his face, you spend all your recuperation with him, reminding him just exactly what he's giving up if he lets you go. And just when you've got him where you want him, you go in for the kill and you push him to give you the answers that you deserve."

I let Effie's advice wash over me, sinking into my gut.

We sat in silence for about ten minutes as I processed what she'd said. She leisurely flipped through a tabloid magazine like she hadn't delivered the kind of profundity I had desperately needed.

Finally I said, my words soft, "How did you get so wise, Effie?"

"I've survived seventy-seven years on this planet," she answered wryly, "and by making the right choices I even managed to *live* for most of them."

The sound of Effie's and Caine's voices carried up toward the bedroom and I braced myself. I strained to hear what they were saying with no luck. I did, however, hear the front door shut and I held my breath. For the past five days when Caine returned from work, the first thing he did was check in on me.

Usually I grumbled that I was bored but fine; then he'd offer to get me something, to which I'd give him an errand; he'd complete the errand, and then leave me to it.

After having turned Effie's advice over and over in my head, I'd determinedly shoved the bitter anger that was desperate to take hold of me to one side, and clawed my way back to my fighting spirit.

My pulse raced at the sound of Caine's footsteps coming up the stairs. The louder those footsteps grew, the harder my heart beat.

Suddenly he was in my doorway looking bone-weary. Like always, that aching pang made itself known in my chest at the sight of him. "Hey," I said.

He gave me a tired smile. "Hey back. How was today?"

I shrugged. "Boring. How was your day?"

His face darkened. "Still nothing."

"You'll get him."

Caine's eyes flared with surprise that quickly transformed into gratitude. "Can I get you anything?"

I took a deep breath. *Here goes.* "How would you feel about vegging out with me? We could order takeout. Watch a movie."

He hesitated.

"Oh, if you have work, I totally get it." I smiled my way through the disappointment.

"No." He shook his head. "It can wait. Vegging out with you sounds great. What do you feel like ordering in?"

I hid my pleased grin and shrugged. "You choose. Movie too."

Not too long later Caine was stretched out on the bed beside me. He'd changed out of his suit and was now in sweats and a T-shirt. Chinese take-out boxes were strewn across the middle of the bed between us, and we were watching an old Jean-Claude Van Damme movie.

"Now, see?" I pointed to the screen with my chopsticks. "If you could do that you could quite possibly rule the world."

Caine gave a huff of laughter. "What? I'm that close? I just need to learn how to do jump box splits and land on a counter in that position?"

"Yes!" I insisted. "Then total world domination will follow."

"Then look out, world, I'm coming."

I giggled. "You can't do box splits."

He threw me a mock-insulted look. "I can do anything I put my mind to, baby."

Pretending not to be thrilled at the return of the endearment, I shook my head in amusement. "You know, your lack of confidence is really quite embarrassing. You should work on that."

Caine just grinned and dug into some of my moo shu pork.

I slanted him a circumspect look.

Effie was right.

I could do this.

It was all about stealth.

I stealthed the hell out of Caine over the next week.

I was getting around a little better now. The doc had said I was supposed to get up and about—gentle exercise, he called it—and I was hanging out downstairs a lot more. Caine was growing progressively more frustrated as he and the police hit a brick wall on the leads for my attacker. I knew wanting to be there for me was taking its toll on his work too. The lack of late nights at the office and lack of business trips had to mean someone else was covering for him, and I knew he was enough of a control freak to hate that.

That meant that when he returned home every evening he wore his dark mood like a black shroud around him. He only ever began to relax once he was out of his suit and kicking back with me to watch movies. We did a lot of movie watching and talking. Yet we never talked about anything serious.

I didn't know if the lack of gravity in our conversations

was what was impeding my stealth attack on Caine, but as far as I could see, despite our closeness he still wasn't any nearer to letting me in.

I thought perhaps I was being too stealthy, so one night while we were watching the Brad Pitt movie about Jesse James I decided to drop the stealth and go in for the kill.

Caine was sitting upright, his long legs stretched out before him on the coffee table. I lay at the other end of the sofa with my legs sprawled across his lap. I studied his profile while he watched the movie and, if I wasn't wounded, going in for the kill would involve a far more physical approach.

Being verbally direct would just have to do.

"Can you deal with this?" I blurted out, meaning could he deal with just friendship between us.

Caine turned to me and I knew he heard something in my voice that alerted him to what I meant. His whole body grew taut. "Alexa."

I smirked unhappily. "I'm always 'Alexa' when you're not happy with me."

"Not true." His eyes glinted and my body flushed.

Oh yeah. Sometimes I was "Alexa" in bed.

"Speaking of . . ."

He looked back at the screen. "Don't ruin this. Outside these walls, life is fucked right now. This here . . . it's the only thing I have. Don't ruin it."

I hesitated, wanting to give him what he wanted since he was caring for me. But I couldn't. "This here . . . it isn't real."

"Bullshit," he snapped, glaring at me. He seemed genuinely affronted by my assessment of our friendship. "It's the only real—" He cursed and cut off his words before returning his gaze to the television.

"If it was real, there wouldn't be secrets between us."

Caine's answer was to gently remove my legs from his lap and walk across the vast room. He disappeared upstairs and all the while my stomach churned with anxiousness.

When he returned thirty minutes later he was dressed in a shirt and slacks, his hair freshly washed and brushed.

"I'm going out," he threw over his shoulder before grabbing his car keys.

The door slammed shut behind him.

I closed my eyes and the movement put pressure on the tears that were filling them. They scored tracks down my cheeks and I burrowed my face into the couch so I could muffle my sobs.

A minute or so later I jerked at the gentle touch on my shoulder and peered out from under my hair to find Effie there. She was perched on the sofa, gazing at me compassionately. "Caine asked me to come sit with you while he went out."

I shifted around with care so I could rest my head on her lap and I just cried harder, hating that the bastard had the power to hurt me so badly.

CHAPTER 29

"Well, it all looks good. No sign of infection," Liz said.

I stared at my outpatient care nurse, a little dazed. I'd been feeling that way since I left the apartment for the first time escorted by Caine, Arnie, and Sly. "I took the Keflex as prescribed," I murmured.

"Good. Now that the staples are out, try not to forget about the injury. You've still got a minimum two weeks of healing to do."

"I don't think I'll be forgetting this anytime soon."

She gave me a sympathetic smile. "I don't suppose you will. Have they found the guy yet?"

"Nope." I stood up and Liz steadied me. "I'm ready to just get on with my life, you know, but with this hanging around my neck . . ."

She squeezed my arm. "I hope they get him soon, hon."

I smiled gratefully and she walked me out into the waiting room, where Caine stood talking quietly into his phone while Arnie and Sly stood by the doors. Their real names were Griff and Don, but they answered with good humor to the nicknames I'd given them.

Caine saw us and quickly ended his conversation. He slipped his phone into his pocket and strode over to us. He homed in on Liz. "Everything's okay?"

"Staples are out. No infection. Lexie's on the road to recovery."

"Great." I gave him a pointed look. "Now I can go home."

He frowned. "If by 'home' you mean my home, then yes, you can go home."

"Caine—"

"No argument." He slipped his arm around my waist, thanked Liz, and started to walk me out.

I glanced over my shoulder to give Liz a grateful smile. The whole time I tried to ignore Caine's body pressed up against mine. I could manage walking by myself just fine, but I didn't want to cause a scene in the hospital by telling him to back off.

After he'd disappeared last night, Effie helped me upstairs and into bed. No words were needed. I think even this time she was pissed at Caine and understood I'd reached the end of my fight on this one. When I heard him return from his drive a while later, I half hoped he'd come to my room. To say what? I didn't know. Something. Anything. However, he didn't, and that was when I decided it was time for me to finally let him go. I lay in bed that night thinking of all the things I needed to sort out in my life that didn't revolve around Caine.

Solving my career crisis seemed like the place to start. Antoine's sister, Renée, had been in contact and had given me these two weeks to mull over her offer before she offered it to someone else. Antoine had e-mailed me a few times over the last fourteen days, each e-mail pontificating on the delights and benefits of living in Paris. I had to admit for the last week I'd made it all up my mind that if I could get Caine to confide in me, then I'd stay in Boston. That would have meant looking around the city for a new job anyway, because there was no way I was continuing on as his PA if we were going to be in a serious relationship.

Now, however, I found myself considering Renée's offer.

Before I even thought about Paris, though, I had to deal with my father. There were too many unresolved issues there. I could not get it out of my head that I would even contemplate that he would hurt me. Yet the thought that the person behind my attack might be him had flittered through my mind, however briefly. Of course upon reflection I was a little horrified with myself for even thinking it. In fact, it more than horrified me—it startled me into realizing that I was never going to get a fresh start anywhere until I found some kind of closure with my father. I had to talk to him, and hoped to God when I did he could make me understand his actions better. If he could, then I might be able to forgive my mother for choosing him over me. After all, the hurt my mother's choices had inflicted on me were at the core of my issues. How could I let go and move on in Paris if I didn't come to terms with that hurt, that rejection? I wouldn't. I'd just take it with me.

"You're quiet. Are you in pain?" Caine asked as we settled into the car.

"It's a little tender but I'm okay. I really wish you'd let me go back to my own apartment, though."

He sighed. "Not until your attacker is found."

"And if we don't find him?"

"We'll cross that bridge when we get there."

"I'm warning you it'll be a wooden rope bridge riddled with dry rot with a big sign that says 'Cross at your own risk.'"

Caine didn't say anything. I looked at him. He was staring out of his passenger window, wearing the ghost of an amused smile.

It was on the tip of my tongue to say, "You're going to miss my smart ass." But I knew his answer—or more likely nonanswer—would sting worse than the staples I'd just had removed.

We traveled back to Caine's apartment in silence. Arnie and Sly walked us up to his apartment and left once I was safely ensconced inside. I was sick of the security. The lack of any leads on my attacker made me suspect I'd been stabbed by some random psycho on the street. The security and lockdown in the apartment felt like overkill.

"I have to get back to work, but Effie will be over soon," Caine said.

"Effie doesn't need to be here anymore." I kicked off my shoes, holding a hand up to stop Caine coming toward me to help. "I can get around on my own now. I'm sure she has better things to do than help you keep me prisoner."

"It's just for a little while longer, Lexie."

"How would you feel?" I scowled, leaning against the wall for support. "Wouldn't this be killing you?"

Instead of answering—not that he needed to, because I knew it would be killing him—Caine reminded me to call if I needed him and then he was gone.

I didn't call him, because I was determined to never need the handsome son of a bitch ever again.

Perhaps in my frustration I moved around the apartment that night more than I should have. Now that I was resolute in my decision to go see my father before accepting Renée's offer, I wanted to do it as soon as I could. The choice was made and I wanted to start living by it, for many reasons, including the fact that it distracted me from thinking about leaving Caine behind for good. Anytime I let myself dwell on the idea of not getting to see him every day, dread and utter desolation crept over me.

Anything was better than that feeling.

To not feel it I'd spent the rest of the day and early evening planning. I'd e-mailed Renée instead of calling—the six-hour time difference meant it was late in Paris. I had my fingers crossed I'd hear something back from her in the morning. From there I'd gone online and started apartment-hunting. Feeling out of my depth, I'd e-mailed Antoine for help and received an enthusiastic response saying he'd start making inquiries for me in the morning.

I'd then done a lot of pacing before heading up to bed early to avoid Caine.

The pacing and the jitteriness were the culprits behind why I'd woken up in the middle of the night in pain. Groaning at my own stupidity, I got up and headed slowly and quietly downstairs, where I'd left my Percocet. I reached the kitchen counter, where I was sure I'd put the pills. No luck.

To my annoyance I spent the next five minutes opening cupboards and drawers, aggravating the pain in my stomach. No luck. I glowered in exasperation around the low-lit room, trying to think where the hell I had put the pills. My eyes alighted on the side table near the dining area. I never used it because it matched the dining table exactly and looked more like a piece of art than a usable piece of furniture, but I wondered if perhaps Effie had put my pills away when she dropped by after Caine left. As soon as she'd appeared I'd told her in frustration that I appreciated her taking so much time for me, but I didn't need a babysitter any longer. Apparently she agreed, because after she made me coffee and pottered around a little she left.

I huffed. I loved Effie to pieces, but every time she came over there was always something I couldn't find because she'd put it away. I couldn't work out how someone with a home as cluttered as hers could be so obsessed with decluttering Caine's.

I pulled open the side-table drawer and pushed around some miscellaneous junk. Nope. No Percocet.

I practically growled.

I was just about to shut the drawer when something shiny caught the light. The realization that it was a bunch of photographs made me stop. Caine didn't have any photos out on display. I'd never even seen any hidden away.

Until now.

Curious, I pulled out the small pile of photographs and held them up under the light. The defeat and disappointment I'd been feeling over Caine suddenly hit brand-new levels of complexity.

Every photo was of me. There were six of them and I remembered they were taken on his phone. Two were ones I had taken. Selfies of us lying in bed. One was of me lying with my head against his, grinning up into the camera while he stared into the lens in smoldering bemusement. The other was of me holding the camera up high while I kissed him.

The other four were photographs Caine had taken of me. In one I was sprawled on his bed on my stomach, the sheet draped across my lower half. It was a modest but sensual photograph because although I was hiding all my good bits I was staring into the camera with a look on my face I'd never seen before. It was filled with desire. For Caine.

I blinked back the tears that suddenly stung my eyes.

The other two pictures were of me at Quincy Market the week before I was attacked. And the last was of me standing in the doorway between Caine's bedroom and master en suite. I wore only his T-shirt. The shoulders were much too big, so it hung down, revealing lots of skin. Caine had made a crack about how he'd never known a guy's shirt could be so sexy. In response I'd turned around and struck a pose, pouting ridiculously, my hair wild around my face.

Crying hard now, I shoved the photographs back in the drawer where he had hidden them.

I kicked the sideboard and immediately felt a sharp burn of pain tear through my abdomen. The tears came faster and I stumbled away into the hallway, suddenly desperate to get my hands on the pills so I had something to do, something else to concentrate on.

I found them immediately on the telephone table, and so I was back at square one with nothing else to contemplate but those goddamn photos.

Attempting to see through my blurry vision and all the while trying to soften the sounds of my crying, I hurried into the kitchen and fumbled with a glass as I pulled it out of the cupboard.

"Lexie?" Caine's questioning voice came to me.

I stiffened, shoving the glass under the tap.

"Hey, hey," he said soothingly, his heat hitting my back as he reached beyond me for the glass. With his other hand he reached for the Percocet, and in doing so trapped me against him. "Are you in pain?"

"I'm fine."

He was silent a moment. And then, "You're not fine. You're crying."

"I said I'm fine. I just need to take the Percocet." I took his hand and tried to peel the bottle out of it. "Give it to me."

"Lex, let me help you."

"I don't need your help."

I did not need to be saved by a man who couldn't even save himself.

"Lex—"

"I said I don't need your help!"

Suddenly his hands were on my arms and he was gently turning me to face him. I resisted, squirming against his hold with as much ferociousness as my wounded body would allow.

"Lexie, stop," he huffed in confusion.

I couldn't stop it now that my emotions had been unleashed on him.

All I could see were those photographs. All I could hear was his denial of how he felt about me. His rejection. His *lies*.

"Get off me!" I yelled, struggling hard now.

His grip on me tightened. "Lexie, stop it."

But I wouldn't. I couldn't.

Every hurt I'd felt in the last few weeks erupted into violence. I was yelling and crying and pounding my fists against his chest.

"Stop it—you'll hurt yourself," I heard him growl.

It didn't stop me.

His hold on me became bruising and he gave me a gentle shake. "Stop it," he commanded hoarsely. "Lexie, stop." And then he was kissing me. Hard. Desperate.

Stunned, I stopped struggling.

I let him kiss me, his hands moving from my arms to my hair, holding me to him as he kissed me like he needed to do so more than he needed to breathe.

Finally my brain blinked back into action and I froze, my lips no longer moving against his. Caine felt my reluctance and his kiss gentled. He brushed his mouth once, twice, over mine before pulling away.

We stared at each other, equally confused by what had just happened.

"I'm leaving" were the first words out of my mouth. "Not the apartment. I mean yes, the apartment, but more than that. Do you remember Antoine Faucheux? I introduced him to you at the airport."

Caine's fingers bit into my arms. I didn't think he even realized. "I remember," he said, his voice gruff.

"His sister offered me a job with her events management company in Paris. I accepted the offer today. I leave in four weeks."

For a moment he searched my face as if attempting to discern my seriousness. Eventually his hands dropped from my arms and he took a step back. "Is that why you were crying?"

Anger flared through me worse than the pain I'd felt earlier. "I just told you I'm leaving Boston and that's your reaction?"

His jaw clenched as he glared at me.

A somewhat better reaction than his previous bland question.

"No, that's not why I was crying," I answered anyway. "I found the photographs."

Confused, he shrugged. "What photographs?"

"The ones you have of me, of us, in the side table."

His reply was to take a few more wary steps back.

Renewed tears trembled on my lashes. "I'm leaving you. So the only thing you'll have left of me are those fucking photographs."

The blank wall came slamming down over his face.

I got it now. It was just like Effie said. Caine was never more cold and distant than when he was determined to hide what he was really feeling.

"I'm not going to stand here and have the same argument with you over and over. What I will say is that when I walk out that door I'm walking out of here hating you for throwing me away when the truth is . . . the truth is you love me. I know you do, even if you deny it. And if it were me, Caine, I wouldn't be able to stand the idea of you ever hating me, no matter how far apart we are, and I will hate you if you don't stop lying. So you either tell me what it is you're hiding or you don't, but you should know I will definitely never forgive you if you don't." I swiped away my tears. "And I'm so tired of the whole concept of unforgiveness."

I waited for what seemed like forever for Caine to answer me. When he did I wasn't sure whether to be relieved or concerned. His eyes hard, he nodded. "Fine, you want the truth, I'll tell you the truth, but take your pills first."

"I can do that," I said, not liking the brittle, snappish tone he was using.

Once I'd swallowed the pills and was seated on the sofa at the other end of the room, Caine paced for a while, back and forth in front of me.

"Are you going to sit down?" My heart had begun to pound at his increasing anxiety.

Oh God, what is he hiding?

Instead of sitting, he stopped to face me.

My stomach felt sick.

When Caine met my gaze, that feeling worsened. He looked angry, and I didn't know if that was because of me or himself.

"Caine," I whispered.

"I'm not the guy for you, Lex," he said, and I knew that he truly believed it.

I flushed with annoyance. "Surely that's my decision to make."

"No, that's my decision to make."

We stared at each other while I bit back an infuriated response.

Caine crossed his arms over his chest. "Only Henry and the people involved know this about my past. I've worked hard to make sure it stays buried."

Oh fuck, oh God, oh hell, oh fuck . . .

"At school I was working as a waiter at this fancy restaurant in Society Hill. I'd gotten into Wharton on my scholarship, but I wasn't living in the greatest student housing in Philly and I still needed money. I needed money to survive, but I also needed money to invest. I met Henry in college and he had connections. He got me the job at the restaurant. It paid better than most . . . While I was there I was propositioned by this older woman. A wealthy older woman."

If it was possible I think my heart stopped for a moment.

Caine's gaze bored into me with some kind of twisted determination. "She offered me a lot of money."

"Oh my God," I whispered, not believing where this confession had led. If I'd placed a bet on what his secret was, I would have lost huge. "You did it? You had sex with her for money?"

He gave a short nod, so tense he looked ready to shatter. "The way she saw it, I was perfect—I was a Wharton man, not some ignoramus off the street, but I was also poor and ambitious. She asked the right questions, worked it out, knew what she was doing, knew I might let her manipulate me. And I did. I thought what the hell? It was just her."

Realization hit me with force. My stomach knotted. "But it wasn't, was it?"

He shook his head. "It was the kind of titillation a bored housewife was looking for. She told a friend she trusted and before I knew it I didn't need the waiter job. I had a *clientele*." He bit the word out bitterly. "It was perfect. There was no chance of it getting out, because none of these women could afford for people to discover they were paying a college student for sex. I made enough money in nine months to invest. I invested wisely and saw a huge return. From there I invested more and so forth."

"A big enough return to start up the bank."

Caine finally looked at me, seeming to dare me to hate him. "Henry walked in on me with one of my clients one time and discovered the whole thing. He's the only one who knows how far I sank to get what I want."

"That's why you're weird whenever I ask about Wharton. Why you hate me around Henry, because he's the only one who could tell me the truth?"

"That and he gets a kick out of pissing me off by flirting with you all the time."

I ignored that, too stunned, reeling from his revelation. "That woman at the Delaneys' party . . . she was one of them, wasn't she?"

"Yes," he admitted, his expression still taunting. "She's from Philadelphia. I rarely cross paths with the women from that time in my life, but I knew she was going to be there—"

"That's why you were in a mood that whole day and at the party . . ." I stood up slowly and he watched me warily. "That's why you ended it with me."

"It could never work between us."

"Because of this?"

"Lexie, I practically sold my soul to get where I am today. I'm a selfish bastard . . . and you . . ." His eyes washed over my face. "You've already lost everything to keep your soul intact."

"Caine." I couldn't say anything for a minute. I was strangled by emotion.

He abruptly started to walk away.

"Don't go," I cried out.

He stopped, turning slightly to look back at me.

"I love you," I said through my tears. "I love you so much. Nothing changes that. *Nothing*."

He huffed in irritated disbelief. "Not even the fact that I was a whore?"

I flinched at the word. It wasn't an easy truth to swallow, and if I didn't know him, know how life had cheated him from the start, maybe I wouldn't have been able to see the big picture. But I could. I didn't blame Caine for what had happened. I blamed them. "They used you," I argued.

If anything, this seemed to piss Caine off even more.

"No, they used you," I repeated. "Yes, you used them, but they used you too. You were just a kid."

"I stopped being a kid at thirteen, Lexie."

"You were just a kid to them. And you *were* a kid, whether you want to admit it or not, and you were hurting. You got through what happened to you because you had ambition to focus on. So you did something you're ashamed of now . . . but it got you where you are. Do I wish it were different? Yes. I wish that wasn't your past. I'm pretty sure right now you do too. But we can't change it. It was years ago. You're not the same person now. We just have to leave it where it belongs. In the past."

"It's not part of the past," he snarled, seeming enraged by

my understanding. "It's who I am—it's what I'm capable of! I use any means to get what I want and I don't give a shit who I hurt in the process."

"No." I shook my head, not believing that for a second. "It's not who you are. Not with me." I reached for him, my fingers stroking through his hair as I curled my hand around the nape of his neck, trying to draw him closer. "You're lying to yourself. You're holding this up as a way to keep me locked out. But it's too late. I'm in. You love me." I smiled softly as he closed his eyes and gritted his teeth against my words. "You love me," I repeated, "and you'll never hurt me. And I will never hurt you. I will never use you like they did, like they all did. Because I want you. Just you." I pressed my forehead against his jaw and held on tighter to him. "No one will ever understand like I do. You're so different with me, baby. You take care of me. You make me feel safe. You're not who you think you are. Didn't you once tell me that people aren't just one thing? You're so much more to me than anything you might have done in the past."

"Lexie," he said, his voice guttural, "I told you this to wake you up. A man like me isn't capable of being your fucking white knight." His fingers peeled my hand from his neck and he gently pressed me away.

I felt the anger boil up inside me. "I'm not looking for a hero!"

He flinched at the emotion cracking my words.

"I never asked for that." I shook, my hands curling into fists at my side. "I just wanted you, because despite what you might think, I see you. And no, you're no fucking white knight, but you're what I want."

When he said nothing I felt my whole body turn cold.

"I won't stay," I warned him. "I won't try to fight for you

anymore. This is it. If you walk away it's not for me. I won't ever think that. I will always, always blame you for this. For ruining us."

The silence of the apartment around us seemed to stretch, expand, and thicken like a monster in the dark. For a while we just stood there facing each other as the monster destroyed any chance of the connection that would stop us from breaking apart for good. Finally Caine wrenched his gaze from mine and turned his back on me.

I walked out of the room, suturing up the gaping wound in my chest with the last of my mental and emotional strength. I made it to the guest room, wound temporarily sealed. I was determined it would stay sealed just long enough for me to get the hell out of Boston.

CHAPTER 30

Caine,

After last night I'm sure you understand why I can't be here anymore. For a while I held on to the hope that if I could just get you to open up to me, to tell me your secrets, then everything would work out for us. Since you're determined to keep us apart, I'm determined to move on with my life.

I'm heading to Connecticut now to see my dad. The attack brought back a lot of those issues, and I need to try to resolve them before I leave for Paris.

I want to thank you for taking care of me these last few weeks, and I want you to know that I appreciate all you've done to try and find the moron who did this. I truly believe he's lost in the wind, but it doesn't matter now since I won't be around long enough for his possible reappearance. When I return to Boston I'm going to fly out to Paris as soon as possible to look at places to rent, etc. Although I truly am grateful for what you've done, I

would appreciate it if you'd stay away when I return to
Boston. I don't want to see you again. I want a fresh
start. You owe me that.

I hope you find peace. I hope you find happiness.

Lexie

❧

Standing out on the lawn of my childhood home, I was still carrying with me that strange mix of fear and resolve. I didn't know what I expected to get out of this. I just knew that if I wanted to move on with my life, I had to talk to him.

Getting out of Boston had been easy. Getting out of Caine's building, not so much. Upon his departure for work that morning, I wrote him a good-bye note, and I headed down to the front desk. Arnie and Sly were waiting for me.

They tried to detain me, but when I reminded them that was illegal, they let me go. It took me twenty minutes of arguing with them before they realized I meant it when I said I'd call the police on their asses. I felt bad since they'd been protecting me for the last few weeks, but once I'd made this decision, no one, and I meant no one, was standing in my way. Still, as I made my way to the bus station I couldn't shake the paranoia that had come as a result of my attack. I found myself constantly glancing over my shoulder and imagining the burn of someone's stare on the back of my neck.

That and the fact that the bus journey was not fun on my wounded body meant I wasn't in the greatest shape by the time I got to my parents' home.

Our house had been very modest. My mom bought it when it was just the two of us and she bought it on her teacher's pay. My father hadn't contributed much over the years, jumping from one job to the next, so we'd never left. It was a one-story, two-bedroom house with a wood-clad triangle brow that sat over the tiny porch. The freshly painted gray wood was mimicked in the attached garage's door, the banister on the porch, and entrance. The house itself was built of quaint pale blond brick. It wasn't much but it was well kept. Even the lawn had been freshly mowed. Clearly my father was more capable of looking after himself than he'd ever let on in the past.

I lifted a hand to tuck away the hair that was blowing in my face and I was surprised to find I was trembling.

Shaking that off, I took a deep breath to try to ease the pressure on my chest. It felt like it was closing on me.

"Come on, Alexa."

Somehow I made it onto the porch and I could hear a television playing from inside. I rang the doorbell. The television noise muted and I heard footsteps coming toward the door.

I was going to be sick.

For some reason there was a painful twinge in my wound.

The door swung open and a tall, good-looking man stood before me. He was slim with broad shoulders, and he had a full head of black hair peppered generously with gray that contrasted sharply with his bright gray eyes. He looked a heck of a lot like Edward Holland. Even in cheap clothes he seemed to radiate a sense of class and money. His features slackened with shock. "Alexa?"

My lips felt numb. Somehow I managed to force out, "Hi, Dad."

"What are you doing here?" He stepped back, allowing me to enter the small living room. A closed door on the left-hand side of the room led into the kitchen. The kitchen led onto a backyard that was massive in comparison to the house. The door directly opposite the front door led into a small corridor, which led onto two small double bedrooms and a family bathroom.

I gazed around, hit by a wave of memories.

The furniture was the same after all these years. Pictures of us as a family still hung on the walls.

"Lexie?"

Our eyes met.

I hadn't expected to find our home . . . well, still as *our* home. I'd built this picture up in my head of the place being stripped back, barren of us, erased by everything that was him. But no. Mom was everywhere here.

This had momentarily distracted me, but reading the wary confusion on his face, I wondered if any emotion he ever showed was actually real.

He gestured to the couch. "Take a seat, Lexie."

"I'd rather stand."

"What's this about? I haven't seen you since your mother's funeral and I think this is the most you've spoken to me in seven years. What's going on?"

"I was attacked," I blurted out.

My father paled. "Attacked?"

I nodded. "I was leaving work and a guy stabbed me. He was wearing a hoodie and I didn't see his face . . . We haven't caught him, but the police are investigating it and think the attack might have been premeditated."

"Stabbed?" He stumbled toward me, his hands reaching out unsurely.

I flinched back from his touch and he froze.

"When?" he whispered.

"A few weeks ago."

"A few weeks ago? Shouldn't you be at home recovering?"

"I had to come see you."

"What was so urgent—"

"The police asked me if there was anyone in my life that had a grudge against me."

Realization dawned on my father with the impact of a swift kick to the gut. He slumped down onto his armchair and stared up at me in horror. "You think I had something to do with this?"

I quashed the guilt his reaction stirred in me. "No. But for a brief moment I did. I wondered to myself what my leaving did to Mom and to your relationship. For a moment I thought about the man who was capable of leaving a woman to die and I wondered if blaming his disloyal daughter for his own crapshoot of a life could make him unstable."

"That's—"

"Far-fetched, I know." I sighed and sat down wearily on the sofa. "But I've been lying in bed these last few weeks and I can't get it out of my head that the thought even crossed my mind. I've been protected and coddled in a friend's apartment, scared of what's outside, but even more scared of how messed up I am over you. So I had to come see you."

Silence fell between us.

Finally my father cleared his throat. His voice was thick. "I am not this monster you've made me up to be in your head."

"No?" Tears burned in my eyes. "How could you leave a woman who had a little boy to take care of . . . How could you leave her to die? I couldn't do that. I couldn't have lived with myself all these years."

His own eyes were bright with tears and I was surprised he maintained eye contact with me. When in the wrong, or lying, or being evasive, my father had a habit of looking at the ground, or anywhere but into my eyes. "I was in the kind of denial I didn't know existed, Lexie. I coped with it because I switched it off. I didn't allow myself to think of her as the vibrant woman she'd been, a confused, lonely, beautiful woman, who loved her kid more than anything in this world. But like me she was weak and she could be selfish. It was many years until she began to haunt me. I don't know what happened, I just know that the excuses I made to myself, the rationalizations, they burned up into ash in my mouth. I couldn't stop seeing her face. That's when I had my breakdown over it, when I told you and your mother."

"So you do feel remorse? Just not enough to apologize to the man who lost his mother and father within months of each other?"

My dad looked away, his fingers biting into his armchair. "Apologize? What the hell kind of apology could I give him now? Not one that would matter. I let a woman die because I was afraid and I was weak." He looked back at me. "You have to come to terms with the man I am, Alexa. I've had to. I'm not a perfect man. Far from it. I never will be. I'm a weak man and for a long time I was spoiled."

Tears dripped off my chin. "Tell me one thing. Did you love my mom? Me?"

His mouth quivered. "I did. I do. I just . . . I was never cut out to be a husband and a father. I'm not built that way."

It was the sad, horrible truth, but there it was. There was no magic solution to finding a father who would take care of me whenever I needed him, whose unconditional love would soothe the rejection of others, whose love for me would always exceed his love for himself.

My father would never be that kind of dad.

Yet there was a small measure of satisfaction in witnessing the change in him since the last we'd spoken seven years ago. There was self-awareness in him that hadn't existed before, and it gave me something at least to know that he was fully aware of his shortcomings. It wasn't enough to ease the ache, and it still didn't give me a father, or bring Caine's family back to him.

I wondered then if that little hole inside me would ever go away, or if I'd just have to get used to it, and hopefully one day meet someone who would distract me from what was missing by giving me a love that eclipsed it.

"Can I get you tea? Coffee?" my father asked uncertainly.

Feeling more pain in my stomach, I nodded. "Tea, please. And a glass of water. I need to take some Percocet."

Somehow he refrained from giving me a scolding look, realizing that any fatherly admonishment would not be welcome from him.

The door at the back of the room closed behind him as he disappeared into the kitchen. Suddenly exhausted, probably from an adrenaline dive, I rummaged through my bag for my phone. I frowned as I flicked the screen open and discovered I had ten missed calls from Caine.

Hadn't he gotten my note?

I sighed, even more exhausted at the thought of dealing with his stubbornness. The man was quite happy to watch me walk out of his life for good, just as long as I'd healed up physically first!

Idiot.

I threw my phone back in the bag and slumped on the sofa.

A loud clatter followed by a heavy thud made me jerk upright. "Dad? Are you okay?"

Nothing.

I heard my pulse start to race.

"Dad?" I said more loudly and cautiously stood up so as not to tug on my injury. "Dad, are you okay?" I made my way toward the door and pushed it open only to freeze at the sight of my father sprawled across the kitchen floor.

I moved, to rush to him, only to be yanked back into the solid heat of a hard body. Strong arms tightened around my chest. The silver of metal flashed across my vision.

Terror and adrenaline shot through me and without even thinking I heaved back with all my strength, slamming our attacker into the cabinets behind me. A male grunt of pain sounded and his grip loosened enough for me to tear away from him.

My feet slipped on the tile floor as I yanked open the door to the living room. I propelled myself forward into the room, just catching myself on the side table. Framed photographs crashed into my mother's favorite vase, the glass shattering behind me as I raced for the front door. I was drawn up sharply four feet from it.

Pain brought stinging tears to my eyes as he grabbed at my hair, hauling me backward. I tugged, crying out in agony at the pressure on my scalp as I attempted to break his grasp.

But it was too late and he clamped an arm around my waist.

Every ounce of fear I'd felt over the last few weeks coalesced inside me, turning from something cold into molten fury. I screamed in outrage, pulling my arm out and then slamming my elbow up high behind me. I connected and heard a satisfying howl of pain as I launched myself toward the door.

It wasn't enough.

Hands clawed at my jacket, dragging me backward. I kicked and screamed, jabbing my elbows back, but he took the blows, and with a strength that overpowered me he wrestled me to the floor.

Shock moved through me as a hooded face came into view. Hard dark eyes glittered down at me. Eyes I didn't recognize in a face that was shrouded by a black ski mask. All I could see were the eyes and thin pale lips.

The nothingness of his face, the emptiness in his gaze, was terrifying.

I fought harder.

I felt the warm trickle of blood, followed by the burning sting of a cut on my arm.

He'd sliced me as I grappled with him.

"Stupid bitch," his deep voice hissed. He let go of one of my arms to drive his fist down into my face.

Fire spread out across my cheek, stinging my nose and eyes and dazing me momentarily. I blinked the overabundance of water out of my eyes, trying to focus away from the pain to the man.

I saw the flash of silver again, this time lowering slowly to my throat.

"Missed last time. Stupid going for the gut. Too many variables."

I couldn't buck, or shrug him off, for fear the knife would slice right through my skin. "Who are you?" I tried to stall him so I could think.

Think, Lex, think, think, THINK!

"Wouldn't a gun have been easier?" I wheezed out, surprised by my thoughts and questions. More than anything, more than who he was or why he was doing this, I couldn't stop thinking about the fact that if he'd used a gun from the beginning he would probably have killed me already.

Lexie, stop! I shouted at myself, feeling insane. I needed to get out of this, not ponder my assailant's reasons for weapon of choice!

The guy's cold eyes suddenly flashed with emotion. "Guns are for pussies."

He pressed down with the blade.

A loud crash behind him made his head whip around toward the front door. As his face tilted upward, a huge fist appeared, slamming down and jerking his head back with so much force blood from his nose sprayed across my face.

His weight was yanked off me, and the knife clattered to the floor from his weakened grasp.

In awe, I struggled to get up, my hand reaching for my throat to feel the small cut that he'd made . . . but my gaze was on the tornado that had just entered my childhood home.

Caine.

Rage unlike anything I'd witnessed before emanated from every pore in Caine's body as he grabbed my attacker by the front of his hoodie and lifted him clean off his feet. He crashed him against the wall so hard pictures shook off from their hooks.

The attacker swung out at Caine, clipping him across the jaw. I reached for the knife and attempted to get to my feet.

I glanced over at Caine, ignoring the ache in my stomach, ready to help if he needed me. The hilt of the knife handle practically melted around my grip with the heat of my emotions.

Caine threw another punch, this time to the attacker's gut, and he winded him. As the attacker's head bent over, Caine brought his knee up and forced the guy's nose to connect with it.

I heard a crack and the agonized muffle it caused.

From there I watched in suspended horror as Caine beat the man. He punched him until he couldn't stand, and once he was on the floor he ripped the mask off, revealing the bloodied face of a stranger. Caine punched him again. And again.

And again.

"Caine," I whispered, wanting him to stop. "Caine, stop!" I hurried over to him and without thought of his reaction I placed a hand on his shoulder.

My touch halted him, however, and he looked up at me.

Tears sprang to my eyes at the stark fear I saw mingling with his fury.

For me.

"He's down," I said softly.

Caine turned back to the man who was making gurgling, choking noises from the back of his throat. He coughed, his lips parting slightly, and a bubble of blood popped between them.

"Who are you?" Caine demanded.

He groaned and shook his head.

I held the knife out to Caine. He took it and reversed the tables on the son of a bitch. Caine pressed it against his throat and repeated, "Who the fuck are you?"

When he got no response Caine pressed harder and blood began to color the blade's edge. "I don't think you realize how much I want to kill you. And I will. It's called self-defense and I've got plenty of money for fancy lawyers who'll make the court see it my way."

Still nothing.

Caine bent down, his nose almost touching the man's. "You touched my woman," he said, his voice guttural with his rage. "I'm itching to send you straight to hell, you piece of shit. I am *not* bluffing."

"O—k—" The attacker coughed, lifting an arm that fell limp before it even got a few inches off the floor. "Matt . . . hew . . . Hall . . . Holland. Hired . . . me."

My knees buckled and Caine turned, shock in his eyes at the revelation, just in time to watch me hit the floor.

"Lex!" He scrambled off the hit man and over to me as I braced over on all fours, trying to catch my breath. His hand slipped through my hair to curl around my nape. "Baby . . ."

My half brother? Someone I'd never even met had hired someone to kill me?

Nausea rose inside me.

I pushed Caine away in time as I vomited bile on my mother's lacquered hardwood floors.

My hair was pulled back from my face and Caine's heat enveloped me.

I jerked my head up at the realization his attention was not on our attacker.

We looked back at the bloodied criminal to see he had struggled up to a sitting position, but he was looking through his one eye that wasn't completely swelling shut toward the kitchen doorway. In unison Caine and I swung our heads around to follow his gaze.

My father stood in the doorway, blood trickling down his forehead, and he had a shotgun pointed at our attacker. "Don't worry," he said gruffly. "This bastard isn't going anywhere."

Assured my father had things well in hand, Caine tentatively touched my arm. "Lex, you're bleeding. You need an ambulance." He curled his arm around me protectively and I leaned my head on his shoulder.

"I'm okay. Let's just call the police to come and arrest this piece of shit. But they might want to send an ambulance for *him*." I stared over at him to see his eyes were still trained on my father. I sneered at the fear I saw in him. Just a bully with a shiny knife. "I bet you're rethinking that gun now, huh?"

CHAPTER 31

They stitched my arm up at Valley, the local hospital, with Caine and my father hovering over me. My dad had a minor concussion, but other than that, and being a little shaken up, he was okay.

Both he and Caine were ignoring the giant elephant in the room and using me as the excuse to do so.

"I'm fine," I assured them for the hundredth time. I had a cut on my arm, a swollen nose and eye, and my stomach was burning, but none of that mattered compared to my emotional state.

The police had taken our statements. Caine stood there in his blood-speckled shirt and told us that he'd jumped on a plane to Chester as soon as he got my note and that was why he'd arrived so shortly after me. We told them everything about my previous attack, and the officers contacted Boston PD to check out our story. We were informed we'd have to wait around a little longer, and a little longer had turned into more than a few hours. I was desperate to get home to Boston.

I'd never felt such bone-weary tiredness, and I wanted somewhere quiet so I could process the violence and the terrifying absurdity of what had just happened to me.

And although there had been times I'd thought about getting Caine in a room with my father and my father apologizing and somehow everything magically working out, the reality was much different. A surge of protectiveness rose inside me for Caine. I didn't want him to have to be in the same room with the man who had destroyed his family. It was difficult, though, because I also was grateful to my father for being there today and for being in charge in a way I'd never seen before. In that moment he'd reminded me so much of Grandpa.

"Miss Holland?" The policemen who had questioned us, Sergeant Garry and Sergeant Tailor, filed into the private room just off the ER ward.

"Hey." I nodded wearily in greeting.

"You doing okay?" Garry asked. He was a big bruiser of a guy with hard, rugged features and kind eyes. His partner, in contrast, was only an inch or so taller than me, wiry, and wore a perpetual look of suspicion.

"Yes." I tried to rein in the impatience I was feeling. "He talked, didn't he?"

"Oh, he was desperate to talk," Tailor replied. "Wants to make a deal."

"So?"

Garry took another step toward me, compassion written all over his face. "The perpetrator's name is Vernon Holts. He's got a record a mile long from petty theft to assault. During a search of his house on one occasion, they found a massive weapons collection." He gave me a pointed look. "Knives, swords . . . anything with a blade."

"There's a surprise," I muttered.

Caine's hand slipped into mine.

"He said he was hired to kill you by a Matthew Holland. Holts claims this man is your half brother."

"He is." I tried to wrap my head around the revelation. It was just too surreal. Like I was standing outside myself, watching this play out in a movie. "But I don't understand . . ." I searched Caine's face for answers. "The article about me came out after the attack. How did Matthew know about me?"

"Maybe he found out some other way," Caine mused.

"That still doesn't explain why he wanted to hurt me." I looked over at my father, who was standing silently in the corner. "Do you know why?"

He shook his head, looking lost. "I haven't spoken to Matthew in years . . ."

"It's my fault." My grandfather's voice startled me, making me jump.

My heart began to pound at the sight of him entering the room. "What are you doing here?"

He stepped toward me, and the officers watched him warily. He was ashen, his expression stark. "Caine called me. I got on a plane." He anxiously searched my face. "Please tell me you're okay."

"I'm going to be okay," I said. "Now, what do you mean it's your fault?"

"I changed my will." His shoulders slumped with guilt and he faced the officers. "I'm Edward Holland. Alexa and Matthew's grandfather." He returned his attention to me. "It was time for me to do something right and not always put the Holland family ahead of everything else. I was proud of you . . . and I felt impotent not being able to take care of you like family should. Matthew wouldn't know a hard day's work if it bit him in the ass," he said with venom. "I changed my will. Matthew has had every advantage in life handed to him and he's a spoiled brat as a result. In the event of my death and my wife's, you would be left with sixty-five percent of our assets. I didn't know Matthew had made a deal with my attorney that included informing Matthew if I changed my will. I found out yesterday during a family . . . discussion . . . about Alexa. The bastard let it slip."

Aghast, I couldn't even speak.

"Sir." Sergeant Garry stepped toward Grandpa. "Are you saying that the motive behind Matthew Holland's attack on your granddaughter is an inheritance dispute?"

"An inheritance dispute." I laughed bitterly. "He hired a hit man to kill me because of money." I glanced over at my father. "Money. It's so fucking toxic."

"Vernon Holts isn't a hit man," Tailor informed us. I stared at him in confusion. "He claims he met Holland in a bar one night and he bragged to Holland about his assault offenses and his skill with knives. Holland offered Holts a hundred grand to take you out."

"But Holland didn't do any research on this guy." Garry shook his head in disgust. "Holts's record show he's had three restraining orders against him in the past six years from women he harassed. Talking to him . . ." His eyes were grave on me. "He admits Holland asked him to stop after the first attack failed. Holts refused. It appears the money became secondary to catching his prey."

"He became fixated on Alexa," Caine's voice growled from above me.

"We believe so." Tailor nodded. "Holts has been very forthcoming. He admits to following Alexa from the hospital to Mr. Carraway's apartment and staking out the property ever since. With his statement and your grandfather's, the Boston PD should be able to get a warrant to arrest Matthew Holland while they investigate."

"Whether they find enough evidence against him to substantiate Holts's claims is another thing," Caine added impatiently.

I froze at the thought, realizing what he meant. "Matthew gets away with this if they can't find physical evidence to connect him to it?"

"It's possible," Garry said, his voice filled with regret. "However, Holts has admitted guilt. We're transferring him to Boston, and the officers on the case there will be taking over."

I nodded, dazed. "Thank you for your help."

When they were gone, Caine rounded the bed to grip my arms. "Alexa, this is all going to be all right."

I scoffed. "How? It's like watching a shitty movie and I'm stuck to the chair and the remote is all the way across the room." I leaned into him slightly. "My half brother hired a crazy ex-con to kill me. Do you know how insane that is?"

"Yes, I do." His eyes blazed with anger. "I know the lengths people are willing to go to for money. I've been a victim *to* it, and a victim *for* it. You're in a room with two other people who have as well."

"This is why I didn't want it," I said, my voice hoarse.

"Alexa, I'm sorry," Grandpa said.

I looked over Caine's shoulder to him. "I know you never meant anything . . . I know you were just trying to make up for . . . but take me out of your will immediately. Promise me."

Tears bright in his eyes, he nodded his agreement. "I'm so sorry I did this."

"No." I shook my head. "Don't take that on."

"She's right," Caine said. "You had her best interests at heart. Matthew and Holts are the ones to blame here."

I could tell Grandpa wasn't quite convinced, the guilt still visible in his eyes, but he nodded gratefully at Caine.

"The sins of the father," Dad suddenly said, his voice quiet, haunted.

We all looked at him.

He seemed wrecked. "Some of us are destined to repeat our parents' mistakes."

"Alistair," Grandpa said sharply. "You made your mistakes, big fucking mistakes, but you did not deliberately attempt to do something so—"

"A woman died anyway."

The muscles in Caine's jaw twitched as he stared at my father like he was staring into hell.

"Caine," I whispered uncertainly, my heart breaking for him.

"I won't apologize." My father met Caine's hard gaze. "Because I know that's not what you want from me. What you want I can never give. I . . . I wish that I could."

The answering silence was so sharp and painful I almost couldn't breathe in it.

Then . . . Caine gave my father this almost imperceptible little nod.

My father, on the verge of tears, looked toward me. "I'm going to leave you two alone, but I imagine we'll see each other soon. I am so sorry this happened to you, Alexa."

Somehow I managed to speak around the strangled feeling in my throat. "Thanks for being there today."

He gave me a sad smile. "Your mother would have killed me if I let anything happen to you."

"Yeah?"

He seemed surprised by the uncertainty in my question. "Yes. You know she missed you every day."

Tears rolled down my cheeks before I could stop them and I buried my chin in my shoulder in an attempt to hide my reaction. Caine, however, was having none of that. His strong arms wrapped around me, pulling me so close I had no option but to wrap my arms around him. Burying my face in his chest, I let the sobs rise from my belly, and I cried for everything. For Caine, for our parents, for Matthew and Vernon's attack, and for the realization that sometimes love really could be too broken to fix, and that you couldn't get a happily ever after with everyone.

But as Caine kissed my hair and whispered soothing, loving words in my ears, I was assuaged by the knowledge that I didn't need a happily ever after with everyone . . . just with *some*one.

"I love you," I choked out against his warm chest.

In answer, Caine gently pulled me away, just far enough so he could look into my face. I was tearstained, swollen-faced, and exhausted. I was a mess. But he stared at me as if I were the only person in the room, and as if I was the most beautiful thing he'd ever seen. His voice was gruff as he confessed, "I love you too."

My arms tightened in reflex around him, and a renewed determination pulsed into my veins. "Let's go home so we can rest. We've got a couple of bastards to deal with who need a lesson in manners."

Amusement curled the corners of Caine's mouth. "There she is," he murmured in satisfaction.

CHAPTER 32

It felt like hours before we were allowed to go home. Once we set foot in Boston we were hustled to the police station, where we had to answer all the same questions all over again. By the time a cab dropped us off at Caine's apartment, I was deadweight.

Caine practically carried me upstairs to his bed. When I flopped down on it he wearily but patiently set about taking off my boots and jeans. I managed to shrug out of my jacket and throw it on the floor while Caine jerked the covers down so I could slide my legs under. The last thing I remembered was Caine getting in beside me and gently pulling me into his arms.

The next morning the sunlight peeked in through the blinds and woke me up. I was sprawled across Caine, unconsciously uncaring of my injury, my head resting on his bare stomach.

My arm was draped across his upper chest and shoulder, and his fingers were drawing little soothing circles on my right biceps.

"You're awake," I said, the words coming out croaky.

His other hand slid down my back to my hip. "Yeah."

Lifting myself off him long enough to look at him, I assessed him carefully. Having heard it in his voice, I wasn't surprised to see the wariness in his expression. My stomach flipped uneasily. "Please don't."

He squeezed my hip, understanding without having to ask. "I'm not. I just want to make sure you understand what you're getting into here with me."

"I'm getting what I deserve," I said, and I meant every word. "And so are you."

Caine moved slowly, easing me onto my back so he could brace himself over me. His gaze moved over my face, and every feeling he had for me blazed in his eyes. It moved me so much I was breathless.

"Don't you get it?" he said, his voice gruff with emotion. "I've never met anyone like you before. There's no one like you. I keep waiting to not feel like this, because there are times I can't bear it. To care this much. To worry about you day in and day out, even before the attack. I love you so fucking much. I sometimes . . . I feel consumed by it. Griff and Don called me as soon as you left the building yesterday, and I felt it. That panic. Like the panic I felt when you went down in my arms and I saw the blood. I felt like I was going to come apart at the seams. I didn't know how I was going to survive it if something happened to you."

"Caine," I whispered, overwhelmed by his confession, but relieved too. I was relieved to know that I wasn't the only one in this who felt so deeply, so strongly.

"I got back to the apartment, I saw your note, and I called everyone I could think of that could help me get a private flight to Connecticut because I was terrified of what might happen to you. But also because"—his voice grew even more hoarse—"when you asked me to stay away from you in your note, it finally hit me. You meant it. You weren't going to try anymore. I'd run out of chances, and I realized that the night before would be the last time I ever saw you. And I couldn't . . . The whole time on that plane I . . . I kept thinking to myself if I could just get to you I would tell you I loved you and I'd get to keep you. I'm that selfish."

"You're not selfish."

"I am . . . and every morning I'm going to wake up feeling like this."

"Like what?"

"Like I'm cheating somehow. Like I've stolen something."

I reached up to smooth away his frown lines. "No more talking about how you don't deserve me."

"But I don't."

It didn't take a psychologist to realize that Caine's fears about his self-worth came from abandonment, his shame at what his ambition had led him to do, and the women who had used him. He was a complex mix of confidence and insecurities. I didn't know if he could ever work through those insecurities, but I was going to do my best to help him try.

"I also don't want to make the same mistakes my father made."

"What do you mean?"

"He loved my mother beyond anything else. He loved her so damn much he had her wrapped up tight and protected in his world. He loved her so much he couldn't see past it to the fact that the woman he loved was desperate to be free. She wanted more. She wanted adventure."

Light dawned.

Finally I got to the real crux of his problem. Cupping his

face in my hands, I poured every ounce of feeling into what I was about to say so that he would never doubt my words. "I am not your mother. I'm not looking for something else from life. I'm not looking for more. I'm not looking for a great adventure. I'm not looking, because I found it. You are my more. You are my great adventure."

Caine stared at me in wonder. "I can't believe that after everything I put you through you're still here."

"You came for me," I whispered, trying not to get choked up again. "Even though it meant facing my father, you followed me to protect me. That meant everything to me. You saved my life."

His own eyes were bright with emotion and his voice was hoarse when he vowed, "I will always protect you."

"No fair," I breathed heavily against the love and desire now pulsing through my body. "We can't have sex yet until this stupid wound is healed, and I really feel like this is one of those moments where intense sex is applicable."

"Anticipation is everything." He laughed, relaxing onto his back and pulling me into his side. "Those first weeks working with you were the best foreplay of my life. By the time I got you naked on my desk, I was harder than I've ever been."

I laughed. "That was really great sex."

"It was."

"I'll miss that desk."

Caine tensed. "What do you mean?"

I soothed him, stroking my hand over his abs. "If we're in a serious, committed relationship now, there's no way I'm working for you. I'll need to find another job."

"But no more Paris?"

I pressed a sweet kiss to his stomach. "No more Paris." I sighed. "I have some e-mailing to do."

"We've both got a lot to do . . . so let's just enjoy the next thirty minutes of peace and quiet."

I snuggled into him. "Now, that I can do quite happily."

To say the Holland family was destroyed by Matthew Holland's arrest was an understatement. My defense lawyers were trying to build a case against my half brother while he was out on bail. He'd been bailed out by his mother's family. They all firmly believed his wails of denial, but my grandfather, although refusing to comment in the media, had taken my side and cut him out of his life and his will. My grandmother was a harder nut to crack. Grandpa said she believed him when he said Matthew had bribed Grandpa's attorney to find out about changes to his will, but she couldn't quite bring herself to believe he was capable of something so despicable as trying to murder me.

The jury was out for her until hard evidence was found against Matthew.

Unfortunately there was no physical evidence yet to link him to the case, but the police were working on it. He hadn't paid Holts in cash but in jewelry, so they were trying to link the pieces that were pawned by Holts to Matthew or anybody connected to him.

I truly believed Matthew Holland was a spoiled idiot who was living so far up his own ass in fantasyland that he'd impetuously hired a man to get rid of the person standing in his way to financial wealth beyond his wildest dreams. I had to wonder if he hadn't thought of me as a person until Holts's attack went awry, and then was forced to see me, to see what he had done. Stupid, naive, and quickly terrified, he'd lost control of Holts and the entire scheme. I didn't think I had anything to worry about regarding my future safety around Matthew.

Holts, however, was a different deal altogether. I felt so much safer knowing Vernon Holts was in prison and, if my lawyers had anything to say about it, would be going away for a long time. That knowledge allowed me to concentrate on starting to put the pieces of my new life together. I contacted Renée and Antoine to tell them I wouldn't be accepting the job. I apologized for messing them around, and they were incredibly understanding about the whole thing.

I'd put feelers out looking for a job in Boston in events management. The last few weeks hadn't brought up anything that sounded appealing financially, and I was beginning to wonder if this career change meant starting from the ground up again.

By week three Caine suggested what Charlie the Red Sox date had suggested months ago—that I start my own events planning company. The idea of starting my own company, however, didn't exhilarate me like it did Caine. All I could imagine was constantly bringing my work home with me, and I didn't want that. I understood work spilled into personal life, but I didn't want my whole world to revolve around my business. That wasn't me. And I couldn't imagine Caine and I would ever see much of each other if we were both running our own companies.

When I said that to him he was quick to agree that I should look at joining someone else's company. To help me along he was using his own connections to see if there were any open positions in that industry. Meanwhile, his offer for me to remain working with him if I couldn't find anything was on the table.

What hadn't been on the table was sex.

By week six into my recovery, although weighed down by the stress of the case against Matthew and Holts, and finding a new job, I was feeling much better physically.

Something I kept trying to explain to Caine.

Although he insisted that I stay at his apartment through-out my recovery, he was very careful with me. I was treated to delicious kisses and gentle caresses but nothing more. After the kissing he'd release me and whisper, "Soon," in my ear.

Well, I was getting sick of "soon." I wanted now. When I'd attempted to push the subject, he got stern with me and told me to be patient, that it was important I made a full recovery.

Of course Caine should have realized by now that telling me what to do outside of the office was never a good idea. My answer was to head home to my apartment and get settled in. I had to admit I'd missed my place. I loved Caine's but only because it was where he was, and I loved his view. Nothing beat his view. Or the fact that Effie was just down the hall.

But my place was home too.

And I was recovered, so it was time to be home. I texted Caine while he was at work.

> Just wanted to let you know I've gone home to my apartment. It's time to get back into the swing of things. Thanks for everything, Roomie. Love you.

Half an hour later he replied.

> Have I told you lately how stub-born you are? Fine. I'll come over after work.

He just can't stay away. I grinned, giddy at his response, and wondered if that feeling would ever go away.

I was less giddy when he showed up late that evening, exhausted by a day trip to New York, and crashed on my bed. I stared down at him feeling a mixture of tenderness and disappointment. Tonight was supposed to be the night we finally had sex after all these weeks. I didn't know about Caine, but I was past the point of frustration.

He looked so tired, though. I stroked his hair back from his face and wondered if we could keep up our pattern of working around his career. We did a good job of making time for each other—Caine did a wonderful job of making sure he spent time with me in spite of his busy schedule. I had my fingers crossed we'd never lose that consideration for each other.

And sex . . . well, we'd just have to be creative.

I smiled in anticipation as I walked around to my side of the bed and set my alarm to low so that it would wake me but hopefully not Caine. I had a far more pleasurable plan of waking for him . . .

Naked from top to toe, I straddled Caine while he still lay in dreamland. It was early in the morning, the sun had just come up, and I intended to make something else come up to say hello. I grinned to myself, desire tingling between my legs, as I gently pushed the hem of Caine's T-shirt up to reveal his hard abs.

I stroked his skin lightly with my fingertips and watched his stomach jerk. I pushed the shirt up as far as I could and bent over to lick his nipple. From there I licked the other, scraping my teeth lightly over it, before moving downward, brushing my lips over his skin, inhaling the familiar scent of him, tasting him.

His dick grew hard against my ass.

Bingo.

Looking up at him, I saw his eyes were still closed but the color was rising in his cheeks and he was moving slightly, a little restless beneath me.

Feeling mischievous and wicked, I brushed my ass over his erection as I moved downward, and had to squeeze my eyes shut against the lust that shot through me at the feel of his hard-on between my legs. I fought for patience, resisting the urge to wake him, pull down his pajama bottoms, and slide him inside me. Instead I tugged down his bottoms and underwear so his cock sprang out. I took him into my mouth, growing increasingly wet at the groans it elicited from him.

For a few seconds I toyed with him, running my tongue down the underside before swirling it around the sensitive rim. Caine began to jerk his hips upward, forcing him farther into my mouth.

I sucked hard.

"Lexie," I heard his surprised gasp, and looked up at him from under my lashes. Caine was awake now and straining against me. "Lex." His sleepy, aroused voice was such a turn-on. "Baby . . ."

I continued to suck him as my fist pumped the base of his erection. His breathing grew ragged, his thighs were rigid, and I knew he was close. I took him almost to the edge and then released him before he got there.

"Lexie," he groaned, his head flopping back on the pillow, "are you trying to kill me?"

"Not quite." I grinned as I shifted back to pull down his bottoms. He helped and then quickly removed his shirt as I crawled back up his body.

"Are you sure you're ready for this?" His eyes cut to the

pink scar on my stomach. It wasn't huge, but it was there. Reminding us. Caine's arms came around me, drawing me up against his chest. His hands caressed my naked back, his eyes filled with desire and tenderness. "We can wait."

I shook my head and leaned down to brush my lips over his. "I'm done waiting." I kissed him with all the fierce love and need I had inside me. My tongue danced with his in a deep, drugging kiss as we crushed tight against each other.

Caine broke the kiss to follow a path down my throat with his mouth. I gasped for breath, my hips surging against his cock as he kissed his way down to my breasts. When he wrapped his lips around my nipple, I lost all control.

I pushed up on my knees, wrapped my hand around him, and guided him to my entrance. I lowered myself down and we panted as he slid inside me. The overwhelming thickness of him took my breath away for a moment and we both held still as my body eased into accepting him.

I sighed when I moved up on him slightly and back down. Pleasure rippled through me.

Caine grasped the back of my head and pulled my mouth back to his, kissing me with a voraciousness that seeped into me—I couldn't get enough of him. I began to ride him hard.

"Easy, baby," he attempted to coax through a groan, apparently still concerned for my injury.

"No," I gasped, my arms wrapped tight around his shoulders as I fucked him with all the desperation that had been inside me for weeks.

We both came fast and hard, the pulsing clench of my climax around his cock wrenching his own orgasm from him.

I collapsed in his arms, my face buried against his neck. I somehow managed to move my languid legs so they were comfortably wrapped around his hips as I sat in his lap.

He twitched inside me at the movement and I smiled. "Round two?"

He kissed my shoulder. "I'll need a minute or so," he said, his voice filled with humor.

"And then round two?"

Caine shook with laughter. "Yes. And then round two." He gently threaded his fingers through my hair to clasp the nape of my neck. He brought my head back and I stared into his handsome face, my gaze low-lidded with satisfaction. Something flared in his eyes at the sight of mine. "Fuck yeah, round two," he said, "but this time I'm in charge."

Not too long later Caine held me down, my hands at the sides of my head while he glided inside me, and it was all with tenderness that brought tears to my eyes. He held my gaze as he thrust gently, taking his time to stoke the flame. It was intense and moving and so much more than we'd had before. Now I knew as he gazed into my face while he made love to me . . . I knew what was working behind his eyes.

I knew it because, as he pushed me in nerve-tingling increments toward climax, he told me.

"I love you, Lex," he said, his voice rough with passion. "Love you so much, baby."

The tears escaped before I could stop them. "I love you too."

He let go of one of my hands to brush his thumb across my temple where the tearstain tracked. The sight of my tears seemed to fan the flames of urgency inside him and he began to pump into me faster.

"Oh God." I wanted to touch him, but Caine knew his control over my pleasure increased it. "Baby!" My cries filled the room, matching his groans as he fucked me harder. The tension inside me snapped and I cried out as the stunning orgasm ripped through me.

Quick on the heels of my orgasm, Caine's hips stilled and then jerked as his own climax tore through him.

I stroked his back in leisurely wonder. "I've never been this happy," I whispered, a little scared by it.

Caine must have heard the fear, because he kissed my neck, tightened his hold on me, and said, "Me neither. But we'll get used to it."

"Promise?"

He lifted his head to meet my gaze. "No, because on second thought I don't want to get used to it. If you get used to it—"

"You forget to be thankful for it," I finished.

He nodded slowly. "Yeah."

I thought about our rough starts in life, Caine's of course more so than mine. I thought about our rough last few weeks, mine more so than Caine's.

I brushed my thumb over his lower lip. "I don't think we'll ever forget to be thankful."

"No. I don't suppose we will."

Later that day while Caine was at work, I received a call from my father. It wasn't the easiest conversation, and I wasn't sure there ever would be easiness between us. My father was going to be in my life when my case against Matthew and Holts went to court because he was obviously a very important witness. But there were no promises from either of us that there would be a future in the cards. Honestly it seemed pretty impossible with Caine between us.

I had to wonder, even if I wanted my father back in my life, would I have tried to make a place for him in it? Or would I have chosen Caine over him? I wasn't sure what the answer would be, but I was stunned and a little disconcerted by the little voice inside me that whispered I would always choose Caine.

And then I realized that wasn't quite true.

I think that I would choose Caine over nearly anyone . . . but if we had children they would always come first. I also knew enough about the man I loved to know that he would feel the same way. So many adults hadn't taken him into consideration when he was a child. In the past few weeks Caine had mentioned "our children" in this offhand manner that made me smile—like kids with me was a given now that he'd admitted he loved me.

He would never put a kid through anything like what he'd been through.

Neither would I.

That realization made me think of my mom. It made me think of what Caine had said to me all those months ago at Good Harbor Beach.

So I sat down to have one last conversation with my mother in the hopes of freeing myself of some that hurt.

CHAPTER 33

Dear Mom,
The greatest lesson you taught me is that parents' actions
and choices resonate into their child's life, sometimes
affecting them in a way it never should. I wish your
greatest lesson to me could be more positive, because the
truth is that's who you were—an optimistic, warm,
sweet woman. But you were also weak. And I have to
forgive you for your weakness, because at the end of the
day we all have our weaknesses. I wanted to tell you that
you hurt me when you chose my father over me. I wanted
to tell you that I'll never understand how you could love
him so deeply when he could never love anyone as much
as he loved himself. And I wanted to tell you that I realize
now that it was never up to me to understand.

I'm sorry for putting you in a position where you
had to choose between us.

You can't help whom you love.

Watching you waste your sweet heart on my father

paralyzed me. For the longest time I deliberately avoided ever feeling about someone the way you felt about him. Because of that I sometimes felt like there were days that I was just sitting watching life pass me by. The hell of it all was that it never even occurred to me to flag it down and ask it for a ride.

Until Caine came along. And there was no choice in it for me. Just as I now realize there was probably no choice in it for you.

I forgive you for loving Dad.

I even forgive you for loving him more than me.

But I'll never forget.

The greatest lesson I teach my kids won't be the same you taught me.

It won't be the lesson Caine's parents taught him either.

I don't know what it'll be yet.

I just know there will never be a day that passes my kids by when they don't know that there is no one in this world they can count on more than me.

I don't mean to make you feel guilty, Mom. I just needed to finally tell you how I feel so I can move on. The past is the past and I'm letting go of it and all the anger that comes with it. I'm trying out this thing called peace, and I'm hoping that wherever you are you can find that peace too knowing that I'm letting the ugliness of the past go, and knowing that no matter what I loved you.

And I know you loved me.

Good-bye, Mom.

Yours,
Lexie

EPILOGUE

"You know, I think we need to lift the ban on showering together," Caine grumbled as he sauntered down the stairs and into the kitchen.

I snorted and held out his mug of coffee before returning my attention to the notes I had spread all over the kitchen counter. "There was a reason we banned it. It was called being late for work," I murmured absentmindedly.

The mug was removed from my hand and I narrowed my eyes on the list of boutiques Nadia had mentioned, wondering how on earth I was going to get around them all in a day.

"I didn't mind."

"You didn't mind what?" I pulled out the map of Boston I'd printed off. I'd used the computer to place the boutiques on the map so I could work out the most efficient route for visiting them all.

"Being late."

"You're the boss," I reminded him. "You can do what you

like. I have a boss who wasn't happy at my excuse for lateness."

"That's because Bree needs to get laid."

"Caine." I looked up at him in admonishment.

He gestured to my face. "Ah, there she is."

Confused, I wrinkled my nose.

"I was wondering if you were ever going to look up from that thing." He tapped the huge folder in front of me. "A 'good morning' would be nice."

I winced. "Sorry. I'm just feeling the pressure with this one." I cocked my head to the side and gave him a soft, flirtatious smile. "And was my good morning this morning in bed not satisfying enough?" I referred to the fact that I'd woken him up with my mouth.

Caine leaned across the counter so our noses were practically touching. "This morning was very nice, but I'd quite like it when I come down to get my coffee in the morning if my wife would look at me. Maybe even throw in a kiss or two."

I smiled and lifted my left hand to cup his face, the three diamonds on my engagement ring sparkling in the light next to my wedding band. "I don't mean to neglect you." I brushed my lips over his apologetically. "And I promise when Nadia returns from the land of Bridezilla you will get me back."

Caine pressed his mouth to mine, his kiss harder, searching. I moaned and melted into him, wishing with all my heart that Nadia's wedding was over already.

Nadia had gone up in the world and was now a cohost on Boston's most-watched breakfast show. In fact, a lot had changed in the thirty months since my whole world turned upside down and Caine finally admitted he loved me.

Not long after I started looking for a new job, I was approached by Henry's friend Bree Stanton, a socialite turned professional career woman who had worked her ass off to create the most elite events management company in Boston. She offered me a job as an events planner and I'd fallen in love with the position almost instantly. We managed many of the biggest events on the social calendar, including weddings. And Nadia Ray's wedding was a huge event, not only because of her celebrity status but because she'd managed to tame the untameable and wring a proposal out of Henry. A Lexington getting married was a big deal. A Lexington getting married to Boston's favorite TV show host was an even bigger deal.

I can't say I was surprised that Henry proposed to Nadia. I'd seen a difference in the way he interacted with her from the beginning. Despite her local fame, Nadia was down-to-earth, fun, and a real friend. I was over-the-moon for Henry and I was delighted for me because it meant I got to keep Nadia in my life too.

It also meant Nadia came to me to organize the wedding. Bree was ecstatic, and I had the promise of a very nice bonus if I pulled the wedding off without a hitch. So I had my friends' happiness and a lovely bonus motivating me to get this day exactly the way Nadia wanted. Ever since Henry had proposed to her, she'd transformed into this crazy woman I barely recognized. I could forgive her for the crazy. My experience in wedding planning in the last two and a half years had shown that most brides (not all, though) transformed into hyper versions of themselves. I had every confidence Nadia would return to normal upon her departure for her honeymoon.

Thankfully I didn't have the opportunity to become one of those brides, because Caine and I didn't have a huge wedding. We invited our closest friends and family—Effie, Henry,

Nadia, Rachel, and Jeff—to witness our very small, very private wedding at Caine's (now our) summerhouse in Nantucket. I didn't invite my grandfather, even though I wanted him there, because it was unfair to Caine. So I was shocked to discover Grandpa there on the morning of the wedding, ready to walk me down the aisle. Caine had surprised me by inviting him for me, and that just made me love my husband a million times more than I already did.

Three months after my attack Caine asked me to move in with him. Actually it was only a few weeks after. It took three months for me to agree. It was more about finally giving up my beautiful cozy apartment than not wanting to live with Caine. We were living together anyway. If I didn't spend the night at his, he was at mine. Finally he got fed up of the back-and-forth and lack of permanency. A month after that he proposed, and two months after that we were married.

His apartment was now our apartment—it was also barely recognizable. Gone were the white leather kitchen stools and the stark black color scheme. In their place was comfortable and gender-neutral furniture with not-so-gender-neutral cushions and throws strewn on them to emulate the coziness of my old apartment.

Caine didn't even say a word.

To be honest, I think he barely noticed.

He was used to my style now, and wasn't a guy who was interested in soft furnishings.

"I don't remember you being this crazy when it was our wedding." Caine scowled down at the massive folder filled with Nadia's wedding arrangements.

"That's because I wasn't. Moreover, Henry and Nadia's wedding is for a hundred and fifty guests. We had six."

"I liked ours better," he murmured, sipping his coffee.

"Me too." I laughed at his petulance, but I really couldn't blame him. Nadia and Henry's wedding seemed to be taking over my life at the moment.

"If they weren't our friends." He eyed the folder again.

"You can't burn it," I said.

Caine grinned at me. "Get out of my head."

"I don't want to." It was my turn to grumble. "I want to dive into your head and take you to bed and have my wicked way with you." I pushed the map away from me. "Instead I'm spending today hopping from one bridal boutique to the next trying to find the perfect bridesmaid dresses because Nadia has become obsessed with using homegrown designs." I bugged my eyes out in frustration. "She's not even from Boston."

His lips twitched. "This is why you shouldn't work with friends."

"We did okay."

"We were lovers. We were never friends." To make his point he got up to put his mug in the sink and as he passed me he pressed a kiss to the side of my neck.

Three years on and he still made my toes tingle. "That's not true. You're my best friend."

In answer Caine wrapped his arms around my waist and drew me back against his chest. "You're mine too, baby. That's why I'm asking you to put the folder of doom aside tonight so we can go out for a nice meal and spend some time together."

There was nothing in this world I'd like to do more. "We can't. We're having dinner with Nadia and Henry."

My husband dropped his forehead to my shoulder and groaned. "There's such a thing as too much 'friend time.'"

I shook with laughter. "We made these plans ages ago. We're going to the opening of that new restaurant, Smoke."

"Oh, that sounds appetizing," he remarked dryly as he pulled up the stool beside me so our knees touched. "A restaurant opening. That means the media will be there."

He looked weary just at the thought of it and I understood. From the moment Caine and I moved in together, the society papers went nuts. It was even worse when we were seen out and about with our friends. Caine, Henry, Nadia, and I would turn up to events together and the photographers would go mad trying to get pictures of us. Of course, it was a juicy story that Nadia was dating a Lexington. It was an even juicier story that the black sheep of the Holland family (that would be me) had accused her half brother of attempting to have her killed, and was now dating one of the wealthiest men in Boston.

Oh yeah, that was good tabloid fodder.

Not so good for my family.

To his credit, Grandpa had stood by me throughout the whole ordeal. Perhaps part of it was to make amends for his involvement in covering up Caine's mother's death, but I knew it was a difficult time for him because my grandmother had left him. Their relationship remained strained and distant up until Matthew's hearing, where it was decided we had enough evidence against my brother to go to trial. My grandmother started to see sense then and she and my grandpa worked on patching things up.

She still refused to meet me, but I didn't need her in my life. If her rejection stung a little, I only had to remind myself that I was used to it, and I'd learned some time ago to only want the people in my life who mattered, who cared.

Vernon Holts and Matthew's case went to trial seven months ago. Holts was convicted of three counts of assault and one count of attempted murder. Six weeks later he was sentenced to twenty-eight years in a maximum-security prison. Matthew was advised by his lawyer to plead guilty because the evidence against him was significant. Not only did we have Holts's witness statement, but there was also the jewelry that Holts had pawned. Every single piece led back to the Hollands and Matthew's wife's family. These were expensive pieces—pieces that were secured in the Hollands' vault where only family members had access to the code. There were witness accounts from my grandfather's staff that saw Matthew removing jewelry. But the real stinger was that he'd stupidly confessed the crime to his father-in-law when Holts got out of control. For whatever reasons, whether it was to protect his daughter and grandson from his son-in-law's stupidity, or his sense of justice, Matthew's father-in-law came forward as a witness in my case.

Matthew was convicted of conspiracy to commit murder and was sentenced a month ago to twenty years, a reduced sentence because he pleaded guilty.

I was just glad it was finally all over.

And as promised, Grandpa had taken me out of his will.

As for my father and me, just as I suspected, we'd lost touch since the trial ended. I intended to send a birthday and Christmas card each year so he knew that he was in my thoughts . . . but I couldn't forge a relationship with him. As sad as it was, sometimes there really was too much damage between people. Sometimes we were better apart than we were together.

My father seemed to be a better man on his own.

That wasn't the fairy tale, but it was real.

And it was okay.

I gave my husband a coaxing smile. "Do this tonight and I promise tomorrow I'm yours."

"All day?" He raised an eyebrow.

I raised my eyebrow right back at him. "You're free all day tomorrow?"

"I'll make myself free." He caressed my knee and I shivered at the heat in his eyes. "I'm sick of quickies. I want to take my time."

"Well, you better switch off your phone. Otherwise Rick will pester us all day." Rick was the young business graduate Caine had hired to be his PA. Yes, he was better than some attractive young female working closely with my husband, but only marginally. He had a giant stick up his ass, and sniffed haughtily at me any time I surprised Caine with an impromptu lunch. Apparently I was, and I quote, distracting him. "I dislike your PA."

Caine grinned. "He's good at his job."

"He's a pain in the neck."

"That is good at his job."

"He doesn't like me very much."

"Good," he said, his voice husky as he slipped his hand under my skirt. "If he liked you I'd have to fire him."

I stopped his hand before it could reach his destination. "If you start that we won't stop," I whispered, already hot and bothered.

He removed his hand only to cup my face so he could press a tender kiss to my lips. His countenance was suddenly serious as he gazed into my eyes. "For the longest time my company is what got me up in the morning. It was what motivated me every second of every day. Since the moment you started working for me, *you* are what has gotten me up in the morning. *You* are what motivates me every second of every day. And still I want more from you. Tomorrow the day is all ours, because I want to talk to you about something."

My pulse fluttered. "About what?"

He kissed me and then released me. "We'll talk tomorrow."

"No, mister." I grabbed his arm and hauled him back down onto his stool. "You can't just say something like that and then think I'll be able to get through an entire day without knowing what the hell you're talking about."

He sighed. "I'd prefer us to have time to talk. We both have to be at work"—he glanced at his watch and frowned—"five minutes ago."

"Caine," I warned, "you tell me now or I will think the worst."

"It's not bad." He rested a reassuring hand on my knee. "Baby, it's not bad at all. I just . . . I've put off discussing it because you've been so busy, but I'm beginning to realize that you're going to be busy right up until the wedding and that's still four months away."

I smiled curiously at the consternation on his face. "What is this about?"

"I want a kid."

I froze at his abrupt announcement.

"I want our kid." He grabbed my hands, searching my face as he attempted to read my reaction. "I want to try to have a baby with you."

The sudden rush of emotion at his declaration overwhelmed me. Any response was strangled in my throat as I fought to fight tears.

"Lexie?"

For the past year I'd pondered the idea of having a baby with Caine, until the pondering became more insistent, until it became a longing. With our schedules I hadn't known how to bring it up. Back in the beginning of our relationship, Caine had mentioned kids in an offhand manner, but we'd never really discussed it, so I didn't know when it would become an option. We'd gone through so much in the last few months with the trial that it just didn't ever seem like the right time.

So his words that morning meant everything to me.

It meant that Caine and I, God willing, would finally have a family.

"Is this real?" I grinned, causing tears to spill down my cheeks.

Caine hauled me to my feet and wrapped his arms around me. He kissed the tears away and held me tight. "Baby, it's real."

It was so real.

Finally.

I had what I'd always wanted.

And Caine . . . he had what he'd always needed.

ACKNOWLEDGMENTS

From the moment Alexa and Caine's story came to mind, I was swept up in it, so I must first thank all my friends and family for putting up with my absence and absentmindedness—much more so than usual. It can be frustrating living inside another world you're so captivated by and have the people around you not quite understand. That's why when the book is finished and it's in their hands, it's a lovely feeling to sit back, relax, and say, "This is where I've been these last few months . . . Hopefully you get it now?" The wonderful thing is that my friends and family always do. I love you for your understanding. I'm very lucky to have you!

In particular I want to thank my friend Shanine for traversing across an ocean to visit and research Boston with me so I could fall in love with the city that Lexie and Caine call home. And I did. Hopefully that fondness comes through in the story.

As always I have to thank my fantastic agent, Lauren Abramo, for believing in me, often more than I believe in myself, for always having my back, and working so hard to make sure my stories find their way into the hands of the readers. Also a huge thank-you to my publisher, Kara Welsh, my editor, Kerry Donovan, and the entire team at New American Library for your incredible support. I appreciate you all more than you'll ever know!

I must also thank experienced ER nurse and avid reader Angela Phillips Lovvorn. Thank you for all your advice and information—it was invaluable to Lexie's story.

Finally I want to thank you, my reader.

You are *my* hero.